MOONLIT SHADOWS

BITTEN

MOONLIT SHADOWS

BITTEN

SHAWNA GAUTIER

Cover design copyright © www.wegotyoucoveredbookdesign.com
Book interior design by www.wegotyoucoveredbookdesign.com

Edited by CLS Editing

Visit Shawna's website to sign up for her newsletter and learn about new releases:

www.shawnagautier.com

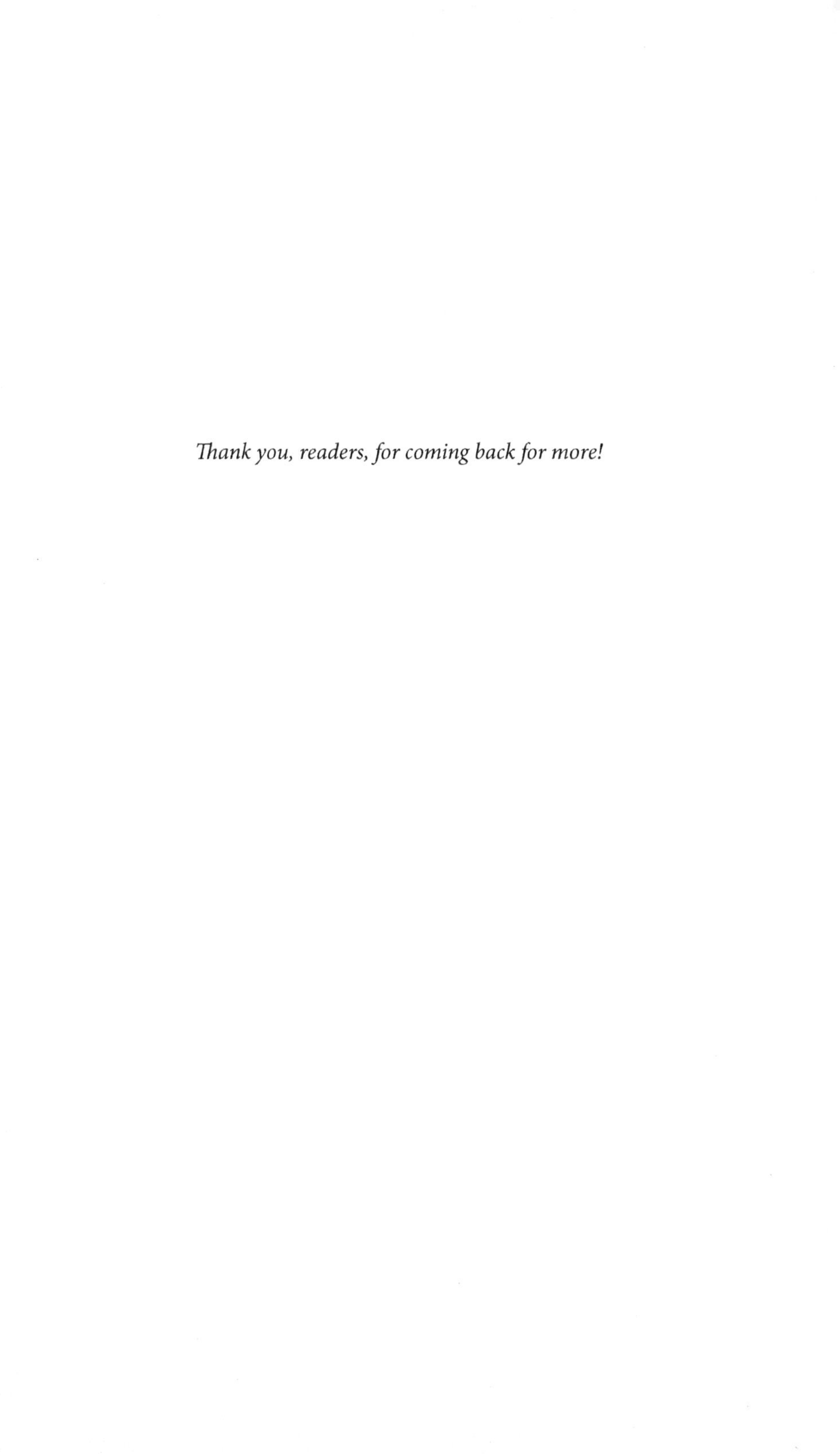

Thank you, readers, for coming back for more!

1

TWO WEEKS had passed since Sami discovered the shocking reality of werewolves, complete with claws, fangs, fur, and sinister, red eyes. Of course, it would take a lot longer than a couple of weeks to get over the horror of being stalked, kidnapped, and tortured by a creature that was only supposed to exist between the pages of a book. Why, then, was she driving right back into the dark depths of where it had all taken place, and in the middle of the night, no less?

She was sure of two reasons. Moving away meant her mom would be all alone in this forsaken town, and more importantly, she couldn't bear the thought of leaving the man she'd fallen in love with. Her heart ached just thinking about it.

Another reason existed, though—one she wasn't ready to admit to herself. For some reason, she was drawn to possibly the creepiest place on Earth, and it scared the hell out of her. Yet, here she was, driving right back to the forest she'd almost died in.

Sami shook the wretched thought from away and flicked off the high beams, relieved to see the lights of the small town finally come into view. Driving at night gave her the creeps, especially since Billy was sound asleep. Even though he was right next to her, she couldn't help feeling somewhat alone. Vulnerable. The pitch blackness of the winding forest road didn't help either.

She tightened her grip on the steering wheel of the '68 Charger and checked the rear-view mirror for any signs of red eyes.

The soft glow of street lights brought a sense of comfort to her tormented soul, but that was short-lived. Before she knew it, the lights were behind them, and she entered the void again—being swallowed whole by the darkness with only the security of dim headlights guiding her to her fate.

A white haze and a streak of red reflecting in the rear-view mirror immediately drew her attention. Body tense, she held her breath, focusing on the tail lights of a car.

Must've just exited a side street. She shook her head and exhaled her tension.

"Get a grip, Sami," she whispered. "This is your home now. Get used to it." She pressed harder on the gas pedal, anxious to get home.

BILLY OPENED his eyes and stretched, focusing on the familiar front porch. "What? We're here already? Why didn't you wake me? I would've driven the rest of the way."

Sami threw a hand over her mouth and yawned. "It's okay. I didn't mind. I didn't wanna wake you. You looked so peaceful."

He glanced at his watch. "Man, it's already after midnight. You must be exhausted. Do you wanna stay here tonight? I'm sure your mom's already asleep."

"I was hoping you'd ask." She arched her back, stretching the stiffness away, and climbed out of the car.

He went to the trunk to get their bags. "Keys please." He held his hand up.

She tossed him the keys and waited in front of the car which seemed too far away in the darkness. He threw a nonchalant glance over each shoulder, eyeing the blackness of the forest for glowing eyes while he retrieved their luggage.

It felt good to be home, but Billy's gut knotted at the thought of having to bring the woman he loved back to the place where she'd almost been killed. He'd become more protective of her since then, not leaving her side once on their vacation except to go to their separate bedrooms at the end of each night and to use the bathroom, of course.

He hated her not being just down the hall anymore. Sure, she only lived next door, but if Jessica *was* still alive, he couldn't get to Sami fast enough if her life depended on it. The mere thought scared the hell out of him.

They went inside and Billy dropped the bags on the floor. He'd been waiting to kiss Sami, like *really* kiss her, since they'd arrived at her dad's house in Monterey. But, even when they'd been alone on the beach, he'd felt as if her dad were keeping a watchful eye on them from the deck. Now, they weren't standing outside a restaurant full of windows, in the parking lot of a busy gas station or rest stop, or at her over-protective dad's house. They were alone in *his* territory.

Without bothering to turn on the lights, he pulled her into his arms and devoured her lips with his, savoring every ounce of her sweet mouth.

"You two are back already?" Mike's gruff voice cut through the darkness and the lights flicked on.

Sami tensed and pushed away from Billy's grasp.

Billy eyed his brother's boxers and sighed. "Yep, we're back. Sami's dad rearranged his business trip to the end of our visit. He didn't want us staying in his house alone together, so here we are, a few days early."

Mike winked at Sami. "Good. I was beginning to miss Sami's company."

She smiled. "I missed you too, Mike."

"What about me, asswipe?" Billy tried to sound as offended as he could through a slight grin.

"The pain in my ass has been gone ever since you left," Mike said with a satisfied smirk. He yawned and headed back down the hallway. "I'll see you two in the morning. I'm going back to bed."

"Hey," Billy called out. "Make sure you're wearing pants in the morning."

Mike's bedroom door rattling shut was the only answer Billy

received.

Sami giggled and put her hands on Billy's chest. "Now, where were we?"

Billy let out a low, devious chuckle and led the way to his bedroom.

2

SAMI OPENED her eyes and stretched, the smell of bacon teasing her senses. Sunshine poured through the window. She rolled over to wrap her arm around Billy, but he wasn't there.

"Uh." She frowned, disappointed. Sitting up, she glanced around his bedroom. Beer cans and soda cans cluttered his desk. His dresser was piled high with clothes. Clean clothes, she assumed, because his dirty clothes were scattered across the floor. A crumpled chip bag teetered on the edge of his nightstand, threatening to fall off.

She climbed out of bed, dug through her suitcase for her white top and any pair of clean jeans she could find, and dressed.

Then, she gathered up his dirty clothes and opened the hamper—which was ironically empty—and dropped them in. She left the lid up, hoping he'd at least try to throw his discarded clothes in their proper place. Next, she picked up the garbage can next to his dresser—also empty—and filled it with the strewn about trash.

"There. Much better. Now, time to find my boyfriend." She went to the bathroom to freshen up first. Her bag of toiletries sat on the counter, along with a folded towel and washcloth. "Aww, Billy," she whispered, delighted with his thoughtfulness. She looked at her reflection in the mirror, admiring her tanned skin and the red highlights in her brown hair. Even her chestnut eyes appeared brighter.

Looks like being at the beach everyday was beneficial in more ways than one. She beamed, but her smile faded when she focused on the faint bruises still lingering on her forehead and cheekbone. Determined to focus on a new day instead of reliving her tragedy, she filled her thoughts with memories of her and Billy frolicking on the beach and turned the shower on.

When she finished showering and readying for the day, she went to the living room, surprised to see Billy had breakfast ready and the table set.

"Good morning." He smiled, wrapping his arms around her waist.

"Good morning." She beamed and snuggled against him, relishing the warmth of his body, along with the intoxicating scent of his sporty soap, wishing he'd swoop her up and carry her back to his bed. "You made breakfast?"

"Yeah, well, I figured it was the least I could do since you drove the rest of the way last night. That and because I love you." He grinned his heart-melting grin and kissed the tip of her nose, before planting a sultry kiss on her lips.

"You two are up early." Mike walked past them, yawning and scratching the back of his head.

"Mike, what a surprise," Billy said in a flat tone. He lowered his lips to Sami's ear and whispered, "We'll finish this later." Then, he pulled a chair out at the dining table and motioned for her to sit.

She grinned and took a seat, noticing Billy was wearing his favorite T-shirt today—the gray one she'd acquired soon after they'd started dating. "I see you found your favorite shirt in my suitcase."

"Yeah, I couldn't find any clean shirts, so I borrowed it. I'll give it back after I do some laundry."

"But it's your shirt."

His brown eyes filled with hunger. "I like you wearing my shirt."

She giggled. "Oh, I hope you don't mind, but your room was kind of messy, so I tidied it for you."

Billy sat next to her with a surprised look on his face. "You did? Thank you. I didn't have time to get to it before we left town. Now, I'm kind of embarrassed."

"Don't be. You saved my life. Picking up some clothes on your floor was the least I could do."

He raised one corner of his mouth. "But you know I would've cleaned it if I would've known you'd be staying, right?"

"I'm sure you would've." She winked.

"No, he wouldn't have," Mike said as he sat down with a plateful of scrambled eggs, potatoes, and bacon. "Say, Sami, my room could use a good cleaning. After all, I saved your life too."

"Ha, ha, nice try!" she said, her tone playful.

A loud banging rattled the front door. Before anyone had time to react, the door opened and Jason barged in. His hazel eyes brightened when they settled on Sami and Billy.

"Jason!" Sami rushed over and threw her arms around his neck.

"Hey, Sami!" Jason lifted her off the ground, before setting her back on her feet. "So, did you bring me any souvenirs?" he asked, rubbing his hands together like an eager child.

"Yes, we did. Hold on." She went back to Billy's bedroom, pulled a blue bag from the suitcase, and hurried back to the living room. "Here's the hot California chick you requested!" She handed him the bag.

Jason grinned and snatched it from her fingers. He shoved his hand inside and pulled out a plastic woman about ten inches tall, wearing a bikini and standing on a surfboard. "Cool! Thanks!" He rocked the doll from side to side, watching her sway back and forth.

"And she was cheap," Billy added.

"We got a girlfriend for you too, Mike," Sami said. "Billy has her in his bag."

"Funny," Mike said with a half-smile.

Jason raised his nose in the air and inhaled. "I smell food." He headed straight for the kitchen.

Sami sat back down at the table and took a bite of her bacon, recognizing the sweetness of the smoked applewood meat—her favorite.

"So, what have you two been up to while we were gone?" Billy asked before he chomped on his bacon, nearly eating the whole slice in one bite.

Jason joined them at the table. "Nothing. We've been up to absolutely *nothing*. Except for work. I am so glad you guys are back. It's been totally boring around here." He shoveled a fork full of potatoes and popped them into his mouth.

"What?" Billy looked at his brother. "I figured you guys would be hanging out, drinking beer, watching TV every night."

Mike flashed a shameful half-grin. "We did a couple of times."

"Yeah, he's been spending most of his time with *Abby*." Jason shot Mike a knowing look.

Billy grinned, and a mischievous flicker filled his eyes. "Oh really?"

Mike glared at Jason, then Billy. "Don't even go there, little brother. I can still kick your ass."

"Abby, huh?" Sami smiled. "I like her. She seems really nice."

"Thank you, Sami. I knew I could at least count on you," Mike said and took a sip of his coffee.

"So, how was your trip?" Jason muttered through a mouth full of eggs.

Sami and Billy took turns talking about their visit with her dad and their daily hikes down to the beach. Not wanting to dampen the upbeat mood, Sami didn't mention their hike along the cliff-side trail to the special beach she'd once visited with her grandpa, where she'd paid tribute to his memory by writing his name in the sand and leaving a bouquet of wildflowers.

When Sami was full, she pushed her plate aside.

Mike jumped up and snatched her plate, along with his, and put them in the dishwasher.

"Thanks, Mike," she said.

Billy smirked at his brother. "You seem pretty damned chipper this morning. So—" he raised his eyebrows "—where're you headed now…*Abby's*?"

"Yep." Jason glowered at Mike. "We're not even close to being finished yet because someone only keeps putting in a few hours a day, so he can go play with *Abby*."

Billy let out a devious chuckle. "Hmm. That's unlike Mike to be half-assed. She must be his *girlfriend*."

Mike gave way to an amusing smile. He shook his head and pointed at Billy. "Watch it!" he warned before strutting down the hallway.

Jason glanced at Billy. "So, are you coming with us today?"

Billy met Sami's gaze with hesitance.

Sami could tell he was torn between whether to work or keep her company. Not even a whole day had passed since they'd arrived back home, and the thought of being alone scared her. But Billy couldn't be at her side night and day, holding her hand until she felt safe in her environment again.

Determined to be strong, she inhaled a breath of confidence. "Go ahead, Billy. It sounds like they could use the help. I'm sure my mom's gonna want to know everything that happened on our trip anyway. And I'm sure that'll take all day."

He paused, studying her expression. "Are you sure? I'll stay if you want me to."

"I'm sure." She stood and pushed her chair in. "I should go see my mom. She should be up by now."

"Okay, I'll walk you home, then. Let me get your suitcase." He took his plate to the sink and went to his room, returning within seconds with her suitcase.

Jason sat back and clasped his hands over his stomach. "See ya later, Sami. I'm glad you guys are back. Please don't leave again. Mike sucks."

"You just now figured that out?" Billy opened the front door.

Sami giggled. "Bye, Jason," she called over her shoulder on her way outside.

Billy followed her to the front porch, and they headed across the yards. "So, you're sure you don't want me to stay?" he asked in a worried tone.

"I'll be okay. It's all behind us now." When he still didn't look convinced she added, "The sun's shining, and it's a beautiful day. I'm happy to be home, Billy. Don't worry about me."

"All right. But I'm only working 'til noon for the first few days just to make sure. You've been having nightmares every night. I wanna be here for you."

"Okay," she said, finally giving in.

When they reached her front porch, she stood on tiptoes to give him a kiss. He leaned down and obliged her request, melting her insides as his tongue rolled with hers. He pulled away, his mouth hovering just above hers, and his warm breath still kissing her lips. Then, he turned the doorknob and the euphoria dissipated.

Billy reached in and set her suitcase on the floor, just inside the door. "I'll see you in a little bit."

"Bye." She watched from the doorway as he jogged down the steps and hurried across the yard.

"You're home early!" her mother boomed.

Startled, Sami screamed and spun around, jumping back out onto the porch.

Her mom stood there, in her bathrobe, beaming.

"You scared me, Mom! I didn't hear you come up behind me."

Out of the corner of her eye, she saw movement. Billy sprinted back into her yard, his eyes wide with fear.

Sami held a hand up. "I'm okay. My mom just snuck up on me, is all." She let out a relieved laugh, her cheeks hot with humiliation.

"You scared the hell out of me." He raised one corner of his mouth and ran a hand through his dark brown hair, his eyes still full of concern. "Okay. I love you. See you soon." He hesitated, but as soon as she nodded with a confident smile he turned and walked away.

Sami went inside and locked the door. When she turned around her mom squished her in a bear hug. She didn't realize how much she'd missed her mother until that moment.

"I'm so happy you're home!" Her mom stepped back and gave her a once-over. "I can't believe your face is almost healed. Only a couple of faint bruises. And you look so well rested. I *knew* this trip would be good for you! I'm so glad you went. Of course, the house has been quiet since you've been gone. Too quiet. But I'm glad you got away for a while. Your father didn't tell me you were coming home early, though. Why didn't you call?"

Sami stared at her mother for a moment, trying to absorb everything she had just said. "I don't know." She shrugged. "I thought I'd just surprise you, I guess. Dad changed his business trip to the end of our visit, so he was home when we got there. And, we had to leave early because he didn't want us staying alone together while he was gone."

Sami plodded over to the couch and flopped down. It felt good to finally be able to relax. And though it seemed crazy to admit it, it felt good to be home again.

Her mom eased onto the recliner. "Well, your dad worries about you, too. He doesn't want to see you settle down at a young age. I'm glad you got to visit with him, though. He misses you."

"Yeah, I guess." Sami didn't bother telling her about the woman who kept calling the house for him.

Her father didn't know it, but every time he stepped out onto the deck to take a call, the woman's shrill voice echoed from his phone through the open bedroom window Sami slept in. Of course, Sami couldn't hear what the woman was saying, and she didn't want to. It hurt too much. So, she wasn't going to tell her mom. She couldn't bear to break her mom's heart any more than it had already been broken.

Sami decided to change the subject. "I met Megan, too. She seems really nice. I didn't know she was only a year older than me. She's thinking about moving back here."

"Oh, really? Aren't things going well for her in California?"

"Yeah, I guess, but her roommate is considering moving in with her boyfriend, and Megan doesn't wanna live alone. Plus, she misses her brothers."

"It'll be nice if she moves back. I know Mike and Billy were both devastated when she decided to move away."

Sami's heart grew heavy at the thought.

"Well, sweetheart, I wish you would've told me you were coming home early. It's too late to find someone to cover my shift today."

"It's okay, Mom. I need to catch up on some sleep anyway."

Carol paused, her demeanor turning serious. "There's something else I need to talk to you about." She stood up from the recliner and sat on the couch.

Worried, Sami straightened from her slouch. "Mom, what's going on?"

"Well…you know I've been seeing Steve. And, I'm sure you know we've known each other for years."

Sami eyed her cautiously, dreading what she was going to say next.

"Well, there's no easy way to say this.... The company Steve's working for is opening a new branch in Seattle, and they want Steve to help run it. He wants me to go with him. He's asked me to marry him."

Sami's jaw dropped. "*What*?" She fumed. "What do you mean he asked you to *marry* him?" She sprang to her feet. "That's *ridiculous*! You just got a divorce from Dad! He can't expect something like that. And to want you to move away with him, that's just...*crazy*! You told him *no*, though, *right*?"

She sat silently for a moment, her eyes ridden with guilt. "No, sweetheart."

"No? What? You mean like you told him *no*?"

"No...I mean I told him *yes*," she replied and lowered her gaze.

Sami let out a heavy sigh and sat back, staring into oblivion. One minute she was returning to her life, to mentally and emotionally rebuild after having been attacked by a werewolf. Now, her life was being turned upside down again.

She wanted to be angry at her mom—to ask her what in the hell she was thinking—but she couldn't get over the shock of it all. She'd moved away from her childhood home, away from her father, and away from all she'd ever known, just so her mom wouldn't have to be alone in this forsaken town. Now, her mother was picking up and moving away, just like that?

"Samantha, I'm sorry. I know you love Billy, but Seattle isn't that far away. You two could always visit each other."

"*What*? You mean you want me to go with you?"

"You can't stay. How would you live?"

"I'm not leaving, Mom! I'll get a job. I'll find my own place to rent. Billy and Mike have an extra room, or maybe I could rent a room from Jason. He has *more* than enough space." The more she ranted, the more upset she became.

"Or, maybe I could find a place with Megan if she moves back, but I'm *not* leaving! I'm *not* moving again! And I'm *not* leaving Billy! It's just like you said when you went out on your first date with Steve—I deserve to be happy too!" Tears blurred her vision, but she held them back.

Her mom's eyes filled with sadness. "You're right. I can't make you come with me. I want you to…but I can't make you. Just because this place isn't for me, it doesn't mean you can't be happy here."

"Why can't you just stay, Mom? Can't he just keep his job here?" she pleaded as the reality of the situation began to sink in. For the first time in her life, she would be without family. Without her mother.

"No, they need him in Seattle. It's a really big promotion for him. He's being promoted from foreman to project supervisor. He has to go. Plus…" She looked down into her lap and began toying with the belt on her robe. "…I *love* him. I *want* to go with him.

"Your father took me away from here when I was your age, and I was so happy. I couldn't imagine living here for the rest of my life. This small town isn't for me. I moved back here to see your grandfather through the end of his life, but it's not my life."

"Well, I don't want to leave here, Mom. When I got back home last night, I was actually relieved. I like it here, and I don't wanna leave Billy."

Her mom stood, and a heavy breath escaped her lips. "To tell you the truth, I was expecting this. I can see, when you two are together, how much you truly love each other. He's good for you."

Sami nodded, still battling with the anger and disappointment flooding through her. Tears brewed, but she had to be strong. If she cried now, she wouldn't be able to stop.

An uneasy moment of silence passed before her mom spoke again. "So…there's nothing I can do to change your mind?"

"No. I'm staying."

"Okay, then. You have a car, and I'm sure you'll be able to find a job. Are you going to school this fall?"

Sami chewed on the corner of her lip. "Actually, I've decided to put it off for a little while."

Carol nodded. "I suspected as much with everything that has happened. It's okay."

Sami smiled half-way, relieved her mother wasn't disappointed.

"Now, all you need is a place to live."

"Yeah." Sami's shoulders slumped forward as the thought of being homeless began to sink in.

"Well, lucky for you, the house is all paid off." Her mom smirked.

"What? What do you mean?" Giddiness filled her chest, and a huge smile crossed her face. "You mean I can stay *here*?"

"Yes, you can stay here! This was my parents' house. Even though I don't like it, I still grew up here. I can't sell it. You get a job to pay for utilities and food, and I'll take care of the property taxes and insurance."

Sami jumped up and down with excitement, giggling like a child. "I can't believe I can stay here. In our house!" She threw her arms around her mother and gave her a big squeeze. "Thanks, Mom! I love you so much!"

"You're welcome, sweetheart."

When Carol pulled away her smile was gone, and her eyes reflected sorrow. "I can't believe my baby isn't a baby anymore." Her lips crinkled into a frown.

Sami's heart filled with a dull ache. "No, I'm not."

"I sure am going to miss you." She sighed heavily, and her eyes glistened with moisture.

"I'll miss you, too, Mom." Sami tried to swallow back the tears threatening to fall. "But, we still have some time together. When are you moving?"

"In two weeks."

Sami's mouth hung open. She felt as if she'd just been slapped in the face. Two weeks wasn't sufficient enough time to prepare or pack, and it surely wasn't enough time to say good-bye. "*What*? I thought it was at least a couple of months away."

"I know. Me too. We're going to move up there to get settled first. Then, we'll fly to Lake Tahoe to get married. I would really like it if you and Billy could be there for the ceremony, but I'll understand if you can't. I know this is all sudden for you."

Sami didn't know what to say. She'd barely gotten used to the idea of her mom dating Steve, and he was taking her away and marrying her—a man other than her father. She shook the gut wrenching thought away and sighed.

"I don't know. I have to find a job and all." Though she'd already had her mind made up on a solid *no*, she didn't want to make things any harder on her mom than they already were.

"It's all right. I understand. There's still time to think about it. Anyway, I need to take a nap before work. I haven't been sleeping well, lately. Oh, and Steve wants to have a farewell dinner at his house. Probably the weekend before we leave."

Sami's jaw tightened, but she hid it with a smile. "Dinner at Steve's…got it." As soon as her mother disappeared down the hall, she squished her eyes shut and silently mouthed *dammit*. Out of respect for her mom, she had to go. There was no getting out of this one.

Sami glanced about the quiet living room, suddenly realizing every day would soon be this quiet. The thought of her mom leaving *and* having dinner at Steve's was too much to fathom. She went out onto the front porch to get some fresh air and to clear her head.

A gentle breeze wafted through the clear blue skies. Sinking into the wicker chair, she stared at the tops of the trees as they swayed. Mesmerized by their carefree dance, her thoughts drifted back two weeks, to when she'd miscarried because of Jessica's brutality.

Lowering her lashes, she looked at her abdomen and rested a hand over it. *I'm sorry, baby.* Tears blurred her vision and ran down her cheeks as the emptiness in her heart awakened. She turned her gaze to the sky.

I'm so sorry I lost you. Even though I never got a chance to meet you, I miss you every day.

She swiped her fingers across her cheeks and pushed the pain back to the corner of her heart, where she kept it locked away. Needing Billy's comfort, she glanced over at his driveway, but his car wasn't there. At times like these, she missed the ocean. While in California, she and Billy had gone to the beach every day. Though she was just there yesterday, she already missed it.

With a heavy heart, she focused on the trail.

Should I go to the lake? Jessica was the only danger around, and she can't hurt me anymore. She hesitated, contemplating what to do. *I could go to Billy's and get a silver knife, just to be on the safe side.*

Before she could talk herself out of it, she skipped down the porch steps and headed next door. If Billy, Jason, and Mike could go traipsing off to the lake anytime they wanted, so could she. After all, it wasn't just a *man's* forest. She had every right to familiarize with it.

Especially, when, in two short weeks, she would have to live in the middle of it alone.

3

WHEN SAMI reached Billy's front door, she found it unlocked. Moving only her eyes, she glanced around the front yard to make sure she went unnoticed. With her heart thumping as the fear of being caught took over, she stepped inside and shut the door.

What am I doing? This is wrong, sneaking into someone's house. I hope Billy and Mike won't be mad at me. I'll just borrow the knife and return it before they even get home. And if they do find out, I'm sure they won't mind. After all, my grandpa made the knives.

She hurried across the living room, to the gun cabinet. She pulled open the top drawer, smiling when the glimmer of silver caught her eye.

She reached in and wrapped her fingers around the cold, metal handle, surprised by its heaviness. Her grandpa had even taken the time to etch a swirling pattern into the handle.

The ringing of a telephone screamed through the silence.

Sami jumped and spun around, focusing on the phone lying on the couch. It rang again, drowning out the sound of her heart pounding in her ears.

A slight laugh escaped her lips, and she clutched her chest to calm the fear. Then, she hurried out of the house and shut the door.

Sami ran home and snatched her backpack from the closet under the stairs and a bottle of water from the fridge.

"Oh no!" She realized she had forgotten to shut the knife drawer at Billy's house. *Should I go back and shut it? No, I'll just make sure I get back before Billy does.* Without a second thought, she dropped the knife and water into her backpack and headed for the lake.

The forest was peaceful. Sunlight filtered through the trees here and there, illuminating it like magic, while birds chirped from somewhere high above. Even though she couldn't see them, their singsong melodies were contenting. And it meant no predators were in the vicinity.

Sami continued along the trail, keeping a fast and steady pace. She needed enough time to enjoy the serenity of the lake and get back before Billy did. Fifteen minutes into her hike, she stopped to catch her breath.

A rustling of leaves caught her attention. She froze and held her breath. Without making a sound, she listened, scanning the nearby trees and brush for movement. Using slow and quiet movements, she slipped the backpack from her shoulders and unzipped it, just far enough to slide her hand inside until she gripped the handle of the knife.

A deer stepped out from behind a nearby tree and stopped to munch on a cluster of yellow flowers.

Sami let out a relieving sigh and smiled. She hadn't seen a deer since she'd moved here. Birds and deer had to be a good sign. The danger was really gone.

The deer lifted its head, its innocent gaze locking with hers, before it pranced away into the forest.

A sudden pang of nausea swept its way from Sami's stomach to the back of her throat. "Oh no!"

She bolted off the trail and leaned against a tree, letting her backpack drop to the ground. She reached in and snatched the water bottle. After a few sips, the nausea subsided.

Well, this was a dumb idea, again! She shook her head and rolled her eyes, frustrated she had to go back for food before she'd even gotten to the lake. *I just ate not too long ago. What time is it?* She cupped her right back pocket for her cell phone, but it wasn't there.

"Dammit! I must've left it in Billy's car last night." She kicked a small rock, sending it flying straight into a cluster of Bluebells. Their rich hue caught her attention. Just beyond them, tiny lavender flowers created a striking contrast. With her favorite color being purple, and her mother's blue, she had to pick them to brighten their home and their spirits.

She dropped the water bottle into her backpack, worked her arms through the straps, and began to pick the flowers.

After she'd gathered a bunch, she noticed some yellow Buttercups, along with pink and white ones close by. She decided to decorate the living room with the blue and purple cluster and pick the others for the kitchen table.

When she finally finished, she had a handful of wildflowers. *These should cheer Mom up.* She beamed.

Feeling a little queasy again, Sami set the flowers on a small boulder. With her backpack dangling from her arm, she reached inside for the water bottle. She took another sip, which seemed to settle the sickness. Wasting no more time, she dropped the bottle back into her pack and slung it over one shoulder. She gathered the flowers and trudged through the brush to the spot she had just been standing at a few minutes ago, but the trail wasn't there.

Confused, she studied her surroundings, breathing a sigh of relief when she spotted the same tree she'd leaned against before she'd started to pick the flowers. When she reached the tree, she headed for the trail only a few paces away, but there was still no sign of the path—only clumps of weeds, ferns, and dead pine needles.

"What the…?" She spun around, looking for signs of familiarity.

Walking along the trail in the past, certain trees and bushes had become familiar—visual markers she'd used to gauge how close or far she was from her destination. But now, she couldn't tell one tree or bush from another. If she were staring right at the tree she'd nicknamed *Fifteen Minutes to the Lake*, she wouldn't know it if came crashing down on top of her.

Just stay calm, Sami! The trail is here somewhere. Just backtrack to where the Buttercups were. She tromped through the brush, retracing her steps, only to find weeds there.

It's not the same spot!

A jolt of fear shot through her. "What am I gonna do?" she whispered and ran a shaky hand through her hair. "I can't be lost. I didn't go far."

With a tight grip on the wildflowers, she scoured the area, tripping over clumps of grass and fallen branches while searching for the trail. Just as hopelessness set in, she stumbled onto a worn path of hardened dirt.

"Yes!" She clutched her chest. "You can be pretty stupid sometimes, Sami!" Eager to get home, she hurried along the trail.

The burden of stress weighed on Sami's thoughts as she hiked toward home. Definitely not the peaceful time she'd hoped for. Nausea gripped her insides, but she pressed on, still rattled about losing the trail. During all the other times she'd hiked to the lake, the thought of getting lost had never crossed her mind. Yet, it had happened so easily.

She rounded a bend in the trail and stopped dead in her tracks. A fallen tree blocked her path.

"Oh no!" Her heart skipped a beat. She spun around, scanning the surrounding foliage, recognizing nothing around her.

"Dammit! This isn't the trail!" She clutched the top of her head and squished her eyes shut, hoping to awaken from her nightmare. When she re-opened them, nothing had changed. She still stood in an unfamiliar part of a vast forest, with no clue on where to go next.

What am I gonna do? She backed up against a tree to rest and collect her thoughts.

Should I go back the other way? She eyed the direction from which she'd come, recalling how backtracking had led her astray in the first place.

Should I keep going? Her gaze shifted past the fallen tree, but a sharp bend in the trail prevented her from seeing any further.

Maybe I should stay here and wait for someone to find me? How could I be so stupid again?

Billy's warnings of not entering the forest alone entered her thoughts, and she frowned. "I'm sorry, Billy," she whispered. *I thought it was just because of the werewolf…because of Jessica. I didn't know I'd get lost, or that I* could *get lost following the trail.*

Another wave of nausea swept through her gut. She dropped the bouquet and braced herself against the tree with one hand, while easing out slow, controlled breaths in an attempt to contain the sickness. Despite her efforts, a sharp cramp forced rank acids up her throat and all over the fern at her feet. Doubled over, she wretched again and again, trying to keep her hair from falling in the way. Just when she thought she'd surely heave up her actual stomach, the gut wrenching subsided.

Hands trembling, she gathered the flowers and headed to the fallen tree to rest and devise a plan.

A few more sips of water settled her stomach again, leaving her with a little over half of the bottle left. She screwed the cap on tight and slid the water into the backpack.

Looking over her shoulder, she followed the unknown trail with her eyes until it disappeared around a bend. According to the suns position in the sky, the trail led northeast, which meant the road to town would eventually appear.

Sami eyed the path. "Well, it *is* a trail. It has to lead somewhere." Determined to save herself from her predicament, she climbed over the dead tree and continued along the trail.

Being in an unfamiliar part of the forest was unsettling. The eerie silence didn't help either. Sami halted, realizing the birds hadn't chirped since she'd gotten lost. And, the farther she journeyed into the unknown, the darker the forest grew.

Looking for signs of life, she gazed into the branches above. They were so thick, not one ray of sunshine passed through the strong barrier. Holding her breath, she shifted only her eyes, listening and searching for movement from any docile creature—a bird, a squirrel, a deer. Any indication to prove she wasn't alone or in danger.

Complete silence engulfed the forest, sending a twinge of fear down her spine. Anxious to get out of there, she bolted forward, hoping to find the road soon.

Rounding a bend in the trail, sunlight filtered through a break in the trees ahead.

"Finally!" Digging her toes in with each stride, she launched ahead. Desperate to reach her goal, she ignored the burn engulfing her leg muscles, afraid if she turned around, she'd be staring at the blood drenched fangs of a killer werewolf right before it chomped on her neck.

The sunlight grew closer and closer until she stumbled into a clearing overgrown with an abundance of weeds.

"Great! Where's the road?" she said through heavy breaths. Lungs burning with each heave, she leaned forward and propped her hands on her knees.

The clearing was significantly smaller than the one at the lake, with only a few clusters of Buttercups and small boulders scattered about. And an eerie aura surrounded this meadow, almost as if life had abandoned it and left it for dead.

Across the way, a white object jutted above the overgrowth. She made her way to it, tromping through the weeds and stopping abruptly in front of a cross. Inscriptions had been carved into each arm it. She knelt and read them.

Rick Holden	*Ann Holden*
Jan 13, 1967 - Sept 13, 2004	*Sept 14, 1968 - Oct 13, 2004*

We love you, Dad and Mom. She silently mouthed the inscription carved at the intersection of the cross.

As sorrow gripped her heart, tears brimmed and fuzzed the words away. A quick swipe of the hand across each eye cleared her view, and she laid the cluster of flowers at the base of the cross.

"Did you know them?" A deep voice broke the silence.

4

SAMI SUCKED in a fearful breath and jumped up to face the intruder. A man she'd never seen before stood about thirty feet away, his dark-eyed gaze locked with hers.

"It's okay," he said, his voice deep, yet gentle. He raised his hands in front of him with cautious movements. "I'm not going to hurt you."

The twinge of fear running through her blood told her to run, but she couldn't even utter a word, let alone move.

"I was just hunting. I saw you crying and came to see if you were all right."

She glanced at his clothing for some indicator he spoke the truth, but a red plaid shirt and worn jeans didn't differentiate a hunter from a serial killer. And his broad shoulders and bulging forearm veins proved he could overpower her.

Could she outrun him? Probably not. She remembered the knife, wondering if she could get to it before he could get to her.

"I thought you might be hurt or lost," he continued, his voice soothing. He motioned with a hand to the graves. "I knew them too."

Still unable to talk, Sami gulped, waiting to meet her fate.

"So…are you all right?" the stranger asked.

Somehow, she summoned the courage to nod, and then, to speak. "I…I'm lost." Her voice quavered, along with her chin. She pressed her lips together to steady them.

"Okay." He smiled and scratched at the stubble along his jaw. "I can help you. Lucky for you, I'm not lost. I've been hunting in these woods for years."

She looked at his empty hands and back to his face. "Where's your gun?"

"I hid it behind the bushes over there—" he looked over his left shoulder "—because I didn't want to scare you." He tromped to the bushes at the tree-line and pulled out a rifle before he made his way back.

The man's honesty didn't ease Sami's trepidation as she stared at the weapon he gripped. But, if he wanted to hurt her, wouldn't he have done it already? Wouldn't he be pointing the gun directly at her instead of at the ground? Or, was he was just toying with her for the sick fun of it?

"I'm Robert Smith. I used to live here a long time ago, but I moved a few towns away." He smiled.

Still leery of his intentions, Sami studied his smile. It appeared friendly enough, nothing intimidating or malicious.

"I'm Sami…Davis." She bit her lip and averted her gaze to the hole in the knee of his jeans, too nervous to face him any longer than necessary.

"Davis? You mean *Samantha* Davis? Greg Davis's daughter?"

Her eyes met his again and she furrowed her brow. "Yes. I'm his daughter."

"I know your mom and dad." He grinned. "Well, *knew* them. Your dad and I went to high school together. Actually, we've known each other since grade school. They're doing well, I hope?"

She focused on the hints of gray in his brown hair and lines around his eyes. He didn't look quite as old as her father, but it didn't mean he wasn't that old. Maybe the man just took really good care of himself. Though still wary, Sami's apprehension lessened, and she felt a little more comfortable in his presence. He seemed genuine. Plus, he hadn't tried to kill her yet.

She decided to trust him enough to utter a full sentence. "Yes, they're doing fine."

"Good." He raised one corner of his mouth. "Seems like another lifetime ago." In one quick movement, he slung his rifle over his shoulder. "Well, Sami, I can show you the way home. I take it you entered the forest next to your grandfather's house?"

She formed a sheepish smile. "Yeah, I wandered off the trail to pick some flowers, and before I knew it, I was lost."

He glanced at the bouquet and his eyes saddened. "They're beautiful flowers. I'm sure the Holdens appreciate the gesture." A heavy sigh escaped his lips. With a nod of the head in the direction from which she'd come, he said, "Follow me."

Keeping a safe distance, Sami followed him back across the clearing to the trail. When they reached the fallen tree, he hopped onto it with little effort, proving his dexterity. So, yeah, he could definitely outrun her.

He held his hand out to help her over the log.

This is it. This is where I either get murdered or find out he really is *just trying to help me.* She sucked in a deep breath and took his hand.

His roughened fingers were strong, yet gentle. He hoisted her up smoothly and kept a firm grip until she hopped down to the other side.

"Thank you." She smiled, glad to still be alive.

"No problem." He winked, jumped down, and continued along the path.

Along the way, Sami tried to think of idle chit chat to absolve the uneasiness in the air, but nothing came to mind. Striking up a conversation with a strange man she had run into deep in the forest wasn't easy. They made horror movies about this sort of thing.

"So, you're Harry's granddaughter, huh?" His deep voice broke the awkwardness.

"Yes."

"I'm sorry to hear about your grandpa. He was a good man."

"Thank you." A dull ache nipped at her soul, but she tucked the pain away, trying to keep clearheaded in case the scenario turned from bad to worse.

"Well, it's a little overgrown." He halted and pointed at the ground in front of him. "I can see how you got confused."

She stepped closer to get a better view. The trail ended with an overgrowth of knee-high weeds and brush.

"But, if you follow it straight through the weeds…" He said as they marched through the tall grass and around bushes. "…you meet up with the main trail again. The one you wandered off from."

Sami breathed a sigh of relief as they stepped onto the familiar path. Glancing back, the trail they were just on wasn't visible through the weeds. "Thank you so much, Mr. Smith! I don't know what would've happened if you hadn't found me."

"It was my pleasure. I'll go ahead and walk you the rest of the way, just to be sure you don't get turned around again. It's pretty easy to do if you're not familiar with the forest. I wouldn't recommend coming out here alone anymore. You don't know how many people become lost and are never found again."

"Believe me, I won't. My boyfriend, Billy, said the same thing, but I didn't listen. I wish I had. I thought I knew the way."

"Billy? Do you mean Billy Holden?"

"Yeah, do you know him?"

"I used to. When he was little. But it sounds like he's grown up to be a very wise young man. You should take his advice."

"Yeah, I know," she admitted with a shameful half-grin.

They walked along in silence, but it didn't bother her anymore. So far, he'd shown no signs of being a threat. After a few short minutes, they reached the beginning of the trail.

Her guide smiled and gestured with a hand to the familiar road past the break in the trees. "Here you are, Sami, safe and sound." His smile faded and their gazes locked.

Something about the intensity of his stare stirred uneasiness again. This man was hiding something. She lowered her lashes and hurried past him, off the trail, relieved to be home. Disappointment took over when she noticed Billy's empty driveway.

"Well, thank you, Mr. Smith, for helping me." She turned to face him, but he was gone.

"What the…?" She stepped back onto the path and scanned the

forest, but didn't see him anywhere. Holding her breath, she listened for movements, but heard nothing. Not the snap of a twig, the rustling of leaves, or the thudding of boots on the hardened dirt.

A wave of goose bumps ran down her arms and she bolted out of the forest, heading straight for Billy's house.

When she reached his front door, she stopped to catch her breath. She eyed the trail one last time for any signs of Mr. Smith, but he wasn't there. By some miracle, she'd made it out of the forest unscathed, but she was sure the ordeal would haunt her with nightmares for weeks. Now, it was time to concentrate on her next feat—putting the knife back before Billy came home.

She opened the front door and peered inside. Aside from the hum of the refrigerator, all was quiet. She removed the knife from her backpack and hurried to the gun case. Her jaw dropped when she focused on the closed drawer. "I know I left it open," she whispered.

"What the hell are you doing?" Billy's voice erupted from behind.

Sami screamed and jumped. The knife slipped from her fingers and stuck through the top of her shoe, sending a searing pain through the middle of her foot.

"Ugh!" She grimaced and bent down to snatch the knife, but it toppled over and clanked to the floor.

"Crap, crap, crap!" she chanted as she hopped on her uninjured foot, attempting to baby the wounded one and lessen the pain, but it didn't work.

Billy hurried to her side. "Sami, I'm sorry! I didn't mean to scare you! I was just surprised to see you standing there, holding a knife. Are you okay?"

"No!" With Billy's arm around her waist, she limped over to the couch, wincing. She plopped down onto the cool leather and eased her injured foot onto the coffee table.

Billy swiped a hand across the small table, sending its clutter plummeting to the floor, and planted his butt next to her foot.

"Let me see it." He wriggled the shoe from her foot, exposing a blood stained sock. "Damn." He slowly peeled it from her foot.

"Careful." She grimaced.

"Well, you don't need stitches. Hold the sock here while I go get the first-aid kit."

She did as he ordered, pressing the sock to the wound and dreading his return. How was she going to explain breaking into his house and stealing the knife or getting lost in the forest?

Billy emerged from the hallway before she had time to prepare an explanation that would lessen the shock.

"That was fast," she said, disappointed.

After easing back down onto the coffee table, he pulled the antiseptic spray from the first-aid kit and propped her foot on his knee. "This might sting." He pointed the can at her wound and pushed the button, sending a cloud of mist into the air.

"Ah." She cringed, body tensing.

"Sorry." Billy lined a gauze pad with ointment and stuck it over the cut. Then, he taped it in place. "What were you doing, anyway?"

She bit her lower lip, dreading his reaction. "I…um…I just needed to borrow the silver knife."

His eyes widened with surprise. "Why? What'd you do with it?"

"Well…uh…" She hated to tell him, but unless she wanted to start lying, she had no other choice. "…I took it with me to the lake, just in case."

From the way his jaw locked and his temples pulsated, Sami could tell he was angry with her.

"What? Sami! I thought you weren't gonna go into the forest anymore? What were you thinking, going to the lake after everything that's happened?"

She flashed an uneasy grin. "Well…I didn't actually make it to the lake." She gulped and stared at the bandage.

"You mean, you didn't go?" He sounded hopeful.

"I did…but I sort of got sick before I got to the lake." She looked him in the eyes again, and his expression went blank as he waited. "I got sick…and then, I kind of got lost."

"What? You got *lost*?" He seethed again—nostrils flaring and eyes narrowed. He looked up at the ceiling and let out a quick breath, before he met her gaze again.

"Sami…" he scolded, but his tone was gentler. He lifted her bandaged foot from his knee and set it back on the coffee table. "How'd you get lost?"

She bit her lip and shrugged. "I sort of stepped off the trail to pick some flowers."

He let out a disbelieving chuckle. "I can't believe you got lost picking flowers. No, wait. Actually, I *can* believe it." With an irritated look on his face, he stood and threw his hands up, letting them flop at his sides.

After everything she'd just been through, his sudden sarcasm and lack of compassion angered her. She glared at him and crossed her arms. "Yeah, well, I thought they'd cheer up my mom. So, I picked some for her. Then, I saw some more nearby, so I picked those. And, I needed the yellow and pink ones to brighten the kitchen!"

He shook his head with a smug *that figures* grin.

"Why is this funny to you?" she snapped. "I didn't mean to get lost! It just happened!"

He pressed his lips together to keep his amusement somewhat contained. "I know. I'm sorry…." He sighed, and his expression turned serious. "I just don't want anything to happen to you, Sami. Do you know how many people get lost in the forest and just disappear? They *die* out there."

"Yeah, someone already educated me on that," she said with a snarky tone. Realizing she'd said too much, her eyes widened.

"Oh, yeah? Who?" he asked.

She lowered her gaze to the motorcycle print on his black T-shirt and brought her fingers to her bottom lip. "Um…just the guy who found me in the forest."

"What?" he boomed. "What guy? Are you kidding me?"

She crossed her arms and decided to put an end to their bickering by explaining the whole story.

"Okay. *Yes*, I got lost picking flowers on my way through the forest that I *wasn't* supposed to enter, even though I live here," she said, still flustered. "I found the trail again…until I realized I was on the wrong one. It took me to a clearing." Her irritation dissipated as she remembered the graves. Her heart grew heavy. "The same one where your mom and dad…." She shook her head, unable to finish the sentence.

Billy sighed, and pain filled his eyes. He sat on the couch and waited for her to finish.

She slid her bandaged foot off the coffee table and scooted next him. "I'm sorry," she said, placing a hand on his thigh.

Billy put a hand over hers and gave it a gentle squeeze. "What else happened?" he asked, diverting the conversation from his sadness.

Though she wondered about the history of the meadow and how his parents came to rest there, she respected Billy's need for privacy and didn't push the issue. "A man came out of the forest. He said he was hunting and saw me crying, so he came to help."

Billy's eyes softened. "You were crying?"

"Yeah, I read the inscription on the cross. I left the flowers for them."

Billy nodded his thank you but remained silent.

Sami turned her hand over and entwined her fingers with his. "The man said his name was Robert Smith, and he knew our parents, my grandpa, and even *you*, when you were little."

"Robert Smith?" Billy drew his brows together. "I've never heard of him."

"It was a long time ago. Maybe you were too little to remember. Anyway, he took me back to the main trail and was even nice enough to walk me the rest of the way. Something strange happened, though. I looked away for a few seconds, and when I turned to thank him, he was gone."

Billy gazed into her eyes and placed a gentle hand on her cheek. "You were so lucky, Sami. Who knows what would've happened if he hadn't found you, or worse, if he'd ended up being some deranged maniac." He shook his head. "Please, *please* promise me you won't go in the forest alone anymore. I *can't* lose you again. I've already lost too much in my life."

Saddened by his pained look and the desperation in his voice, she whispered, "I promise."

He leaned forward and kissed her. As his mouth caressed hers, his love flowed like an energy traveling straight from his heart to hers, and she wanted more of it. She wrapped her arms around his neck and pressed her chest against his, deepening their kiss.

Billy grunted and entangled his fingers through her hair. His lips left hers to leave a trail of soft kisses down her neck, causing her to shiver, before he crushed his lips to hers again. He loosened his grip from her hair, ran his hands down the length of her back to her butt, and effortlessly lifted her into his lap. They kissed fervently, mouths colliding this way and that, while hands roamed and fingertips caressed. In one swift move, he stood with her in his arms and carried her down the hallway and into his bedroom.

5

STARING AT the ceiling fan above his bed, Billy tightened his hold on Sami as she snuggled against his chest, her bare flesh pressed against his.

She sighed as if something were bothering her.

"What's wrong?" He stroked her hair, enjoying the silkiness.

She was quiet for a moment, deepening his concern. He looked down at her, waiting for a reply.

She let out another heavy breath and frowned. "I'm sorry I snuck into your house while you were gone and took your knife."

Relieved it wasn't anything serious, he laughed under his breath. "Don't be sorry. My house is your house. And I'm glad you thought to protect yourself with something other than a pocketknife. With something that could actually save you."

"But I cut myself with them both." She looked up into his eyes, crinkling her forehead.

"I know. I think you need to consider taking a knife safety course. Or maybe I could make a butter knife out of silver for you?"

"Uh! What*ever*!" She propped herself on one elbow. "You just think you're so funny, don't you?" She snickered.

"Mmm hmm." He gloated while eyeing her red lips. Wanting to feel them on his again, he pulled her toward him.

She obliged him with a quick peck before drawing her head back. The distress in her eyes proved she was still troubled.

"Is something else bothering you?"

She let out heavy breath and shrugged. "I just wanna make sure you know that I'm *really* sorry. I thought I knew the forest enough to go out there alone." She shook her head. "When I figured out I was lost, I was so scared. And when I ran into the hunter—" she furrowed her brow, highlighting the distress in her eyes "—I had no idea what might happen to me. What if I'd ended up in a cage again? Or worse… if I never saw you again? I was so stupid, Billy."

"Don't be upset, Sami," he said as he caressed her cheek. The thought of her out there—alone, vulnerable, and possibly close to death—made him cringe on the inside. Even though his gut twisted into a tangled mess just thinking about it, he gave her a reassuring smile to ease her worries.

"I know how scared you must've been, but nothing bad came out of it. You're safe now, in my arms."

She gave him a soft smile, though he could still see the uncertainty in her eyes.

"Yeah, you're right," she whispered.

"You know, before you came back, I knocked on your door. Of course, no one answered. I knew you weren't with your mom because Mike and I passed by her on the road. I figured you went to the lake, so I ran home for my rifle and some food and water. When I saw the knife drawer open, I knew you were up to something. Mike takes pride in the weapons and cleans and polishes them regularly. He wouldn't have left the drawer open."

She lowered her lashes and stared at his chest.

With a careful finger, he raised her chin until her gaze met his again. "I would've found you. I know I would've," he whispered and pulled her on top of him. "And as long as you always take me with you, I can keep you safe. Promise me you'll never go alone again."

"I *promise*," she said as if she'd just gotten a second chance at life.

"Good." With both hands on either side of her face, he guided her mouth to his, devouring their sweetness. Then, he rolled over until she was under him and lowered his lips back to hers.

BILLY STROKED Sami's back as they lay in each other's arms, enjoying the blissful silence of their post-lovemaking. The sudden churning and grumbling of her stomach disrupted the quiet. She moved to look in his eyes, her cheeks flushing.

He smirked. "Are you hungry?"

"Yes, I'm starving!" She climbed off him and gathered their clothes from the floor, hobbling on her injury.

"How's your foot?"

"It only hurts a little when I flex it to walk." She handed Billy his shirt and jeans before getting dressed.

"I'm sorry," he replied, feeling like an ass for causing the injury in the first place. When they were fully clothed again, he picked up his injured woman, ignored her protests, and carried her to the dining table. After he set her on her feet, he pulled a chair out for her, and went into the kitchen. Behind him, the legs of the chair screeched across the floor as she got comfortable in her seat.

"So, why'd you feel the need to go to the lake anyway?" he asked, opening the cupboard next to the refrigerator.

"My mom's leaving."

"What?" He set two plates on the counter and stared at her in disbelief. "She's leaving? As in—moving away?"

Tears filled Sami's eyes, but she didn't let them fall.

"Yeah. Steve asked her to marry him. He's getting a promotion in Seattle and wants her to go with him. She said yes."

Billy felt bad for her. After all she'd been through, she needed stability in her life, not to have it disrupted again. "Sami, that really sucks. I know this is hard for you."

Her eyes displayed uncertainty, as if she were holding something back.

"Are you moving with her?" He dreaded the answer but had to know.

Her soft smile immediately eased his worry.

"No. I'm staying. My mom's keeping the house, so I can still live there."

He grinned. "Good! You scared me there for a minute." He pulled the package of deli ham from the fridge and held it up. "Is ham and cheese okay?"

"Sounds delicious."

He grabbed the rest of the items out of the fridge. After piling everything on the counter, he began building their sandwiches. He glanced over at Sami, and though she watched him work, her thoughts were clearly elsewhere.

"I'm sorry your mom's leaving. Did she even invite you to go with her?"

Sami nodded, her face crinkling with stress. "She did, but I said no. I don't know why she asked, though. I could never live with Steve. If anything, I'd move back to California. But I like it here, even with everything that's happened. Plus, I don't wanna leave you."

"I don't want you to leave me either."

"Really?" she asked.

"Are you crazy, woman? Of course, I want you to stay." He gathered everything up and carried the items to the dining table.

Sami snatched the soda cans tucked under his arm and set them down. "Thank you for lunch." She picked up her sandwich and took a bite.

"You're welcome." He sat next to her and chomped on his double-decker sandwich.

The familiar rumble of a car approaching rattled the front window.

"Good!" Billy said, relieved. "Mike has successfully brought my car back in one piece again."

"Yeah, I was wondering where it was."

"I wanted to get back to you, so he brought me home early and went back to work." He winked.

She smiled. "Awww, I love you too."

Mike and Jason laughed as they burst through the front door, wearing dirt-smudged T-shirts and tan canvas workpants.

Jason raised his eyebrows. "What? You mean, you two actually have your lips on something other than each other?"

Billy narrowed his eyes. "*Your* lips are about to make contact with my fist."

Jason let out a devious chuckle on his way to the kitchen. "Dude, you're too easy to rile up."

"You are," Mike agreed with a smug grin as he followed Jason.

The stranger in the forest crossed Billy's thoughts. "Hey, Mike? Have you ever heard of a Robert Smith?"

"Robert Smith?" Mike was quiet as he made a sandwich. On his way to the table, he shook his head. "Nope. Why?" He took a seat and shoved the sandwich into his mouth.

Sami sat silently, chewing her food, eyes on her plate.

"Sami got lost in the forest today, and some hunter named Robert Smith found her and brought her back. He said he knew her parents, Harry, and me."

Jason sat down, his eyes wide. "What? Sami! I thought you weren't going out there by yourself anymore. What if something had happened?"

She opened her mouth to speak.

"What were you thinking?" Mike cut in. "You could've gotten yourself kidnapped or killed."

She stared at them for a few seconds, surprised by their sudden outbursts. "I just wanted time alone to think, but I took the knife with me."

"What, your pocketknife?" Jason sneered.

She glared at Jason. "No! The *silver* knife!"

"Really?" Jason's smirk turned into a proud grin. "Good thinking." His smile fell flat. "Still wasn't a smart thing to do, going out there by yourself. You'd still be lost right now if it weren't for that Robert guy."

"It must've scared the *crap* outta you, running into a strange man like that," Mike said with a blatant attitude.

"Hey!" Billy interjected. "What the hell guys? Ease up!"

"Yeah! Ease up!" Sami snapped and her eyes filled with warning. "Yes, it did scare the *crap* outta me, *Mike*." She stood and limped to the kitchen, carrying her empty plate.

Her ability to brazenly stand up to Mike impressed Billy. No one else had never done that in the past and had gotten away with it. But, from the heightened tone in her voice after she'd said his brother's name, Billy knew she wasn't finished. He sat back and crossed his arms, eager to watch his girlfriend unleash her wrath.

After setting her plate in the sink she limped back to the table and put her hands on her hips. "And, yes, I could still be lost at this very moment, *Jason*! But, I'm *not*! And, lucky for me, I came across a *friendly* stranger. Now, if I wanted someone to scold me, I would go home and tell my *mom*! So, back off!" She crossed her arms and glared at the two jackasses.

Billy's lips curled into a satisfied smirk.

Jason grinned sheepishly. "I'm sorry, Sami." His tone was genuine. "Just, after what happened with Jessica…" He shook his head and sighed. "I'm glad you took the silver knife. That was a pretty smart thing to do."

Mike still looked like a prick, but his sigh was heavy with guilt.

"Yeah, me too, Sami. I'm sorry," Mike said.

Billy raised his eyebrows, taken by surprise. "Wow, I think that's the first time I've ever heard you apologize to anyone, especially after they just ripped you a new one."

Mike glared at him. "Don't get used to it."

Sami sighed away her frustration and uncrossed her arms, letting them rest at her sides.

Jason stood and gave her a hug. "Forgiven?"

"Yeah, I guess." She squeezed him and sat back down. "I can't stay mad at you guys." She smiled.

They both grinned.

"So, what happened to your foot anyway?" Mike asked.

To spare Sami from another chastising, Billy answered before she could. "She dropped the knife on her foot, *but*—" he put his hand up, warning them to let him finish before they said anything "—it was *my* fault. I came up behind her and scared her."

They both narrowed their eyes.

"By *accident*," Billy added.

"What'd you do, scare her in the forest?" Jason asked with a confused look on his face.

"No, she snuck in the house to put the knife back. She didn't know I was home."

"You mean she took it? While we were gone?" Mike asked, his eyes bright with amusement.

Jason smirked. "So, Sami, you broke into their house while they were gone and stole their knife?"

"No! It wasn't like that *exactly*. The door wasn't locked. I just *borrowed* it."

Mike grinned. "It's okay, Sami. Our house is your house."

Feeling the need to both protect and comfort her, Billy winked at Sami and jerked his head to the side, motioning for her to sit on his lap.

She bounced up from her seat and planted her cushiony bottom on his thighs.

He wrapped his arms around her, throwing Mike and Jason a warning glance, before filling them in on Carol's plans to move away and Sami's plans to stay.

JASON STARTED his car and headed down the road toward Sami's, glad to be off early for the day. He'd been working long, hard hours at Abby's and couldn't wait until the remodeling was over.

Looking in the rear-view mirror, Abby's massive farmhouse disappeared around the bend. The sharp corner up ahead marked the part of the forest where the trees were denser, somehow making the already cloudy skies seem darker.

"Why in the hell would anyone want to live down here? Not even the forest around my house is as sinister looking."

He wondered if he could ever really rest easy again, knowing danger could be lurking nearby.

Not wanting to scare Sami and cause her any more undue stress, Billy had ordered him and Mike to keep their mouths shut about the possibility—or rather the *probability*—of Jessica still being alive. They were just supposed to go about their casual lives as if nothing had happened, making sure Sami didn't notice when they suspiciously eyed their surroundings for any dog-faced predators with sharp teeth, waiting to devour them alive.

He and Mike thought Billy's reasoning was a stupid idea. They had insisted Sami know of their suspicions to keep her safe. Especially since her last escapade in the forest had gotten her lost and she'd come across a stranger. But Billy wouldn't budge. He didn't want Sami to be terrified every time she stepped outside or at night in her own bed.

Jason had also suggested they take turns watching over her—*physically* watching over her. But that would mean her being guarded twenty-four hours a day. And for how long? The rest of her life? That wasn't feasible. Besides, Sami and Carol would eventually notice their lack of privacy.

Whoever that Robert Smith guy was, Sami's lucky he turned out to be a good guy. It could've easily went the other way—him being a serial killer, rapist werewolf. Sami would've either disappeared without a trace, or been strewn about the forest, half-eaten.

Jason shook the morbid thought away. For now, Sami was alive and safe. And it was his job to keep it that way—along with Billy and Mike. But, with Sami striving to gain her independence and traipse off to the lake every chance she got, how in the hell were they gonna keep her safe without her knowing what they were up to?

All they could do was keep tabs on where Sami was at all times, constantly check in on her, and hope Sheriff Briggs could *really* keep Jessica away. Or better yet, hope he'd *really* shot and killed the bitch.

Jason eyed the shadows in the forest, wondering if there were other monsters out there waiting for their chance to strike or eat. Thankfully, aside from Jessica, there was no evidence to prove their present existence.

His thoughts drifted to the day he'd taken Sami swimming at the lake.

Man, was she beautiful. I should've taken things slower when we'd first met, and not been so quick to make a move. Then, maybe I would've stood a chance.

But I'm glad Sami and Billy hooked up. They're good together. Besides, I'm the reason Billy's parents are dead, and the cause of Billy's suffering since then. Billy deserves to finally have some happiness in his life. He deserves to be with Sami.

Jason knew he'd get over her eventually. One day, some other woman would have his full attention. But, with the way his heart fluttered every time Sami was around, that day couldn't come fast enough.

He parked behind the red and white Chevy Bel-Air. As he climbed out of the car, Sami's shrill scream ripped through the air. Jason's heart jumped in his throat. He bolted across the yard and up the porch steps.

I LOOK up at the deep blue sky. The sun shines brightly. Slowly, I ascend the porch steps. The front door is open. I walk inside and look around. Everything is quiet, peaceful.

Billy stands at the bottom of the staircase and greets me with smile. I want to go to him, but I can't. Something is keeping me from him.

I walk past him, down the hall, and into the bedroom. The sliding-door is open, its curtains blowing gently in the wind. I look behind me for Billy, but I can no longer see him.

Drawn to the door leading outside, I walk through it. Cold air whooshes all around me. Suddenly, the sun fades and darkness surrounds me. I sense something in the forest, hiding...lurking...waiting.

"Sami...," a deep voice calls out from the shadows.

Chills run down my legs. I want to turn and run, but I can't.

"Sami!" the voice snaps, and a wicked laughter echoes all around.

Frozen with fear, I shout for help, "Billy!" But there's no answer. Terrified, a blood-curdling shriek rips from my lungs.

Sami screamed and sat up. She took a second to grasp her surroundings, eyeing the recliner across the room, the flat screen TV, and the couch beneath her. "It was just a dream," she whispered and clutched her chest, trying to calm her breathing.

The front door flung open and Jason burst in.

"What the hell!" she shouted, eyes wide.

"Sami! Are you okay?" he asked with a horrified look.

Realizing Jason must've heard her scream, she let out a heavy sigh and sat back. "Just another nightmare."

Jason plopped next to her and ran a hand through his hair. "Holy shit! You scared the hell outta me."

"Sorry."

"Don't be sorry. Are you okay?"

"I'm fine."

"Good." He hopped to his feet and shut the front door.

She glanced at the clock on the wall above the hallway. The short hand pointed to twelve and the long hand to one. "Aren't you supposed to be at work?"

"Yeah, Abby's making a big lunch, and she invited you over. Billy had to finish up something he was in the middle of, so he asked me to pick you up. If you're up for it, I mean."

"Oh." She forced a smile, still shaken from her nightmare.

"So, are you up for it? Are you sure you're okay?"

"Yeah, just give me a minute." She headed upstairs to freshen up and gather her thoughts. After brushing her teeth, she went to her room and changed out of the T-shirt, wrinkled from her nap. She chose a navy eyelet blouse to match her faded jeans. Then, she wriggled her feet into a pair of navy flats, which left the bandage on top of her foot uncovered and comfortable.

Feeling somewhat better, she went back downstairs.

Jason was waiting by the front door.

"All ready." She smiled.

"Now, that's the Sami I know." Jason grinned. "You had me worried there for a minute." He held his arm out and looked down. "I see your foot's feeling better."

"Yep, it only hurts a little." She grabbed his arm and they headed to the yellow Mustang parked behind her car. As soon as they settled in their seats, Jason glanced in the rear-view mirror and ran a quick hand through his tousled, dark blond hair.

"You look pretty, Jason." Sami snickered. "And so does your car. Did you both get a bath today?"

He smiled through one corner of his mouth and pushed the start button, revving the engine to life. "Very funny." He backed out of the driveway and threw her a wicked grin. "Now hold on." The tires spun and the car thrust forward.

Sami clutched the handle and giggled. "Slow down!"

"Fine." Jason stopped at the end of their road and made a right, keeping a slower pace.

Sami stared out the window, watching the forest whir by, still shaken over her nightmare. She'd had the same dream as last night. Though she knew Jessica couldn't hurt her anymore, the feeling something still lurked out there, waiting for her, was too strong to ignore.

Maybe there are more of them out there, waiting for their chance to kill me? Maybe they want revenge for what happened to Jessica? Or maybe there's nothing out there, and I just need to get a grip.

"You okay, over there?" Jason glanced at her, his brow creased with worry.

"I'm fine. Still just a little tired, I guess."

"You'll probably feel better after you eat."

"Probably." She focused on her surroundings. The forest on Farmington Road appeared thicker and eerier than at her house. *Darker* even. She hoped Abby's house was more cheerful than the drive.

She thought of Abby, wondering how they'd get along. When they'd met two weeks ago, all had went well. But, since the kidnapping, Sami had become socially cautious.

What if Abby mistakes my wariness of strangers for just being flat-out weird? It would be nice to have one female friend in this town.

"What's going on in that head of yours?" Jason asked.

Sami chewed on her bottom lip, wondering if she should bother Jason with her reservations.

"Come on, out with it," he said, his tone playful and coaxing.

Needing reassurance, she decided to confide in him. "Do you think Abby will like me?" *Now that I'm broken,* she added silently.

"Of course, she will. Why wouldn't she?"

"I don't know." She shrugged.

"Don't worry, Sami. Abby's a nice person. You two will get along just fine."

"But I won't know what to say."

"Trust me, there's not a moment of silence with Abby around. Why do you think it's taking us so long to finish the house?" He grinned.

She giggled under her breath. "Yeah, you're right. I just get a little nervous meeting new people now. It's silly." She shook her head, embarrassed.

Jason's smile faded. "It's not silly, Sami. You have every right to be leery of strangers. Don't worry. Aside from her constant, energetic yabbering, Abby's a good person. You'll be fine. Just be yourself, and she'll fall in love with you like I did." His jaw dropped. "Uhhh, I mean, not that I'm in *love* with you or anything. I just love you like a friend, or *like* you like a friend." He chuckled nervously. "You know what I mean."

"Yes, Jason, I know what you mean." She grinned, yet deep inside she felt as if he was hiding the truth.

The first time she'd gotten the hint Jason held deeper feelings for her had been at the lake when he'd kissed her. And, when he'd found her in Jessica's basement, she'd *heard* the love in his voice and had *felt* it in his touch as he'd stroked her cheeks. Since then, he hadn't given the slightest indication that he was in love with her—which was a good sign. Either way, all she could offer him was close friendship.

She looked out the window into the dark shadows of the forest, feeling uneasy again. "It sure is creepy out here."

"Yeah, it gives me the creeps too. The forest is denser here or something. I can't wait until we're done with the house."

"Well, *I* can't wait until we're done with *lunch*. I don't know how she can live out here all alone. How much farther is it anyway?"

"Another mile."

"Another *mile*? You can't be serious?"

"Dead serious. Which is fitting in these woods."

Sami scanned the edges of the road, looking for driveways. She didn't remember seeing any so far. "Is her house the only one out here?"

"Yep! Creepy!" he said as the house finally came into view. "And here we are…Creepsville!"

They slowed, and the tires crunched across the long gravel drive lining the vast, grassy yard.

"Wow! The front yard is almost big enough to play baseball on. Does Abby mow all this?" Sami asked.

"Mike does. The back yard is even bigger. And, if you put the side yards together, they're just as big as the front." Jason pulled up next to

Billy's black Charger and shut the engine off.

Sami stared at the large, three-story farmhouse. Four, if you counted the attic with the eerie looking octagon-shaped window. "I almost expected to see a ghost standing there, in the attic window."

Jason peered up. "Yeah…me too…now that you mention it. Thanks for ruining it for me." He continued to stare at it with his mouth hanging open.

The wrap-around porch of the traditional house had been freshly painted a pale blue-gray. But the white paint covering the rest of the house had dulled and flaked over the years, allowing old gray wood to show through in spots.

"It's really big," Sami said, amazed.

Jason chuckled. "That's what she said."

She rolled her eyes and giggled under her breath. "Your dumb, Jason."

Jason stopped smiling. "Yeah, I know."

They climbed out of the car, and Sami followed Jason up the porch steps and into the house.

Though the outside looked like a big farm house, the inside was elegant with a modern touch.

The spacious foyer opened all the way to the third floor, and a grand mahogany staircase stood in the middle of it. Gray swirls danced across the white marble flooring. And crystal vases stood on mahogany end tables against the walls on either side of the staircase, each holding bouquets of beautiful flowers in a multitude of bright colors.

"Wow!" Sami exclaimed. "This is so beautiful. And *huge*!"

Jason smirked.

She glanced at him and shook her head. "Don't even."

He laughed and motioned with a quick nod to a door on the left. "Come on."

Sami followed Jason into a spacious, modern kitchen. The light hickory floors contrasted well with the white cabinets and black granite countertops. A matching oversized island sat in the middle of the room. Behind it, Billy, Mike, and Abby sat in the black leather chairs surrounding a long dining table near the window-filled wall.

Billy grinned. "There she is!"

Jason made a beeline for the table, leaving Sami standing by herself. Feeling vulnerable, her stomach flip-flopped with nerves. She forced a slight grin and proceeded with caution.

"Hello, Sami!" Abby's blue eyes lit up and she crossed the room.

"Hi, Abby," Sami said. Trying to show confidence, she stuck her hand out, waiting for Abby to shake it.

Instead, Abby wrapped her arms around Sami in a polite hug. "No need to be formal. I've heard so much about you that I feel like I know you already."

Sami glanced at the three men standing behind Abby, wondering what they'd said about her. "Yeah, I get that a lot around here."

They all flashed cheesy grins.

"You've healed nicely from your car accident." Abby smiled. "You are very beautiful."

"Thank you." Sami pinched her lips together, feeling awkward as memories of her battered face flashed through her mind.

"Anyway, come sit down." Abby took Sami's hand and led her to the table.

Various platters of sandwiches, fruits, vegetables, and even a round chocolate cake sat in the middle of the table.

Sami sat next to Billy, eyeing the formal place settings. "It looks really nice."

"Thank you!" Abby beamed. "It's just a little something I threw together."

Everyone glanced at each other for a moment, not knowing quite how to proceed. Finally, Mike reached out and took a couple of sandwiches.

"It does look good, Abby." Mike winked. He reached over and patted Abby's hand.

She smiled a silent thank you.

Billy and Jason followed Mike's lead and began filling their plates. Sami took a sandwich, carrot sticks, and strawberries. She chomped on a carrot stick, enjoying its sweetness.

"So, Sami," Abby said, "Mike tells me your mother is moving to Seattle?"

"Yeah." Sami covered her disappointment with a smile, trying to appear more enthusiastic about the situation. Abby had gone through a lot of trouble to prepare lunch, and she didn't want to ruin it by talking about personal problems.

"I guess I'll be on my own soon." Sami raised her eyebrows and shrugged.

Abby's eyes sparked with giddiness and she flipped her blonde hair back from her shoulder. "Oh, how exciting! I remember when I first lived on my own. Of course, I was a few years older than you, and it was after I had graduated from college. What college are you enrolled in?"

"Well, I..." Sami glanced at Billy, silently asking for help. So far, it seemed every topic of conversation had been about the depressing issues she was trying hard to forget. Feeling uncomfortable, she was at a sudden loss for words.

Billy reached under the table and squeezed Sami's hand. "She's taking time off from school, Abby," he said.

"Oh, well, there's nothing wrong with that." Abby smiled.

Jason glanced at Sami and winked. He cleared his throat. "So, Abby, what do you want us to do next?"

Abby's eyes twinkled. "Well, I had originally wanted one of the upstairs bedrooms completed next. But then, I was thinking maybe one of the upstairs bathrooms should be done first. There's one in particular, on the second floor, that looks as if it were very elegant at one time. I'm anxious to see what it would look like restored. Of course, most of the house will be more modern, but some of the rooms will hold their original touch."

Sami glanced at Jason and gave him a silent *thank you* through a subtle smile.

Jason winked again.

They focused their attention back on Abby and their sandwiches. For some reason, the food tasted better than Sami had been accustomed to and she savored every bite. "Are you a chef?" she asked Abby.

"I'm flattered, but no. Maybe someday?" She made eye contact with the three men staring at her before she continued. "I'm so happy you all finally finished the kitchen though! It looks so beautiful. I just couldn't go one more day without it. I *love* to cook."

"It does look beautiful," Sami said, finally feeling a little more at ease in Abby's presence. Especially since Abby had stopped making her the target of conversation.

"Doesn't it?" Abby agreed. "You should see what Billy did with the family room in just a few days' time. It doesn't even *look* like the same room."

"Ah." Billy tried to hide his grin through tight lips. "It's just work. Mike's the one who taught me everything I know."

Sami reached under the table and patted Billy's thigh. "I'm sure it looks great." She nudged her empty plate aside.

"Are you finished, Sami?" Abby asked. "I can show you around the house." She stood and pushed in her chair.

Sami glanced at Billy, and his lips curled into a reassuring smile. Then, she glanced at Jason, who raised an eyebrow and smirked.

She wasn't so sure she wanted to go on the house tour now, but she couldn't come up with an excuse to get out of it. "Uh, sure. Can't wait to see it." She stood and followed Abby into the next room.

Even though exploring an old house kept her interest satisfied, the tour seemed to last forever. Abby moved from one room to the next, and from floor to floor, explaining in detail what each room would become—guest bedrooms, a library, an office, a possible nursery. She even showed Sami the attic which would just be used for storage for now.

Sami went to the creepy, octagon-shaped window and peered down through it. She spotted Jason standing next to his car in the driveway, talking to Mike. They were both laughing and having a good time.

Jason casually glanced up at the window and froze, his expression filled with fear. After a few seconds, he placed a hand on his chest and grinned. He pointed up to the attic window, drawing Mike's gaze to it.

Mike started laughing.

Jason waved at Sami.

Sami giggled and waved back.

"What's so funny?" Abby asked.

"Jason saw me standing in the window and got scared. I think he thought I was a ghost." She giggled again.

Abby snickered. "Come on. Let's go back downstairs."

When they reached the final staircase, Sami was relieved to see Billy waiting for her at the bottom, wearing a huge grin.

"Pretty cool, huh?" Billy asked.

"Very," Sami said as she jogged down the last few steps and stood next to him.

Abby joined them.

Another door behind the staircase stirred Sami's curiosity. "What's behind that door?"

The excitement in Abby's eyes dimmed. "Oh, that's just the basement. You don't want to go down there." She laughed but with a nervous undertone. "It's just used for storage."

"Don't feel bad, she won't let us go down there either." Billy shot Abby a knowing glance.

"Just a clutter of boxes. I don't like going down there myself. It's kind of scary," she replied.

"I'm sure it is," Sami said.

Billy wrapped his hand around Sami's. "Are you ready to go?"

"Yes!" Sami said, more than ready to leave but trying not to sound too jovial. "Thank you for lunch and for showing me around, Abby. You have a very beautiful home."

"Thank you, Sami. I enjoyed giving you a tour. We should have lunch again sometime," she suggested.

"Yeah, that would be nice," Sami said, hoping not anytime soon. Though Abby was friendly, Jason was right, the constant chattering was mentally exhausting.

"Maybe this weekend?" Abby suggested with excitement in her eyes.

Billy looked at Sami as if he could read her mind. "Actually, Abby, her mom is leaving soon, and she's already promised to spend time with her."

"Oh, that's right! I forgot. Maybe sometime after that."

"Sure." Sami nodded, dreading the day already. She hoped Billy, Jason, and Mike would be invited along, to take some of the pressure off.

Jason and Mike walked through the front door.

"You guys ready to head out?" Jason asked.

"Actually, I'm gonna stick around for a while." Mike winked at Abby, before he turned to Billy. "Little brother."

"Yeah, yeah," Billy muttered and rolled his eyes. He fished keys from his pocket and tossed them to Mike.

"Okay, guys—" Jason headed out the front door "—bus is leaving. Especially after the near heart attack I just had." He stopped on the porch and glowered at Sami.

"Boo!" Sami snickered.

Mike and Abby laughed.

"Screw you guys." Jason headed for his car.

Billy looked confused. "What was that all about?"

"Jason saw me standing in the attic window and thought I was a ghost. You should've seen the look on his face." Sami giggled again.

Billy smirked. "I wish I would've." He looked at Abby. "Thanks for lunch."

"You're welcome. See you tomorrow."

Billy led the way to Jason's car. He climbed into the back seat and let Sami sit up front.

"Now, do you see why we come home from work completely exhausted?" Jason asked. He stepped on the gas and sped away.

Billy chuckled. "Because you're afraid of ghosts?"

Jason glared at Billy through the rear-view mirror. "Very funny."

"Abby's not so bad," Billy said. "She talks to Mike most of the time."

"I'm glad it's a big house. There are *lots* of places to hide from her," Jason said. "Except, I don't think I'll be hiding in the attic anymore."

"Is that why I can't ever find you?" Billy asked.

Jason flashed a sheepish grin. "I seriously don't know how Mike does it."

When they arrived back at Sami's house, they all went inside.

Her mom was at the kitchen sink, setting dirty dishes into the dishwasher. Wisps of hair had fallen from her ponytail, framing her face, and her lavender dress complimented her rosy glow. Happiness exuded from her again, something Sami hadn't seen for over a year.

Her mother welcomed them with a warm smile. "Well, what are you all up to today?"

"We went to Abby's for lunch," Sami said. "It was nice. You should see her house. It's humongous!"

"That's what she said," Jason said and chuckled under his breath.

"Seriously?" Billy stared at Jason, his expression flat. "What are you, like, twelve?" Without warning, he punched Jason in the shoulder.

"Okay!" Jason laughed and winced, rubbing his arm.

"Oh!" Her mother's eyes lit up. "Steve's having dinner at his house tomorrow night. Billy, Jason, we'd like you to join us." She looked at everyone with a hopeful smile.

Sami had forgotten all about dinner at Steve's, and she dreaded it.

"Ummm." Jason hesitated, clenching his jaw and causing his temples to pulsate.

Her mom's eyes filled with desperation. "Please, Jason. It's sort of like a going away dinner. I'm going to miss you, too, you know."

Jason's temples calmed, and he raised one corner of his mouth. "Sure. I wouldn't wanna miss your going away dinner…at Steve's house."

"Sounds good to me, too," Billy said.

"Great," Sami muttered under her breath and rolled her eyes. Having the pervert in *her* house was difficult enough, but now she had to travel into *his* territory? Had her mom forgotten that Steve had attacked Jason's mother a few years back? And, that he'd knocked Jason unconscious for defending her? Sure, Steve had been drunk and had later apologized to Jason and his family. But, in Sami's eyes, no apology was worth forgiving such vile actions.

"Come on, Samantha. He just wants to get to know you before—"

"Before what, Mom? Before he moves you to another state?" Sami snapped.

"Give him a chance, please? For me." Her mom let out a weary sigh. "Oh, and I just got off the phone with Mike. He and Abby are coming also."

Jason's smile faded.

Billy smirked at him.

"Well, guys, I'm going home to take a shower," Jason said. "I worked up a sweat hiding from Abby today. She's getting faster at finding me. I think she's figuring out what I'm up to."

Carol gave Jason a questioning look.

"I mean, I worked hard today, hence the sweat. And, most of the time, she can't find me because her house is so big…and spread out. It's like you're *hiding* from everyone. You know? Hard work." He let out a guilty chuckle and headed for the front door. "I'm just gonna go now. See you guys tomorrow."

Sami giggled. "Bye, Jason," she shouted before the front door shut all the way.

"Hmmm." Her mom snickered and shook her head. "Anyway, Steve's taking me to dinner tonight. You both are more than welcome to join us."

Sami tensed and scrambled to come up with a viable excuse to get out of it without hurting her mother's feelings, but nothing came to mind.

"I'm making her dinner tonight," Billy said.

"Oh." Her mom smiled. "That sounds nice."

Sami felt bad for rejecting her mom, especially since she'd be moving away soon. They needed to spend time together, but she couldn't fathom the thought of seeing Steve any more than she had to. "Well, Mom, maybe you and I could watch a movie later tonight?"

A pleasant smile crossed her mother's face. "That's all right, sweetheart. You two have a date planned. I don't want to cut your night short. Besides, Steve is taking me out of town for dinner. I don't think I'll be back until late. But we can do breakfast tomorrow. At the diner," she said, sounding hopeful.

"Just me and you?" Sami asked.

She nodded. "Just me and you."

"Sounds good. I'll see you in the morning, then. Have fun tonight."

"I will," Carol said. She looked at the clock on the wall. "Oh, Steve will be here any second."

Sami grabbed Billy's arm and opened the front door, anxious to leave before Steve arrived. "Okay, bye, Mom!"

"Bye, sweetheart. You too, Billy."

"See you tomorrow, Carol," Billy said as he closed the door.

They jogged down the steps and hurried across Sami's yard, into Billy's.

"Thank you for getting us out of dinner tonight," she said. "There's no way I could take two nights in a row with him."

"Now, you owe me."

"Oh, really?" Sami raised an eyebrow. "And how do you expect me to repay you?" Not hearing his heavy steps crunching on the grass anymore, she turned around to see why he'd stopped.

A devious grin formed, and Billy charged straight toward her.

"What are you doing?" Sami screamed and ran across his yard, giggling, with Billy on her heals. She didn't stop running until they were in the privacy of his bedroom.

7

A FAINT groan escaped Sami's lips as they trudged up the porch steps to Steve's house. "Two awkward meals, two days in a row. This is definitely *not* my idea of a good time." She smoothed out the skirt of her pale blue summer dress decorated with purple flowers.

"I'm with her," Jason said with an irritated look. "First lunch with Abby, now dinner at Steve's? Someone put me out of my misery!"

Billy squeezed Sami's hand. "You look nice. It won't be so bad. We'll leave right after dinner." His gaze shifted to Jason and back to her. "Okay guys?"

"Yeah, sure. Easy for *you* to say," Jason said.

Sami reached up and unfolded the collar of Billy's smoke-colored, buttoned shirt, flattening it back down in its proper place. "You look nice, too."

Jason eyed Billy's shirt. "And did you have to wear the same color as me? We look stupid!"

Sami snickered.

The front door opened, and the moment Sami had been dreading was here.

"Hey, guys!" Steve grinned. "Come on in. Make yourselves at home." He stepped aside.

They proceeded through the door and into the living room. Pictures of the forest, framed in black, hung on the walls, black curtains covered the windows, and a black leather couch and loveseat faced a large, flat-screen TV. Even his shirt was black.

Must be his favorite color. Fitting! Sami thought.

"Everyone's in here," Steve said, leading the way through a doorway to the left.

Sami nudged Billy in front of her, making him go in first.

The dining room was more formal than the living room. More paintings hung on the walls, but these were of the ocean. An elegant chandelier dangled from the tray ceiling. The hutch practically overflowed with china and crystal. And an oversized dining table, fit for a king, dominated the middle of the room.

Her mom sat at the table, along with Abby.

"You made it!" Her mom's eyes sparked to life when they walked in.

Steve sat at the head of the table next to her mother.

"It's about time you guys showed up!" Mike said as he entered the room from a door on the opposite wall, while holding a glass of water and a bottle of beer. The slate hue of his shirt almost matched his brother's and Jason's. He took the open seat between Abby and Steve.

Sami glanced at Jason just in time to see his face pucker with disgust when he noticed Mike's shirt. She bit her lip to keep from laughing and took a seat next to her mom. Billy sat next to Sami.

Jason took the only other seat available, on the other side of Abby. He gave a quick nod and a polite smile. "Abby."

"Hello, Jason!" Abby beamed. "Did you know you all match tonight?" She motioned to Billy and Mike before gesturing toward Jason's shirt. "Maybe I should've worn my gray dress instead of this red one." She peered down and smoothed the wrinkle across her middle.

"That would've been a great idea," Jason said with a flat undertone.

"Anyway," Abby continued, "I was just telling Steve what a beautiful home he has." She turned back to Steve. "If you ever want me to sell it for you, just let me know."

"Huh, you sell houses for a living?" Jason raised his eyebrows. "It suits you."

"Thank you." Abby smiled and took a sip of her wine.

"Wine, Jason?" Sami's mom held up the bottle.

"Please!" Jason said, almost begging. His eyes lit up as she filled his glass to the top.

"Billy?" She held the bottle to his glass.

"No thanks. I'm driving," he said. He reached across the table and snatched Mike's full glass of water. "This is fine."

"Sweetheart?" her mom asked.

Sami's eyes widened. She'd asked her mom for a sip of alcohol here and there since she'd been seventeen, but the answer had always been no.

Sami studied her mom's calm expression, wondering if it were some sort of joke. Or wine with no alcohol in it. *Is there non-alcoholic wine? I've never heard of it. That would just make it grape juice, right?*

Sami shrugged. "Sure."

Her mother poured the burgundy liquid, stopping when it neared the top. She hadn't noticed until now that her mom's dress matched the color of the wine.

Steve handed Sami the bowl of spaghetti.

"Thanks." She smiled, trying to be amicable for her mother's sake. She scooped a pile of the steaming pasta onto her plate and handed the bowl to Billy. After everyone filled their plates, they all dug in to enjoy the food and each other's company.

Much to Sami's surprise, aside from the bitterness of the wine, dinner was pleasant. The warm swimming feel of her head helped. She finally realized why her mom had poured her a couple of glasses in the first place—so she would enjoy herself. Her mother probably had Jason in mind too, when she'd set a full bottle within his reach.

Sami glanced at Jason. He was actually enjoying a conversation with Abby and Mike. Billy was in the middle of talking to Steve about his promotion in Seattle.

A gentle nudge to Sami's elbow drew her attention to her mom.

Carol leaned in and whispered, "Thank you for coming tonight."

Sami nodded and pointed to her empty glass, raising her eyebrows and awaiting her mother's approval.

Her mom hesitated and narrowed her eyes, but gave way to a hint of a smile. She grabbed the bottle and filled Sami's glass.

"Thanks, Mom." Sami beamed and took a sip.

Abby's cell phone rang, and the room fell silent. She pulled her phone from her purse and looked at the number. "Excuse me," she said as she stood up from the table and went into the other room for privacy.

Billy sighed. "Well, it's been a long day. Are you about ready, Sami?"

"Sure." Sami took a few more gulps of the wine, trying to polish it off, until the bitterness became too overwhelming. Her mouth puckered, but she stifled the reaction between tight lips before anyone noticed.

Abby reentered the dining room, her face wrought with distress. "Uh, Mike. I need to go. Can you get a ride back with Billy?"

"Sure." Mike's brow creased with worry. "Is everything all right?"

"Just a bit of a family emergency. I have to go out of town for a few days." Abby snatched her purse from the back of the chair. "I'm really sorry I have to leave so suddenly. Steve, Carol, thank you for the lovely dinner."

"You're welcome," Carol said with a look of concern. "Is there anything we can do for you?"

"No, thank you." She smiled. "I'll see you all when I get back. And, if I don't get back before you leave, have a safe journey."

"Thank you, Abby," Carol said. "It was nice to meet you."

"I'll walk you out." Mike hopped to his feet and followed Abby out of the dining room.

"We should get going." Billy stood and pushed in his chair.

When Sami stood, her legs weakened, and her mind clouded with dizziness. As she gripped the edge of the table to steady herself, Billy's hand clamped around her arm, providing extra support.

He gave her a reassuring smile and handed her his glass of water.

Luckily, no one else noticed. Her mom was talking to Steve, and Jason was finishing the last of his wine.

Sami gulped down the contents of Billy's glass, wishing she hadn't asked her mother for more wine. Thankfully, the water cleared the fuzziness enough for her to bid farewell without appearing drunk. "Bye, Mom. Thanks for dinner, Steve," Sami said, trying to avoid eye contact.

Her mother gave her a hug. "I'll see you at home."

"Okay." Sami gave her a quick pat on the back, anxious to get out of there.

"Thanks for dinner." Jason made his way to the front door.

"You're welcome, Jason," Steve said.

Without looking back, Jason raised a hand over his head, gesturing a single wave good-bye.

Billy wrapped one arm around Sami's waist, giving her much needed support, and led her outside to his car where Mike was waiting.

Carol and Steve followed them out, stopping on the front porch to wave.

They all waved back and piled into the car. Jason and Mike climbed into the backseat, and Sami sat up front with Billy.

Sami eyed her wide-open door, wishing the handle wasn't so far away. Under normal circumstances, closing the car door would've been an easy task. But being somewhat intoxicated made the simple feat seem impossible.

With jerky movements, she tugged at the long, heavy door until it swung shut. She eased against the seat and yanked the seatbelt across her torso. The metal clanked together and slid around as she tried to latch the harness into place. *How is this not working? Is it broken?*

Patience growing thin, she gave a final shove and the two ends clicked together. "Huh." She let out a long breath to calm her frustration. The potency of the wine intensified as time went by, rather than diminishing as she had hoped.

"Is everything all right with Abby?" Billy glanced at Mike through the rear-view mirror.

"I don't know. She just said there was some drama going on with her sister and she would call me in a couple of days. She left me her key, so we can keep working on the house."

"I'm sure everything's fine," Billy reassured. He started the car and headed down the road.

"I'm not so sure. She was acting kind of strange," Mike added.

"That's because she *is* strange," Jason said.

"Come on, Jason," Billy said, sounding irritated. "Now isn't the time for smart-ass comments."

Sami giggled.

Billy glanced over at her and furrowed his brow.

Jason let out a slight chuckle.

"What the hell?" Mike snapped. "This isn't funny!"

Sami clamped her lips together to stifle her amusement, but laughter sputtered through them.

Billy eyed her warily. "Come on, Sami, it's not funny."

She puckered her lips, trying to keep a straight face. "You're right. It's not funny."

Jason guffawed, making it impossible for Sami to contain her laughter. She threw her hands over her mouth to hide it.

Billy's expression turned flat. He sighed and looked at his brother through the rear-view mirror. "Great! They're drunk!"

"What? How in the hell can they be drunk?" Mike glared at Jason. "How much did you drink?"

"Don't know." Jason muffled a laugh, forcing a snort of air from his nose. "Just a few glasses. No one even noticed me refilling my glass. You know, I've never had wine before. But it's really, really good. You want some?" He pulled a bottle out from under his jacket. With a flick of his thumb, he popped the cork off and proceeded to guzzle it.

"Dude!" Billy said with a shocked look on his face. "You *stole* a bottle of wine from Steve's?"

"What the hell's the matter with you?" Mike snapped.

Sami found it entertaining. She laughed so hard, tears rolled down her cheeks and she gasped for air. When she finally gained a little self-control, she snatched the bottle from Jason's hands.

"I'll have some!" She raised the bottle to her lips and took a few gulps.

"Sami!" Billy reached for the bottle.

She huddled against the window, clutching the bottle.

Suddenly, she bounced violently in the seat and her shoulder slammed against the door as Billy swerved onto the grassy shoulder.

"Shit!" He corrected his steering and found his way back onto the road. "Is everyone okay?"

"Yeah," Mike said, his tone bitter.

"I'm good!" Jason patted the back of Billy's headrest.

Sami cringed. "Oops. Sorry."

Mike's arm appeared over her shoulder and he yanked the bottle from her fingers.

"Hey!" She pouted, sticking out her bottom lip.

"You're gonna thank me in the morning!" Mike stuck the bottle out the window and tipped it upside down.

Jason glared at Mike. "Oh, dude, that was so not cool!" He burst out in sudden laughter.

Sami giggled.

"Mike, have I ever told you what a *great* big brother you are?" Jason enunciated every word. "Because…you're like a brother to me. Did you know that?"

"Awww. That is so sweet! I bet he loves you too, Jason." Sami unbuckled her seatbelt and turned around to face Mike, kneeling on the seat. "Do you? Do you love him like a *great* big brother should love a little brother?"

"Sami! What the hell are you doing?" Billy roared and the car slowed. "Sit back down!"

Mike unfastened his seatbelt, grabbed her firmly by the shoulders, and forced her back into a forward-facing position. Then, he yanked her seatbelt across her chest and clicked it into place. "Well, this night is turning out to be a nightmare!"

"Geez, you don't have to get so pushy, Mike!" Sami harrumphed and crossed her arms.

Jason snickered with his hand cupped over his mouth. "You got in trouble."

Billy shook his head.

"Good! We're home!" Mike belted out as Billy pulled into the driveway.

Billy shut off the engine and got out of the car, leaving the headlights on. He went around to the front, carefully inspecting the front end.

Sami climbed out, but her legs wobbled, offering little support. She shut the door and leaned against it, trying to focus as everything spun around her.

Jason slithered out of the back seat and stumbled toward his driveway.

"Bye, Jason!" Sami shouted.

Mike bolted out of the car and caught up to him. "You're not going anywhere!" He picked Jason up, threw him over his shoulder, and headed toward the house.

"Dude, put me down!" Jason laughed.

"If you puke on me, I'm knocking your ass out and leaving you here!" Mike said.

Sami pointed to Jason. "Ha, ha! *You* got in trouble this time!"

Billy shut the headlights off and made his way around the front of the car to where Sami stood. He shook his head and sighed, his eyes filled with disappointment.

"Awe, Sami, I'm sorry you're so drunk."

She smiled at him, swaying and trying to steady herself against the car. "Don't be sorry. I feel great!"

"You won't feel this way in the morning," he said with regret.

"Are you mad at me?" She puckered her bottom lip.

"No, I still love you very much." He kissed her on the forehead, carefully scooped her up, and carried her into his house.

8

SAMI OPENED her eyes to blinding light and a pounding headache. She pushed herself into a sitting position and stared at Billy's dresser, and then, his desk, wondering how she'd gotten into his room. Nausea knotted her gut and rose to the back of her throat, hitting like a tidal wave. She threw a hand over her mouth and sprinted for the bathroom.

As soon as she reached the toilet, she fell to her knees and vomited sour acid—heaving over and over until her stomach cramped so violently she was sure it had ripped in half. With shaky arms and legs, she pushed herself up from the toilet and flushed away the sickness. She abolished the rancid aftertaste with mouthwash and trudged into the living room, using the wall as support with one hand and holding her achy head with the other.

"Good morning!" Mike shouted from the kitchen table, grinning. "Feel better?"

"Shut up, Mike!" She grumbled and flopped onto the couch.

Jason was sprawled across the recliner, snoring.

"How do you feel?" Billy came out of the kitchen with a tall glass of water. He handed it to her, along with two acetaminophen tablets.

"I feel like I'm gonna die," she croaked. "Why didn't anyone tell me this is what drinking too much feels like?" She dropped the pills into her mouth and washed them down, drinking half the liquid in two gulps.

"Easy on the water," Billy warned and took the glass from her. "You might get sick again."

"So, are you hungry?" Mike grinned. "Bacon? Sausage? Maybe some runny eggs with another bottle of wine?"

The repulsive thought sent Sami's stomach flip-flopping. She shot Mike an evil glare and laid her head back on the couch, waiting for the pounding in her brain to stop.

Billy rubbed the back of her hand. "I'm sorry you're so sick. I remember my first hangover. Haven't had one since."

"How long is this gonna last?" She let out an unsteady breath and held her stomach, trying to stay the building nausea.

"A few hours," Mike replied.

She glared at him. "Why are you being so mean?"

"Probably because you weren't being very nice last night, Sami," Billy said.

"What? What do you mean? What'd I do?"

"You and Jason made fun of Abby, and you were major pains in the asses all night until you finally passed out," Billy said.

Sami covered her open mouth with her hand, before clutching her upset stomach again. "Oh no! I don't even remember any of it. I *like* Abby. Really. I'm such a jerk."

"Don't worry about it, Sami," Mike said in his normal tone, as if he had a change of heart. "I know you were just drunk. You guys didn't actually say anything too bad. You just thought *everything* about Abby was hilarious and that everything else was too."

"I'm *so* sorry! I don't think anything about her is funny. Not at *all*! I feel so terrible." She closed her eyes and shook her head. Another wave of nausea struck full force. She jumped up and ran for the bathroom, slamming the door shut behind her.

When she finished heaving for a second time, she made her way back to the couch again, her entire body weaker than ever.

Billy frowned. "Sorry. I tried to take the bottle from you last night but almost wrecked. I wish I could make you feel better." He handed her the glass of water.

"You almost wrecked because of me? How could I have been so *stupid*? I could've gotten us all killed. I am *so* sorry!"

"Don't worry about it. Luckily, no one was hurt, and my car's fine. I'm sorry you're hurting now, though. You should drink some more water." He gazed at her with sympathetic eyes and frowned.

She stared at the water, afraid the nausea would return as soon as the liquid hit her stomach. The next few sips settled just fine. After a couple more, she handed the glass back to Billy. "I'm just gonna rest here for a little bit." She laid back on the couch and closed her eyes, hoping to fall asleep before the urge to vomit returned.

BILLY SAT in the lawn chair in the backyard to watch Mike work on his motorcycle. "So, did Abby call yet?"

"Not yet. Can you hand me the wrench?"

Billy picked up the wrench from the toolbox next to his chair and handed it to his brother. "I'm sure she's just caught up with her family. She doesn't ever talk about them. Probably just a private person."

"You've got *that* right. I didn't even know she *had* a sister." Mike swiped the sweat from his forehead with the back of his hand and let out a burdened sigh. "Abby's different somehow. Almost like she's void of emotion or something. It's a good thing this isn't going anywhere serious. As a matter of fact, as soon as we're done with the house, I think I'll call it off."

"Maybe something bad happened to her in the past?"

"I don't know." Mike cocked his jaw to one side, deep in thought. He shook his head and turned his attention back to his bike.

Billy had never seen his brother so upset over a woman before. Which meant Mike really cared about her. "Sorry, bro."

"Holy hell!" Jason grumbled as he trudged down the steps. He plopped down in the chair next to Billy. "Wine is truly evil!"

"Want a beer?" Billy asked.

Jason grimaced.

Mike chuckled.

"Guys, whatever I did last night…whatever I said…I'm sorry." Jason laid his head back and closed his eyes. In an instant he jumped to his feet again, bolted across the yard to the edge of the forest, and vomited.

Mike and Billy laughed.

"Shut up!" Jason tromped back toward them and eased onto the seat, his expression sour.

"Wasn't that exactly what we were telling Jason to do all night—to shut the hell up?" Mike asked.

"Yep! That about sums it up. Oh, and you'll have to be sure to tell Sami you're sorry," Billy said, staring at Jason.

"Shit! What'd I say to Sami?"

"It's not what you said, it's what you *did*," Mike said as he continued to work on his motorcycle.

"What'd I do?"

"Well, let's just put it this way—" Billy narrowed his eyes, recalling what he'd said to Jason at the lake a few weeks ago when Jason had tried to kiss Sami "—you're lucky I didn't break your jaw!"

"No!" Jason said, his eyes as wide open as his mouth. "I *didn't*! Please tell me you're frickin' joking!"

Billy continued his cold stare.

"Dude, I am *so* sorry!" Jason sighed and ran a hand through his hair. "I don't even remember kissing her."

Mike grinned. "How does your jaw feel?"

Jason rubbed his chin and opened his mouth wide, stretching it as if he could feel an ache. His eyes met Billy's. "Did you hit me?"

"No." Billy smirked. "Sami did."

"She did? Son of a bitch! I guess I'll apologize when she wakes up." His pained expression proved he was disgusted with himself.

"Apologize for what?" Sami shut the backdoor and made her way to the chair on the other side of Billy.

"Do you feel better?" Billy asked.

"Yes! Much! No more headache and no more throwing up." Sami smiled. Focusing on the back of her hand, she closed her fingers into a fist and opened them again. Her smile faded, and a puzzled look formed. "My hand kind of hurts though."

Mike chuckled.

"I'm sorry, Sami," Jason said.

"About what?" She looked at him, confused.

Jason shrugged. "Uh, you know, for anything I might've said or done to offend you last night?"

She looked at him as if he were crazy. "You don't have to apologize for anything. The last thing I remember was the drive home. Barely."

Billy shot Jason an evil glare.

Jason ignored him. "So cool? We're all good, then, right?"

"Sure." She smiled, turning her attention back to the faint purple hue of her knuckles. "Did I hit something last night?" She looked at Billy.

Billy eye's bore into Jason's.

"Okay!" Jason said, frustrated. "Apparently, I kissed you last night, and you punched me for it. I don't remember any of it, and I'm sorry!"

"What?" Sami's mouth fell open. "You kissed me?" Her worried eyes shifted to Billy's again.

"Don't worry, Sami," Billy said. "I'm all right with it. It wasn't your fault."

"You can hit me again if you want." Jason jumped up and leaned down close to her. He squished his eyes shut, waiting for the impact.

"If you don't wanna hit him, I will." Mike formed a devious grin.

"No, I don't wanna hit you, Jason. Don't worry, I forgive you. I wish you hadn't even told me because I can't remember a thing anyway." Her cheeks flushed pink.

"Billy made me." Jason pointed at him and sat back down. He rubbed his temples and squished his eyes shut before opening them again.

"I didn't make him do anything." Billy shrugged. "I just looked at him." He narrowed his eyes, silently warning Jason to stop causing trouble.

Sami giggled.

"On second thought..." Using the armrests for support, Jason pushed himself to his feet. "I have to go home and recuperate. I don't feel so hot."

"Do you need a ride, Jason?" Mike asked.

"*Please*! There's no way I can walk down that *looong* driveway under the smoldering sun," he complained. "Who has a driveway that long anyway? It's just…weird."

Billy dug keys from his front pocket and tossed them to his brother.

Jason and Mike disappeared around the side of the house.

"Don't puke in my car!" Billy shouted.

"Will you come home with me while I shower and brush my teeth?" Sami asked, begging with her eyes. "You can wait for me in my bedroom."

A wanton urge awakened, and he grinned. "I was hoping you'd say that."

9

"YOU LOOK nice, sweetheart." Her mom beamed, though her eyes held a hint of sadness. "I can't believe my little girl has grown up." She stuck out her bottom lip and sighed. "I'm sure they'll like you. And you have experience from working in the deli last summer. That's a very good start."

"Huhhh," Sami groaned as her chest fluttered with anxiety. She ran a hand down the front of her white blouse and across the waist of her lavender skirt, assuring all buttons were buttoned and everything was tucked in neatly.

Lifting one foot at a time, she inspected the black heels she wore, satisfied there were no scuff marks. "Thanks for letting me use your heels, Mom, but don't you think I'm a little overdressed? It's a waitress position."

"Trust me, how you dress for an interview makes a big difference when it comes to whether or not they'll hire you."

"All right, then. Wish me luck!"

"Good luck, and don't worry. You'll do fine."

Sami flashed a nervous smile and headed out the front door on wobbly legs, trying to keep her balance. She stood on the porch, eyeing the red and white '57 Bel-Air in the driveway, wondering if she'd reach it without falling flat on her face.

Dark clouds filled the sky. Luckily, it wasn't supposed to rain until later in the day, and the air was still warm. "Here goes nothing." Sami gripped the porch railing and clomped down the steps and across the gravel drive.

Billy crossed the yard, wearing his heart-melting smile and easing her worries.

"Aww. You came to wish me luck?"

"Of course." He leaned down and gave her a light peck on the lips, being careful not to smear her lipstick. "You look beautiful."

"Thank you. I think it's a little much, but you know my mom." She noticed a button undone on his blue plaid shirt and buttoned it for him.

"You didn't over do anything. You look… Well, actually, you look pretty *hot*!"

She giggled. "That's not quite the look I was going for today."

He opened the car door for her. "Maybe not, but I think it'll get you the job."

"Don't jinx me." She climbed into the driver's seat and started the car. "I'm so nervous!"

"Don't worry, Sami. You'll do fine. I love you."

"I love you, too."

"Oh, and we shouldn't be too long at Abby's today. We'll get a lot more done now that she's gone."

"Okay." She sighed, wishing he could come with her. "Here goes nothing."

He winked and shut her door.

Sami threw the shifter into reverse and backed out of the driveway, heading toward town.

On the drive, she mentally prepared for a possible interview, trying to recall the different questions asked by the manager of her last job and coming up with reasonable answers.

Before she knew it, she was staring at the diner. The drive had gone by too fast. But thankfully, only one silver car and one older Dodge pickup were parked in front of the diner, which meant fewer prying eyes inside. The beachfront deli she had applied at last summer was crowded when she'd asked for an application, causing her fear and trembling hands to be more obvious than she had hoped.

Not wanting to draw attention to herself, she parked across the lot instead of right in front of the door. She took a deep breath and exhaled slowly, trying to calm her nerves. *Okay, Sami, you can do this.*

She climbed out of the car and walked with careful steps across the pavement, heels clicking with each step. As soon as she gripped the handle of the front door, her heart rate quickened, and apprehension took over. Determined to be brave, she straightened her shoulders and yanked the door open.

A waitress stood behind the counter, her back to the front door. Sami remembered being waited on by her soon after she'd moved here.

The woman looked around Sami's age, maybe a little older, with dark curly hair, almost black. So far, she was one of the few townspeople who were actually friendly.

Sami made her way to the counter.

The waitress turned around, and her hazel eyes lit up. "Hello, Samantha! Just one today?"

Sami lifted one corner of her mouth, feeling guilty the waitress already knew her name, though she had never taken the time to read the woman's nametag. As nonchalantly as she could, she glanced at the nametag before flicking her eyes back up.

"Actually, Sharon, I wanted to apply for the waitress position."

Sharon smiled. "Sure. Let me just get you an application." She reached under the counter and pulled out a form. She set it down, along with a pen from her apron. "Here you go. You can just sit here at the counter and fill it out."

"Thank you." Sami took a seat on the stool and began the arduous task of trying to remember detailed information while under pressure. Out of the corner of her eye, she noticed the elderly couple in a booth along the front window. They glanced at her and back to each other, their conversation never ceasing. By the way the woman shook her head and looked Sami's way again, she was sure they were talking about her.

Sami turned her attention back to the application. When she was finished, she waved at Sharon, who stood at the far end of the counter.

Sharon took notice and headed back over.

"Let me just get Henry, the manager." She picked up the form and disappeared through a swinging door behind the counter.

Sami tapped her fingers on the counter as she waited. *Please don't let this end bad. Please let me get the job.*

The door swung back open and a familiar man, with gray hair on the sides of his head and balding on top, stepped up to Sami, with Sharon tailing behind.

Sami suddenly recalled seeing him eating lunch with Sheriff Briggs in this very diner. *Great, he's a friend of the enemy.*

She cringed inwardly as her hopes of getting the job were doused. Bolting out of the diner to save herself the humiliation seemed like a great idea, but she didn't want to look like a coward. Deciding to remain dignified, she straightened her posture and held her head high, facing Henry with all the courage she could summon.

"Hello, Samantha." Henry's gruff voice and expression lacked any sort of emotion.

"Hello." Sami smiled.

"Your Harry's granddaughter, huh?" he asked, eyeing her.

She nodded.

"I'm sorry, but we've already filled the position," he said, his tone flat.

"But the sign is still in the window." Sami pointed over her shoulder with her thumb, toward the front door.

"Sharon, go take the sign down," he ordered.

"Yes, sir." Sharon's eyes dimmed with disappointment and she rushed to the front of the diner.

Sami couldn't believe what had just happened. She was *crazy* Harry's granddaughter, enemy to Sheriff Briggs's niece, and everyone in town knew it.

Humiliated, she stormed away, pushing past Sharon on her way out the door, thankful the tears blurring her vision didn't fall until she was outside. Despite wearing heels, she somehow managed to run to her car. She jumped in and slammed the door shut.

A banging on the window gave Sami a heart-stopping jolt.

Sharon stood there, with a sympathetic look on her face.

Sami wiped the tears with the back of her hands and rolled down the window.

"Hi." Sharon's voice was gentle. "I am so sorry about that. I feel so awful for you. Are you going to be all right?"

Sami sucked in a ragged breath and sighed. "Thanks. I'll be okay."

"Sharon!" Henry's voice bellowed from the doorway of the diner. "If you value your job, I'd suggest you get back in here and start doing it!"

"Sorry, again," she whispered and hurried away.

Having Sharon was on her side was comforting, but it couldn't undo the damage. If she had known Henry was the manager of the diner, she wouldn't have applied. She'd seen him eating in there from time to time, but aside from a tucked in dress shirt, there was never any indication he actually worked there.

"What am I gonna do now?" Going home jobless, with her head tucked in shame, was out of the question. Someone out there had to be willing to hire her.

Sami started the car and pulled away from the diner.

"Where to now?" She paused at the stop sign and looked down one side of the road, then the other. The grocery store caught her attention.

None of the employees there had been rude so far. She made a right and headed toward it.

She pulled into the parking lot and parked up front for a quicker getaway if needed. Only a few cars, a minivan, and a couple of trucks were parked along the outer edge of the lot.

Probably just employees.

Peering in the rear-view mirror, she used her fingertips to wipe away the black smudge under her eyes, hoping she'd have better luck with the store manager. Henry's spiteful face rattled her thoughts, and she let out a heavy sigh.

Forget about him. He's just an ass. She practiced smiling in the mirror. Not wanting to appear too eager, she decided to go with the *closed mouth* smile. She climbed out of the car, noticing a *Now Hiring* sign taped to the window.

Good, they're hiring. Okay, Sami, you can do this...again.

The automatic door opened, and a handsome young man—tall and lean—tipped his cowboy hat to her. "Ma'am." He smiled, his bright green eyes a striking contrast against the hue of his skin. After a quick wink he strutted away.

Sami smiled, stunned another citizen of this town showed her kindness. She watched him walk across the parking lot to a heavy-duty truck parked in the corner, trying to recall the last time anyone in town had gone out of their way to be nice to her. Only Sharon came to mind.

Someone else in Wolf Hill isn't bothered by my presence. It's gotta be a good sign, right?

With renewed determination, she sucked in a confident breath and went inside.

A handful of employees stood up front, gathered in a meeting. They were of various ages, anywhere from still in high school to graying, and were all wearing green smocks over white dress shirts. One heavyset man wore a tie. Probably the manager.

She focused on his familiar weathered face and balding head with gray hair on each side. His features were almost identical to Henry's.

"Dammit," Sami whispered under her breath, growing discouraged before she'd even had a chance to speak to the man. *They're obviously related. Why bother?* She was just about to leave when they all zoned in on her.

A surge of fear shot through her, and she froze. She couldn't even breathe. Somehow, she managed to gulp and force a pathetic smile. "Hello. I was wondering if you were hiring?"

The manager approached, eyed the length of her body, and smirked. "Well, now, you must be Harry's granddaughter?"

Sami didn't respond. He already knew the answer. But, before he humiliated her in front of the group of employees, she had a question for him. "Are you related to Henry from the diner?" she asked, surprised at her boldness.

He narrowed his eyes. "Yep. Why?"

She shook her head. "You just look alike is all."

"Yeah, I get that a lot," he replied, his tone flat. "But we're not hiring, so I won't have you bother with an application. Now, if you'll excuse me." He headed back to his meeting.

Feeling like an idiot, she rushed out of the store. Just before she reached the safety of the car, her heel caught in the cracked asphalt, and she tripped and fell on her hands and knees.

"Crap!" She winced from the sting biting her skin.

A steady clomping of boots echoed behind her, the sound growing faster and louder as it neared.

Wanting to get to her feet before the stranger approached, she snatched the shoe lying behind her and wriggled it back on her foot, but she wasn't quick enough.

"Are you all right, ma'am?" The green-eyed man grabbed her just above the elbows and lifted her with little effort.

Even though her knees felt as if they'd been ripped open, along with her pride, Sami nodded. She bent down and dusted the bits of asphalt away, trying to hide her flushed cheeks and moisture filled eyes.

The man gave her a couple of gentle pats on the back. "There's no blood. You okay?"

She bit her lip to steady its trembling, trying to keep from crying. She wanted to thank the stranger, but if she spoke now, the tears would flow. Avoiding eye contact, she nodded again, hopped into her car, and shut the door.

Out of the corner of her eye, she watched the stranger strut across the lot and climb into his truck.

Unable to keep the pain in any longer, tears blurred her vision and rolled down her cheeks. She started the engine and backed away from the store, intent on never returning again. At least not without Billy at her side.

The clouds darkened, and heavy drops pelted the windshield.

"Great! That's all I need today!" A quick sob and more tears escaped. She pulled the headlight knob next to the steering wheel. At the stop sign, she paused. "Now, where are the windshield wipers?" she whispered, scanning the dashboard. When she found the knob, she turned it on, but nothing happened. "What the…?" She tried again—nothing.

"Dammit! Why is all this *happening* to me today?" she shouted. She stepped on the gas and sped up, trying to get home before the rain completely hindered her view. A mile out of town, the steady pang of droplets on the metal roof grew louder and heavier, until a continuous sheet of water rippled down the windshield.

"Shoot! Nooooo!" she pleaded with the angry sky.

Up ahead, she recognized Abby's mail box. She took the immediate right onto Farmington Road and rolled down her window to get a better view. As the car crept forward, she stuck her head out and scanned the edges of the road for somewhere to park, but deep ditches lined both sides. All of a sudden, the engine lugged and fell silent.

"What the…?" Sami jerked her head back inside just as the dashboard lights dimmed and disappeared. She pressed on the gas pedal, but nothing happened.

"You've got to be kidding me!" She cranked the window handle the opposite way, until the rain stopped shooting in at her face, and wiped a palm across her wet forehead. When she threw the shifter into park and turned the key, nothing happened. The annoying echo of the clanging rain intensified, adding to her frustration. She wanted to scream, but instead, she slumped in her seat.

"I'll just call Billy." She snatched her purse from the passenger seat and dug through it until her fingers curled around the smooth case of her cell phone. A quick swipe illuminated the screen. Using a thumb, she jabbed the phone icon with Billy's picture. The background colors shifted from green to blue as the phone dialed his number.

A few seconds passed, and the colors continued to shift, but no sound echoed from the speaker. *Why isn't it ringing?* Her gaze shot to the top corner. An *x* lay where the *4G* symbol should be, and there were no visible service bars.

"No service in the middle of this thick, creepy, haunted looking part of the forest. Would never have guessed," she said, her voice heavy with cynicism. She groaned and rested her head back, wishing the nightmare would end.

She stared at the rain streaming down the windshield, smearing the surrounding forest into a dark blob, wondering whether to wait for someone to pass by or to seek help.

It's only been about an hour at most since I left the house. Billy will be at work for a few more hours. Guess I have no other choice.

She peered in the back seat for any sort of protection against the elements—an umbrella or a jacket—but found nothing.

"Of course, just my luck." She had no job, no windshield wipers, no umbrella, no jacket, no cell phone, and she was stranded in the creepiest forest on earth, with the dreaded knowledge that there really are monsters out there.

She wanted to cry again—to be home in her cozy, warm bed, curled up on her side, and crying her eyes out.

Instead, she embraced her dignity, put her fear in check, and took a deep breath. "You can do this, Sami. It's just water. No big deal." She shoved her purse under the seat, slid her phone into the front pocket of her skirt, and headed on foot to Abby's.

10

WEARING THREE-INCH heels, Sami wobbled as fast as she could down the middle of the road, hoping the pounding rain would let up soon. It didn't.

She warily eyed the forest as memories of red eyes flashed through her mind. Shaking the thought away, she quickened her pace and focused on the road in front of her. The tip of her shoe caught in a small rut hidden under a puddle of water, sending her flying to the ground on her hands and knees.

"Ahhh," she groaned, gritting her teeth through the sting. The fresh bruises from the first fall intensified the pain, and the cold made it worse.

She sat back and rubbed the specs of rock away. Her palms were only skinned, but her knees were bleeding. A lot.

"Just great!" She let out a hopeless sigh, watching as the rain mixed with her blood and sent streaks of pink running down her shins. She remembered the first aid kit in the trunk, but at this point, she was just as close to Abby's house as she was to the car.

Billy would freak if I walked up to him with bloody legs. Eyeing her favorite skirt, she frowned and grabbed a firm hold of the hem. A quick jerk tore the delicate fabric, ripping a good six-inches off the bottom—enough to make two makeshift bandages to tie around her knees.

When she finished, she stood and inspected her work. Sure the bandages would stay, her gaze settled on her soaking wet mini-skirt, which stuck to her thighs and buttocks.

"Just great." She shook her head and focused on her white top—suctioned to her skin and hugging every curve.

"Can this day get any *worse*?" she yelled, staring up at the menacing clouds.

A bolt of lightning shot across the sky and a thunderous *crack* boomed.

She screamed and jumped back from the unexpected fury.

"What is going on today?" She cringed and continued on her way, limping to ease the ache in her knees and her soggy, blistered feet, while periodically checking her phone for service.

Squishy step after squishy step, she pushed on until the pain became unbearable.

Ready to give up and plop down in the road until someone found her, Abby's house came into view.

"Finally!" She tried to run, but ended up hobbling along instead, not stopping until she was standing in the middle of the empty gravel driveway. Neither Billy's nor Jason's car were anywhere in sight.

"No! This can't be happening! What the hell am I gonna do now?"

She checked her cell phone for service again. Still nothing. She shoved the useless device back into her pocket.

Shoulders slumped, dignity disheveled, and still trying to hold back the tears, she limped along the walkway, up the stairs, and across the front porch to the door. She tried the knob, but it wouldn't rotate.

"Figures." She let out a heavy sigh and focused on the large windows lining the porch. "Please let one of you be unlocked." She made her way along the wrap-around porch, checking each window and the back door, but none of them budged.

She stared at the narrow window next to the front door. *Should I break it…? No. Not yet. They probably had to stop for supplies first or something. I'm sure they'll be here soon.*

At the far end of the porch, a creaky wooden swing swayed in the wind. She limped to it, laid down with her legs curled to her chest, and cried.

BILLY STOOD on his front porch, watching the fury of the storm pouring down only inches from his face. "Huh. I wonder what's taking Sami so long?"

Jason shrugged. "Don't know? Maybe she had to stop at the store or something?"

"It's raining pretty hard. She shouldn't be driving in this storm."

"Have you tried calling her?"

"Yeah. It went straight to voicemail. Maybe he hired her on the spot, and she's already working?" Billy suggested, though he knew it wasn't likely.

"Maybe."

Billy shook his head. "Nah, not with the heels she had on." He glanced down the street, hoping to see his brother drive up at any second. "Where in the hell is Mike? I wish he'd get his own car, so he wouldn't have to keep borrowing mine."

"Where *is* Mike, anyway?" Jason asked.

"He had to exchange the tiles for Abby's bathroom." He let out an impatient breath. "I wish she'd make up her mind and stick to something."

"I feel your pain, buddy," Jason agreed. "Well, let's go." He gave Billy a solid swat on the back and headed for his car.

"Go where?" Billy furrowed his brow.

"What do you mean, *go where*? You wanna look for Sami, right?" Jason hopped into his car and revved up the engine.

Billy looked at the clock on his phone, contemplating whether he should give her a little more time. Eleven forty-five. Sami had been gone for over three hours. Even if she'd applied at every business in town, he was positive it wouldn't have taken this long. He hopped over the porch railing and hurried to Jason's car.

As soon as both of Billy's feet were in, Jason sped off toward town.

The blaring rock song on the radio made it hard for Billy to think straight, adding to his worry. Plus, if Sami tried to call, the high-pitched screeching would drown out the ringing. He turned the music off, ignoring Jason's glare.

Are we overreacting by going off to search for her? Maybe she just had some sort of new hire orientation and decided to have lunch afterward…? Nah. In the pit of his stomach, he knew they were doing the right thing.

When they reached the diner, Jason slowed and pulled into the busy parking lot. They crept through it, searching for Sami's car.

"She's not here, dude," Jason said. He pulled into an empty spot and shut off the engine. "Try her cell phone again."

Billy dialed Sami's number. When he reached her voicemail, he hung up and tried again…. He grunted in frustration and ended the call.

"I just keep getting her voicemail!"

"It's okay. Don't worry. Let's just go in and see when she left," Jason said.

Billy couldn't shake the uneasy feeling that something had happened.

They went into the diner and approached the waitress at the counter.

"Hi, Billy. Hi, Jason." The waitress smiled. "Just you two today?"

"Uh, no." Billy shook his head, wondering how the waitress knew his name. He glanced at her nametag. "We're looking for my girlfriend, Sami. She was in here applying for a job. We were wondering if you can tell us how long ago she left?"

"Hmm, let's see…" She looked at her watch. "It's been about three hours. Why?"

"*Three* hours?" Billy said, growing anxious.

Her eyes widened. "Oh, I hope she's okay. She left in tears. Then, it started pouring down rain. I've just been worried about her all morning. If you see her, tell her I'm sorry, again. Poor thing."

"I'm sure she'll be fine—" Jason's eyes flicked down to her chest and back up again "—Sharon. Thanks for the info."

Billy hurried out of the diner with Jason right behind him. They hopped into the car.

"Well, I guess she didn't get the job," Jason said flatly.

"Something's not right, Jason. I have a feeling Sami's in danger again."

Jason backed out of the parking space. "Where do you wanna look next?"

"Just head back toward the houses. Maybe she ran off the road or something?" Billy cringed at the thought.

"I didn't notice her car anywhere on the way in."

"Just go, dammit!"

The tires screeched as Jason pulled onto the main road. They scanned every parking lot of every business they passed, hoping to catch a glimpse of the red classic.

When they reached the edge of town, Billy began to fear the worst. "Slow down. You look on your side, and I'll look on mine."

They drove for a couple of miles in the pounding rain, searching for tire tracks leading into the forest or any other signs of Sami or her car.

They rounded a bend, and Abby's mailbox came into view. "Turn here," Billy said.

"Why would she be here?" Jason slowed the car and turned right.

"Because she thought we were working today."

The headlights reflected off the bumper of Sami's car. "That's her!" Billy said.

"What's she doing?" Jason pulled up behind her car and threw the shifter into park, leaving the engine running.

Billy jumped out and ran to the passenger door. He peered in through the window at the empty front and back seats. His heart suddenly dropped.

Jason got out of the car.

"Sami?" Billy yelled, straining to see through the fury of the storm for anything resembling a human shape.

"Dude, what's going on?" Jason asked. "Where's Sami?" He peered through the car windows.

"Sami?" Billy yelled louder, waiting for her reply. He stood there, scanning the ditches and forest on each side of the road, praying he didn't find her lifeless body.

"Sami?" Jason joined the search. He jogged up the road a way before heading back.

"Sami!" Billy waited for an answer, but the splatters of rain grew louder, lessening the chances of hearing her.

"Dammit!" Billy ran his fingers through his hair. "This can't be frickin' happening again!" he yelled.

"Billy, it's okay! We'll just check Abby's. She thought we were working today, right? Her car just broke down, so she had to walk. Come on."

They both rushed back to Jason's car and hopped in.

Billy kept the window down, scouring the forest along the way. Jason did the same on his side, while keeping an eye on the road in front of him.

"This can't be happening again, Jason," Billy said with a shaky voice.

"It's not, Billy. We'll find her. See, the rain's letting up now. We'll find her."

"There's the house," Billy said. "Hurry!"

Jason sped past the driveway, up and over the walkway, and right to the base of the porch steps.

Billy jumped out of the car, bolted up the steps, and to the front door with Jason on his heels.

Please be here. Billy jiggled the knob. "Shit! It's still locked."

"Billy?" Sami's raspy voice broke the silence.

Billy snapped his head to the left, relieved to see Sami laying on the porch swing.

She sat up and a soft smile formed. "I'm so glad to see you!"

"Sami!" Billy rushed to her side and wrapped his arms around her. "We've been looking everywhere for you."

"We thought something happened to you again," Jason said as he approached them.

Billy let go of her, his gaze immediately drawn to her wet see-through blouse and white lace bra. His gaze fell to her ripped skirt, also see-through and revealing her panties. Blood soaked bandages covered her knees.

Jason tensed, and his hands flew over his eyes. "Sorry. I didn't see anything! I promise!"

Billy's jaw fell open. "What in the hell happened? You're bleeding!

And your skirt is ripped! Did somebody hurt you?"

"What?" Jason lowered his hands, and his eyes widened when he saw the damage. "Sami? What happened?"

"No. Nobody hurt me. Not *physically*."

Billy shrugged off his zippered hoodie and draped it around her shoulders.

"It's just…" Her chin started to quiver, and tears filled her eyes. She sucked in an unsteady breath and began to cry. "I didn't get the job because I'm Harry's granddaughter. The manager was Sheriff Briggs's friend. So, I tried the grocery store, but the manager there was related to the manager of the diner. I was so humiliated, Billy!

"Every employee was staring at me. I ran out of the store and fell. And my windshield wipers broke, and I couldn't see. Then, my car broke down. I tried to call you, but I had no service, and I had no umbrella, so I had to walk in the pouring rain." She ran her fingers over her cheeks to dry them and took a deep breath.

"Then, I fell *again* and had to rip my favorite skirt for bandages. And when I got here, you weren't here, and the door was locked. I was scared, wet, and cold." Her shoulders shook with each hiccup of a sob. She buried her face in her hands and wept.

Billy's heart grew heavy. He pulled her against his chest and kissed the top of her head.

"Shhhh, it's okay, Sami." He held her tightly, trying to comfort her and wishing he could rip the heads off Sheriff Briggs and his posse. "I'm so sorry about the diner and everything. It's gonna be okay. Let's get you home." He encircled her waist with a strong arm and guided her to Jason's car.

Jason rushed past them and opened the passenger door.

"You sit up front," Billy said and folded the seat forward to climb in the back.

Jason flipped the seat back to upright. When Sami was in, he shut the door and hurried around the front of the car to the driver's side. As soon as he opened the door, Sheriff Briggs pulled up behind them.

"Shit," Jason whispered under his breath. He leaned into the car and looked at Billy. "What the hell do we do?"

"Lift the seat!" Billy hit the back of the driver's headrest.

Jason pulled the lever and the seat sprung forward.

"Jason," Sheriff Briggs said. "I noticed Samantha's car broke down in the middle of the road back there, but there's no sign of her. Have you seen her?"

Billy climbed out of the driver's door and stood next to Jason.

"Yeah, she's right here." Jason pointed into the car. He went around the front of the car and stood next to the passenger door.

"Huh?" Sheriff Briggs wrinkled his brow. "She was with you two the whole time?"

"Uh, no," Jason said. "Billy and I just found her."

"Just found her?" He narrowed his eyes. "Where?"

"Here!" Jason snapped.

"I was here not too long ago. There was no sign of her." He continued his wary glare.

"You were *here*? Before *we* even got here?" Billy scowled. The thought of Sheriff Briggs being so close to Sami while she was alone and vulnerable made his skin crawl.

Sheriff Briggs didn't offer a reply.

Jason cleared his throat. "We didn't see her either at first. She was asleep on the porch swing."

"Let me take a look at her," Sheriff Briggs ordered.

"Why do you need to look at her?" Billy snapped. "You can see her right there!" He pointed through the window.

"Open the door, Jason," the sheriff warned.

Jason opened the door and helped Sami out of the car.

She kept her head down, avoiding eye contact.

Sheriff Briggs eyed the length of her body and his lips curled into a devilish grin.

Billy seethed with anger, ready to lunge at him. Sami was unaware that the hoodie she wore hung open, exposing her wet clothes.

Jason followed the sheriff's gaze and snatched the hoodie closed.

Billy narrowed his eyes and took a step forward.

"I wouldn't do that if I were you! You just stay put! Both of you!" Sheriff Briggs warned with his hand hovering over his holster.

Billy did as ordered and stopped. "What do you want, sheriff?"

Sheriff Briggs grinned. "Just wanted to make sure Samantha was okay, that's all. You look hurt, Samantha. Did these boys do that to you?" He gestured to her knees.

"What? No! I fell."

"Do you need me to call a tow truck?" he continued, enjoying his form of harassment.

She shook her head.

"Well, good thing the rain let up." He winked. "I suggest you all hurry and get the car out of the middle of the road before it causes an accident. Billy, Jason, Samantha...I'll be seeing you." He flashed a cocky grin, climbed back into his car, and drove away.

"That was just too damned close for comfort!" Jason gritted his teeth.

Billy rushed around the back of the car to Sami. "Are you okay?"

"No, I think I've just had the second worst day of my life, and it's not over yet," she said, letting out an unsteady breath.

Jason opened the door while Billy helped her in.

"Don't worry, Sami," Jason said. "The worst part of today is over. I promise."

Billy and Jason went around the back of the car toward the drivers-side.

"Dude," Billy whispered to Jason. "What in the hell was that all about? Should we be afraid of Sheriff Briggs? Do you think he's a werewolf, too?"

"I don't know, man." Jason shook his head. "At this point, anything's possible. I do know one thing for sure. We all need to watch our backs, especially Sami's. Damn pervert."

Billy's stomach knotted as he recalled the way Sheriff Briggs eyed Sami like she was a piece of meat. Yet, there was nothing he could do about it. Feeling helpless and disgusted, he got into the car, wishing he could bash Sam Briggs's face in.

11

THE NEXT few days went by quickly—too quickly. Sami had been dreading this day, wishing it would never come. But now, *moving day* was here and there was no stopping it.

Sitting on the top step of the front porch, she toyed with a loose thread hanging from the navy blouse she wore—her mother's favorite.

"Well, sweetheart." Her mom eased next to her. "This is it."

Sami frowned and nodded. "I'm gonna miss you, Mom." Tears stung her eyes and rolled down her cheeks. She wrapped her arms around her mother, never wanting to let go.

"Aww, Samantha. I'm going to miss you, too." Her mother gave her a big squeeze and pulled away to face her again. "Just remember, I'm always just a phone call and a state away." She sniffed and swiped at the tears staining her cheeks. "Did you know Seattle is only about a seven-hour drive from here?"

"Yeah, it's not as far as it seems, I guess," Sami said, her voice quavering. She pressed her lips together to stifle her trembling chin.

"Oh, I almost forgot. I made lasagna. It's in the fridge," Carol added through sniffles.

Mike walked by with a suitcase in his hand, and a box of tissues in the other. He winked and held out the tissues on his way down the steps.

"Thanks, Mike." Carol smiled and took the box. She set it on the step below her.

Sami snatched a few tissues and patted her eyes dry. She and her mother continued to keep each other company while they watched the men load the back of Steve's truck with suitcases, bedroom furniture, and boxes. Sami was grateful her mom had given her the rest of the furniture and everything in the kitchen.

"Are you ready?" Steve asked her mother as he approached them.

Sami hated his cocky stride, with his brand-new cowboy boots clomping along the walkway with each step he took. She eyed the red plaid shirt tucked into his black jeans. *Maybe he's walking that way because his jeans are too tight?* She shrugged the thought away and turned her attention back to her mother.

Her mom wore a navy summer dress—something casual and comfortable for the long drive—with her sandy hair draped loosely about her shoulders. She looked beautiful. The ache in Sami's heart grew.

"Are you sure you have to go, Mom?"

Her mother's eyes filled with a sadness Sami hadn't seen since her grandpa's funeral.

"Oh, Samantha..." Carol frowned.

Sami threw her arms around her, dreading the inevitable. "Bye, Mom. I love you."

"I love you too, sweetheart. Just remember, this isn't good-bye forever...just for now." Her mother gave her a kiss on the forehead before pulling away.

Steve held his hand out and helped Carol up. "This is for you, Sami." He handed her a thick envelope.

Sami took the envelope, leaving it unopened. The fact that it was about an inch thick and a generous weight startled her. Unless the bills were all ones, he'd just given her a hefty sum.

Steve shifted his feet and cleared his throat. "You're Carol's daughter, and I worry about you, too. I know you've had a hard time lately. You probably shouldn't take on too much too soon anyway. Your mom and I want to make sure you'll be okay for a while. If you need any more help, just call."

Unsure of what to think of Steve's kind gesture, she looked at her mother for approval.

Her mom gave an encouraging smile and nodded.

"Thank you, Steve," Sami hopped to her feet and gave him a quick hug—which she immediately regretted. Wrapping her arms around a man she considered a creep was almost nauseating. She did it mostly for her mom's sake, and partly because she figured she owed him something other than a *thank you* for the monetary gift.

Steve grinned. "Oh, and I made a few calls. When you're ready, there's not one business in this town that won't hire you. The jobs are yours for the picking. I know everybody here, so…" He shrugged.

"You called *everyone*?" Sami asked.

He gave a stoic nod.

Sami raised her eyebrows, baffled as to why he would go out of his way to ensure everyone in town treated her better. Maybe he wasn't such a bad guy after all. Even so, now, she was more humiliated than ever. There was no way she could swallow her pride and work for anyone who secretly despised her but had been coerced into hiring her.

Sami eased back down onto the step, not knowing what to say.

"Just think about it…when you're ready." Steve took Carol by hand and guided her down the steps.

Wearing a cheerful grin, Jason met her mother at the bottom of the stairs. "Carol." He hugged her and lifted her off the ground.

Carol giggled. "I'll miss you, too, Jason."

He set her back down, trudged up the steps, and plopped next to Sami.

Mike stood in the middle of the walkway, waiting for his turn to say good-bye.

"Mike." Carol smiled through tears as she hugged him. "You take care."

"Don't worry, Carol—" Mike hugged her back "—I'll take care of everyone."

She let out a heavy sigh and patted his shoulder. Then, she made her way over to the truck, stopping in front of Billy. "Billy, you take care of my daughter." She sucked in an unsteady breath.

"I will, Carol," Billy promised as he hugged her. "She'll be safe." He smiled and added, "And, I promise I won't let her forget to eat."

Carol's soft laughter was halted by a quick sob.

Billy opened the truck door for her.

Sami couldn't stand seeing her go. After twenty years, this would be the last time her mother would be a part of her everyday life, and the thought was unbearable.

"Wait!" Sami yelled. With tears streaming down her cheeks, she jumped up and bolted across the yard into her mother's loving arms again. "I'm gonna miss you so much, Mom."

"I'll miss you, too, sweetheart," her mother cried, tightening her grip. She kissed Sami on the forehead one last time and climbed into the truck. The door banged shut and her mom didn't look back.

Sami felt as if a part of her had just been ripped away. She clenched her jaw to stop the trembling.

Steve had already climbed in and started the engine. Slowly, the truck rolled forward.

"Bye, Mom," Sami whispered as she watched them drive out of sight. Devastated, she buried her face in Billy's chest and cried.

Billy held her tightly, comforting her until she lifted her head and wiped the tears away.

"Do you wanna go inside?" he asked, his voice soothing.

Sami nodded and sniffed. "Yeah, sorry. I didn't think it would be this hard, you know?"

"Yeah, I know. Saying good-bye to people you love is never easy." He sighed, long and forlorn, but then his eyes lit up. "We could move your things into the master bedroom now. It would help get your mind off it."

His sudden upbeat mood brought a smile to her face. "Yeah, I don't really wanna sleep upstairs at the end of the dark, creepy hall tonight."

"I don't know how you did it for so long," he teased. "Come on." He wrapped his hand around hers and led her inside.

Mike and Jason had just exited the master bedroom.

"Hey, you guys wanna help me move Sami's stuff downstairs?" Billy asked.

"Already done." Mike winked at Sami as he passed by them.

"What? You did?" Billy asked. "That was fast."

Mike paused at the front door. "I'm heading out for some beer. I'll be back." He pulled the door shut behind him.

"We moved some of the stuff before Carol left," Jason said. "But, we left the desk. We figured you'd probably turn one of the rooms up there into an office or something." His eyes softened. "We just wanted to do something nice for you, Sami. Make it easier on you and all."

"Awww. Thanks, Jason." She smiled.

"No problem." He winked. "Anyway, I'm gonna catch up with Mike before he leaves. I'm tired of that light beer crap he keeps buying. Light beer is for chicks!" He hurried out the front door.

"Tell Mike I said thanks, too," Sami shouted right before the door closed.

"Well, let's go see your new room," Billy said, motioning with a hand for her to go first.

She hurried down the hall, eager to see her bedroom. The queen-sized bed had been centered against the right wall, along with her nightstand in the far corner, and the dresser sat opposite the bed, against the left wall. The bed had been neatly made, with both the purple and blue throw pillows set carefully in place, just the way she'd had it upstairs.

"They even made the bed for me," she said with awe as she smoothed out a wrinkle in her gray comforter. She plopped down on the foot of it, enjoying her new space. She even had a bathroom in her room, right next to the bedroom door for easy access. Now, she wouldn't have to run all the way upstairs every time she had to go.

Billy opened the closet door, next to the dresser, and peeked inside. "They brought your clothes down." He shut the door and sat next to her on the bed. "Are you okay?"

"Yeah. I'll be okay. It's just gonna be hard living in this big house all by myself. I imagine I won't be getting much sleep anymore, especially during the full moon…or the new moon…or *any* moon."

She eyed the sliding glass door, which led right out to the backyard, and beyond that, the forest. "Maybe I should've kept my room upstairs?"

"Well." Billy raised his eyebrows and nudged her shoulder with his. "I can always stay the night."

She bit her lip to hide a coy smile and wrapped her arms around his neck. "Yes, you can," she whispered.

He grinned and captured her mouth with his, indulging in a deep kiss. With his lips still on hers he lay back on the bed, pulling her on top of him.

She giggled and lifted her head to look him in the eyes. "So, what are you gonna do? Stay here every night?"

The twinkle in his eyes faded, and his demeanor turned sober. "I can…if you want me to."

Her heart skipped a beat when she realized he was serious. What was he saying, exactly? Did he want to move in with her? Were they really about to face the next huge step in their relationship? The thought excited her, but she was scared—just like she had been when he'd first kissed her and the first time they'd made love.

"Ummm, do you want to?" An anxious flutter buzzed through her. She chewed on her bottom lip. "I mean, you don't *have* to, but if you want to…then, I want you to."

He sat up with her in his arms and gazed into her eyes. "Marry me, Sami," he whispered.

Body tense, her breath caught in her throat. He'd skipped right over the *moving in* part and jumped right into marriage. She wanted to say something, to give him an answer, but she was terrified.

He caressed the side of her cheek with the back of his fingers. "I love you…more than anything. I've loved you since the day I saw you. But I didn't know exactly how much until I almost lost you. And when we lost our baby…." He swallowed hard and his eyes filled with tears.

"I knew I wanted another chance to have a baby with you. To have a chance to recreate the life we lost, someday. I need you in my life, Sami. Now and always. I can't imagine life without you. I don't *want* a life without you. Marry me. It doesn't have to be now. It can be ten years from now if you want. I just need to know *now* if I can love you for the rest of my life."

Tears welled and made their way down her cheeks. His declaration of love abolished her trepidation and created an ache in her heart so deep she thought it might actually break. But it didn't. It just filled with more love than she'd ever thought possible. She smiled and gazed into his eyes, not being able to imagine life without him in it either.

"Yes," she whispered softly. "I want to marry you, Billy. More than anything."

A quick rush of air escaped his lips as if he'd been holding his breath. Suddenly, he crushed his lips to hers and entangled his fingers in her hair, kissing her with such intensity that she could feel their love deepening. Then, he pulled away, wearing a proud grin.

"I was hoping you'd say that," he whispered.

She pinched a smile between her lips, her cheeks flushing with warmth. "And yes," she added. "I want you to."

He furrowed his brows. "To what?"

"To stay here every night. Move in with me, please," she asked with the biggest puppy dog eyes she could muster.

He smirked and laid her back onto the bed, covering her body with his. "Yeah, I'll move in with you, Sami," he said, his voice husky.

"I was hoping you'd say that," she whispered.

Lust engulfed his eyes, and a subtle smirked formed. In one swift move, he yanked his shirt over his head and chucked it behind him.

She ogled his chiseled torso with her eyes and fingertips, anticipating what was to come.

Slowly, he lowered his lips until they hovered over hers, teasing her with the slightest of kisses. Then, his mouth left hers and brushed against her neck, his warm breath tickling her nape and sending a wave of chills down her arms. He gently pulled her to a sitting position and unbuttoned her blouse, guiding it from her shoulders and tossing it aside. He pressed his lips to her bare shoulder, showering it with soft kisses while his hands made their way to the middle of her back. After a quick tug, her bra loosened and slipped down her arms, the cool air spreading goose bumps across her chest.

As if he could read her mind, he gathered her into his arms, and she shuddered, relishing the warmth of his bare skin on hers.

"I love you, Sami," he whispered and molded his mouth to hers, not giving her a chance to reply. Not with words anyway. She pressed harder against him and deepened their kiss, rolling her tongue with his. He grunted and kissed her hungrily as he lowered her back onto the bed....

12

BILLY WATCHED Sami as she stood from the kitchen table and put the leftover lasagna in the refrigerator. She looked troubled. He feared she might be having second thoughts about him moving in with her, or worse, marrying him.

"Maybe I should just stay home while you tell him?" Sami suggested.

"Ah, is that what's been bothering you?" Billy let out a subtle sigh. He pondered his brother's possible reaction to his moving in with Sami, recalling how angry Mike had been when their sister had announced she was leaving.

"Maybe you're right." He gathered the dirty dishes from the table and took them to the sink. "This'll probably be hard on him, you know, since he raised me and all."

"Yeah, I know. I feel bad." She frowned.

"Don't feel bad." He wrapped his arms around her waist. "We're starting a new life together. You should be happy. Mike will be all right. As soon as Abby comes back, that is." He chuckled lightly. "Whenever she's here, he stays at her house most of the time anyway."

Her worried expression lessened. "Yeah. I guess it's a good thing Mike has a girlfriend now." She gave Billy a peck on the lips and finished clearing the table.

"Don't let Mike hear you call her his girlfriend." Billy went to the refrigerator and grabbed a cola. He gulped down half of it before he finished. "My arm still hurts from that mistake. He likes to say they're just *dating*. He doesn't seem to want things to get too serious with her."

"Well, I doubt he'd punch me in the arm, but thanks for giving me the heads-up." She hesitated as if she were still struggling with something. "Billy…do you think maybe we could keep the *getting married* part a secret? You know, since we're gonna wait awhile anyway? It's just gonna be hard enough when my parents find out we're living together, and you know how Mike and Jason can get. Maybe we should just give them one big piece of news at a time?"

"I was just thinking the same thing." He crossed the room, wrapped his arms around her, and kissed her on the tip of her nose. "It's getting dark. Maybe I should go tell Mike now, so I can get some of my things moved over?"

She nodded. "Okay."

He indulged in the sweetness of her mouth and tongue before he headed for the door.

Pausing halfway out the door, he looked back. She was tracing a finger across her lip.

"There'll be more of that when I get back." He winked.

She giggled. "I can't wait."

He pulled the door shut behind him and headed across the yards to the single story next door. It seemed weird to think of the place he'd lived in all his life as Mike's house now, and not his own. He was more than ready to move in with Sami. Eager even. But as he neared his childhood home to gather his things, his chest grew heavy.

He hopped up onto the porch and stopped at the front door. With his hand on the knob, he took in a deep breath and exhaled to calm his nerves. Then, he went inside.

"What's up, little brother?" Mike said as he sat in the recliner with a beer in hand.

Billy closed the front door and shrugged. "Nothing." He gulped, dreading having to tell Mike the news. "Well, there is *one* thing. Sort of."

Mike gave him a questioning glance.

"Uhhh." Billy didn't know how to proceed.

His brother's look went flat, and he let out an impatient breath.

Billy formed an uneasy half-smile. He headed along the back of the couch, about to make his way into the living room, when he noticed his suitcase sitting on the floor. Confused, he looked at Mike.

"Yeah, I thought I'd save you a little time and pack some stuff for you," Mike said casually and took a sip of his beer.

"What?"

"Well, you *are* moving in with Sami, aren't you?" he asked, unfazed by the notion.

"How'd you know?"

"'Cause, I just know these things. That's why," he said. "So, when are you two getting married?" He was still as cool as could be, sprawled on the recliner, swigging his beer.

"Uhhh." Billy gulped. "Well, we didn't actually set a date. It's just something that's gonna happen when we're both ready." He shook his head, wondering if Mike had been eavesdropping outside of Sami's bedroom. "How in the hell did you know all this?"

Mike grinned. "Brother's intuition."

Though Billy was glad the conversation had gone better than expected, he was a little upset that Mike showed no discord over the matter. But he'd never admit to being offended by Mike's lack of compassion. He let out a quick breath of air, relieving the last of his burden.

"Well hell, this was easier than I thought it was gonna be." He went to the fridge and grabbed two beers from the door. "A little too easy," he mumbled so Mike wouldn't hear.

On his way back to the couch, he set one of the beers on the end table next to his brother's recliner. Billy plopped down and stretched his legs out as he took a sip of the crisp, refreshing ale. "I'm gonna miss this, though."

"I'll always be here, little bro," Mike said with a hint of sadness in his voice.

But just a hint. Something only someone close to him could notice.

Which for Billy, meant a lot at the moment. His brother did care after all.

"Oh, and don't tell anyone we're, you know, getting married. Sami doesn't want anyone to know yet. She wants to let the shock of us moving in together settle in with her parents first."

"No problem."

"So, when does Abby get back?"

"Tomorrow. Oh, and I need to borrow your car in the morning to pick up more supplies."

"Dude, when are you gonna get your own car?"

"This weekend. I'm gonna go look at an old truck Joe's selling."

"You mean Joe, the paramedic?"

"Yep!" Mike tilted his head back and polished off his beer. He set it on the end table and grabbed the unopened one.

"Huh, that's cool. Need a ride?"

"See, brother's intuition. You have it too." Mike flashed a huge grin.

Billy chuckled and finished his beer. He snatched Mike's empty can as he passed by and went to the kitchen.

"I'm gonna miss having someone clean up after me all the time," Mike teased.

"Maybe you should invite Abby over more often," Billy teased back and chucked the bottles into the trash can.

The front door swung open and Jason barged in. "So, are you ready?" He stared at Billy with his eyebrows raised.

Billy crinkled his forehead. "Ready for what?"

"To move your stuff over to Sami's." Jason pushed past Billy and grabbed a beer out of the refrigerator.

"What the hell? How'd *you* know?" Billy stared at him through squinted eyes, irritated by the casual tone in Jason's voice.

"It's only obvious." Jason took a few gulps of beer and burped.

"What's only obvious?" Billy asked.

"That you and Sami were gonna move in together, and you're gonna get married," Jason said, shaking his head and looking at him as if he'd lost it. He gave Billy a solid swat on the back and headed into the living room. "Anything good on tonight?" He asked Mike.

Billy clenched his jaw as irritation brewed. He stormed into the living room and eyed Mike and Jason. "What the hell do you mean it's only obvious? Sami and I didn't even know until a couple of hours ago!"

"Geez, Billy—" Jason took a sip of his beer "—no need to get your panties in a bunch."

"Yeah." Mike smirked. "What's the big deal?"

Billy glared at them and shook his head. "You guys are assholes!" He stomped off to his room to gather some of his things, mumbling more obscenities under his breath along the way.

Mike and Jason's laughter followed him down the hall.

SAMI SAT on the couch and stared at the clock on the wall, anxious to find out how Mike took the news, positive he'd handled it better than her parents were going to. She dreaded telling them. Especially her father. He was going to flip when he found out she'd dropped out of college before she'd even started, was about to shack up with a man, and that they were engaged to be married.

Emotionally exhausted, she let out a weary sigh. Deciding to occupy time until Billy returned home, she went upstairs to her old room to see if there was anything else that needed to be brought down. She turned on the light and went into the bedroom, which echoed with emptiness after each step she took. Except for a few pictures, the mirror, and the desk, the room was hauntingly desolate.

The closet door stood slightly ajar. She pulled it open, surprised to see her red tank top dangling alone from the rod.

Huh, I haven't seen this for a while. It must've been hiding behind my jacket or something. I wonder why they didn't bring it down with the other stuff? Maybe they just missed it? She shrugged. *Or maybe they don't like this shirt and they left it on purpose?*

A quick tug and the top slid from the hanger. Holding the shirt against her torso, she went to the mirror and swayed from left to right, admiring the shimmer of the sequin heart. "Hmmm…I like it," she said, smiling.

A sudden burst of cold air wafted across her bare arms, followed by a wave of fear. She spun around to face the wide-open window. "Awww, come on," she whispered. *They must've gotten hot and opened the window when they were moving my stuff.*

"Thanks for leaving it open, guys," she said with sarcasm.

The window had to be closed, but thanks to nightmares of wolves jumping through it to rip her to shreds, she was afraid to go near it. Using cautious steps, she moved toward the window, stopping a few feet away.

A soft light illuminated the pine trees towering in the backyard, which probably meant a full moon. Leaning forward, she peered through the top of the window, catching a glimpse of the glowing orb.

"Great! Just great!"

She hung her shirt back in the closet to free her hands. When she turned back to the window, green eyes stared back at her from the edge of the forest.

She tensed and opened her mouth to scream, but her breath caught in her throat and she froze.

What is it? Is it dangerous? Without another thought, she slammed the window shut and locked it. Then, she ran over to the door and flipped the light switch on the wall, engulfing the room in darkness. She tiptoed back to the window, just far enough to peer out again. The green eyes were gone.

She let out a shaky breath. *Probably just a deer or something, right? I'm sure there are lots of animals with green eyes. It's gotta be better than red.*

She shuddered at the thought and rushed out of the room, down the stairs, and straight to the kitchen window to look for Billy. Her car and the trees in Mike's front yard were highlighted silver by the moonlight, making them almost as visible as they were in the daytime. Unfortunately, all remained still and calm. No movement from Billy.

"Hurry up, Billy," she muttered. With nervousness buzzing through her, she tapped her fingertips on the counter and glanced around the kitchen and living room, contemplating what to do next to keep her mind off all things scary.

I could watch some TV. She eyed the black screen and shook her head. *Naw, I'm too anxious to concentrate on watching anything.*

She glanced out the kitchen window again. *Should I just go over there? No, they need this time together. I could just call.... No, I don't wanna bother them.*

The thought of hot water engulfing her tense muscles brought a smile to her lips. *A nice hot bath in my new huge tub—that's what I need!*

She headed for her bedroom but halted before she even stepped foot out of the kitchen. If the green eyes did belong to a werewolf, being alone made her vulnerable. Less vulnerable if she was armed. She slid open the knife drawer and gripped the handle of the butcher knife. It wasn't silver, but if Jessica really was gone as the sheriff had assured, she had nothing to worry about. But if she needn't worry, why was she arming herself?

"Ah, what the hell." She shrugged. Having a knife in her possession, silver or not, gave her a sense of security. With a firm hold on the handle, she headed down the hall to her dark bedroom. She hesitated in front of the door, summoning the courage to go inside. Whatever had been staring at her had only been a couple of dozen feet from the sliding door.

I hope it's not dangerous.

Moving only her arm, she stretched as far as she could around the doorjamb until her fingertips rested on the cold plastic switch. A quick flick and the room brightened. Everything appeared to be in order, just as it had been an hour ago.

Movement at the sliding door caught her eye. The curtains rippled before settling back into place.

Sami tightened her grip on the knife and gulped. *Did Billy open the sliding glass door? Why would he do that? Why would he just leave it open? What was he thinking?*

Bolting out the front door straight to Mike's seemed like a good idea at the moment, but she didn't want to look stupid.

Billy just forgot to shut the sliding door, is all. Probably.

She repositioned her hold on the knife, with the blade pointing down. That way, if something came lunging for her, she could block it with her arm and swipe at it with the knife.

With her knees trembling, she crossed the room. Afraid to pull back the curtain, she reached through it and fumbled until her fingers clutched the handle. She yanked the door shut and locked it. Then, she leaned against the wall to catch her breath.

Mew.

"What the…? Is that a kitten?" Sami held her breath and cocked her ear toward the door.

Please don't let there be a kitten out there. Let it just be a bird chirping or something.

Mew.

The helpless whimper both tugged at her heart and made it race faster. Maybe it had been the kitten's green eyes she'd seen? The poor baby was probably lost. She couldn't leave it out there. But the thought of going outside sent a chill down her arms.

She pulled back the curtain just enough to peer outside. The moonlight created too many shadows. The kitten could be anywhere. She flipped the switch next to the door to turn on the porch light, but of course, it didn't work.

Mew.

"Crap," she whispered, frustrated and afraid. She went to the nightstand and snatched the flashlight from the drawer. After a couple of deep breaths to prepare herself for what she was about to do—for the very *stupid* thing she was about to do—she went back to the sliding door and opened it, along with the screen door.

A crisp breeze blew her hair back. *Definitely too cold for a kitten to be out in all night.*

Stepping only one foot out the door, she shined the light across the backyard. Other than the moving shadows created from the flashlight, there was nothing unusual—just the trees in the yard, and beyond that, the forest. No monsters with fangs and claws.

She peered over at Mike's house, hoping to catch a glimpse of him or Billy, but the back half of the house was dark, and she couldn't see the front half from her angle.

I'll just find the kitten and head straight over there.

Mew.

She aimed the light in the direction the cry had come from, toward Mike's backyard. The feline still wasn't visible. Summoning all the courage possible, she planted the other foot onto the back step.

"Here, kitty." She held her breath, waiting for its reply.

Mew…mew.

Following the cry, the beam of light illuminated the mouth of the basement steps.

"Shoot!" she whispered through clenched teeth as she eyed the shadowy corridor. Taking another step down, she leaned forward to peer around the wall, but wasn't close enough to see the bottom.

"Here, kitty, kitty," she whispered louder, hoping the kitten would find its way to her. "Kitty," she said in her normal tone, but the kitten didn't answer back. "Crap!" One final step down and the grass crunched under her shoe.

"What are you doing?" a deep voice asked from behind.

A scream tore from Sami's throat, and she spun around.

Billy stood on the top step, staring down at her with a horrified look on his face.

Mike and Jason bolted out the door, pushed past Billy, and scanned the backyard.

"What is it?" Jason rushed over to Sami, grabbed her by the shoulders, and gave her a quick once-over.

Sami opened her mouth to speak, but Jason released her and darted to the edge of the yard, continuing his frantic search.

"I—"

"Is it Jessica?" Mike asked, not giving Sami a chance to finish. He disappeared around the side of the house bordering the forest.

Billy jogged down the steps and took the butcher knife from her. "What's the matter? Are you okay? Was it Jessica? Was it another werewolf?" he asked as he anxiously glanced around.

"No," she said.

Mike and Jason walked back over to them, both taking deep breaths to slow their breathing.

Sami suddenly found the entire situation ridiculous. She pressed her lips together to hold back the building giggle, but it forced its way through, and she sputtered into laughter.

Mike raised an eyebrow, but his expression remained serious. "Oh, this is all funny now?" He shrugged.

Sami managed to stifle her amusement, but she couldn't erase her grin. "No. Jessica can't hurt us anymore, remember? And I heard a kitten. Coming from the bottom of the basement steps." She pointed the flashlight at the basement.

"Geez, Sami!" Jason placed a hand over his heart. "You scared the crap outta me!"

Mike chuckled and shook his head. He took the flashlight and disappeared down the dark corridor.

"Are you serious?" Billy handed Jason the butcher knife and wrapped his arms around her, lifting her off the ground. "Ahhh," he groaned playfully. "I thought something happened to you again. Especially when I saw the size of that knife."

"Is this what you were looking for?" Mike approached, holding an orange tabby. "It's a boy." He grinned.

Billy set Sami back down.

She took the trembling baby and held it to her chest. "Awww, it's so cute…and scared. It's okay," she said to the kitten. "I won't hurt you."

"A cat? You mean our first pet is gonna be a cat?" Billy sighed and scratched it between the ears.

Jason smiled. "Cute little fella."

"So, you mean you wanna keep it?" Sami asked.

Billy let out a soft chuckle as the kitten licked his finger. "Sure, why not?"

"Yay, our first pet!"

Mike scanned the forest, his face full of worry. "Let's go back inside."

With Sami leading, they all went back into the house. Mike locked the door and yanked the curtain closed.

"So, what are you gonna name it?" Billy asked.

"I don't know." She shrugged.

"Can I hold it?" Jason asked, his tone eager.

"Sure." Sami giggled as she handed him the kitten.

"Hey there, little buddy." He perched the fur-ball in the crook of his neck and stroked its back.

"That's a good name," Sami said. "Buddy."

"Hey." Jason grinned. "Did you hear that?" He lifted the kitten up to look it straight in the eyes.

Mew. Buddy cried and placed a paw on Jason's nose.

Jason handed him back to Sami. "I think he wants his mommy."

"Aww...." She took Buddy and snuggled him.

Billy scratched Buddy under the chin. "We don't have a litter box."

"I have some cat litter," Jason said.

Billy looked at Jason like he was crazy. "You have a cat?"

"Nooo," Jason said with wide eyes. "I'm not a cat kinda guy. The litter's for oil spills in the driveway. I'll be right back." He headed out of the bedroom and down the hall.

"He could've fooled me." Billy chuckled under his breath.

Sami suddenly remembered the green eyes. "Oh, I almost forgot. I saw green eyes from the window upstairs."

"Green eyes?" Mike asked.

Billy furrowed his brow and looked at his brother.

"Do you think it's something dangerous?" she asked. "I thought maybe it was just Buddy."

Mike paused before he answered. "We can't be sure. It could've been Buddy, Jessica, or another werewolf."

"What?" Sami asked. Growing suspicious, she narrowed her eyes. "You guys said that outside. How can it be Jessica?"

Billy glared at his brother.

"We can't hide this anymore, Billy," Mike said. "Sami was out back, in the dark, by herself. It's too dangerous to keep it from her any longer."

"To keep *what* from me?" she demanded.

Billy squished his eyes shut and opened them again while letting out a heavy breath. "We're not so sure Jessica is dead," he said, his tone full of guilt.

A twinge of fear shot down Sami's spine. "You're kidding me? All this time, I've felt more comfortable here because I thought Jessica couldn't hurt me anymore. So comfortable, I even traipsed off into the forest by myself and wandered out back, in the dark, during the *full* moon—a time when *Jessica* goes on *killing* sprees. What do you mean you don't think she's dead?" she snapped.

Regret haunted Billy's eyes. He opened his mouth to speak, but no words came out.

Mike cleared his throat. "We're not so sure Sheriff Briggs was telling the truth. And we think there could be others like her."

Sami clenched her jaw and tapped her foot, trying to remain calm. "Why didn't you guys tell me sooner?"

Billy let out a heavy sigh. "You've been through so much already with Jessica and the miscarriage. I just wanted you to enjoy life and be happy again. We thought just keeping a watchful eye out was good enough. I'm sorry." He lowered his head in shame.

Sami's anger dissipated. She squished her eyes shut, trying to keep the pain from resurfacing. When she was sure she had a handle on her emotions, she opened her eyes to find Billy still staring at the floor. All of this time, he was only trying to protect her, and because of that and his genuine remorse, she couldn't stay mad at him. "It's okay. I understand."

Billy's gaze met hers and a soft smile formed. "You do?"

"Yeah." She gave him a half-smile. Not wanting the conversation to drift back to the tragic events again, she turned to Mike. "So, do you think what I saw could've been Jessica?"

Mike rubbed his chin. "I'm not sure, but it's a possibility."

"But Jessica's eyes were red," Billy reminded him.

"Yeah, and when she was human, they were golden brown. Who's to say they can't be green too?" Mike said. "And maybe Sheriff Briggs did shoot her. But we did too, *remember*? She didn't die from it. We just pissed her off."

Visions of Jessica as a werewolf flooded Sami's thoughts, spreading goose bumps up her neck. "I'm afraid, Billy. What if she's out there again?"

"Don't worry, we'll keep you safe," Billy said.

"How are you gonna do that?" she asked, her gut knotting. "You were both there in the forest. None of us stood a chance against her. She just came in, overpowered everyone, and took me!"

"Shhh." Billy hugged her. "Don't worry. We have the silver knives this time."

Mike sat on the corner of the bed, his eyes fixated on nothing in particular, as if he were in a deep trance.

"Hey, bro?" Billy nudged his brother's leg with his shoe.

"Yeah?" Mike snapped his head up, focusing on them again. "I have an idea. Sami, do you have anything silver around the house?"

"Uh, I think my mom left her silverware for me in the kitchen and her silver tea service. They were her grandmother's. Why?" She dreaded what she was about to hear.

"Because we're gonna need them. Billy, call Jason before he leaves his house and tell him to bring over all the silver he can get his hands on."

Billy went into the living room to call Jason.

"I'll be right back." Mike winked at Sami. "I'm gonna go get the knives."

"Okay…," Sami said, watching as Mike headed down the hallway and out the front door.

Soft purring drew her attention to the fur-ball cuddled in her arms. Buddies eyes were half closed. "Aww, you're so sleepy," she cooed as if talking to a child. "Lucky for you there's some extra blankets and an empty box under the stairs." She moseyed down the hall and gathered the items from the closet.

After Sami lined the box with the blanket, she set the kitten inside. "There you go, Buddy." She carried the box to her room and placed it on the floor next to her bed.

"Here," Billy said as he re-entered the bedroom and handed Sami a small bowl of water. "He's probably thirsty."

"You're so thoughtful." With steady hands, she put the bowl into the corner of the box and watched Buddy eagerly lick the water.

Jessica entered Sami's thoughts again. She stood and turned to Billy. "How are we gonna stay safe, Billy?"

"With these." Mike walked in with the knives, handing one to Sami and another to Billy. "I found some old sheaths they'll fit in." He gave them each a case. "Hook it onto your belt and keep it on you at all times."

"What?" Sami looked at Mike as if he were crazy. "Are you serious? I'm supposed to wear a knife all day? What about when I go shopping? Do I wear it then?"

"No," Mike said. "But you do need to wear it around here. Just to be on the safe side. When you go out, you can keep it in your purse.

Jason and I'll stay here tonight and see if the green eyes come back. If that's all right with you?"

Sami hadn't expected her first night alone with Billy to be a big sleepover for everyone. She let out a dismal sigh and nodded.

"It's just until we're sure. Okay?" Billy said.

"Yeah, I guess. It just seems a little extreme, that's all. I mean, it could've been a deer or just Buddy," she tried to reason with them in a final attempt to avoid the slumber party.

"Maybe, but we're not taking any chances," Jason said as he barged in with a bulging bag slung over his shoulder. "Where do you want the silver, Mike?"

Billy's eyes widened. "Shit. Did you remember to bring the silver spoon from your mouth, too?"

"Fun-ny," Jason said in a snarky tone before he turned his attention back to Mike.

Mike smirked. "Downstairs in the basement. Sami, do you have the key?"

"Yeah." She wriggled the car keys from her jeans pocket and handed them to Mike.

"What's down in the basement?" Billy asked.

"You'll see," Mike said as he hooked the knife onto his belt.

Billy and Jason did the same.

Sami stared at the knife and sheath in her hand, feeling uneasy about being armed just to be safe in her own home. But, unless she wanted to risk dying, there was no other choice. She unbuckled her belt and attached the weapon, pleased with the sense of security and confidence that came with it. A slight smile formed, but not enough for anyone else to notice.

"Follow me." Mike unlocked the sliding door and pulled it open.

Fear crept back into Sami's bones. She grabbed Billy's hand and squeezed it.

"Nothing's gonna happen to you," Billy reassured.

Jason put a hand on her shoulder. "Don't worry, Sami. I've got your back."

Putting faith in the three men surrounding her and the weapon strapped to her hip, she proceeded to the basement.

13

"THIS IS what's in the basement," Mike said, flipping the light switch on.

Billy, Sami, and Jason followed him inside.

Sami grimaced as the musty odor of the dim room blasted her senses. The shelves along the walls and the two work tables in the middle of the room were cluttered with boxes, various tools, and old machinery. She'd never been down here before, yet everything looked familiar.

She recalled the nightmare she'd had shortly after moving here, about being in a basement. Though she couldn't remember the exact details, the rooms were the same.

"I had a dream about all of this!" She flipped open the flaps of a box on the table and peeked inside. Old, greasy engine parts were piled in a heap.

"What?" Billy sounded surprised. "You dreamed it? Maybe you've been down here before?"

"No." She shook her head. "I've never been down here." She spun around, settling her gaze on a door across the room. "And that door! In my dream it was locked." She hurried over to it, curious to see what was on the other side. If it was significant enough to have entered her thoughts as she slept, it had to mean something. She gripped the knob, but the door wouldn't budge.

"Still locked."

"Huh?" Jason raised his eyebrows. "That's strange. Maybe you saw the basement in an old picture?"

Sami tried to recall seeing the basement in her mom's photo albums, but nothing came to mind. "I don't think so, but I can't be sure."

"Anyway—" Jason looked at Mike "—I don't see anything special down here."

Mike crossed the room and shoved a key into the locked door. After a click, he pushed it open and went inside.

Sami grew wary. She wanted to see what was in there, but she was scared. After all, it wasn't a locked door in some fairy tale, rainbow land dream. Apparently, she was facing her nightmares. Even so, she couldn't resist the temptation.

She entered the room and froze. A large cage shimmered under the lights, stirring memories of Jessica kidnapping her and holding her captive. She took a step back, bumping into Jason as he walked in.

"Whoa!" Jason steadied her with firm hands on her shoulders before he focused on the cage. "What the hell?"

Sami's legs trembled with weakness. She took in slow breaths, trying to calm the panic slowly building in intensity. Jessica's fangs, claws, blood-stained fur, and the gaping gunshot hole in her forehead that had magically vanished, all flashed before Sami's eyes.

"The cage is still here?" Billy said. "I thought they would've hauled it away for evidence or at least taken it apart. I can't believe they just left it." He went over and ran his hand along a bar. "I wonder what—"

Though Sami could hear Billy talking, his words were muffled by the pounding of her heart in her ears and the fog jumbling her thoughts.

"Sami?" Mike's voice echoed.

Feeling numb, Sami shook her head, trying to make sense of the distorted world around her. She stumbled backward and leaned against something soft.

"Sami?" Jason's voice bounced through her thoughts.

For a moment, she felt at peace—as if she were effortlessly floating while watching the fluorescent lights sway above her.

"Sami?" Jason said, eyes wide.

She was in his arms, and her entire body tingled with numbness.

"Sami?" Billy's face was wracked with worry.

Mike turned to the nearest table and pushed its clutter onto the floor.

Jason rushed over to it and laid her down.

She looked around, dazed. "What happened?" Her voice quivered.

"You fainted, Sami. How do you feel?" Billy asked, standing over her. He took her hand and squeezed it.

"Don't try to sit up yet," Mike ordered.

"Ummm, I feel fine," she said. The buzzing throughout her body slowly receded. "I don't know what happened. When I saw the cage, I just couldn't stop thinking about Jessica."

"I think you hyperventilated," Mike said. "Your breathing was erratic before you fainted. Just lie still for a minute and take in even breaths."

She nodded and concentrated on regulating her breathing.

"It's okay." Billy gave her a reassuring smile. "You were just shocked to see the cage is all. Things are gonna get better, okay? I promise. You're safe."

Jason took his hoodie off, balled it up, and placed it under her head.

"Thanks." She gave him a weak smile, feeling silly for fainting.

Jason winked.

"So, brother," Billy said. "What's your big plan?"

Mike went to the corner of the room and pushed a bookshelf out of the way, revealing a hidden door, half the height of a regular door. He opened it and reached in, dragging out a large box.

Sami sat up to get a better view as Mike opened the box.

"Feeling better?" Billy asked.

"Yeah," she said, thankful the numbness had subsided.

"Everything we need to make silver bullets." Mike stood and dusted his hands off on his jeans. "If silver knives can kill werewolves, so can silver bullets."

"Cool!" Jason reached into the box and pulled out a large bowl.

"Crucible—" he handed it to Mike and continued to sift through the contents "—bullet moldings, knife moldings." A huge grin crossed his face. "Cool! A soldering torch." He held it up and carefully set it back into the box.

"That's not all." Mike set the crucible down and went back to the half-door, reached in until his cheek was pressed against the wall, and pulled out a large duffle bag. He unzipped it and opened it wide, revealing dozens of silver knives.

Billy's jaw hung open. "Holy shit! It looks like Harry was preparing for battle."

"Yeah, I found all this stuff when I repaired the basement door that night. I didn't realize all this actually meant anything. Just thought Harry had really lost it." Mike swiped a hand over his mouth. "I'm sure he was going to make bullets too, but just didn't get to it in time. Or maybe they're hidden somewhere else, but I've searched everywhere and didn't find any."

"Maybe we should hide some of the knives in different places around the house, just to be safe," Billy suggested. "It looks like there's enough there for all our houses."

"I like the way you think, little brother," Mike agreed. "But it's too late tonight to get started on the bullets. I'll come down here first thing in the morning."

Soft buzzing filled the air. Mike pulled his phone from his pocket and read the text. He let out a heavy sigh.

"Everything okay?" Billy asked.

"Abby got held up. She'll be here the day after tomorrow." Mike shoved his phone back into his pocket and slung the duffle bag over his shoulder.

"Bummer," Jason said.

"No big deal," Mike said. "You okay to head back up now, Sami?"

"Yeah." Sami swung her legs over the side, but before she could hop down, Billy grabbed her by the waist and hoisted her off the table. With his fingers interlocked with hers, they all went back upstairs.

Billy wasted no time before digging into the duffle bag. He strategically hid each knife in different spots around the house.

Sami followed close behind, so she would know exactly where they were hidden, while Mike and Jason went home to gather their sleeping bags, pillows, extra clothes, and guns. When the men returned, they went upstairs to set up camp in her old bedroom, overlooking the forest at the edge of the backyard.

Bored, Sami strolled into her new room to check on Buddy. He was curled into a ball with his eyes closed and a content smile on his face.

Billy approached from behind. "Jason brought over a litter box and some cat food."

She turned to face him. "Really? He had cat food, too?"

"I guess there used to be strays around his house that his mom fed." He shrugged.

"Maybe this is one of their kittens?"

"Maybe." He put his arms around her and pulled her close. "I've missed kissing you tonight."

His seductive grin and the feel of his warm body pressed against hers stirred an ache inside of her. "I can tell." She stood on tiptoes, so his lips could easily reach hers.

"Hu-um." Mike cleared his throat.

Billy let his arms fall to his sides and glared at his brother. "What?"

Mike snatched the duffle bag off the bed. "We're starting our watch. I'm taking the first shift, and Jason's taking the second. Since tomorrow night is the full moon, we'll watch tomorrow too. If it's all right with you, Sami?"

She crossed her arms and nodded. "But what if it was just an animal? Like a *normal* animal? It seems like so much trouble to go through."

"After what I saw in the forest that day," Mike said as he put his hand on her shoulder and looked her square in the eyes, "I know *anything* is possible. And I am never gonna let what happened to you before, happen to you ever again."

"He's right, Sami," Billy added. "We can't take any more chances. Our lives could be at stake here." He swallowed hard, and his eyes softened. "Your life."

"Yeah, I know," she agreed, wishing such extreme measures didn't have to be taken. Maybe privacy had been an issue before, but not now. Now, she couldn't help feeling like a nuisance, burdening Mike and Jason by making them go out of their way to keep her safe.

"I'll see you two in the morning." Mike strutted out of the room.

Billy yawned and stretched his arms in front of him. "We should try to get some sleep, I guess. It's gonna be a long night." He went to the sliding door to make sure it was locked and pulled the curtain back to peer into the backyard.

Sami sat on the foot of the bed, remembering the door being open earlier. "Hey, did you open that door before you went over to Mike's tonight?"

He turned, wearing a sheepish grin. "Sorry. It was kinda hot in here. I forgot to shut it."

"It's all right. I'm glad it was you, and not something else." She flopped back onto the bed, enjoying the plush comfort on her weary muscles, ready to put the exhausting day behind her. "This isn't how I imagined our first night together here."

Billy closed the curtain and plopped next to her. "I know."

She sat up and nudged his shoulder with hers. "But this is only the first night, right?"

"Right." He smiled and wrapped an arm around her shoulder, pulling her against his chest.

"I feel like I'm being a pest, though, making everyone go through all this trouble."

"What? Are you crazy, woman? You are *not* a pest. We *want* to keep you safe. We want to keep *all* of us safe. And did you forget, I promised your grandpa I'd protect you?"

"You're right," she said, feeling a little less guilty.

Billy sighed.

"What?" She looked up at him.

"Ahh, I was just thinking…it's nothing."

"What is it, Billy? Tell me."

He sighed again. "…Maybe it'd be safer for you in Seattle?"

"What?" She jumped up off the bed to get a better look at him, upset he'd even suggest such a thing. "No. I'm *not* leaving. Who's to say that, if it is another werewolf, it can't just follow me to Seattle? You saw how fast Jessica was. I'm *not* leaving, Billy. I *want* to stay here, with *you*."

"It's okay. It was just a thought is all," he said with a soothing tone and caressed her arm. "But you're right, it doesn't mean you'd be safe there either. I'm sorry. I didn't mean to upset you."

She wrapped her arms around his neck and settled onto his lap. "I know you just want me to be safe, but I only feel safe when I'm with you."

Without another word, his soft lips pressed to hers, engulfing them with tender kisses.

Remembering they weren't alone, Sami pulled away and hopped up from his lap. "I'll be right back." She shut the door, locked, it and eagerly returned to his arms.

IN THE moonlit bedroom, Mike sat in a chair, staring up at the shadows on the ceiling created from the giant sugar pine outside the window. The shadows looked more like crooked arms with claws for fingers, reaching down to grab him.

"What the fuck?" he whispered.

"What the fuck, what?" Jason mumbled with his nose buried in his cell phone, his mind clearly elsewhere.

"You should try to get some sleep," Mike said.

"I just need to finish this level," he replied as he jabbed his thumbs across the screen, over and over. "Dammit! See what you made me do." He tossed his phone to the foot of his sleeping bag.

Mike smirked. "So, are you going back east to live with your parents after the summer?"

"Ah, I haven't thought about it much. I don't particularly like the east coast, but there's nothing here for me either." Jason sighed and lay back on his sleeping bag with his arms folded under his head. Looking up at the ceiling, he furrowed his brow. "What the hell? No wonder why Sami has so many nightmares."

Mike turned his attention back to the forest just outside the window. He wondered how in the hell life had brought him here, to this point in his life. *Both my parents are dead. My sister ran away. And now, I'm sitting here in an old house in the middle of the creepiest forest on Earth, protecting my brother's girlfriend from a frickin'* werewolf *of all things.*

This is sure as shit isn't what I thought life would be. I should've been an electrical engineer by now, running my own company. Maybe even married with a couple of brats running around.

Life seemed stale lately, the only excitement being *werewolf watching*. He let out a burdened sigh. *Time to make a change and stop feeling sorry for yourself, asshole! You're not a big-wig engineer, so fucking what! You're one hell of a carpenter with enough money to open your own business just like you've always wanted.*

He glanced at Jason, who was still staring at the ceiling, his eyes roaming the shadows. *Maybe he'd be willing to be a part of this business venture?* "You know, you could always find a permanent job here to keep you busy."

Jason exhaled, long and steady. "Aside from helping you with Abby's, there's not much work in this small town. And I can't just live off my parents' money for the rest of my life. I mean, I *can*, but what kind of man would that make me, right?"

"You could go into business with me and Billy. There's a vacant building downtown I was thinking about buying. Right now, we have all our tools stored in Megan's old room. But if she comes back—"

"What?" Jason sat straight up, like a vampire from its coffin. "Megan's coming back?"

Mike shot him an intimidating glare. "You stay the hell away from my sister."

"Heh, heh, heh," Jason let out a guilty laugh and lay back down. "Billy didn't mention you guys opening up a shop downtown."

"I didn't mention it to him. I've just been thinking about it, is all. Work's been steady lately with all these old houses around here needing to be renovated. Billy and I could really use another set of hands. You do good work."

"I'll think about it," Jason said as he got comfortable in his sleeping bag. "Wake me when it's my turn."

Mike chuckled under his breath.

"What?" Jason asked.

"I was just thinking—here we are hunting the same bitch you dated a couple of months back."

"Ugh! Why'd you have to remind me? Thanks, asshole!" Jason

snapped.

"You have pleasant dreams, now."

"Yeah, whatever," Jason mumbled and rolled onto his side.

Mike smirked and turned his attention back to the forest.

14

BILLY SMILED when Sami entered the kitchen with Buddy in her arms. She wore a white top with denim cutoffs. Her hair fell loosely over her shoulders, and her warm brown eyes danced with liveliness, proving she'd finally had a good night's rest.

"Good morning," he said with jubilance, admiring her beauty.

"Good morning." She stuck her nose in the air and inhaled. "What smells so delicious?" She set Buddy down to explore.

Buddy pounced to the corner of the kitchen when he caught scent of his food bowl.

Billy pointed to the table where Mike and Jason were eating and drinking their coffee.

She peered into the kitchen.

"Good morning," both men said in unison. Then, they both yawned.

"Morning, guys." She smiled and joined them at the table. In the middle of scooping eggs onto her plate, she looked at Jason and frowned. "I'm sorry you didn't get much sleep."

Billy sat next to her and noticed the dark circles around Jason's eyes. "Yeah, I'm gonna take watch tonight to give you a break, dude."

"Ah, you don't have to do that, Billy." Jason yawned again. "You should stay with Sami."

"I'm taking a shift," Billy argued. He stabbed a sausage link with his fork and took a bite.

"I'll take a shift too," Sami said.

Mike shook his head. "No, Sami. You need to sleep. Billy can relieve Jason, and I'll just get a nap in today."

Jason's eyes lit up and his lips curled into a mischievous grin. "Yeah. And I'll take Billy's place down here tonight."

Billy balled up his napkin and threw it across the table. It bounced off Jason's forehead and onto the floor.

Sami giggled, trying to swallow her food so she wouldn't choke.

"Careful." Billy handed her a glass of orange juice.

She took a sip and cleared her throat. "No, but seriously, I *want* to help. Plus, I don't really wanna stay in the room downstairs all by myself."

"Like I said—" Jason grinned again "—I'll be happy to take Billy's place."

Mike punched Jason in the arm.

"Ow, man!" Jason chuckled under his breath, wincing. "That really hurts when you're exhausted."

Billy rested his hand on Sami's thigh. "You can sleep upstairs too."

She grinned. "Yay. It'll be like a big slumber party!"

"Hey, you got any girlfriends you can invite over?" Jason teased.

Sami frowned. "No. So far, the only girl I've met tried to kill me, remember? No one here seems to like me anyway." She shrugged.

An awkward silence engulfed the room.

Jason's eyes filled with remorse. "Sorry."

"It's okay," Sami said through a slight smile, yet she couldn't hide the glum tone in her voice.

Billy patted her thigh and gave it a light squeeze.

Mike cleared his throat. "You can't really trust anyone in this town, anyway. It's best to just keep to yourself."

"Yeah," Jason agreed. "We're all the friends you need."

One corner of Sami's mouth lifted. "You guys are pretty awesome."

Jason stuck his chest out proudly. "I'm the only awesome one here."

Mike smirked. "You're the only *loser* here, maybe."

Sami giggled.

"Yeah, yeah." Jason yawned again.

Mike stretched his arms above his head. Then, he lowered them and rolled his head from side to side.

"Rough night?" Billy asked.

"I'm good," Mike said, his voice gruffer than usual. He looked at Jason. "So, you up for making bullets?"

"Yeah, if I remember how." Jason gulped the last of his coffee and set his mug on the table with a clank. "I was just a kid when my dad last showed me. It's a lot less hassle to just buy them, you know?"

"Don't think there's a big market for silver bullets at the moment, Jason," Billy said.

"There *should* be in *this* town," Sami added.

Billy winked at her.

"Well, I guess I'll clean up from breakfast." Sami gathered everyone's dirty dishes and took them to the sink.

"Thanks, Sami," Jason said.

"What he said." Mike motioned with his head toward Jason.

"Do you want some help?" Billy asked.

"Thanks, but I'm okay. You cooked breakfast. The least I could do is clean up the mess."

"You guys sound like you're already married," Jason teased.

Sami spun around to face Jason, her mouth wide open. "What do you mean?"

Using one swift movement so Sami wouldn't notice, Billy kicked Jason in the shin.

"Mmm." Jason muffled the pain with tight lips. "Uh, I just meant that, you know, since you guys live together and all, you act like a married couple?"

"Oh." She smiled warily and turned back to the sink.

Jason narrowed his eyes at Billy and smirked.

A searing pain shot through Billy's shin. He tensed and gripped the sides of the table, resisting the urge to spout all the curse words building behind his clenched teeth.

Jason grinned.

Sami glanced over her shoulder, her brows crinkled with curiosity before she turned back to the sink.

"Jason, you ready?" Mike's chair screeched across the floor as he stood.

Jason sighed. "Ready as I'll ever be." He sniffed his armpit. "But I could use a shower first. Sami, do you mind if I use the shower upstairs?"

"Sure. The clean towels are in the hall closet up there."

"Thanks. I'll meet you in the basement, Mike." Jason rose to his feet, stretched his arms over his head while groaning, and headed upstairs.

Mike disappeared down the hallway.

Billy approached Sami and wrapped his arms around her waist. He nuzzled his chin in the crook of her neck. "I'm gonna shower, too. Are you gonna be okay by yourself?"

She leaned her head against his. "You're just down the hall. Jason's upstairs. Mike's downstairs. Besides—" she turned, pointing to the sheath at her side "—I have my knife on me."

Billy grinned to hide his apprehension. Ever since he'd found her alone in the backyard last night, and knowing something with green eyes was out there, her safety was a constant worry.

I wonder if I could hear her scream over the shower spray? I'll leave the bedroom and bathroom doors open, just in case.

"Okay, I won't be long." He gave her a quick kiss on the neck and hurried to the bathroom. When he finished showering, shaving, and brushing his teeth, he went to the closet, threw on a gray T-shirt and a pair of jeans, and wriggled his feet into a pair of cross-trainers. Anxious to check on his woman, he hurried back to the kitchen.

Sami had just finishing wiping down the counters. "That was fast." She draped the blue dish cloth over the sink.

He shrugged, trying to appear casual.

She furrowed her brow and glanced toward the stairs. "I don't think Jason even took his shower yet."

Billy peered up the stairway, at the open bathroom door. "I wonder what he's doing?" He jogged up the steps and peeked into the bathroom. Jason wasn't in it. No moisture on the mirror either. The door to Sami's old bedroom was shut. Billy went down the hall and opened the door.

Jason was sprawled on his sleeping bag, snoring, with Buddy curled into the crook of his neck.

Billy shook his head and went back downstairs.

"Where's Jason?" Sami asked.

"Sleeping."

She giggled. "He did look pretty tired.

"Yeah, I didn't think he'd be able to make it through the day. Come on, let's go tell Mike." They strolled to the bedroom, into the backyard, and down the basement steps. When they entered the basement, Sami slung the metal door shut behind them.

Light flickered from the other doorway. They crossed the basement to the other room.

Mike sat on an empty milk crate, hunched over the crucible with silver trinkets, utensils, and platters spread about the floor. A high velocity fan propped in the corner blasted him with air. He lifted his face shield and wiped the forehead sweat on his sleeve.

"Jason's passed out," Billy said.

"I didn't think he was gonna make it through the day." Mike grinned.

"You need some help?" Billy asked.

"Naw. You keep Sami company." A quick nod set the shield back in place and the torch sparked to life again.

Sami walked over to the cage and ran her hand down one of the bars. "Is the cage made of silver?"

"Yep," Billy said. "I guess it's the only thing that can contain werewolves?" He shrugged.

"Where did my grandpa get so much silver?" she asked.

"I don't know. Maybe the same way Mike did? Or antique stores?"

"Hmm." Sami nodded. "So, now what should we do?"

After last night, Billy didn't want to make Sami stay in the basement, staring at the cage, any longer than she had to. "It's a little hot down here. You wanna sit on the front porch and get some fresh air?"

Her eyes lit up. "Sure!" She wrapped her soft fingers around his, pulling him toward the door.

Billy chuckled at her child-like mood. She didn't seem to be affected by the cage this morning, despite all the precautions they had to take.

"Hold on," Billy pulled the opposite way and tapped on Mike's shoulder. He sprawled his fingers in front of his brother's mask, motioning a small wave good-bye.

Mike nodded without lifting his head.

Tugging him along with a smile on her face, Sami led him out the door into the other room. Suddenly, she stopped.

"What's wrong?" Billy asked.

"I could've sworn I shut that door when we came in," she said, staring at the open door leading to the stairs. "Something's not right, Billy."

The door moved, and a man stepped out from behind it.

Billy froze, feeling as if he'd just been punched in the face. A faint echo of Sami saying, "Mr. Smith," reached his ears. The rest of her words faded, as did everything else in the room.

Tears stung Billy's eyes and rolled down his cheeks as he stared in shock at the familiar man. "Dad?"

"What?" Sami belted out.

"Hey, I almost forgot—" Mike entered the room, but stopped dead in his tracks when he focused on the man. "What the fuck?" His face drained of color.

"Hello, boys." A man who resembled their father, Rick Holden, smiled through tear-filled eyes.

Billy stared at the man, wondering what kind of sick joke this was. It couldn't be him, his dad was dead. Yet, he looked just like him.

The man stood as tall and broad as Billy and Mike. His dark hair mixed with silver looked just like their father's had. This guy even wore the usual buttoned shirt, jeans, and worn work boots as them. The only difference was the stubble on his face. Their father had always been clean shaven for their mother.

"How can it be?" Billy's voice trembled. He was sure he was staring at a ghost. "I-I don't understand."

"Mike…Billy…." The man nodded, his eyes beaming with pride as he took the time to get a good look at them both. A few seconds passed, and his demeanor turned serious. "I didn't die that day in the forest thirteen years ago. Not exactly."

Billy took a step toward him. Then another. "*Dad*? Is it really *you*?"

"It's me, kiddo." Rick smiled, bright and warm, though his eyes reflected sorrow. "It's really me."

Billy had often dreamed about getting another chance, just one more moment to spend with his dad. To be able to hug him again and tell him how much he loved him. This man looked like him, sounded like him, and in his gut, Billy knew it was him. Wasting no more time, he rushed over to his father and threw his arms around him.

"I can't believe it!" he cried and sank into his father's tight squeeze. "I can't frickin' believe it!"

"I've missed you, Son!" His voice shook.

"I've missed you, too, Dad!"

Rick pulled away to get a good look at him. "You've gotten so damn big!" He grinned and wiped the tears away with his hands. His gaze shifted to Mike, and his smile faded. With cautious steps, he approached Mike. "Son." He gave a firm nod and held his hand out.

Mike's eyes welled up with tears. He took his father's hand and yanked him into a firm embrace.

"It's so good to see you again," Rick said as he patted Mike firmly on the back. "I'm sorry I stayed away for so long."

Smiling, Sami sniffled and gave Billy a reassuring squeeze on the arm.

Mike pulled away to face his father. "What in the hell happened, Dad? Where'd you go all these years?" he asked, his voice wracked with anguish.

Their father let out a heavy breath. "That day in the forest, thirteen years ago, I was attacked…but not by a wolf. Not by a *normal* wolf."

Billy's chest tightened with dread. He envisioned Jessica as a werewolf—long snout, pointed ears, claws curled—and he prayed his father wasn't the same. He held his breath, waiting for his dad to continue.

Rick lowered his stare, unable to look anyone in the eyes. "The sheriff got to the scene first, and when he told me what I'd become, I knew I couldn't come home. He covered everything up, took me up north, and held me captive for a while until he knew how I'd handle what had happened to me. When he finally released me, I stayed up north. I just couldn't chance anyone I knew seeing what I'd become. Especially you." He lifted his head and looked at his sons. "I'm not the same father you used to know. I'm not even human anymore."

Billy stared at his Dad in disbelief and gulped. "What are you saying? Th-that you're a...a werewolf?"

His father nodded with shame in his eyes.

"What?" Mike boomed. "So, are you like Jessica? Are you here to *kill* us?"

Billy yanked the knife from his sheath and pushed Sami behind him.

"No!" Rick boomed, and his eyes turned green.

Mike whipped his knife out and stood shoulder to shoulder with his brother.

"Shit!" Billy tightened his grip on the knife. "It was *you* in the forest last night!"

"I'm *not* like Jessica! I don't kill people!"

"Your eyes, th-their green," Sami's voice quivered.

"I won't hurt you." Rick took a deep breath and closed his eyes. When he opened them they were brown. "I'm sorry I lied to you in the forest, Sami—the day you were lost. I was visiting my wife's grave when I heard you coming. I wanted to make sure you made it home safe without getting lost again. Then, a few days ago, when Abby came to me and told me what Jessica did to you, to *all* of you—" he looked at everyone "—I came back to protect you."

He lowered his gaze and shook his head, clearly disappointed with himself. "I had no idea that Jessica had been so much trouble, otherwise I would've come back sooner."

Mike stared at his father with his jaw wide open. "Abby? You mean *my* Abby?"

Rick met Mike's shocked gaze. "She's Jessica's half-sister. Sheriff Briggs ordered Abby to watch over you all since you know their secret. They think, since Abby's family, that she's on their side. They don't realize Abby is good-hearted. After she met you all, she knew she had to protect *you* from *them*. Especially Jessica. But Jessica's too strong for her. That's why Abby came looking for me. As soon as she got word Jessica was planning to come back, she knew she needed my help to protect you."

"So, Abby's like Jessica?" Mike asked, his eyes saddened with the pain of betrayal.

"No, Son. She's like me," he said with regret.

Mike grabbed a nearby folding chair and eased onto it. With his elbows propped on his knees, he rested his forehead on his hands, hiding his inner turmoil.

Billy took a deep breath and exhaled to relieve his tension. He scratched his head, trying to make sense of it all. "So, Jessica's not dead? And you keep saying *they*. There's more of them? More werewolves? What about Mom? Is she alive?" He held his breath, praying she was.

His dad's eyes filled with remorse and he shook his head. "No. I'm sorry."

An ache filled Billy's heart as his hopes were crushed. He swallowed back the building tears.

"Billy, please put the knife down. I'm not here to hurt you."

Billy hesitated, wondering if he could really trust his father. A werewolf. Whatever he was. He stared into his dad's pleading eyes. Slowly, he lowered the knife and slid it back into the sheath.

Rick pressed his lips together and gave a slight nod. "Jessica is still alive. Sheriff Briggs just sent her away, so she couldn't cause any more trouble. And yes, there are more werewolves out there. A lot more. But I'm not like Jessica. I'm not evil. I'm a protector."

"So, you just protect people from other *werewolves*?" Billy furrowed his brow.

"Yes, that's what I do…or that's what I was supposed to be doing all these years," he admitted with a shameful look. "But I'm here, now, to keep you safe."

"So, some of you are good and some of you are killers?" Billy asked.

"Yes. Just as there are good and evil people, there are also werewolf opposites, I guess you can say. It just depends on who you truly are deep down at the time you're bitten. The evil one's have red eyes, and as you've just seen, protectors have green eyes. That's the only real way to tell."

"So—" Mike finally lifted his head "—Abby's been a werewolf for *how* long now?"

"For about a year. She's still new and inexperienced, but full of energy. Which is another reason why I'm here. Abby's in trouble. She needs our help."

Mike jumped up, his eyes wide with worry. "What do you mean? What happened to her?"

"Jessica. I tried to get Abby to come back here with me, but she was adamant on seeing her sister first. She wanted to find out exactly what Jessica's plans were, so we'd be better prepared. But what Abby didn't realize—Jessica already knew we were conspiring against her. That someone had tipped her off. Abby walked right into a trap.

"And even worse, Jessica's holding her in a silver cage, which has sickened her. I can take you there and hold off Jessica, but I can't open the cage. If I touch silver, it renders me powerless for a minute."

"How did Jessica get her in there?" Mike asked.

"I'm not sure. Probably has human help. Someone not affected by silver."

"How'd you find all this out?" Billy asked.

"When Abby didn't return, I knew something must've happened, and I had to look for her. But I didn't want to leave you all unprotected for so long. So, when I saw Sami standing in the bedroom window last night, I revealed my green eyes, hoping you would be on alert after that and protect yourselves with the silver knives. And that's exactly what you all did."

Billy grew irritated. "Why the green-eyed game? Why didn't you just tell us all this last night? Or sooner?"

Rick lowered his gaze to the floor before looking at Billy again. "You thought I was dead. Abby was supposed to tell you about me before I revealed myself, so it wouldn't be so much of a shock. And—" he motioned with a quick nod to the knife hooked to Billy's belt "—to lessen my odds of being stuck with a silver knife. I was hoping to just find her and bring her back. Instead, I found her caged. And now that silver is involved, I need someone not affected by it to help with the rescue."

Mike jumped to his feet. "I'll help. Let's get Abby!"

Rick shook his head. "We can't tonight. It's the full moon. Jessica's too strong. It's too risky."

"But I have silver knives and silver bullets. We can do this!" Mike demanded.

"No!" Rick ordered and his eyes turned green. "I will *not* risk you. We'll go in two days when Jessica's anger has subsided."

Mike threw his hands up and let them fall to his sides. "But what if it's too late?"

Rick took a deep breath. When he looked up, his eyes were brown again. "It won't be too late. Jessica doesn't want to kill her sister. If she did, Abby would be dead by now. She just wants to keep her out of the way, so she can deal with me one on one. If she overpowers me, there'll be nothing standing in her way."

Sami's eyes widened. "Is she coming here tonight?"

"No. I think she's waiting for *me* to come to *her*. She knows I'll try to rescue Abby. You're safe for now."

Sami breathed a sigh of relief.

Rick glanced at each of his sons. "How's Megan?"

"She moved to Santa Cruz, California with a friend as soon as high school was over," Mike answered.

"Is she okay?"

"Yeah, she's doing good," Billy said. "She's been talking about maybe moving back home. I'm sure she will when she finds out you're alive."

Rick swiped a hand across his chin. "I would love to see her again. But, for now, let's not tell her about me and the fact that werewolves do exist. It's safer for her this way, and she's safer where she's at."

Billy couldn't imagine his strong-headed sister being thrown into the werewolf mix at the moment either. "I won't say anything."

Mike nodded his agreement.

A steady thudding drew their attention to the ceiling. Heavy footsteps jogged across the floor, upstairs in Sami's bedroom. They followed the sound with their eyes until it stopped. The whoosh of the sliding glass door being opened rumbled the ceiling.

JASON POPPED his eyes open and sat up. "Oh shit! I was supposed to help Mike!" He jumped to his feet and grabbed his backpack. Then, he hurried down the hall to the bathroom, snatching a towel out of the hall closet along the way. He quickly showered, dressed, and brushed his teeth. He slathered deodorant over his armpits, paused for a few seconds, and slathered on an extra layer just to be safe.

Using his towel, he cleared the moisture off the mirror and combed through his hair with his hands, giving it a tousled look on top. His eyes fell to his white T-shirt, all wrinkled from being in his backpack.

"Crap," he said, smoothing the wrinkles out with his hands. "Oh well." He shrugged. Satisfied he was presentable enough, he hurried to the basement, jogging the whole way.

"Dude, sorry, I fell asleep," Jason said as he rushed into the basement. He grinned and placed a hand on his chest to catch his breath.

Billy, Sami, and Mike all stared at him with stunned expressions. They were obviously taking his falling asleep more seriously than expected. His smiled faded. "Come on, I said I'm sorry."

"Hello, Jason." A deep voice echoed behind him.

Jason spun around to face the stranger.

Rick Holden stood there, smiling.

"What the hell?" Jason sucked in a breath and suddenly he couldn't breathe. Somehow, he was staring at a man who'd been dead for the last thirteen years. With his heart pounding in his ears, he stumbled back, bumping into a shelf and knocking over its clutter.

Billy was suddenly in front of him with a firm grip on his shoulders. "Jason, it's okay! It's my dad. It's Rick! He didn't die that day, Jason. He didn't die."

In complete shock, Jason stared at Billy until the words finally sunk in. His lungs started to cooperate again and finally allowed him a full breath of air. "Rick?" he whispered. Tears blurred his vision. "You mean…he didn't *die*? He didn't die because of *me*?"

Billy shook his head, and his eyes glistened with sadness. "No, Jason, he's alive. And it was never your fault."

Jason fell to his knees and ran trembling fingers through his hair. In utter disbelief, he stared at Rick for a long moment. Then, he buried his face in his hands and cried as the tremendous guilt he had carried on his back for the last thirteen years suddenly lifted.

Billy dropped to his knees and put his arm around him. "Hey, bud. It's all right."

Rick crossed the room and knelt in front of them. "It was never your fault, Son. *Never!*" He pulled Jason into his arms.

Jason hugged him back, trying to control his sobs, still not sure if he was dreaming or not. "I can't believe it. I can't *frickin'* believe it!" he said through his tears, chuckling lightly.

Rick patted him on the back. "Believe it. It's really me." He stood and held his hand out.

Jason gripped Rick's hand and rose to his feet.

"I'm just sorry I didn't come sooner. I'm sorry I put you through all this pain—" Rick looked at each one of them "—all of you."

Jason wiped his eyes dry on his shirt and took a couple of deep breaths to collect himself. He lifted his arms at his sides and dropped them, letting them smack against his thighs. "Okay, if you didn't die... what the *hell* happened?"

With a quick hand, Mike squashed away a lost tear and cleared his throat. "Maybe we can go upstairs and talk?"

"Sure." Sami wiped her cheeks dry with her fingers and everyone followed her upstairs.

They all sat around the kitchen table while Rick explained the details.

Jason smacked his palms on the table. "Okay, I'm in! I'll go with you to get Abby."

"No," Rick replied. "Abby will be busy getting Mike out of there as fast as she can. It'll take a minute or two before her strength comes back. I'll be busy dealing with Jessica. It's just too dangerous."

"While you're dealing with Jessica, I can sneak up behind her with the knife," Jason argued.

"There's no sneaking up on a werewolf, Jason," Rick said with a flat expression. "She can smell and hear you coming. Besides, you need to stay here with Billy and Sami. As soon as we rescue Abby, this is where Jessica will head next. We'll make sure we get back before she does, but you three will need to be prepared."

"So," Sami spoke up. "Does this mean Jessica will come for me again?"

"No, not the way I understand it. Jessica never wanted you, Sami. She just wanted you out of the way. She wants Billy."

"What?" Sami bolted to her feet, nearly knocking over her chair.

"She can't take Billy! We have to stop her!"

Billy grabbed Sami's arm. "Hey. She's not taking me. Everything will be okay."

"No!" Sami yanked her arm away. "It's *not* okay, Billy. *Jessica* is coming back." She let out an unsteady breath and tears filled her eyes. "She's coming back…."

15

SAMI SHUT the front door and set the pizzas on the counter. Buddy pounced into the kitchen and flopped onto his back.

Mew.

"Silly boy." She smiled and picked him up, nuzzling him into her neck. "Are you lonely? I'm have to go downstairs for a minute. I'll be right back." She set him on the ground, went to her bedroom, and out the back door.

The setting sun sent red and orange streaks across the clouded sky. She took a second to admire the beauty, feeling more at ease now that Rick was here to protect them.

A cool breeze picked up and sent a chill down her bare arms. Tree limbs creaked and moaned, awakening the quiet forest. Eyeing the dark shadows, she decided not to take any chances and hurried down the basement steps.

"Pizzas are here," she announced.

Billy, Jason, Mike, and Rick all looked up with smiles on their faces and sweat beading their foreheads. They'd been busy making bullets all day.

"Good! I'm starving!" Jason dropped the tool he held, letting it clank to the ground, and went to a sink in the corner. He washed his hands and splashed water on his face. Grinning, he headed upstairs.

"We're just about done here," Billy said. "We'll be right up."

"Okay." Sami smiled and hurried back upstairs, trying to catch up to Jason. When she reached the backyard, Jason wasn't there. She jogged through her bedroom door and didn't stop until she reached the kitchen.

Jason was already sitting at the table, eating.

She grabbed a piece of pizza and sat down to join him.

"This is so good!" he said, shoving half the slice in his mouth.

She forced a smile, trying to be happy with him, but she couldn't get her mind off Jessica.

Jason looked at her and frowned, seeing right through her fake smile. "Don't worry, Sami." He gulped down his food. "We have two days to plan."

"You mean two days until we meet our doom?"

"Billy and I won't let that bitch lay another hand on you," he said.

"I just keep remembering that day in the forest. She just came in and overpowered everyone. There was nothing we could do."

"Don't worry," Rick said as he entered the kitchen with his sons. "You have me to help now. I'll make sure I get to Jessica before she gets to anyone. And there are more of us to stop her now."

Sami nodded and gave him a slight smile. They had a werewolf on their side now, easing some of her worries.

Billy went to the cupboard and grabbed some plates. He handed one to his dad and brother and filled his own plate with as much pizza as it could hold. On his way back to the table, he picked up a barstool.

Mike and Rick joined them at the table.

"So, you eat regular food, huh?" Jason asked Rick.

Rick's eyes twinkled with amusement. "What'd you think that I ate?"

"Same thing as Jessica. People." Jason shrugged and kept eating.

Rick chuckled under his breath. "Jessica doesn't eat people. She could if she wanted to, but she does eat food. And, when the moon is full, wild animals."

Jason grinned. "You mean like *live* wild animals?"

Rick nodded and took a bite of pizza.

Billy gulped and eyed his dad. "Do you eat wild animals?"

"I have, when I lived in the forest, in a cave." Rick replied, his tone dismal. "It's hard to get used to the hunger at first, especially when you have no one to guide you through it. You get so ravenous that you can't control it."

The room fell silent. All eyes were on Rick. Sami was sure everyone's minds were envisioning the same thing—Rick living as a beast in a cave, tearing into the flesh of a wild animal with his fangs.

"But pizza's my favorite," Rick said, interrupting the silence. A smile formed in the corner of his mouth, and he winked at Sami.

Afraid Rick somehow knew exactly what she'd been thinking, her cheeks turned hot with embarrassment. She pinched a smile between her lips. "It's my favorite, too."

A comfortable silence filled the air as everyone enjoyed their hot cheesy meal.

"Hey, do you got any beer?" Jason jumped up and went to the fridge. "Yes!" He grinned when he found them. "Anyone else?"

"I'll take one," Mike said.

Billy shook his head. "No thanks. I'll take a soda though."

Jason looked at Rick and furrowed his brow. "Do werewolves drink beer?"

Rick smirked. "I'll take a soda too. Thanks."

"Good, more beer for us, then." Jason walked back to the table with an arm full of canned beverages and sat down. He slid a beer across the table to Mike and set sodas down for everyone else.

"Thank you, Jason." Sami smiled at him. She popped the tab on the cola and took a long swig.

"Well, Dad," Mike said, "I have your old room, but Billy's room is available tonight. We can switch 'em back around tomorrow."

"Thanks, but Billy's room is fine. As soon as all this is behind us, I'll look for my own place."

"No, Dad. It's *your* house," Mike argued. "Billy lives here with Sami now. There's more than enough room."

"You're a grown man, Mike. You need your own space. Besides, there are too many memories of your mother in that house. It'll be hard enough just staying for a few nights."

Heavy silence filled the air. Sami sensed the pain of loss radiating around the room from the four men.

"You can stay here," she said, her voice gentle.

"Thank you, Sami. I appreciate the gesture. I'll be fine though." Rick winked again, obviously trying to lighten the mood. "Well, I need to get some rest. I haven't slept in a couple of days." He rose and set his plate in the sink.

"I'll help you get settled in." Mike stood and headed for the front door.

"Goodnight, Dad." Billy smiled.

"Goodnight." He gave a quick nod. "Oh, and don't worry about Jessica. I'm sure she won't come here, but I can sense when she's near. You're safe."

"That's a huge relief," Billy said.

"Yeah, that's pretty awesome!" Jason grinned.

"You all get some good sleep tonight," Rick said. He followed Mike outside and shut the door behind him.

"Well, I should get going, too." Jason guzzled the rest of his beer. "Last night was rough."

Billy crinkled his brow. "Are you sure you should be alone with Jessica still out there? Your house is farther away. My dad can't be in two places at once."

"Neither can Jessica," Jason said. "Besides, she wants you, not me. Remember? Anyway, she's busy guarding Abby, and your dad can sense if she's near. I think we can all use some good rest before doomsday." He gathered up the empty plates on the table and set them in the sink. "See you guys in the morning."

"Bye, Jason," Sami said.

Jason went to the front door and opened it. Half-way out, he paused and stepped back inside wearing a sheepish smile. "Just in case, can I borrow your car, Sami? Mike gave me a ride back here last night, so I don't have mine. And it's already dark out."

"Dude, why don't you just stay?" Billy asked. "That way we won't be up worrying about your sorry ass all night."

"Tempting, but no. Besides, you two lovebirds need your privacy, and I can't wait to get into my own bed tonight." Jason grinned and raised his eyebrows up and down.

Sami snickered. "The keys are hanging by the wall, Jason. But, if you change your mind, the house key is on there too."

"Thanks, Sami." Jason shut the door on his way out.

"I'm gonna see him off." Billy went out onto the front porch. When he came back inside, he locked the door.

Sami wondered what purpose the locks held now. If a werewolf wanted to get in, they could easily push the door open. Probably with one hand.

She shook the thought from her head and bounced up to look for Buddy, realizing she hadn't seen him in a while. "Here, kitty, kitty," she called out, peering into the living room. "Buddy...."

"Can't find him?" Billy asked.

"No, I haven't seen him for a little while. I'm pretty sure I accidentally left the back door open when I came to get you guys for dinner. Do you think he got out?"

"I'm sure he's just sleeping somewhere." Billy's arms encircled her waist, and he pulled her against him.

She sighed and sank against his chest, enjoying his touch. "Yeah, you're probably right."

Billy let out a long exhale, as if something were bothering him.

"What's the matter?" Sami lifted her head to look him in the eyes.

He exhaled again, his face full of worry. "I'm just afraid I'm gonna wake up tomorrow and my dad won't be here. It's still hard to believe this is all real. I just don't want it to be a dream, you know?"

"Don't worry, Billy. He'll be here. Okay? He's home for good."

Billy nodded and sighed away his worry. "You're right. He'll be here."

She gave him a peck on the lips. "Do you wanna watch some TV?"

"Nope. I wanna do this—" He leaned down and kissed her. When he gazed at her again, his eyes were full of lust.

Her lips curled into a knowing smile.

Billy smirked and led her toward the bedroom.

SOMETHING IS scratching at the sliding glass door. I climb out of bed and walk slowly toward it. When I open the door, a burst of cold night air crawls up my arms, and I shiver.

"Sami...," a woman's voice calls out to me.

She's somewhere in the forest, but I can't see her.

"Sami...," she calls out again.

Though I am afraid, I glide to the edge of the grass and watch the shadows of the trees, waiting for her to appear.

Mew, mew....

Sami tensed and opened her eyes, blinded by a ray of sunshine trickling through the curtain. She raised a hand to block the light and sat up.

"Did you have another nightmare?" Billy placed a hand on her back and rubbed it.

She nodded and exhaled, relieved to be safe in her bedroom, with Billy at her side. "I dreamed Buddy was in the forest. He was crying. And a woman was calling my name." She glanced at the empty box on the floor and frowned before she lay back down and snuggled against Billy's chest.

He kissed the top of her head and sat up, planting his feet on the floor. The bed shook while he fumbled with something in front of him. As he stood, he slid his jeans to his waist and zipped them.

"Where are you going?" She pouted.

"To look for Buddy." He winked.

"That's so sweet." She climbed out of bed and put her robe on. "I'll help."

"Okay, you look down here, and I'll go upstairs."

"If he was in the house, I think he would've come when we called him."

"Maybe. But, before I look outside, I wanna make sure he's not hiding in here somewhere." Billy opened the door and headed down the hallway.

"Here, kitty, kitty," Sami called. "Buddy!" She dropped to her hands and knees to peer under the bed. "Darn it, where is he?" She peeked into the closet. Next, the bathroom. Buddy was nowhere in sight.

On her way to the living room she searched the storage space under the stairs, looking alongside the stacked boxes. Still no Buddy. Disappointed, she went into the living room. "Buddy…."

"Did you find him?" Billy asked as he jogged back downstairs.

"No." She pouted, sticking out her bottom lip. "I think he got outside, Billy."

"I'll go look." He went into the bedroom and out the back door.

Sami followed him and watched from the doorway.

"Here, kitty, kitty," he called out.

"Buddy!" she shouted.

Billy looked around the backyard and down the basement steps but came back empty handed.

Sadness tugged at Sami's heart. Buddy hadn't been with them long enough to become familiar with his surroundings. If he ventured out into the forest, he probably wasn't coming back.

"He's gone, Billy." She frowned.

"He'll come back." Billy hopped up the steps and put his arms around her.

"I don't think so." She thought of her dream. Buddy's cry had come from the forest, along with the woman's voice. Previous nightmares came to mind, and their similarities to reality were too coincidental to ignore. "My dreams, they seem to be real somehow. Almost like… they come true."

"What?"

"Well, when I first moved here, I dreamed I was in the forest and a wolf was chasing me. Then, it really happened—Jessica chased me through the forest and got me. And I dreamed about the basement, all the clutter, and the other door. Yet, I had never been down there. This morning, I had a dream about some woman deep in the forest, calling my name. Buddy was out there too. He's lost in the forest somewhere. I *know* it. We have to find him." She pleaded with her eyes, hoping to persuade him to search for the helpless kitten.

He pursed his lips, his eyes filled with uncertainty. "I'm sure it's all just a coincidence. And I know you wanna find Buddy. But I don't think it's good idea to go out there looking for him," he said, motioning toward the trees. "He could be anywhere. Or maybe he even found his way back to where he came from."

"But what if he's hungry and cold? Or what if he gets eaten by some wild animal? Or something worse?" She envisioned Jessica sinking her fangs into the helpless kitten and shook her head to clear the thought.

"Sami…" Billy placed his hands on her cheeks. "If something *worse* is out there and Buddy's life is at stake because of it, so is ours."

Her hopes crumbled, but Billy was right. It'd be stupid to go traipsing through a werewolf's playground to look for a kitten. "Yeah, I know. I don't wanna put us in danger."

Billy lowered his hands to her waist. "I'll tell you what. We'll put food and water outside for him. And we'll keep calling for him. I'm sure he'll be back when he's hungry enough."

"Okay," she agreed, clinging to the last bit of hope. Her cell phone chimed. Surprised to see her mother's face on the screen, she snatched it off the dresser and answered it. "Hi, Mom…. Yes, I'm doing fine…. No, the first night was okay…. What? So soon…? Well, I'll talk to Billy and see…. Okay, I'll call you back a little later…. Love you too, Mom…. Bye."

"That was a quick call." Billy sat at the foot of the bed.

"Yeah, she was in the middle of something. She just wanted to tell me that she and Steve are getting married in a couple of days. They're flying to Lake Tahoe tonight. She wants us to go."

"Do you wanna go?"

Sami cringed at the thought of Steve becoming her stepfather. But she also couldn't bear the thought of disappointing her mom. "No…. Yes…. I don't know. I don't want her to marry him!" She threw her arms up, frustrated.

"We can go if you want. With Jessica being alive and all, maybe it wouldn't be such a bad idea. I'm sure we'd be safer there than we are here."

Sami plopped on the bed next to him. "I don't know. I'll think about it."

Billy grinned. "Come on, let's go get some food set out for Buddy and get ourselves some breakfast. You still have time to decide."

Her stomach rumbled at the thought of food and she smiled. "Okay. I *am* getting hungry."

Billy took Buddy's food and water dish outside. He rattled the food around in the bowl and called out to the lost kitten a few more times, before he set the food on the top step and came back inside.

Sami stuck out her bottom lip.

"He'll come back," Billy reassured and slid the door shut. "Let's go eat."

When they opened the bedroom door, the smell of bacon filled the air.

"What the hell?" Billy hurried down the hall to the kitchen, with Sami following behind.

Jason stood at the stove, flipping bacon. He turned and grinned. "Good morning! I hope you don't mind. Thought I'd make you guys some breakfast for letting me stay last night and all."

Billy looked confused. "Dude, you came back? I didn't even hear you come in."

"Yeah, it was kinda late. I ended up watching a werewolf movie on TV and thought maybe you two would feel a little safer if I was here. You know, to help. Just in case." He let out a nervous laugh.

"Billy?" Sami crossed her arms. "If he stayed the night, and you checked upstairs for Buddy, how come you didn't know Jason was here?"

Billy flashed a sheepish grin. "Well, the guest room door was shut, and I know cats can't open doors. So, I figured I didn't need to look in there?" He cringed.

"Why? Is Buddy missing?" Jason looked worried.

"Sami left the back door open yesterday, and we haven't seen him since," Billy said.

"Bummer. I'll keep an eye out for him. Okay, Sami?"

"Thanks, Jason." She managed a half-smile, but it faded as her stress mounted. Worried about Buddy and having Steve as a stepdad, a hot shower to relieve the tension sounded perfect.

"Billy, I'm gonna go take a shower before breakfast is ready."

"Okay. After we eat, do you wanna go with me to talk to my dad? I wanna find out more about their plans to rescue Abby."

"Sure." She gave him a peck on the lips and went to the bedroom.

Sami showered and readied for the day, choosing to wear jeans and a lavender top, with a camisole under the thin fabric. When she finished, she went back into the kitchen to join Billy and Jason for breakfast. Afterward, they all pitched in and cleaned the mess, before heading next door.

16

BILLY OPENED the front door of his brother's house and went inside, followed by Sami and Jason.

"Good morning," Billy said, relieved to see his dad sitting at the dining table, alive and well, and that it hadn't been a dream after all.

"Good morning," Rick beamed and pushed his empty plate aside.

Mike stacked his plate on top of his dad's and leaned back in the chair.

Billy sat at the table along with Sami and Jason. He ran a quick hand through his hair, wondering how he was going to get his dad and brother on board about Lake Tahoe without upsetting Sami. The anger on her face after the conversation with her mom was a sure sign she didn't want to go. But with danger lurking so close to home, Sami being mad was the least of his worries.

"So, Dad, I was thinking—maybe it'd be better if the three of us didn't stay here and wait for you guys to rescue Abby?"

Rick's smile dimmed. "You can't come with us. It's too dangerous."

"I know, but Sami's mom wants us to join her in Lake Tahoe for her wedding. Maybe it'd be safer for us there, out of the way. No one would even know we left."

Rick rubbed his chin while he thought. "I think it's a good idea."

Sami squished her eyes shut for a brief second and put her head down.

Billy reached under the table and squeezed her hand. She didn't pull away—a good sign she wasn't too pissed at him.

"We want all three of you to be safe," Mike said, looking directly at Sami.

After a few seconds she lifted her head and let out a tiresome sigh. "I guess you're right."

"Awesome!" Jason shouted. "Lake Tahoe here we come!"

Sami's strained expression softened, and a hint of a smile formed in the corners of her mouth as she watched Jason's excitement. "So, when should we leave?"

"I don't want to leave any of you unprotected. So, the sooner the better," Rick suggested.

"I guess we'll leave when we're done packing," Billy said. "We should make it there by nightfall."

Jason's eyes lit up. "I'll drive. My car's better on gas."

"All right, then, let's go pack." Billy pushed away from the table and headed for the door.

Sami followed him. "Oh, I almost forgot—" she turned back to the table "—Buddy got out, and we can't find him. If he comes back, can you put him back in the house? And his food and water dish too? We left them out back for him."

Mike furrowed his brow. "That sucks. We'll keep an eye out for him."

"Thanks," she said and went outside.

"Hey, Mike? Can I get a ride home?" Jason asked.

"I guess."

"See you guys in a few." Billy pulled the door closed. With Sami's hand in his, he kept a steady pace across the yards, anxious to get his woman away from danger for a few days.

As soon as they stepped inside the front door, Sami called her mom to tell her the good news. When they finished packing, they met Jason at his car.

Jason popped the trunk and put their suitcases inside, next to his.

"So, we really have to do this, huh?" Sami asked, her eyes full of worry.

Billy felt bad for her, wishing he'd come up with some other plan. They could've just went somewhere out of the way and laid low for a few days. They didn't actually have to go to Lake Tahoe. But at least Sami would be able to spend time with her mom again.

"It'll turn out okay. You get to see your mom, and we might even have a little fun while we're there," he said.

She gave way to a soft smile. "All right, let's go."

He grinned and gave her a quick peck on the lips. "Jason's getting his own room though."

She giggled.

Rick and Mike exited the single-story house and crossed the yards.

"You guys are all ready, huh?" Mike said as he approached them.

"Yep." Billy sighed. The thought of leaving his dad and brother to fend off a werewolf by themselves made his stomach turn. He wished there was some other way. That he could stay and help ensure they would both make it back alive.

"I'm sure you'll be much safer than you would be here," his dad said with a strained look, as if he were trying to convince himself of the notion. "Just don't stop unless it's necessary."

"Do you have the knives and handguns?" Mike asked.

"Yep! Got 'em!" Jason motioned toward his trunk.

"Just drive carefully, Jason," Mike warned. "You don't wanna get pulled over."

"Maybe we should keep that bag up front with us?" Billy suggested.

"I have a couple of knives under the seats and a gun in the glove compartment," Jason said. "The ones in the bag are for the hotel room."

"Good." Rick turned to Billy and hugged him. "You take care, Son. We'll see you soon."

"I will, Dad." Billy hugged his father, afraid to let go.

After a couple of firm pats his dad stepped aside. "We'll be back, Billy. Abby and I are strong and damn near invincible."

Billy nodded and turned to Mike. Instead of the usual half-hug, he threw both arms around Mike and hugged him tight. "You take care, big brother."

Mike gave him a swat on the back and pulled away. "Don't worry, little bro." He grinned. "I'll see you when you get back. Don't waste all your savings gambling."

Billy stood with his hands in his pockets, watching as everyone else said their good-byes. And just like that, the moment he dreaded had come. He swallowed the lump in his throat and climbed into the backseat of Jason's car.

Sami slid into the front seat, and Jason sat behind the wheel.

The engine revved to life, and the car rolled forward.

Looking through the rear window, Billy waved as his dad and brother disappeared into the distance, praying it wasn't the last time he'd ever see them. Tears slipped from his eyes, but he swiped at them before anyone noticed.

Sami reached around the seat and grabbed his hand. Without uttering a sound, she mouthed the words *I love you*.

He winked and gave her hand a quick squeeze, letting her know he'd be all right. With an ache in his chest, he settled back into his seat and stared out of his window into the forest.

AFTER DINNER, Mike flopped onto the recliner to relax. Thoughts of Abby, caged like an animal and miserable, flooded his thoughts. His father had ordered they wait until tomorrow to rescue her—two days after the full moon, when Jessica was no longer at her strongest point. But Mike couldn't stand sitting idly by, staring at the clock above the front door, helpless.

Punching something sure would relieve some stress. He glanced around, searching for a target. But, other than the couch, everything else was breakable. Besides, he couldn't risk a broken hand. Abby needed him.

His dad passed by him and sat on the couch, deep in thought. "I was thinking, Mike, maybe we should leave tonight. I can't leave Abby locked up in that cage another night. The full moon was last night, so

Jessica won't be quite as strong tonight."

A burst of energy jolted through Mike's veins, and he sprang to his feet. "I'll get Billy's car loaded."

"No, Son." Rick hesitated. "We won't be taking the car. It's not fast enough. By the time Abby gets her strength back, she's going to have to get you out of there as fast as she can while I hold Jessica off. There won't be time to get in the car, pick up speed, and follow the winding road out of there."

Mike's energy fizzled and wariness took over. "So, what are you saying?"

"I'll have to carry you in on my back."

"You mean as a werewolf?"

Rick nodded.

Mike eased onto the edge of the recliner. He tried to envision himself climbing onto the back of a huge, hairy beast, but the thought was surreal. Until recently, werewolves just hadn't existed in his world. And now, his own father was one. Mike knew his dad wouldn't shred him to pieces, but it didn't make the situation any less freakish.

"Sorry, Son. If there was any other way...."

Mike's reservations of playing piggy back with a werewolf diminished as his thoughts drifted. Sami had been in bad shape after they'd found her in Jessica's basement. He couldn't stand the thought of finding Abby in the same condition. He jumped to his feet.

"Let's go, Dad!"

Rick grinned. "I'll take the shortest route there. There's a hidden cave just a few miles from where Abby's being held. No one else knows about it. We'll stop there to go over our plan of attack. Just bring a jacket, and fill a backpack with the weapons and a lock pick. Oh, and a set of clothes and shoes for me, just in case."

Pushing his worries aside, he followed his father's instructions and placed extra clothes and shoes into the backpack. He went back out to the gun case in the living room and placed two handguns, loaded with silver bullets, and two silver knives into the bag.

"Are you sure you're ready for this?" Rick asked.

"Yep," Mike said, ignoring the tornado of nerves in his chest.

"You'll have to get on my back after I morph."

"I already saw Jessica as a werewolf. It'll be just the same, right?"

His dad nodded. "Except for one thing."

Mike's trepidation grew. "What?"

"I'm quite a bit larger than Jessica." He winked, wearing a smug grin.

Mike shook his head and chuckled. "So, should I grab the ladder?"

His father's smile faded along with the humorous moment. "I'm gonna change in the room. Don't be scared when I come out. I'll still think and feel like me inside. I'll just be a werewolf too. Oh, and don't worry about the sounds that might come from the room. Changing can be a little painful. And though I won't be able to talk to you, you can still talk to me. I'll comprehend everything you say." He disappeared down the hallway.

Mike swallowed the lump in his throat, mentally bracing himself for the ride of his life. He put on his jacket and slid his arms through the backpack. Exhaling to ease the tension, he stared down the quiet hallway and waited.

Deep groaning cut through the silence, and a heavy thud rattled the front window.

Afraid his dad had fallen, Mike started toward the bedroom. A low growl stopped him dead in his tracks. Mike's eyes widened, and his heart raced. Not ready to see his dad as a werewolf yet, he went into the kitchen and leaned against the counter with his arms folded across his chest.

The bedroom door creaked open, breaking the silence, followed by heavy stomping as his dad made his way down the hall.

A humongous werewolf, standing as tall as the eight-foot ceiling, rounded the corner and towered over him.

"Shit," Mike said under his breath. His dad's shoulder span had to be about five feet across. But the thick, dark fur covering his body made it hard to tell. He focused on his dad's vivid green eyes, which appeared to be glowing.

The beast before him unclenched his long-clawed fingers and a low growl rumbled from his chest.

Mike gulped, glad he wasn't bearing his fangs too.

His dad let out another low growl and motioned to the kitchen door with a jerk of the head.

Mike nodded, realizing he was wasting valuable time staring like a fool. "Let's do this." He grabbed a kitchen chair and hopped up on it.

With trembling hands and legs, Mike climbed onto his father's back and clamped his hands around his neck. His dad's thick fur felt softer than its rough appearance. Contrarily, his body was rock solid, pure muscle and strength.

His father went to the kitchen door and opened it, pulling it shut behind them as soon as they were outside. He paused, eyeing the darkening forest.

Without warning, they thrust forward.

Mike tightened his grip as the gray of the impending night whizzed by. They flew so fast everything blurred together. After about a minute, the fear subsided, and a new sense of thrilling adventure overcame him. He sucked in a huge breath, enjoying the exhilarating rush.

They jerked to a stop, and reality surrounded them again. Trees, bushes, everything came into focus.

Mike jumped to the ground. "Are we here already?"

His dad shook his head and pointed above his head.

Mike looked up.

Buddy peered down at them from inside a small cage, hanging from a branch by a rope.

"Son of a bitch!" Mike shouted. "Was it Jessica?"

His father nodded. With a quick swipe, he sliced through the rope with his claw and handed the cage over.

"That means she was here." Mike pulled the trembling fur-ball from the cage and held him against his chest. "Do you think she might've gone after Billy and them?"

He nodded again.

"We have to warn to them!" Mike shrugged the backpack from his shoulders and carefully placed Buddy into the netted outer pocket. The kitten fit comfortably, and it even zipped shut.

After he worked his arms back through the straps, he dug his phone out of his pocket and called Billy.

"You've reached Billy—"

"Shit!" He hung up and tried Sami's phone.

"The person you are trying to reach—"

"Dammit! Answer your fucking phone, Jason!" He pressed Jason's number and held the phone to his ear.

"The mailbox of—"

"Fuck!" He gritted his teeth and shoved his phone back into his pocket. "I can't get through. They must be out of range. Let's go."

His dad knelt as far as he could.

Mike hopped onto his dad's back and held on tight.

With lightning speed, they darted through the forest until they reached the edge of town. Remaining hidden behind the veil of trees lining the highway, they travelled the same route Jason had mapped out. After a few minutes, Mike's cell phone rang, and his dad skidded to an abrupt stop.

Mike jumped down to answer the call.

17

SAMI STARED out the passenger window, mesmerized as the sky transformed from bright orange, to deep pink, to red. She shifted in her seat, trying to get comfortable. Up ahead, a truck stop sign illuminated from the headlights. Stopping to eat and use the bathroom, *again*, was the last thing she wanted to do on the desolate drive, but she couldn't wait any longer. "Um, I know your dad said we shouldn't stop unnecessarily, but I'm getting hungry. And I have to use the bathroom again."

"Yeah, me too," Billy agreed.

"Good. I need a break," Jason said. "Anyone up for a diner?"

"Sounds good to me," Sami replied, eager to get some food in her stomach.

Jason pulled up to the truck stop diner, and they all piled out of the car. Compared to the unpopulated highway, the parking lot full of cars and semi-trucks was a welcome sight.

Sami eyed the darkness of the trees at the edge of the lot, and an uneasy feeling swept over her. "Is this safe?"

Billy put an arm around her waist. "The danger is back at home, remember?"

"Yeah," she agreed with uncertainty. She knew Billy was skeptical too because he gripped her tight. And Jason kept glancing around, eyeing the shadows surrounding them. None of them felt completely safe. Yet, stopping was an unavoidable duty.

Jason pulled the door open and they all went in. The mumble of voices and clanking of silverware on porcelain gave Sami a sense of security. Following the directions of the *Seat Yourself* sign in the entryway, they sat in a booth along one of the front windows.

A server from behind the back counter spotted them and made her way around the tables in the middle of the room, with three menus in hand.

Sami smiled at the young woman as she approached. "Thanks, but I don't need a menu. I'll just have a cheeseburger, fries, and a cola."

"I'll have what she's having," Billy said as he sat back and put his arm around Sami's shoulder.

"Same here." Jason grinned.

The woman smiled. "Well, I think you're all just about the easiest customers I've had all night. I'll be right back with your sodas."

Jason smirked as soon as the waitress left. "I think that means she won't spit in our drinks."

Billy shook his head. "Shut up, dude. You're gonna make me lose my appetite."

"I wonder how Mike and your dad are doing?" Sami asked. She'd been thinking about them the entire drive.

"I'm sure they're doing fine," Billy said. "My dad and Abby can handle Jessica."

"I never thought I'd say this," Jason said, "but I sure am glad there are other werewolves out there because we didn't stand a chance against Jessica by ourselves."

Billy shot him an intimidating glare.

Jason's smile faded. "Of course, I'm sorry it had to be your dad... and your brother's girlfriend."

Sami patted Billy's thigh.

Billy cocked his jaw to one side. "I'll get used to it...eventually. I'm just glad he's alive."

Jason nodded. "I hear ya, bro."

"I'm gonna go to the restroom before our food gets here," Sami said.

Billy stood so she could slide out of the booth. With her eyes on the gray speckled linoleum under her sneakers, she headed for the bathroom. Glancing out of the corners of her eyes, she noticed no one was paying attention to her. No glares, no shaking of heads, no silent judgments. Everyone ate their meals and worried about their own lives.

I sure could get used to this. She pushed the door open and headed for an open stall.

After she finished in the bathroom, Sami went back out into the dining area. She held her head high as she walked, feeling more confident than she had in the last two months. Just as she slid back into the booth, the server arrived with their food.

Sami picked up the burger and took a huge bite, enjoying her meal without worrying about who was sitting in the diner with them. Even Billy and Jason seemed relaxed as they chatted and laughed. For the first time since she'd moved to Wolf Hill, they didn't seem to have a care in the world—aside from their minds being on the harrowing rescue about to ensue.

When they were full, they filled the car up with gas and were back on the road.

Driving through the eerie forest at night still gave Sami the creeps, but she felt a little safer when they reached maximum speed. Nothing could stop them now. She let out a long breath, trying to relieve her stress.

"Don't worry," Jason said. "I loaded up on snacks in the mini-mart. Next stop, Lake Tahoe!"

"Good," Sami said, more contented now as they drove along, listening to the soft clatter of classic rock on the radio. She relaxed her tense muscles and sank comfortably on the seat with her head against the headrest. After a few minutes of watching the forest whir by, her eyelids grew heavy. She blinked rapidly, trying to keep them open as the lull of the radio faded.

The beast sneers wickedly, bearing pointed fangs. Breathing heavily, it runs along, galloping in and out of trees and effortlessly over hills and mountains. Its eyes glow like red fire as it runs faster and faster through the dark forest, under the light of the full moon.

"*Huh*!" Sami tensed and opened her eyes, focusing on the full moon shining through the windshield.

"You okay?" Jason asked.

"Did you have another nightmare?" Billy sounded worried.

"Yeah." She ran a trembling hand through her hair and peered out the passenger window for any signs of red eyes. Blue dashboard lights reflected off the window, inhibiting her view.

"What'd you dream about? Was it Jessica?" Billy asked.

"Yeah, I think so. She was running through the forest," Sami replied, unable to keep the fear from her voice.

"What happened?" Jason asked.

Sami stretched her neck as far as she could and scanned the road behind them, startled to see red eyes in the distance.

"She's right behind us!" she shrieked.

"Holy shit!" Billy turned around to see.

Jason slammed his foot on the gas pedal, causing the car to jerk as they thrust forward. "Sami, the gun! In the glove box! Get the gun!"

She opened the compartment and pulled out the gun, pinching it between two trembling fingers. "What do I do?"

"Give it here!" Billy yelled as the red eyes grew closer.

She quickly handed him the weapon.

Billy took aim at the red eyed beast and pulled the trigger.

A piercing *crack* and a shattering of the rear window rang Sami's ears. She screamed and covered them, preparing for the next blast.

"Shit!" Billy shouted. He unbuckled his seatbelt and turned around, his hair whipping about from the rush of air streaming in. Another loud *crack* erupted.

Sami screamed again as the blast rumbled through her chest.

"Fuck!" Billy yelled. "Go faster!"

"I'm going as fast as I can!" Jason shouted. "Keep shooting!"

Billy pulled the trigger again and again. *Crack! Crack!*

The werewolf barreled toward them, darting from side to side as if it could see the bullets coming. Within seconds, the beast was right on their tail.

"The knife!" Jason shouted.

Billy reached under his seat for the knife, but he wasn't quick enough.

The beast jumped onto the back of the car, reached through the window, and grabbed Billy around the waist.

"Fuck!" Billy yelled as he struggled to get free. "Jessica, don't do this!"

"Nooo!" Sami screamed. Desperate to free Billy, she wedged herself between the two front seats and frantically pulled and punched the beast's hairy arms.

"Shit!" Jason shouted. He reached under his seat and pulled out a knife. "Sami, take the wheel!"

As soon as she wriggled back into the passenger seat and grabbed the wheel, Jason turned around and sliced through the werewolf's right arm.

The werewolf roared, yanking its wounded arm from Billy's waist.

"Let go, you bitch!" Billy balled his hand into a fist and jabbed at its throat, again and again, while trying to squirm free.

Jason shimmied further into the back seat and lunged with the knife again. The werewolf dodged the blade and sunk its fangs into Jason's left forearm.

"Ugh!" Jason yelped and dropped the knife to cradle his arm.

"Nooo!" Sami screamed and jerked the car over to the side of the road, waiting for it to come to a rolling stop.

"Fuck!" Billy yelled, pounding its snout with his fists. "You crazy bitch!"

The beast leaned back, avoiding Billy's punches while pulling him through the back window.

Billy gripped the headrest, trying to hold on.

With both hands, Jason clutched Billy's arm, grunting as he pulled against the werewolf's mighty force.

The car stopped and Sami dove over the web of arms and into the backseat, fumbling for the knife on the floorboard, straining and stretching until she gripped the handle. Then, she scrambled out of the back window and shoved the silver knife deep into the werewolf's side.

A ferocious roar tore through the night. The werewolf narrowed its fiery eyes and bashed Sami across the face with a solid fist.

Sami screamed from the searing pain as she flew backward and slammed into the ditch. Clutching her chest, she gasped for air, while staring in confusion at the commotion taking place on the back of Jason's car. The car, werewolf, and Billy all appeared upside down and moved in slow motion, while faint growls and voices echoed. She gasped, and her chest expanded with a full breath of air. She rolled over onto her stomach, wincing from the ache in her throbbing jaw.

"Let me go, dammit!" Billy shouted, trying to gouge out the beast's eyes with his thumbs.

Jason climbed out of the back window and swiped at the werewolf with the silver knife, but it leaned out of the way and knocked him to the ground. Struggling with Billy, the werewolf rammed its fist into his jaw.

Billy's body went limp.

"No! Billy!" Sami shrieked.

The beast leapt off the back of the car and landed in the middle of the road, about fifty feet away, with Billy draped across its arms.

Jason jumped up and bolted toward them. "Billy, wake up!"

"Please, nooo!" Sami scrambled to her feet and sprinted toward Billy.

The werewolf turned, and its raging eyes bore into Sami's. All of a sudden, it darted into the forest.

Mouth agape, Sami stood in shock, waiting to wake up from her nightmare. Her legs wobbled, and she fell to her knees.

"No!" Jason ran to the edge of the forest where he'd last seen the werewolf and stopped. "Shit!" he yelled. "Shit, shit, shit!" He ran a shaky hand through his hair and lowered his head. With his shoulders slumped, he headed back to Sami and sank next to her.

Staring into the forest, he shook his head and gritted his teeth. "Fuck you, bitch!" he screamed, his voice echoing off the trees. He looked at Sami, his eyes full of tears. "I'm so sorry, Sami. I'm so sorry."

"Please tell me this isn't happening, Jason!" She buried her face in her hands and broke down sobbing. "Please tell me this isn't happening!"

"Shhh, shhh," Jason whispered shakily. He pressed his hand to her back and rubbed it, trying to comfort her. "We'll get him back. We'll find Billy."

Sami lifted her head and looked him in the eyes. "She hit him hard. What if she killed him?"

"It wasn't hard enough to kill him, Sami. He's alive."

"What if we don't find him? She could've taken him anywhere. What if she kills him later?" She cringed at the thought.

"Billy's gonna be fine. Let's just get back home. Rick will know what to do."

She nodded and focused on a dark streak across Jason's arm. Blood oozed from gaping holes and dripped to the ground. "Oh, Jason, she bit you! You're bleeding a *lot*."

Jason stared at the wound with wide eyes and sucked in a ragged breath. "Shit. I forgot. She bit me. The fucking bitch bit me! What does this mean? What in the fuck does it mean?"

Sami yanked her shirt over her head and pressed it to his wounds. "Keep pressure on it. We have to get you to a hospital." She stood and helped him to his feet.

They got back into the car and sped toward the next town.

"What does this mean?" Jason sat in the passenger seat, still staring at his arm. "Does it mean I'm like *her* now? Am I a werewolf too?"

Sami knew the answer but couldn't bear telling him. Instead, she held on to a childish thread of hope that, if it weren't said aloud, it wouldn't happen. "I don't know. We'll get you stitched up, and we'll go back home and talk to Rick. Call Mike and tell him what happened."

With a trembling hand, Jason grabbed his cell phone from the center console and called Mike.

"Put it on speaker phone," Sami said.

"It's about time! I've been trying to get a hold of you guys!"

"Mike..." Jason's voice shook. "Jessica was just here. She got Billy."

"What do you mean she got Billy? Is he dead?"

"No, she took him! She jumped through the back window at over a hundred miles an hour and took him!"

"Fuck! Why didn't you shoot? What about the knives?"

"Billy shot at her over and over! She must've dodged the bullets. I cut her in the arm, and Sami stuck her in the side, but the bitch got him anyway."

"Dammit! Hold on.... Dad, we're too late! Jessica got Billy!"

"Mike, what do you mean you're too late?" Jason asked.

"It was a trap, Jason. Jessica led us away, so she could get to you guys. I tried to call, but I couldn't get through to any of you."

"What are we gonna do?" Jason wiped the tears from his eyes and lowered his head.

"We need to get Abby, so that we have more help. Come back immediately. We'll be at the house when you get there."

"Why can't Rick just come here and hunt her down?" Jason argued.

"What if Jessica's using a car to hide her tracks, like she did with Sami? By the time we got there, she'd be long gone. It'd be easier for us to get Abby now, while Jessica's distracted with Billy. You and Sami get back home as fast as you can!"

Jason took in a ragged breath and more tears slid down his cheeks. "Well, we sort a have to go to the hospital first."

"What happened? Is Sami okay? What the hell happened?"

"Sami's okay. It's me, Mike. I was bitten. The fucking bitch bit me!" Jason threw his head back against the headrest, his face wracked with agony.

"Shit, Jason! Hold on...."

Sami shook her head and wiped away the tears blurring her vision, trying to keep her sobs quiet enough to hear Mike's voice echo from the phone. "What's he doing?"

"I don't know, he said to hold on. I think I hear growling."

"Jason, it's Rick. Just get to the hospital to get stitched up so you don't lose too much blood. You've got plenty of time."

"I've got plenty of time for what?" Jason wiped his cheeks dry on the shoulders of his shirt.

"Don't panic. You're gonna be okay. We have until the next full moon to fix this."

"To fix what, Rick? What happens if I don't get fixed before the next frickin' full moon, huh? Am I gonna be like you and Jessica? Huh, Rick? Am I gonna be a fucking werewolf too?"

"Yes, Jason. I'm sorry."

"Shit!" Jason's mouth hung open. He stared at his arm, eyes wide with shock. "I can't do this! I can't! Rick, there has to be something you can do."

"There is. We just have to kill Jessica before the next full moon. Abby and I are gonna hunt her down and kill her. Do you hear me? Now, pull it together. Tell the doctor your dog bit you. That it got into a fight with your other dog and you stepped between them to break it up. That way, they don't need to get the police involved or give you a rabies shot."

"What?" Jason boomed. "Rabies?"

"Don't worry! You don't have rabies. Mike and I have to rescue Abby. We need her help more than ever now. And don't worry about Jessica. I'll take care of her."

The call ended. Jason tossed his phone back onto the center console. "Dammit!" He put pressure on his arm again and threw his head back against the seat. "I can't believe this is happening."

"I'm so sorry, Jason," Sami said, feeling helpless.

A blue hospital sign glowed in the distance. She slowed the car and took the exit.

"It's up here on the right." Jason pointed at his window.

Sami pulled into the lot and parked in front of the doors. She shut off the engine and slouched back against the seat, hoping a few seconds of rest would calm the tension gripping her nerves. It didn't work.

"Are you gonna be okay in there?" Jason asked, his voice more subdued. He stared up at the hospital as if he were dreading going in.

She shook her head and looked at him as if he were crazy. "How can I be okay, Jason? I'm not okay!"

"If you can't go in there and face everyone, I understand." He turned his attention to her, and his eyes widened. "Holy shit! You have a huge bruise across your cheek. That bitch!" He clenched his jaw, and his temples pulsated.

Sami peered into the rear-view mirror at the purple and black splotch extending from her jaw to the top of her cheek bone. It hurt, but she didn't care. Her measly bruise was nothing she hadn't experienced before. All she cared about was getting Billy back alive and whether Jason was going to turn into a monster.

"It doesn't matter." She clutched the door handle. "Let's go in."

"Hold on. Let me get you a shirt. Pop the trunk."

She'd forgotten all about being shirtless. She eyed the thin camisole she wore and tugged it back in place over the top of her bra.

Jason got out of the car, and Sami pushed the button, unlatching the trunk. A few seconds later, the car jerked as the trunk slammed shut.

"Here," he handed her a red top through the open car door. "If they ask about your face, just say you tried to help during the dogfight but got knocked down and hit your face on the coffee table. But try not to sound nervous. We don't need them thinking I abused you."

"Right." She put the loose-fitting tank top on and climbed out of the car.

When they approached the entrance of the emergency room, the doors slid open, and they proceeded to the front desk. Sami stood behind Jason, trying not to be seen by the receptionist.

"Looks like we're the only ones here," Sami whispered.

Jason turned and glared at her. "Yeah, lucky us." He rolled his eyes and faced forward again.

Offended by his rude behavior, Sami lowered her gaze to the floor and bit her lip, trying to hold back the tears forming. With the emotional rollercoaster swirling inside of her at the moment, Jason's haughty remark was the last thing she needed.

He let out an impatient sigh and turned back around. "Sorry. My arm just hurts is all. I didn't mean to be a jackass. Okay?" He squeezed her hand.

The receptionist motioned him forward. "What happened?" She eyed the blood-soaked shirt around Jason's arm.

"My dogs were fighting over a piece of bacon, and I tried to break them up."

The woman winced. "It's always the bacon. Let's get you checked in." She continued to ask Jason a series of questions, while tapping away at her keyboard.

In her mind, Sami practiced how to answer the receptionist if asked about the bruise. After going over it a few times, she was sure she'd be able to handle the task.

"Oh, honey, what happened to your face?"

Sami's heart skipped a beat as she peered around Jason and focused on the way the receptionist's face puckered with worry. *Here it goes. Don't mess this up.*

She stepped next to Jason, clasping her fingers together on the counter to hide the trembling. "The dogs knocked me down during the struggle, and I hit it against the coffee table. But what are you gonna do, right?" She shrugged, trying to act nonchalant.

"We're gonna get you an icepack, that's what," the woman replied in a matter-of-fact tone and disappeared through the door behind the desk.

Jason gripped his forehead and groaned. "This is too intense. My hearts been beating a hundred miles an hour since this all happened. I think I'm gonna have a heart attack."

"It's all gonna work out," Sami whispered and rubbed his back, trying to sooth him.

The door opened, and Jason lowered his hand and straightened.

The receptionist handed the icepack to Sami. "Keep this on your cheek for about fifteen minutes or until you can't stand the cold anymore. It should help with the swelling. Do you want to see a doctor?"

"Thank you, but no. I'll be fine." Sami pressed the icy bag to her cheek, wincing at the initial sting, which was followed by a deep, searing ache.

"They'll call you back shortly," she said to Jason.

Jason led Sami to two nearby chairs.

Sami eased onto the seat without uttering a word. Haunting visions of the werewolf biting Jason and taking Billy reeled through her mind. *I should've done something more to save Billy. Tried harder. Shoved the knife through her heart instead of her side.*

"Jason McAllister."

A man's voice cut through Sami's thoughts. Jason's sweaty palm wrapped around her fingers, and he led her to the door the nurse held open.

The man guided the way to a nearby room. He took Jason's vital signs and removed the blood-stained shirt to inspect the damage. "Ouch," he said. "Dogs are a man's best friend until they're fighting over a piece of bacon."

The nurse held up the bloody shirt. "Do you still want this?"

Sami shook her head. "No."

He tossed the make-shift bandage into the infectious waste bin next to the sink and pressed sterile gauze pads against the wounds.

The doctor entered the room, flushed Jason's wounds clean, and stitched him up. Before they knew it, Sami and Jason were back on the road again, heading for home—without Billy.

Sami guided the car along the highway in silence, her thoughts on Billy and whether he was okay or even alive for that matter. The more she thought about him, the more her heart ached. A constant stream of tears rolled down her cheeks, and she had to wipe them away as quickly as they fell to regain a clear view of the road.

"Sami," Jason's soft voice interrupted the silence. "We'll get Billy back, alive and human." He patted her leg.

She grunted to clear her throat and regain composure, but the tears kept falling.

"Pull over and let me drive."

"No, your arm," she croaked. "You should take a pain pill like the doctor said. And your antibiotics."

"I don't need any pills right now. And I always drive with one arm. Now, pull over. You can barely see the road in front of you."

He was right. After everything they'd been through, getting into a car accident was the last thing they needed. She pulled onto the shoulder and climbed out of the car, meeting Jason in front of the headlights.

"Sami…everything's gonna be okay. You'll see." He pulled her against his chest and held her.

Emotionally frazzled, Sami buried her face into his neck and cried. "I hope so, Jason. I hope so."

He rubbed her back for a moment before placing a finger under her chin and guiding her eyes to his. "Let's go home."

"Okay." She sniffed.

They both climbed back into the car and continued homeward.

18

MIKE SAT alone in the dimly lit cave, staring into the moonlit forest. "Don't worry, little brother," he whispered, "we're gonna kill that bitch if it's the last thing we do."

"Someone else is guarding Abby," Rick said as he entered the cave.

"Shit!" Mike jumped up, knife in hand.

"Someone I don't recognize. Jessica isn't there."

"You scared the hell outta me!" Mike clutched his chest to calm his thudding heart. "What took you so long? I thought you were captured too."

"Sorry, Son. I wanted to make sure there were no other werewolves around. I didn't pick up Billy's scent either. Jessica has him somewhere else. I'm sure of it. She knows we'll rescue Abby. It would be stupid of her to take Billy to the same place."

Mike sighed. "So that means, until we find out where Billy is, we can't kill Jessica."

His father swiped a hand over his mouth. "You're right."

Mike recalled Jason saying he'd cut Jessica, and that Sami had stabbed her. "Dad? If Jason and Sami both stuck Jessica with the silver knives, why didn't it render her powerless?"

"Sometimes it can take a few seconds for the effects to take over. I've been able to last half a minute until I lost my strength."

"Damn." Mike shook his head.

"Are you ready to get Abby out of there?"

"More than ready."

"Okay, I see you have your knife. Do you have your lock pick?"

"Got it."

"Remember, we aren't stopping until we're there and reach the cage. I'll be right back." His dad left the cave to morph.

Mike worked his arms through the backpack, trying not to disturb the sleeping kitten. He paced back and forth, his thoughts on the rescue plan. Shuffling drew his attention to the mouth of the cave. His werewolf father stood mightily, blocking the entire entrance with his massive body.

Mike gulped. "I can't wait 'til I get used to this shit."

His father crouched down and Mike climbed onto his back, grabbing a firm hold around the neck.

Suddenly, they were speeding through the dark forest. Afraid of being whacked in the face by pine tree branches or anything else, Mike kept his head ducked, thankful for his dad's monstrous-size.

After a few minutes, they jerked to a stop. Mike hopped off his dad's back and eyed his surroundings.

Lanterns hung from branches, illuminating an open area guarded by trees. A small cabin stood off to one side, and the silver cage sat next to it. Recognizing Abby's silhouette on the floor of the cage, Mike rushed to it.

Abby looked at Mike and moaned, her eyes shadowed black with exhaustion. The white nightgown she wore was smudged with dirt.

"Dammit!" Mike snapped. He slid the backpack from his arms and carefully set it down, wanting nothing more at that moment than to see Jessica dead and to shove the knife through her cold heart himself.

He slid the lock-pick from the side pocket and began toying with the lock.

Towering over him, his dad scanned the area.

A large werewolf with black fur and hungry red eyes lunged from the forest, heading straight toward them.

Mike snatched the silver knife from his sheath and held it up, ready to spar.

His dad leapt through the air and tackled the beast, sending it crashing to the ground. They wrestled, viciously growling, snarling, and tearing through flesh with fangs and claws.

With his heart beating wildly in his chest, Mike set the knife down and continued with his task. Out of the corner of his eye, he watched the two monstrous figures continue to tumble over one another. Mike shook his head to clear it and carefully picked at the lock. A loud clunk rattled through the metal tool, and the lock opened. He dropped the lock pick into the backpack and yanked open the cage door.

"Abby, it's okay. I've got you." Mike gathered her cold limp frame into his arms and ran from the battle.

Abby's eyes turned green. She lifted her head, sucking in deep breaths while her entire body shook with convulsions.

"Holy shit!" Afraid Abby would fall out of his arms, Mike set her on the ground. He looked to his dad for help, just in time to see the two engaged beasts soaring through the air, headed straight for him and Abby. Giving Mike no time to react, they plowed into him, sending him flying backward and crashing to the ground.

"Ugh!" Mike groaned, arching his aching back. They'd knocked him clear over to the cage again—a good fifteen feet away. Gripping one of the cage bars, he pulled himself to a sitting position and looked for Abby, but she was gone.

He loosened his grip, and his hand slid down the bar, landing on the backpack. "Oh shit!" He picked it up and peered through the netted pocket. Buddy was trembling but safe. "It's all right, Buddy."

An enormous, sandy-colored werewolf appeared out of nowhere and peered down at him.

"Abby?" Mike gulped, clutching the backpack. "You better fucking be Abby!"

The werewolf scooped him up and darted away. By the time Mike knew what was happening, he was sitting on the hard ground in complete darkness and away from the turmoil.

"What in the hell just happened?" He took a few deep breaths to steady his racing heart while waiting for his eyes to adjust to the moonlit forest. Aside from Buddy, he was all alone.

A deep sting in his leg drew his attention to the bloody rips in his jeans. He set the backpack aside and lifted his pant leg to inspect the wounds. From what he could see through the darkness, the gashes weren't too deep, but they were narrow and long.

Dammit! Are these fang or claw marks? He gritted his teeth and shook his head. *It doesn't matter either way.*

He shrugged off the plaid flannel he wore over his T-shirt and wrapped it tightly around the wounds.

"Fuck!" he shouted as the reality of the situation sank in. *I'm gonna turn into a fucking monster!*

Mew. Buddy's timid cry caught his attention.

He set the backpack in his lap and eyed the trembling fur-ball. "You're gonna be okay, cat."

A loud roar, followed by a whimper, echoed throughout the forest. Then, silence engulfed the night.

Mike didn't move a muscle. "Please be alive. Please be alive," he chanted in a whisper. A gust of wind blew in his face, and two werewolves with green eyes were suddenly staring down at him.

"Dad? Abby?"

The larger, taller beast nodded, followed by the other.

Mike let out a sigh of relief, but his heart stopped when he saw the deep gashes in his dad's chest. A steady stream of blood oozed out of them. "Dad, you're hurt!"

Rick turned his head from side to side in slow, deliberate movements. Within seconds, his wounds vanished.

"What the—?"

Abby yanked Mike from the ground before he could finish, and they darted through the forest again.

"I'm pretty sure I was bitten, Dad," Mike yelled through the rushing of the wind against his face. "On my leg."

His father shot him a quick glance.

Mike remained silent the rest of the way, hoping the other werewolf, and not his father, had wounded him.

When they reached the back door of his house, Abby set Mike on his feet.

On wobbly legs, Mike opened the kitchen door and went inside, with his dad and Abby right behind him. He placed the backpack on the table. Buddy was sleeping. Either that or he was dead. Mike leaned in close, relieved to see the kitten's body expand with each breath.

"Hold on while I get you some clothes." Mike went to his room and grabbed a T-shirt and a pair of sweat pants for Abby. He went back into the living room and handed them to her. "You can change in my room."

Abby darted down the hall.

Mike pulled his dad's clothes from the backpack, being careful of Buddy. He handed them over and his dad disappeared in an instant.

"Damn werewolves." Mike shook his head. He went to the bathroom, retrieved the first aid kit from under the sink, and went back to the dining table. With a good yank, his jeans ripped farther up his leg to expose the wounded area. The bleeding had stopped, but the make-shift bandage had fallen off somewhere along the route home.

"Are you okay?" Abby asked with a gentle voice as she entered the kitchen.

Glad to see his blonde-haired beauty again, Mike jumped up and gave her a hug. "Oh man, I've missed you," he whispered, holding her tight.

Abby sank into his arms. "You mean you're not mad or completely disgusted with me?"

He pulled his head back just far enough to look into her deep blue eyes. "I'm not mad at you, Abby." He brushed a loose strand of hair from her cheek. "And I could *never* be disgusted with you. A lot of things that didn't seem right before make sense now. But I still care about you. I still wanna be with you."

Tears filled her eyes. "All this time, I was afraid once you found out what I really was—"

"Shhh." He leaned down and pressed his lips to hers, taking in her sweetness one slow mouthful at a time.

"Sorry to interrupt." His dad's voice cut their reunion short.

Mike pulled away from Abby and winked, happy to see her eyes filled with life again.

She suppressed a smile between her lips, but she couldn't hide the pink spreading across her cheeks.

"We need to get your wound cleaned as soon as possible," Rick said.

Mike sat back down and threw his leg up on the table.

Abby opened the first aid kit and pulled out the bottle of iodine solution.

Spotting paper towels on the counter, his dad ripped off a few squares from the roll. He held them under Mike's leg as Abby poured the disinfectant directly into his wounds.

"Son of a bitch!" Mike clenched his jaw, bearing through the sting.

"It doesn't need stitches." Abby smiled.

"But the other werewolf is dead, right?" Mike eyed them warily.

"Yes, Mike," Abby said. "He is."

Rick walked across the kitchen and threw the soiled paper towels into the garbage while Abby bandaged Mike's leg.

"So, Dad, that means I'm gonna be okay, right? Because he's dead now—before the full moon." Mike let out an uneasy breath, still unsure of his fate.

"Mike—" Rick took a seat across from him "—I scratched you."

Dread shot through Mike's chest.

"What?" Abby belted out. "You could've killed him, Rick!"

"I know." His dad shook his head. "I wasn't careful enough."

Mike squished his eyes shut for a second and clenched his jaw. "Dammit!" He slammed his fist on the table. Needing the comfort of an icy cold beer, he went to the fridge.

"Son, everything will be okay."

Mike opened his beer and gulped it down within seconds. "How is me being a werewolf unless we kill you, okay?" He crumpled his empty can and threw it against the wall, sending it tumbling against the floor and coming to rest at his dad's feet.

"You're not going to be a werewolf." Rick picked up the can and tossed it across the kitchen into the garbage.

"Why? Because you think I'm gonna kill you before the full moon? That's not gonna happen!"

Rick furrowed his brow. "No, Mike. You have to be *bitten* to become a werewolf."

Mike threw his head back and let out a disbelieving chuckle. "What a frickin' relief! So, I'm fine—just a scraped leg?"

Rick nodded. "But I'm glad you weren't going to kill me, Son."

Abby's lips curled into a slight smile.

"Damn werewolves," Mike muttered under his breath. After snatching two more beers from the fridge, he sat down in the recliner and propped up his throbbing leg. He glanced at the clock above the front door. "Where in the hell are Jason and Sami?"

19

SAMI OPENED her eyes and sat up. She pulled the lever below her and the back of the passenger seat sprung to an upright position. The cold night air whooshed over her bare arms, and she shuddered.

"Are you cold?" Jason asked.

"Billy?" She turned around and stared at the empty backseat. Images of the attack flooded her thoughts. "It really happened," she whispered. Tears blurred out Billy's empty seat and rolled down her cheeks. With her heart shattered, she faced forward and stared at the dark road in front of her.

"Sorry, Sami," Jason said, his voice full of sympathy. He pushed the heater button and warm air gusted across her arms and face, making the cold tolerable.

"I'll pull over and grab a jacket out of the trunk for you."

The car slowed.

"No!" The thought of it taking longer to get home just for a stupid jacket was agonizing. "I just want to get back as fast as we can, *please*!"

"Okay, okay." He pressed harder on the gas pedal. "I won't stop. I'll go faster, all right?"

She nodded and wiped away the tears, focusing on the familiar markers—a bent tree over-hanging the road and a reflective arrow sign marking the sharp turn ahead. She furrowed her brow. "We're almost there already?"

"Yeah, we're here actually." Jason glanced her way, his soft smile illuminated by the street lights of Wolf Hill.

"I didn't think I slept that long." She began tapping her fingers on her thigh, anxious to get home.

I hope Rick has a plan to rescue Billy. Or maybe he already found him when they rescued Abby? No, they would've called. Unless they had bad news. They wouldn't call if something bad happened to Billy. She shook the thought from her head. *Billy's alive. I know it. I can feel it.*

"This is taking forever!" She threw her hands up and let them fall into her lap.

"My thoughts exactly!"

Jason didn't slow through the empty streets of town. He kept a steady speed until he turned onto their road.

When they finally pulled in front of Billy's house, a weight lifted from Sami's shoulders. Not all the weight she carried, but enough to keep her moving forward.

She climbed out of the car and leaned back to stretch her stiff muscles. Billy's car shimmered in the moonlight. She went to it and ran her hand along the smooth black paint. A slight sob erupted from her throat, and another, as the possibility of never seeing Billy again hit full force. She fell to her knees and cried into her hands.

"Hey, heyyy." Jason knelt beside her and pulled her against his chest. "Sami, shhhh."

"I got her," Mike said. He scooped her up and headed for the house.

"I'm fine, Mike." She wiped the tears away with the back of her hands.

Jason held the screen door open for them.

"I think you're still in shock." Mike set her on the couch. "Don't worry, we'll get Billy back."

"Promise?" She clenched her teeth together to stifle a sob.

"Promise." Mike inspected her face and cringed. "That's one hell of a bruise." He headed for the kitchen.

"You're telling me." Jason pushed the front door shut. "Did you guys get Abby?"

Mike nodded. "Yeah. She's taking a nap. So is my dad."

Abby and Rick emerged from the hallway, both yawning as if they'd just woken up.

"Oh, Sami!" Abby frowned. "I'll get some ice for you." She hurried to the refrigerator.

Jason plopped down on the couch next to Sami. "What a fucking day!" He sighed and rested his head back.

"I'm sorry, Sami." Abby walked in with a bag of ice and handed it to her. "Jessica can be such a bitch. Just wait until I get my hands on her." She sat on the arm of the couch and draped an arm across Sami's shoulders. "It's all going to work out. You'll see."

For a moment, Sami felt at peace, almost as if her own mother were comforting her.

"Oh, and Buddy is at your house," Abby said. "He's so cute."

Sami raised one corner of her mouth, relieved. "You found him? I'm glad he's okay."

Abby pulled away and patted Sami's arm. "Put the ice on your bruise."

Sami bit her lip, preparing for the sting. As soon as the frigid bag touched her tender skin, she winced.

Mike came back in and handed Jason a beer and Sami a tumbler filled with brown liquid. He glanced down at Sami's shirt and furrowed his brow. "Where in the hell did you get that shirt?"

Sami glanced at the red top, decorated with a shimmering sequin heart. "Uh, from my closet. You guys left it up there when you brought all my stuff down." She held the glass to her nose and sniffed the liquid. The pungent, gasoline-like smell blasted her sinuses and she grimaced. "Ewe, it smells terrible."

"It's whiskey. It'll help you to relax and sleep tonight," Rick said. "You've been through a horrific ordeal, and you need to rest."

Mike looked confused. "We didn't leave anything in your closet, Sami. The last time I saw that shirt was in Jessica's bedroom when we rescued you a few weeks back."

A wave of goose bumps ran down Sami's arms. If they didn't leave it her closet, then, Jessica must've put it there. "Are you saying Jessica was in my house?" She handed Abby the glass and jumped to her feet, her eyes glued to the top. Disgusted to be wearing the same thing Jessica had worn, she yanked it over her head and threw it across the room as if it were poisoned.

Everyone stared at her with blank looks on their faces.

Feeling awkward, she shrugged. "I don't want it now." She sat back down, crossing her arms to cover her camisole.

"I'll get you a shirt," Abby said and hurried down the hall.

Mike looked at his dad. "How could Jessica have gotten in and left the shirt if you were nearby?"

Rick swiped a hand over his mouth. "It must've been when I left yesterday afternoon to eat." He shook his head and clenched his jaw. "Damn! I wasn't gone for long. I didn't even sense she'd been here."

"Don't be so hard on yourself, Dad. You're doing everything you can possibly do."

Rick nodded, but his eyes still reflected disappointment. "I know."

Abby returned with one of Mike's T-shirts and handed it to Sami. "Here you go."

"Thanks." Sami took the shirt and slid it over her head.

"Now, drink." Abby held out the glass of whiskey.

Sami took the glass and sniffed the liquid again, wrinkling her nose.

"Go ahead," Abby urged.

Jason popped open his beer and clanked it against Sami's glass. "To Billy, and to keeping him safe until we get there." He winked and took a swig.

Sami went along with the ritual, feeling she'd jinx Billy's safe return if she didn't. She took a sip and puckered her face as soon as it touched her taste buds. She'd never wondered what gas tasted like, but she was sure this was it. The acrid warmth made its way down her throat and into her stomach.

"Yuck!" She shuddered from the bitter aftertaste. "I'm not gonna feel like I did when I drank wine, am I?"

"No, you're not gonna drink that much. Just sip it, and take your time." Mike gave her a half-smile.

"Fuck this!" Jason slammed his beer on the coffee table. "I'll have what she's having, but a lot more of it!"

Mike went to the kitchen and retrieved a tumbler from the cupboard.

Sami took another sip, which wasn't as harsh as the first one. The warmth travelled down her throat and through her chest, easing some of the tension.

Mike came back in and handed Jason the filled glass. "How's your arm?"

Jason drank half of the whiskey in one gulp. "It's gonna feel much better after this kicks in." He looked at Rick and held up his bandaged arm. "How are we gonna fix this? Oh. And why did Jessica still have powers after we stuck her?"

"Sometimes it takes a minute for the silver to take effect. She either had a car close by or she stopped somewhere and waited to regain her powers." Rick's eyes filled with guilt as they settled on Jason's bandaged arm. "I'm sorry you were bitten. Jessica was leading us into a trap the whole time, and I fell for it. But I'm going to find her. Abby will stay here with all of you while I scour the forest. As soon as I pick up her scent, I'll come back for you, Abby. We'll have a better chance of defeating her if we go after her together."

"But I don't want to leave them alone," Abby protested as she put her hands on her hips.

"Jessica's got what she's wanted all along," Mike said. "Don't worry about us. We'll camp out in Sami's basement and lock ourselves in the cage until you get back, if we have to."

"Wait, will silver affect me now?" asked Jason.

"No, you'll be fine," Rick said. "It shouldn't affect you until you change, which won't be until the next full moon nears. We still have plenty of time to fix this."

"You better be right." Jason took another sip of his whiskey. "Ahhh. Just what I needed."

Rick headed to the kitchen door and opened it. "I'll be back before sunrise." He went outside, pulling the door closed behind him.

For the next couple of hours, they all sat around Mike's living room and talked about what had happened with each of them earlier in the night. When there was still no word from Rick, they began to worry.

"I think we should gather up all the weapons and go to your house, Sami," said Mike. "I like the idea of being close to the silver cage if we need it."

"Okay." Sami yawned, watching as Mike rummaged through the gun case. She suddenly remembered the whole reason for leaving Wolf Hill in the first place—to go to Lake Tahoe for her mom's wedding. "Oh no! I forgot to tell my mom we're not coming. What do I say? She doesn't know about the werewolves."

"Just tell her we were in a little fender bender, but we're all okay," Jason said. "That Mike picked us up and we had my car towed back. I'm sure that's good enough reason to miss her wedding, right?"

"Yeah," Sami said with guilt in her heart. "I'll call her when I get back home."

Mike slung a bag over his shoulder, along with a couple of rifles. "Okay, let's go."

On their way across the yards, Jason went to his car to gather the knives and guns.

Sami stopped at her front door and hesitated, afraid to go in. Their houses had been left unattended earlier in the night. What if Jessica or another werewolf was inside, waiting to get them?

"I'll go in first," Abby said. She went inside and turned on the lights. "It's all clear." She smiled and stepped aside, waiting for everyone to enter.

Sami puttered through the front door and made her way to her bedroom, hoping to see Billy sleeping peacefully on the bed. Only two days ago, he'd asked her to marry him. Now, he was gone. Tears filled her eyes, but she held them in.

Buddy was curled up on the soft blanket in his box. She wanted to cuddle him, but she didn't have the energy. Her broken heart and complete exhaustion made it nearly impossible to care about anything else around her.

Glancing in the mirror, she focused on Mike's oversized T-shirt. She took it off, threw it into the hamper, and opened the closet. The somber site of Billy's shirts hanging there made the emptiness invading her soul nearly unbearable. Not being able to hold them in any longer, tears slipped from her eyes.

Spotting Billy's favorite gray T-shirt, she slid if from the hanger and put it on, taking in a deep breath of his manly scent as she pushed her head through the neck hole. Then, she crawled across the bed and clutched Billy's pillow as she flopped onto her side.

On the nightstand, a picture of her and Billy cuddling on the couch together caught her eye. He was smiling his handsome, chin-dimpled smile, and his deep brown eyes sparkled with his love for her. She squeezed his pillow tighter as the pain in her heart grew.

"Please be alive, Billy. Please be alive."

Footsteps clomped down the hallway toward her bedroom.

"Sami?" Jason's voice was full of sorrow. He sat on the bed next to her and patted her arm. "Don't worry. Billy will be back before you know it. Maybe even tomorrow." He sighed. "Please don't be sad. I can't bear to see you sad anymore."

"Sorry. I just miss him so much." Her voice cracked with exhaustion. "I-I feel so empty inside."

"I know." He lay back on the bed and interlocked their fingers together. Staring at the ceiling, he said, "We're gonna get him back. Rick's out there, right now, looking for her scent. As soon as he finds it, he'll be back. Then we'll save Billy." He turned his head and looked into her eyes. "Okay? Billy's coming home."

Sami nodded, hugging Billy's pillow and holding Jason's hand. A spark of hope awakened somewhere deep in her broken soul.

MIKE AND Abby peeked into the bedroom. Jason and Sami were sound asleep with a pillow between them. Mike raised a finger to his lips.

Abby smiled and nodded.

Mike closed the door to just a crack, and they went back out into the living room to wait for his dad's return.

"What about Carol?" Abby asked. "I'm pretty sure Sami forgot to call her."

"Shit." Mike let out a weary sigh. "I'll call her and let her know." He retrieved his cell phone from his pocket. The battery light flashed at one percent. He eyed the house phone sitting on the breakfast bar and picked it up. "Now, where is her number…?" He scrolled through his cell phone until her name popped up and pushed the corresponding buttons on the house phone. Only one ring chimed before he heard a click.

"Hello? Samantha? Why are you calling from home?"

"Carol, its Mike."

"Mike? Where's Sami? What happened?"

"Everything's okay, Carol. They just had a little accident."

"Accident? Oh God! Are they all right? What happened?"

"Just a couple of bruises. Sami's fine. They got into a little fender bender, but they're all fine. I picked them up, and Jason's car was towed back home. They were so exhausted when we got here, they went to straight to bed. I thought I'd give you a call so you wouldn't worry."

"Thank God they're okay! I can't believe it! Oh, I was so looking forward to Sami being here. Maybe we should postpone the wedding?"

"No, Carol, Sami doesn't want that. She wants you to be happy. Besides, you know how she feels about Steve. Maybe it's better this way? I'll wake her so you two can talk it over."

"No, Mike, don't wake her. Maybe you're right. I'll talk to Steve and see what he thinks. I'm so glad everyone's okay. Give my love to everyone and tell Sami to call me in the morning please."

"I will. You have a good time in Lake Tahoe."

"Thank you for calling, Mike. Good-bye."

"Bye." Mike set the phone back on its base and headed over to the couch. Exhausted, he plopped next to Abby. She snuggled her soft body against his chest, which seemed to melt some of his worries away. He wrapped an arm around her and rested his chin on top of her head, taking pleasure in the intoxicating scent of her sweet, freshly shampooed hair.

"I'm sorry about Billy. We'll find him."

Her soft tone was like a melody to his ears. He didn't know why he'd ever thought of breaking up with her. Werewolf or not, she was good for him. Since he'd met her, his constant anger and disregard for life's purpose had slowly turned into him waking up and actually looking forward to each new day. And, when he'd found out Jessica had locked her up like some animal, the thought of losing her forever had made his gut wrench.

"Rick's the best tracker there is," Abby said.

"That doesn't surprise me. He was the best damn tracker when we used to go hunting, too." He sighed and squeezed her tighter. "I know we'll get Billy back, but I'm afraid of what condition he'll be in when we do. Sami was pretty beat up after just one day with Jessica." He shook the image from his head.

"He'll be okay. I'm sure of it."

"I hope you're right, Abby." Fatigued, Mike opened his mouth wide and pushed out a yawn.

"Maybe we should get a little sleep while we can?" she suggested.

"There's a guest bedroom upstairs, but I don't wanna leave them down here alone, unprotected."

"Don't worry." Abby stood and held her hand out. "Red-eyed werewolves may be a little stronger than us, but we have a secret sensory that lets us know when another werewolf is near. Something they don't have," she said, wearing a smug grin.

Mike clutched her hand and let her pull him to his feet, surprised at how worn out he was. Damn near every muscle ached. With slow steps, almost limping, he headed upstairs. "So, how do you know when another one is around?"

"Hmmm, it's sort of similar to when you fear something so much a chill runs over your entire body. Well, that's the way it feels when killer werewolves are around. The feeling isn't as strong when protectors are near. But if I were in werewolf form at the time, the hair on the back of my neck would stand on end. For some reason, I think because Jessica's my sister, the feeling is stronger with her. I can sense her coming for a few miles. That's why she led me away from here."

Mike entered the first bedroom on the left and sat on the bed, pulling Abby down next to him. "If you can sense her, how did she capture you?"

"I didn't know she was a danger to me at the time. While Rick came back here to protect you, I went to her, sister to sister, trying to get her to confide in me. To tell me what her plans were for all of you. That way, Rick and I would have known exactly how to prepare.

"But, somehow, she found out I alerted him. That I was a traitor. Probably a human contact since I didn't sense any other werewolves around when I notified Rick. Or maybe my crazy uncle found out I had left town and told her I was coming? Who knows." She shrugged.

"I walked right into her hands and didn't know it. She had someone come up to me, while I was asleep on her couch, and drape a silver necklace across my leg. Took all my powers away in an instant. It's funny how that works. I can sense a werewolf coming a mile away, but I didn't pay any attention to the one human friend she had staying with her. Being a werewolf, I didn't think I had to.

"Anyway, I tried to run, but didn't make it far before she caught me. Then, she dragged me through the dirt and tossed me into the cage like a wild animal."

"I'm sorry, Abby. I wish we could've gotten to you sooner," Mike said. "My dad thought it'd be too risky during the full moon. He wanted to wait two days after it passed to rescue you, but neither of us could bear to leave you caged up another night."

"He was right to be cautious, and he should've waited. The guy she had guarding me was very strong, and the fight could've been much worse. You both could've gotten killed, Mike." She leaned against his shoulder, hugging him across the abdomen.

Mike kissed her on her forehead and sighed.

"You know, I'm surprised I was able to keep the fact that I was a protector a secret from Jessica for so long. Until I came here, I had to pretend to be a killer. To be uncaring and spiteful. I'm glad I never had to morph in front of her."

"Who ordered you to come here to protect us?"

"My so called *uncle*. I hate calling him that. It sickens me to think of someone like him as a family member. He's not really family anyway—not by blood. Just a close family friend. I'm just going to call him Gordon Briggs or sheriff from now on. He's a reformed red-eyed werewolf."

"What do you mean reformed? And why would Sheriff Briggs want anyone to protect us?"

"Well, I'll explain reformed first. He was bitten several years ago, and two weeks later, his eyes turned red. But it all depends on your inner self, who you truly are deep down as to whether you'll be a protector or a killer. Anyway, on the eve of the full moon, and in the middle of the sheriff's transformation, the one who bit him was killed, and the sheriff turned human again. Since then he has struggled between keeping the peace for the human citizens of Wolf Hill and pleasing the killer werewolf population. He tries to be good for the sake of his badge, but the evil within him is still very real."

Uneasiness crept into the pit of Mike's stomach. "What do you mean *population*? How many werewolves are out there?"

"In general? A lot. Nothing I can put an exact number on. But I would say at least a few thousand in this country alone. As for Wolf Hill, there are some protector's who live around here. I've picked up on a scent here and there, but I haven't come across them yet. And I don't know who they are. Some werewolves just pass through town. The sheriff promises to keep quiet about their secret and allows them to hunt wild animals in the surrounding forest if needed. But once Jessica turned and," Abby sighed and shook her head, "killed our parents—"

"What? Jessica killed your parents? Her *own* parents?"

Abby nodded. "It happens from time to time when a red-eyed werewolf turns. They have so much new strength and rage growing inside, they don't know how to handle it. They just go on a killing spree, and it all gets blamed on an animal attack." She wiped away a tear rolling down her cheek.

"Anyway, that's one of the reasons Sheriff Briggs took Jessica in—to keep an eye on her. The other was to keep red-eyed werewolves just passing through town, from actually *moving* to Wolf Hill. Because they're so territorial, they like to live away from others of their kind.

"At the same time, they are very lustful and are always looking for a mate. Once they find one, they are loyal to one another. But, since they like to dominate, they fight and disagree all the time.

"Sometimes, they do band together with other werewolves to create a strong force if they feel threatened. The most powerful one will lead them. The one who guarded me while I was in the cage had the hots for Jessica. The idiot had no clue she was just using him.

"And as for why Sheriff Briggs ordered me to protect you—I don't know. Jessica has gotten out of hand. Maybe he really doesn't want to see her hurt you all. He has known you all your lives. Or maybe, since you know about werewolves now, he wanted to keep a closer eye on you. Whatever the reason, I'm glad he did."

"So, will you and I fight for dominance?" Mike asked warily.

She giggled as she pulled back the covers and climbed under them. "No. We aren't angry dominators. We're loving protectors. We live well with society and with each other."

Mike turned off the light and climbed under the covers with her. "Abby?"

"Yes?" She cuddled against him.

"Who turned you?" He put an arm around her and pulled her close.

"Jessica," she said, her voice full of loathing. "It was a year after she'd turned, and I trusted the sheriff's word that she'd gained control over her anger. So, I allowed her to come visit me one weekend. I wanted to confront her about what she'd done to our parents.

"I was so stupid. It all happened so fast, I didn't even see her do it. Apparently, she darted into my room while I was sleeping, scraped me with her fangs deep enough to draw blood, and darted away. When I got up to look for her, she was gone.

"You know, before she visited me, I had actually begun to feel sorry for her. I mean, she didn't ask for some werewolf to bite her. She was a victim, too, at one point. But I was so naïve to think she wouldn't hurt me." Abby sucked in a ragged breath.

"What in the hell was I thinking, Mike? She killed my parents. What made me think I could trust her?"

Mike's eyes burned with tears. He gritted his teeth, wishing he could bash Jessica's face in. But all he could do at the moment was try to lessen Abby's pain. "Because you're kind-hearted and she's your sister," he whispered.

"I hate her, Mike. So much that I want to kill her myself." She took in an unsteady breath, then another.

As his shirt grew damp with Abby's tears, Mike encircled his other arm around her waist and held her tight. "Shhh. Don't be sad, Abby. Jessica will get what's coming to her, and she'll never hurt anyone again."

Through the darkness, he cupped her face with his hands and guided her sweet lips to his, tasting the salt from her tears. He showered her mouth with tender kisses, trying to heal the pain in her broken heart. He pulled away just long enough to discard their clothing before he molded his bare flesh onto hers. Then, he lowered his lips to hers again, determined to show her just how much she was loved.

20

THE COLD, dark forest surrounds me. I follow the overgrown trail at my feet, effortlessly floating along for miles and miles—over hills, through deep valleys, and across creeks and rivers.

"Sami..." Billy's voice surrounds me. "Sami..." he calls again.

"Billy!" I shout, desperate to find him. "Billy!"

"Billyyy!" Sami sat up screaming, staring at the picture of the ocean hanging above the dresser.

"Huh?" Jason bounced up from the bed, his eyes wide with panic. He reached over and grabbed Sami's arm, pulling her into a hug. "It was only a dream, Sami. Just a dream," he said, voice trembling.

"No! He's still gone, Jason. It wasn't just a dream. It's a living nightmare!" She cried on his shoulder.

Mike and Abby burst through the bedroom door.

"Is everything all right?" Mike glanced around the room, his breathing ragged.

Jason pulled away from Sami and ran a hand through his hair. "Just a nightmare."

"Shhh!" Abby held her palm up to hush everyone. She stood completely still, deep in concentration. The corner of her mouth curled upward. "Rick's coming."

Mike went to the sliding glass door and yanked the curtain aside. Darkness still shadowed the forest, but a hint of gray loomed in the distance—the first light of morning.

Rick's face appeared at the door.

Mike tensed and jerked his head back. "Damn werewolves." He shook his head and slid the door open.

Rick stepped in and shut the door, his eyes dark with exhaustion.

"Well, did you find them?" Mike asked.

"No," said Rick, his voice lined with defeat. "I was only able to pick up old scents of her here and there and the scent of other werewolves."

"Maybe she used a car?" Mike suggested.

"Or maybe she had someone else take Billy to wherever she's keeping him?" Abby said.

"Dammit." Rick turned his attention to Jason and Sami. "I'm going to the last place you saw her in California to try to track her from there. It'll take a lot longer, but there's no other choice."

"Dad, you should get some rest first," Mike said.

Rick shook his head. "I'll rest later."

"But what if it's like Mike said—what if she took off in a car?" Jason asked.

"Maybe I can find the direction she headed in," Rick said.

"Rick," Abby said, hesitating, "maybe I should go? I can sense Jessica's presence from farther away than you can."

"No, you need to stay here to protect everyone."

"She's right," Mike spoke up. "We'll be fine here. The longer Jessica has her slutty hands on Billy—" His eyes widened and he looked at Sami.

Sami's heart sank as she envisioned Jessica touching Billy. She had been so wrapped up in the thought of him being turned into a werewolf, or worse, *dead*, she'd forgotten Jessica was obsessed with him.

Tears brewed, but she swallowed them back. She glanced at the four people staring at her, then to the sliding door, yearning for the privacy she needed to hide and overcome her humiliation.

"I need some fresh air." Sami climbed out of bed and headed for the door.

Rick moved aside and pulled it open.

"Thanks," she whispered and stepped outside, curling her toes as the cold concrete bore through the soles of her feet. Knowing they wouldn't let her get far while unattended, she perched on the second step and crossed her bare arms to shield them from the cool morning air.

She shuddered as she stared at the shadowed forest, the conversation ensuing in her bedroom fading to a distant muffle.

To ease some of the pain, she closed her eyes, her thoughts on Billy. She could almost hear his voice again as if he were there with her—as if he'd never left her side.

"Marry me, Sami.... I just need to know now if I can love you for the rest of my life. Marry me. It doesn't have to be now. It can be ten years from now if you want. Marry me. I love you, Sami. Marry me...."

Not being able to stand the torture any longer, she shook Billy's image from her thoughts and cried into her hands.

"Sami," Mike whispered, his voice full of sorrow.

She took in a ragged breath and pulled the neck of her T-shirt over her eyes to pat them dry.

He sat next to her and pulled her into a hug. "Don't worry. Billy's coming home."

"I just miss him so much it hurts." She pulled the shirt back down to her chin and sank against Mike's chest, welcoming the comfort and warmth.

"I know it does. But it's gonna get better. My dad will find him. I'm sure of it." He gave her a couple of pats on the back before he stood and extended his hand. "Come on. Let's get you warmed up and get some food in you so you don't get sick."

Food had been the least of her worries since the attack. It didn't even sound good at the moment. Nothing did. Even standing up and walking back into the house seemed too much of a burden. All she wanted to do was sleep. To just lay on her side, right where she was at, and close her eyes.

She shook her head. "I'm not hungry."

"You have to keep strong, for Billy," he said, his hand still extended.

"Besides, he'd kick my ass if he came home and you were withered away to nothing."

She gave in, knowing Mike wouldn't stop trying until he actually saw her shoveling food into her mouth. "I'll be there in a minute."

"I'm not leaving you here by yourself. Either you come with me, or I'm sitting back down."

Too exhausted to argue, she threw her hand into his and let him pull her up from the cold concrete.

They went inside and locked the door. She didn't know why. A door lock wasn't going to keep a werewolf out. Everyone else had gathered in the living room, their voices trickling down the hall.

Sami followed Mike, but she stopped at her bedroom door, not ready to face anyone yet. She couldn't hide the pain in her heart, and she knew it. They knew it too. And she was tired of being the fragile, broken-hearted child everyone catered too. She needed time alone to deal with her heartache until she could control it enough to be strong in front of others again.

"Mike, I'm gonna take a shower."

He studied her face, his eyes squinted with reluctance. After a long pause, he nodded. "All right. Just yell if you need us. Oh, and I called your mom for you last night, so she wouldn't worry. I told her you were in an accident and you're all fine but you wouldn't make the wedding. You should call her."

"Thanks, Mike. I'll call her later today."

He left the room and closed the door.

A glimmer on her dresser caught her eye. She focused on the locket.

"What?" she whispered, wondering who had put it there. She trailed her fingertip along its smooth surface, realizing from the bright glint that it wasn't the same locket her mother had given to her. This one was made from silver.

Taking a closer look, she noticed an inscription carved onto it. A *B* followed by a heart, then an *S*. "Billy loves Sami," she whispered. Tears blurred the locket into a shimmering blob.

She brushed the tears away with the back of her hand and opened the locket. A gasp escaped her lips as she stared at Billy's handsome smile. The picture had been taken while they were at the beach. Billy stood behind her with his head on her shoulder, his cheek pressed against hers, and his arm extended far in front of them to snap the perfect shot.

Emptiness tugged at Sami's heart, and her memory faded. "Where are you?" she whispered, staring into his eyes. She couldn't stand the pain and loneliness any longer. There had to be something she could do. To get to him somehow. To find him and bring him home.

If there are others out there, then, maybe I can get one of them to take me to Jessica? Or at least get them to tell me where she is.

She caught her bottom lip in her teeth, and a tingle of anticipation awakened in her chest as her heartbeat quickened. Was she really contemplating possibly the worst idea ever? Rick and Abby could sense other werewolves nearby, so she'd have to travel at least a mile away. The lake was a little farther than that.

But Rick would track her down in no time as soon as they discovered her missing, so if she was going to do this, she had to act now.

She glanced out the door. Pink hues of light filtered through the trees. The forest would still be somewhat dark, yet just light enough to see her way through it.

"I'm coming, Billy." She snapped the locket shut and clasped it around her neck. Then, she tiptoed to the bedroom door and turned the lock slowly, trying to avoid its *click* from drawing any attention.

"Where's my knife?" she whispered, spotting it on the dresser. She tucked it into the back of her jeans and wriggled her feet into her running shoes.

"The shower." If they didn't hear the water running they'd become suspicious. She hurried to the bathroom and turned on the shower, locking the door on her way out. Keeping her footsteps light, she crossed the room to the glass door and pulled it open just far enough to slip her body through.

Before she closed the door, she listened for footsteps, a knock on the door, or any indication someone was coming. All she heard was the spray of water bouncing off the bathtub floor and trickling down the drain. She let out a steady breath and slid the door shut.

With a watchful eye over her shoulder to make sure she still went unnoticed, she made her way around the outer edge of the yard to the trail.

When she reached the dirt path, she picked up her pace, not giving a second thought about the possible dangers lurking around her. Her focus was on saving Billy.

If all went according to plan, whoever Jessica had keeping an eye on them from the forest would capture her. Then, she'd be taken to where Billy was being held captive and could use the knife to kill Jessica or to escape somehow.

A sudden cramp in her side slowed her pace. She stopped to catch her breath, propping her hands on her knees to hold herself up. She glanced around and listened for movement, but so far, the forest was quiet. The pain subsided and she continued forward. Plodding breathlessly along, each step grew heavier as she neared exhaustion.

A couple of minutes later, the cramp returned with a vengeance. Clutching her side, out of breath, legs burning, she pushed on. Just when she thought she'd collapse, she stumbled into the clearing at the lake.

On wobbly legs, she trudged to the middle of the meadow and stopped, trying to catch her breath just enough to speak.

"Is anyone there?" She placed a hand over her burning lungs, trying to gain control of her breathing. "I need to see Jessica!" Her voice echoed across the lake.

"Will I do?" A gruff voice answered.

Sami gasped and whirled around to face the stranger.

A brawny man—with black eyes, hair, and clothes—stood not more than fifty feet away. His lips curled ominously, and his eyes filled with hunger. "I'm sure as hell not Jessica, but I can be if you want." He took slow steps toward her.

Sami suddenly realized she'd made a terrible mistake. She had been so wrapped up in finding Billy, she was certain if anyone were here, they'd take her to him. Afraid of the bold giant approaching her, she took a couple of long strides backward, toward the boulders overlooking the lake.

"Who are you?" she asked with a shaky voice.

"I'm Jessica." He grinned devilishly, continuing his slow pace.

Sami gulped. "Do you work for Jessica?"

"Oh yeah." He winked. "Me and Jessica, we go way back."

As she took another step away, she tripped over one of the boulders and fell to the ground. Feeling vulnerable and unable to protect herself, she shuffled away on her hands and feet, facing the stranger as he grew dangerously near.

"Are you a, a werewolf?"

"Do you want me to be?" He smirked, and his eyes turned red.

Sami let out a terrifying scream and scrambled to her feet. Without looking back, she sprinted for the trail.

The man suddenly appeared out of nowhere, and she plowed right into him. With a violent jerk, he grabbed her waist, crushing her against his solid frame.

A screech tore from her throat and echoed across the lake.

"Mmm, mmm, mmm. What a tasty treat you're gonna be!" He picked her up and threw her to the ground.

The blow knocked the air from her lungs, and she struggled to take a breath. She tried to scream again, but the faint squeal caught in the back of her throat. Pulling herself along clumps of weeds with tight fists, she made a desperate attempt to scramble away. Her lungs finally expanded, and she sucked in a huge breath.

Stone-like fingers clamped around her ankles like a vice, and in one swift move, he flipped her onto her back.

She screamed again, frantically kicking and trying to break free.

The man straddled her and grabbed her flailing arms. Using one of his over-sized hand's, he pinched her wrists together and pinned them above her head. Then, he leaned down and licked her cheek. "Mmm, tasty!"

Terrified, Sami shook her head from side to side, trying to keep his filthy tongue away from her.

His head jerked back and he released her wrists. "What the hell is this?" he snapped and ripped the neck of her shirt open. "A silver necklace? Stupid bitch!" He pulled his hand back, ready to strike.

Sami slid her knife from behind her back and stuck him in the gut, sawing the blade downward with all her might.

He roared and struck her across the cheek with a forceful blow.

Intense pain and a flash of light engulfed her head, followed by darkness.

21

MIKE AND Abby set the bacon, sausage, eggs, and toast out on the breakfast bar.

"You're right, Abby," Rick said. "It would be best if you searched with me. We'll leave right after breakfast. We need all the energy we can get, so eat as much as you can. It's gonna be a long day."

Abby smiled. "I knew you'd come to your senses. Maybe we'll get Billy back today."

"Breakfast is ready, Jason," Mike said.

Jason drew his gaze from the window and pushed himself up from the recliner, using one arm rest for support. His movements were slow as if he were in pain. Dark circles surrounded his eyes.

"I'll go tell Sami," Jason said, his voice strained.

"No." Mike put his hand up to stop him. "You eat and rest. I'll go get her."

Jason sighed and arched his back to stretch it. "Good idea."

Mike went down the hall and knocked on the bedroom door. "Sami, breakfast is ready." He listened for a reply. A steady hum of water rushed through the pipes. He sighed and went back to the kitchen to eat.

"Is she coming?" Jason asked through a mouthful of food.

"She's still in the shower." Mike piled food onto a plate and joined everyone at the table.

"She's probably just enjoying the relaxing hot water," Abby suggested. "Maybe trying to get her thoughts and emotions together? She's pretty distraught."

"Is that what girls do?" Jason asked.

Abby shrugged. "Sometimes. I guess."

"Huh." Jason turned his attention back to his food and continued to devour it. In less than a minute, he'd cleared his plate. "Man, I'm really hungry this morning." He went to the breakfast bar for seconds.

"It's a side effect from the bite," Rick said.

Jason hesitated as he held the serving spoon over the pan of eggs. With a worried look on his face, he forced down the last bite of food in his mouth with a big gulp. "What are you saying, Rick? That this is a werewolf thing?"

"That's exactly what I'm saying, Jason. You need more calories now to keep your body healthy until we kill Jessica. As a matter of fact, because the healing powers haven't developed yet, if you don't eat within a day or two of being bitten, it can be fatal. You're still basically human, but your body is burning a lot more calories to prepare for the transformation."

"That's just great," Jason mumbled in an angry tone. He slopped more food onto his plate and sat back down.

Mike crinkled his brows together, disgusted by Jason's pig-like face stuffing. Half of the food he shoveled into his mouth fell back out onto his plate. He looked at his dad. "Is this the way werewolves usually eat?"

"At first."

"I'm glad I was only scratched," Mike scoffed.

Jason stopped eating and narrowed his eyes. "*I'm glad I was only scratched*!" he mocked. "Shut up or I'll bite you myself! Rick, if I bit him now, would he become a werewolf too?"

"Not until you've transformed."

Mike grinned, enjoying the fact that Jason was easy to rile up now.

Jason sighed and began wolfing down his food again.

"Don't worry, Jason," Abby said. "I still eat like that when no one else is around."

"You do?" Mike asked.

"Well, a werewolf's gotta eat." She shoved a whole piece of bacon into her mouth.

Mike shook his head and let out a slight chuckle, hiding the fact that he was a little turned on now. *I think I can get used to my girlfriend being a wild beast.* A subtle smirk formed, but nothing anyone else would notice. He took a bite of his toast, the crunching filling his ears, and his thoughts went back to Sami.

What in the hell is she doing? He stopped chewing, trying to distinguish sounds coming from her room but couldn't hear anything over the clank of silverware and the incessant gnawing and gulping of mouthfuls of food. He put a hand up to silence them. "Wait, wait. Shhh."

The room fell silent and the steady rush of water through the pipes filled the air.

"The shower's still running. It took us at least thirty minutes to cook breakfast." Mike jumped up and ran to Sami's bedroom.

"Sami!" Mike pounded on the door. When she didn't answer, he turned the knob, but it didn't budge. "Sami!"

The only sounds he heard were everyone's footsteps approaching from behind. "Dammit!" He took a step back and kicked the door open with so much force it separated from the top two hinges.

He scanned the room, but she wasn't in it.

Mike went to the bathroom door, also locked. He slammed his boot against the door. It bounced off the wall and came back at him, but he barged right through it.

"Sami?" He yanked the curtain back and stared at the empty shower. "Son of a bitch!" He turned the water off and went back out into the bedroom.

Jason lifted his arms and let them drop at his sides. "Where in the hell is she?"

Rick went to the sliding door and pulled the handle. The door slid open. "It's not locked."

"I locked it when we came in," Mike said.

"Abby, you got anything?" Rick asked.

"No, but if she's more than a mile out...." Her face tensed with worry.

"The lake!" Mike boomed. "She always goes there when she's sad. To be alone and think."

"Let's go, Abby," Rick ordered.

"Should we morph?" she asked.

Rick nodded.

"Wait! You're taking me with you!" Mike demanded.

"No, Son. It could be dangerous."

"Abby, you're taking me! You guys can't just surprise Sami looking like werewolves. She might have a silver knife on her. You need me to let her know it's just you guys."

"Okay," Abby agreed, avoiding Rick's harsh green-eyed gaze. "Come on, Mike." She hurried out the back door.

Mike followed her to the middle of the backyard.

"I'll be right back. I have to change." She disappeared into the woods.

Jason hopped off the top step, into the grass.

Rick stepped outside and pointed a finger at Jason. "You're staying! Go to the basement and get in the cage until we get back."

Jason nodded and headed straight for the basement.

"I'm gonna morph," Rick said and darted back into the bedroom.

Twigs snapping drew Mike's attention to the edge of the yard. Abby stepped out from behind a tree—complete with green eyes, pointed ears and snout, and head-to-toe sandy fur covering her monstrous frame. He wondered if he would ever get used to the shock of seeing his girlfriend in her beast form.

A dark brown blur darted from the bedroom and disappeared into the forest—his dad was already on his way to the lake.

Before Mike knew it, he was in Abby's furry arms, cradled against her rock-hard chest and watching in disbelief as the green and brown hues of the forest whirred by. Not even a minute had passed before the faint sound of Sami's blood curdling screams nearly stopped his heart.

"Sami!" Mike said as dread filled him.

They broke through the barrier of trees and into the clearing.

Across the meadow, a man hovered over Sami's motionless body.

"Nooo! Sami!" Mike fell from Abby's arms and thudded to the ground. He looked up just as his dad plowed into the stranger and tumbled down the hill with the man in his clutches.

Abby raced down the hill to assist Rick.

Mike jumped to his feet and sprinted to Sami, falling to his knees when he reached her side. Blood splatters covered her face and stained her clothing. "Oh shit! Sami?" He lowered his ear to her chest, listening for signs of life. The steady beat of her heart pulsated against his cheek. "Thank God!"

A vicious roar drew his attention to the shoreline. His dad struggled with the red-eyed man, who now shook with convulsions.

"Oh shit, don't morph," Mike whispered.

Abby grabbed the man from behind and slammed him to the ground on his back.

Rick straddled the attacker and rammed his claws straight into the man's chest.

A loud whimper echoed across the meadow, and the battle was over.

Mike turned his attention back to Sami. "Sami?" He couldn't control his shaky voice or trembling fingers. With a gentle hand to her chin, he turned her face toward him. A purple and black bruise covered her cheek, and blood dripped from the cut the blow had created. "Son of a bitch!"

A sudden shadow blocked the sunlight as his dad and Abby towered over them.

"She's alive, but she's covered in blood." Mike inspected Sami's torso, arms, and legs for any signs of blood spilling from gaping wounds. Dark fingerprint bruises covered her waist, wrists, and ankles, but no other wounds were visible. He focused on the silver locket around her neck and the bloody knife at her side before eyeing her blood soaked clothes.

"The blood must be his," Mike said, throwing a quick nod to the lifeless stranger.

Rick nodded.

"I think she's okay. We got here just in time." Mike picked up the knife and wiped the blade clean across a clump of grass. Then, he carefully tucked it under his belt. "Let's get her home." He gathered Sami up and held her out to his father.

Rick stepped back and growled, shaking his head.

"What are you doing?" Mike asked. "You have to carry her home."

Using a claw, his dad pointed at the silver locket around Sami's neck.

"Oh, right." Mike gently set Sami on the ground and tried to unclasp the locket, but his jittery fingers made the task difficult. "Come on, dammit!" Trying again, he picked at the clasp with his thumbnail until it finally unlatched.

"Damn adrenaline!" He shoved the necklace into his front pocket, scooped Sami up, and handed her over.

With Sami draped across his arms, Rick took off across the meadow.

Mike jerked forward, and he was in Abby's strong arms with the wind rushing over his face. He felt foolish, being carried like a helpless loser by his girlfriend. But, unless he wanted to get home in forty minutes, he didn't have a choice.

The sensation of flying blindly though the air came to a sudden halt, and he was on his feet again, standing in front of the sliding glass door of Sami's bedroom. "I don't think I'll ever get used to this shit." He yanked the door open and stepped aside to let his dad in with Sami, followed by Abby.

"Jason, it's clear!" Mike shouted toward the basement before he went in to check on Sami.

Jason came barreling around the corner and stopped in the doorway. "Did you find her? Is she okay?" He froze, his wide eyes focused on the two beasts in the room.

"It's just my dad and Abby," Mike said.

Jason's gaze settled on Sami's motionless body, and his face drained of color. "Oh shit! There's so much blood!"

"She's fine," Mike said. "The blood isn't hers." He went to the bathroom, yanked the towel off the hook next to the door, and tossed it to Jason. "Spread this out on the bed." He snatched a washcloth from the rack above the toilet and doused it with water from the sink.

"What in the hell happened to her? Whose blood is it?" Jason asked.

Mike pushed by him and perched on the bed next to Sami. As he wiped away the blood smeared across her cheek, he filled Jason in on the details.

SAMI MOANED and fluttered her eyes open. A blurry figure hovered over her. She sat up and screamed, trying to back away from her attacker.

"Sami!" Mike gripped her shoulders. "It's me. Mike. You're safe."

She let out a ragged breath and looked around. Jason stood in the doorway, leaning against the doorjamb. She was in her own bed, in her own bedroom, safe. "I'm in my room. It was just a nightmare."

"No, Sami, it wasn't." Mike's tone was harsh. "You went to the lake by yourself. What in the *hell* were you thinking? He was gonna *kill* you!"

Humiliated and ashamed, she lowered her lashes to hide her forming tears and shook her head at her own stupidity. "I…I…" She bit her lip to steady the quiver. "I wanted to find someone that could take me to Jessica—to where she was keeping Billy—so I could rescue him. I just need to see him and know he's alive."

Mike clenched his jaw, causing his temples to pulsate.

Jason sat beside her and gave her a hug. When he pulled away, his eyes were filled with angry tears. "Sami." His voice held a scolding tone. "You almost *died* out there." He paused to clench his teeth, trying to keep the tears from falling.

"How do you think Billy would feel after he was finally rescued and got to come home to start his new life with you but he came home only to find you dead and lying in the ground next to your grandpa?" As he spoke, his words became harsher. "Or what if Rick, Abby, and Mike had been killed trying to save you? There would be no one left to even *rescue* Billy."

Sami hung her head, trying to hide the shame. "I'm so sorry." Her voice cracked, and the tears fell. "I was so *stupid*! I put my life and everyone else's lives in danger. I'm sorry."

Jason wrapped his arms around her, and she buried her face in his chest, unleashing her sorrow.

Abby came in and sat on the edge of the bed. "Here." She held out an ice pack. "This goes on your other cheek this time."

Sucking in a sob, Sami pulled away from Jason and took the ice pack. She pressed it to her aching cheekbone, wincing at the frigid sting. "Is it as bad as it feels?"

Jason raised his eyebrows. "Worse. Both sides of your face are bruised now, Sami. It looks like you were in a fight with an aluminum baseball bat."

She pressed her lips together to keep her chin from trembling. "I don't know what I was thinking."

"You can say that again," Jason said with underlying cynicism.

Mike reached out and hit Jason's shoulder.

"Ow, dude! Come on. That's the only arm I have left," Jason said, clutching his shoulder.

Mike dug into the front pocket of his jeans pocket and stuck his fist out.

Sami held out her hand, palm facing up.

"I think this helped save your life today," Mike said as he dropped a locket into her palm. "And this…." He pulled the knife out from his belt and tossed it onto the foot of the bed.

Jason raised one corner of his mouth. "I heard you finally got to use your knife."

"Oh, she used it all right," Mike said, his eyes still on Sami. "You stuck your attacker in the gut and sliced him open. My dad finished the job by ripping out his heart, but if he hadn't, the asshole would've died from the knife wound anyway."

Jason grinned. "I'm impressed. You've graduated from using a pocketknife to defend yourself from wild animals to using a silver hunting knife to stop a werewolf dead in his tracks."

"Yeah, well, I was still stupid," Sami replied, not seeing the situation in the same light they did. "I'm sure he would've killed me before he died, if you guys hadn't gotten there on time." She stared at the locket in her palm and her heart grew heavy. "I found this on the dresser this morning. I think Billy meant for me to find it."

"He made it, you know," Jason said. "He was waiting for the perfect time to give it to you. When we decided to go to Tahoe, he was gonna give it to you there. I held onto it for him, so you wouldn't find it. But I figured if you had it now it might help you through this tough time. And, apparently, it did."

Sami tossed the ice pack aside to admire the piece of jewelry again, wishing she could wrap her arms around Billy and thank him. The necklace slipped through her fingers and landed on her thigh, drawing her attention to the navy sweatpants and white T-shirt she wore. Images of her attacker ripping her shirt open flooded her thoughts and her hand flew to her neck.

"He ripped my shirt—Billy's favorite shirt. These are different clothes."

Jason cleared his throat. "Bummer about the shirt, but the only thing we noticed was the fact that you were unconscious and covered in blood."

Her mouth fell open. "Covered in blood?"

"You did shove a knife into him," Mike reminded.

Abby patted Sami's foot. "Don't worry. I made them leave when I took you to the bathtub and cleaned you up."

"Thanks." Sami turned her attention back to the locket. She opened it, and a soft smiled formed. "There's a picture of me and Billy inside." With a heavy heart, she snapped it closed and clasped it around her neck. "Wait a minute." She recalled putting it on before she'd headed to the lake. She looked at Mike. "How did you get it?"

"I had to take it off you, so my dad could carry you back," Mike said.

"Oh.... Maybe it helped save my life too," she replied in a glum tone, sure she would never let herself live this one down. *And neither will anyone in this room. Or Billy, when he finds out. If he finds out.*

Mike cleared his throat. "Sometimes, when our loved ones are in danger, we do things we normally wouldn't do and take risks we normally wouldn't take in order to save them. And we're not always smart-headed about it. Anyway, now that I'm *finally* convinced you'll never go into the forest alone *ever* again..." He paused, letting an uneasiness fill the air before his expression softened and a half-smile formed. "...are you ready for breakfast?"

Sami nodded and a hint of a smile formed. "Yeah, no tricks this time."

Jason reached his hand out and helped her off the bed.

As soon as her feet touched the floor, she winced from the deep ache in her ankles. Even her waist hurt. She lifted her shirt to her navel and inspected the damage. Dark purple and red splotches covered each side.

"Damn!" Jason cringed.

Sami lifted each leg of her sweatpants, exposing her discolored ankles. "Oh my gosh!"

"Son of a bitch!" Jason spouted.

Sami shook her head. "You're right, Mike, I'll never do anything like that again."

"I know you won't," Mike said.

With each step, a painful throb pulsated through her ankles. She winced, limping along.

"You look pathetic," Mike said. "Do you want me to carry you?"

"Thanks, but I'll get through it." As they went through the bedroom doorway, she noticed its crooked appearance. "What happened to my door?"

Jason gave her a knowing glance over his shoulder.

"Oh yeah." She flashed a cheesy grin. "I guess my bathroom door looks pretty much the same way?"

"Pretty much," Mike said flatly.

22

"WHAT THE hell?" Billy said, staring at the stone walls surrounding him. He sat up from the cold, hard ground and arched his back to stretch the ache away. "Where in the fuck am I?" he snapped, his voice echoing down the dark corridor. The back of his head throbbed in one particular area. He touched the sensitive spot, wincing when he found a lump.

Images of being attacked on the way to Lake Tahoe flashed through his mind. A wave of panic shot through him, and he jumped to his feet. "Sami? Jason?" Their names echoed off the walls and faded down the corridor.

A lit lantern sat on the ground behind him. He picked it up and proceeded through the dark tunnel. Not knowing what to expect, he kept a slow pace while tossing a periodic glance over his shoulder for any furry beasts creeping up on him.

"Sami? Jason?" he shouted, peering into little dens here and there as he passed by them.

"This cave just doesn't end," he said, growing impatient. "What the hell, Jessica? Is this some sort of a sick joke?" Billy boomed. His voice bounced back at him from all directions. Frustrated, he continued through the tunnel until he came to a fork in the path.

"Just my luck," he said, his tone lacking enthusiasm. Choosing the tunnel to his right, he followed it for a couple of minutes, calling for Sami and Jason along the way before it came to a dead end.

"Dammit!" He swiped his sweaty forehead across the shoulder of his shirt and headed back to the fork, choosing the opposite path this time around.

The tunnel leading left seemed twice as long. Up ahead, a bright light filtered through. "It's about frickin' time!" He quickened his pace toward the visible blue sky.

When he reached the exit of the cave, he stopped dead in his tracks. The ground was well over forty feet below, straight down the face of a cliff.

"Fuck!" Anxiety clutched his chest and he took a step back. Gripping a protrusion of rock on the wall, he peered down at the tops of the pine trees extending like a sea of green to the horizon.

He glanced upward, following the cliff-side for dozens of feet until it met the blue sky. Not wanting to chance slipping to his doom, he took another step back and set the lantern down.

"Hello?" he yelled with his hands cupped around his mouth and scanned the forest for any signs of rescue. "Hello? I need help! Is anybody there?" The echo of his voice faded into an eerie silence.

Billy went back into the cave, a few feet from the edge, and sat down with his back against the cold, stone wall. He stared out across the tops of the trees, waiting for help.

He thought of Sami and Jason, praying they were alive and unharmed. Tears brimmed, but he swallowed them back.

"I'm so sorry, guys," he said aloud, his voice laden with regret. "I'm sorry I let that bitch get to us."

The rustling of trees in the distance drew his attention.

"What the hell?" He stood and held his breath, searching for more movement. About fifty feet closer than the first disturbance, another treetop shook. Then another. All were in a line, headed straight for him.

Dread filled him when he realized what was out there. "Jessica!" He backed away from the entrance, looking for somewhere to hide before she showed up, but he knew it was pointless.

Within seconds, her large, furry figure blocked the entrance, engulfing him with her monstrous shadow. A ferocious growl ripped through her saliva drenched fangs.

Billy stood his ground, determined to be strong. But fear crept its way through his blood, and he backed up—trying to think of a way to save himself.

Hitting Jessica upside the head with the lantern seemed like a fairly good idea. But pushing her out of the cave seemed like a better one.

He envisioned running toward the lethal beast, gaining speed and plowing right into her. The impact might send her over the edge, but would she grab hold of his arm and take him with her? Would she live because she could heal while he ended up a splattered and bloody mess at the bottom? Pushing the thought aside, he eyed the lantern at his feet.

Jessica sneered wickedly, showing off her long, pointed fangs. She moved toward him and disappeared into a den near the entrance. Seconds later, vicious growling and snarling radiated through the corridor.

Billy cupped his hands over his ears, shielding them from the horrific sounds, until all went quiet again.

"Sorry about that." Jessica smiled as she stepped out of the den, while fluffing her long black curls until they sprawled about her shoulders. A blood-red dress hugged her every curve, stopping just below her buttocks. "How do you like it?"

Lust filled her amber eyes, and she ran her fingers down the slender strap to the middle of her cleavage before propping her hand on her hip.

"Where are Sami and Jason?" Billy demanded.

Her smile fell flat, and her eyes narrowed. "How in the hell should I know? They're probably back at home, in each other's arms and in your bed!"

He closed his eyes, thankful Sami and Jason were safe. Determined not to let on, he met her cold glare. "What do you want with me?"

"Oh, I have lots of things in store for you." She grinned.

Realizing hostility wasn't the route to take with a killer beast, Billy clenched his jaw, suppressing the rage building within. "Why'd you kidnap me?" he said, his voice more subdued.

"Kidnap you?" She scoffed. "I didn't *kidnap* you, Billy. I rescued you from that *whore* who tried to have your baby."

"She is *not* a whore! And my baby's gone because of you!" He lunged for Jessica, knocking her to the ground. Before her stunned look wore off, he clenched his fingers into a fist and bashed her in the face.

A fierce growl erupted, and her eyes turned red.

He pulled his fist back again and thrust it straight toward her jaw.

Wearing a smirk, she caught his hand with little effort and squeezed.

He gritted his teeth, bearing through the bone-crushing torture. A quick *snap* sent a sharp jolt of pain through his hand. "Ugh!" He grimaced and squished his eyes shut, trying to hold back tears of agony.

"You've been a bad boy!" Jessica scolded as she kicked him off of her.

The forceful blow sent him flying backward and crashing into the hardened dirt. "Ugh!" he grunted and rolled to his side to cradle his throbbing hand. "You broke my hand, you bitch!"

Jessica stood and dusted off her dress. She sauntered over to him, her red eyes full of fury. "Call me a bitch again and I'll break your other hand! Do you hear me?"

"Yeah," he croaked through a grunt.

"Do you have anything else to say?" She glared at him with her hands on her hips.

He couldn't stand the thought of apologizing. His disgust for her ran deep, and he struggled to hide it. To ease the difficulty, he envisioned Sami standing there instead. "I'm sorry."

"You better be!" When she blinked, her eyes switched back to amber. "I knew you'd see things my way," she said in a soft tone and smiled. "So, did you find which den I hid the food and water in?"

This is just a damn game to her. A sick, fucking game! He imagined himself lunging for her again and beating the twisted smile off her face. Instead, he took a deep breath to keep calm. "No, I didn't."

"Oh, too bad." She pouted, sticking out her bottom lip. "Well, I guess I'll just have to show you where it is since you're too stupid to find it. Come along."

Nausea overcame him when her sweaty fingers wrapped around his. Not wanting to irk her further, he swallowed back the sickness and let her help him up.

Luckily, she remained silent as they walked. The pain shooting through Billy's broken hand was too intense for him to speak without showing weakness. He rested his arm against his chest to keep it still, with his hand just above the heart. After a few minutes of plodding along, the pain dulled to a slight ache.

"And we're here!" She motioned with a swoop of her hand to a large den on the right.

Skeptical to see what she had in store for him, he peered around the corner. A cot sat along the far wall, covered with a sleeping bag and a pillow. Along the right wall was a folding table with two chairs. Another table had been pushed against the left wall, housing a box of food on top and an ice chest underneath.

"What do you think?" she grinned. "Cozy, isn't it?"

Billy forced himself to be kind. "Yeah. Thanks."

"I knew you'd like it." She let go of his hand and sauntered over to the ice chest. She slid it from under the table and flipped the lid open. "I even got you a surprise." She snatched a beer from the ice and handed it to him. "Here you go, dear."

Caught off guard by her delusion, he stared at her with a blank expression before he focused on the beer.

Man, this chic has really lost it!

Using caution, he took the beer and smiled a half-smile. "Thank you."

"See! I knew this was going to work." Beaming, she pranced to the cot and lay down on her side. "And, if you're really good, then maybe, just maybe…" She eyed him seductively as she slowly pulled up the hem of her dress, revealing her bare hip.

Billy swallowed hard and fought back the urge to chuck his can of beer at her.

Jessica bounced up from the cot and straightened her dress. "But that's only if you behave."

As she passed by him, her shoulder brushed against his, and her hand cupped his butt. He tensed and jerked from her grasp.

"I have to go now, but I'll be back later. I'll bring extra clothes for you. Oh, and if you have to use the bathroom, there are some buckets a few dens down." She pointed down the corridor, opposite the way they'd just travelled.

"Thank you." He showed a polite smile, though the only thing he was thankful for was her leaving.

She raised her eyebrows as if pleased. "You're welcome." Without warning, she grabbed his jaw, pulled his face close to hers, and pressed her lips to his.

Disgusted, he stiffened and pulled away, wiping his mouth with the back of his hand.

Jessica narrowed her eyes and pushed him with so much force he crashed to the ground on his right side.

"Ugh!" Billy grunted as an intense pain jolted through his broken hand. Afraid to move, he lay still, waiting for Jessica to leave.

"You had better rethink your actions and be ready to cooperate when I return!" Her eyes flashed red and she disappeared.

Billy moaned and gritted his teeth, trying to bear through the agonizing throb. "Shit!" He winced. On both knees and using only one arm, he crawled to the cot and pulled himself onto it. He leaned against the wall and cradled his black and purple hand against his chest.

On the ground, next to the cot, another box caught his attention. He flipped the flaps back. Inside were matches, a first aid kit, paper plates, plastic utensils, a mirror, and extra batteries for the lantern.

Praying he'd find something for pain, he opened the first aid kit, relieved to find a bottle of ibuprofen inside. He pinched the bottle between his chest and the bicep of his right arm and worked the lid off with his unbroken fingers. After shaking four pills onto the cot, he popped them into his mouth and gulped them down. He went to the ice chest and dragged it to the bed before easing back down.

He opened the lid and stared at the ice. His swollen hand needed it, but the thought of anything touching the throbbing injury sent a twinge down his legs. *You have to do it, Billy. Just man up and do it!*

Preparing for the pain, he forced air in and out of his nostrils like a bull about to attack. He shoved the beverages aside and laid the back of his hand on the ice.

"Ahhh." He grimaced through the torture and placed a few cubes in his palm to reduce as much of the swelling as possible. The agonizing burn consumed his every thought, almost to the point of being unbearable.

Alcohol will dull the ache faster than the pills. He snatched a beer, pulled back the tab, and guzzled it. A loud belch burst from his throat, and he tossed the empty can aside before grabbing another one.

After chugging the second, his head began to buzz with the first signs of intoxication. Eyeing another can, he contemplated drinking it. With Jessica being mentally unstable, he needed to keep his wits about him. *Ah, fuck it! Just one more to dull the pain.*

Billy slammed back the ale and crumpled the aluminum vessel, tossing it next to the other.

His body warmed as the buzz intensified, and just as he'd hoped, the pain in his hand lessened to tolerable. After nearly fifteen minutes, the ache had diminished to a slight throb. Not being able to bear the cold any longer, he lifted his hand from the ice.

Now what can I use to make a brace? He focused on the box of supplies. An idea came to mind. He ripped off a side of the cardboard box, folded it in half, and grabbed the roll of gauze from the first aid kit. Carefully, he set his arm on the sturdy cardboard brace, positioning it so his fingertips were exposed at the top. He wrapped it in place with the gauze, leaving a few inches of material at each end to tie into knots. Using his teeth, he pulled each knot tight.

"Stupid bitch!" he said, staring at his makeshift cast, his voice heavy with cynicism. His stomach churned and rumbled, diverting his attention to the food box on the table. He dug through it, choosing an apple, beef jerky, and crackers. After scarfing down the food, he went to look for the den housing the buckets.

Just as Jessica had said, they were two dens down. "I don't know how the hell I missed this one earlier," he spat, staring at the five gallon buckets sitting in the middle of the den.

On the ground, behind the buckets, rolls of toilet paper formed the shape of a heart. Billy crinkled his face in disgust.

"You are seriously whacked." He shook his head and unzipped his jeans. The task of using the bathroom wasn't easy with one hand, but he managed.

When he finished, he went back to his room for the mirror and continued on to the mouth of the cave.

He planted his butt in a spot where the dirt was soft and his back rested flat against the stone wall. The sun shined from almost directly overhead, which meant the day was still early. He held the mirror up, angling it just right so the sunlight reflected across the forest, and scanned the horizon, watching and listening for any signs of rescue.

Sami filled his thoughts and he smiled. He remembered the first day he'd met her, and how he'd known he was in trouble as soon as she'd opened the door and their eyes had locked. His memory drifted to the night of their first kiss and the surge of energy that had shot through him. At that moment, he'd known she was the one for him. And after the first time they'd made love, he'd known that he was the one for her.

He let out a heavy sigh, staring at the treetops, and continued to pass the time by thinking about Sami. Periodically, one of their tragic experiences worked their way into his thoughts, but he quickly squashed them with more good memoires.

Sitting forward, he stretched his stiff back and gauged the position of the sun in the sky again—only about two hours had passed. It didn't matter though—two hours or ten—he saw and heard nothing. Not the blast of a hunter's gunshot or the engine of a flying craft overhead. Hell, there weren't even any birds squawking around.

A loud yawn escaped his wide open mouth. Just as he was about to close his eyes for a few minutes of rest, the top of a tree rustled in the distance.

"Dammit!" He jumped up and rushed to a nearby den, looking for somewhere to hide the mirror. A crevice caught his eye and he shoved the mirror into it. He ran back to the mouth of the cave and sat back down, trying to appear nonchalant. The protrusion of the cave wall digging in his spine made it impossible to relax.

"Son of a bitch!" he muttered, flustered and knowing it was too late to find a different spot.

Jessica's monstrous hairy frame blocked the entrance. She took a menacing step toward him and growled.

His eyes widened. Hoping to avoid pissing her off again, he decided to explain his recent choice of words. "*Son of a bitch* wasn't directed at you, Jessica," he said, his tone soft. "My hand hurts is all." He eyed the bag slung over her shoulder, ready to change the subject. "I see you brought me some clothes?"

She narrowed her red eyes and disappeared into the same den as earlier—the one he'd hid the mirror in.

Billy covered his ears to filter the grizzly sounds echoing through the cave, hoping he'd hidden the mirror well out of view.

"Here." Jessica reappeared again, wearing a red satin negligee which dipped low across her breasts. The thin fabric hugged every curve, leaving almost nothing to the imagination.

She tossed a black backpack at his feet. "You can change, and there's some baby wipes in there also. I thought maybe you'd like to freshen up a little. Oh, and I put my favorite cologne in there too. Make sure you use it please. It really puts me in the mood."

Billy gulped, realizing what she had planned.

What the…? I can't have sex with this crazy bitch! And there's no way I'd cheat on Sami. What in the hell am I gonna do?

He scrambled to come up with a diversion, but no ideas came to mind.

She picked up the lantern and headed down the tunnel. "Come here. I have a surprise for you."

With no choice but to obey, Billy stood and slung the backpack over his shoulder. He followed her through the cave, remembering to be polite when responding to her idle chit chat about the comfort of his new room, if he had enough food and supplies, and whether he'd found the bathroom.

They passed Billy's room and continued on until she made a sharp left around a wall of rock which jutted out and curved back in. With just a quick glance, it appeared to be a solid wall. But, as he followed the curvature into the shadow it created, another passageway opened up.

"Wait here until I call for you." She handed him the lantern and hurried down the new tunnel.

He sighed and rolled his eyes, dreading what was to come. *Shit! What am I gonna do? Think, dammit!*

A dim light illuminated in the distance.

"I'm ready!" Jessica beckoned.

"Damn," he whispered and headed toward the light—around a corner and into another den.

Jessica lay in the middle of a large bed which was covered with black satin sheets. Propped on her side, she ran her fingers against the side of her breast, along her hip, stopping at the hem of her skimpy negligee.

Billy froze, not knowing what to say or do. Most importantly, he wasn't sure how to get out of this mess without having every bone in his body broken. He eyed the posts of the metal headboard and footboard, wondering if they could break easily and be used as a weapon against her.

A flicker out of the corner of his eye caught his attention. He focused in on the lighted disturbance—dozens of lit candles on the ground along the walls.

How in the hell did I not notice those when I came in?

"Do you like what you see?"

Not wanting to agitate her, he nodded.

"Awe, don't be shy, Billy." She smiled. "I just couldn't wait to show you your surprise. Now, hurry off to your room and get freshened up for me. I'll be waiting."

Without another word, Billy hurried away, not stopping until he reached his den.

What the fuck am I gonna do? I can't go through with this! I'll die before I touch that skank!

He sat on the cot and ran his fingers through his hair.

I guess I'll just have to piss her off again and hope she knocks me out this time.

He slumped against the cave wall and waited, while going over in his mind possible outcomes of the upcoming mutiny. One thing he knew for sure—he had to keep his other hand from being broken or Jessica would have to care for him day and night. Same outcome if she broke his legs. So, basically, he was screwed. The only thing that could save him was a miracle. Or death.

Jessica entered his room with her hands on her hips. "What's taking so long?" she snapped.

Startled, Billy opened his mouth to speak but couldn't utter a word. *This is it—I'm gonna die.*

"Well?" She glared at him.

"I'm not feeling so well," he finally managed to say. Which wasn't a lie. The thought of dying, possibly seconds from now, made his stomach sick.

"Is that so? Well, you're just going to have to suck it up like a real man. I don't have time to wait until you're feeling better!" She stormed toward him.

"I think it has something to do with my broken hand. I think I need to see a doctor."

"That's fine. You'll see a doctor in a couple of days. Now let's go!"

Her sweaty fingers gripped his and he jerked his hand back. "What do you mean *in a couple of days*? Are you letting me go?"

"No." An impatient breath shot from her lips. "I guess so." She shrugged with an attitude and crossed her arms like a spoiled child. "My *uncle* says I have to get you back or *there'll be hell to pay*. Frankly, I could give a rat's ass about what the *boss* thinks!"

"The boss?"

"Never mind!" Her eyes turned red. She grabbed his hand and pulled.

Knowing dying wasn't an option anymore gave him the advantage. He yanked his hand from her filthy paw. "No! I said I'm not feeling well."

Jessica clenched her jaw and backhanded him across the face.

Billy stifled the groan, not wanting to give her the satisfaction of causing him pain. He held the upper hand now, and it was time for payback. An idea came to mind, but he hid his smirk of anticipation behind a tender gaze. "I'm sorry." Reaching out slowly, he caressed her cheek with gentle fingertips.

A soft smile formed, and she closed her eyes, enjoying his touch. "That's better."

His lips curled deviously, and he popped her in the jaw.

"Ah!" Jessica stumbled back with a dumbfounded look on her face.

Oh Shit! Billy's heart raced as he mentally braced himself for his fate.

With fury in her eyes, she stormed up to him and rammed her fist into his jaw so quickly he didn't even see it coming.

23

AFTER SAMI ended the phone call with her mother, she went out to the front porch and eased onto the wicker loveseat. "I can't believe you went through with it, Mom," she whispered and frowned.

Deep inside, she had held onto the glimmer of hope that her mother would come to her senses and run the other way. Instead, she became Mrs. Carol Garrison.

Sami shook the disappointing thought away and glanced at the sky. The sun loomed almost directly overhead now, meaning the day wasn't even half over yet. Running a finger across the smooth heart shape of her locket, she stared into the forest.

Billy entered her thoughts and a soft smile formed. She recalled the day he had come to her front door to introduce himself. When she'd first opened the door, she had been startled to see a tall, muscular guy staring down at her. But his gaze had been so intense, she'd felt as if he were staring right into her soul, which had awakened an immediate attraction for him.

Her thoughts drifted to their first kiss during the storm in front of her bedroom window, and how it had sparked a desire in her she'd never known existed. All she'd been able to think about for the rest of that night had been whether he would kiss her again. And, when he had, she had known he'd stolen her heart.

She thought of their first lovemaking, of how it had consumed every inch of her being like magic, bonding them so deeply their love could never be broken.

A crow squawked by, jolting her back to reality and taking her momentary happiness with it. Now, the emptiness in her chest felt worse than before, and guilt riddled her conscience for enjoying a fleeting moment of pleasure while Billy was probably suffering.

Is Jessica torturing him like she did to me? Is he locked in a filthy basement, being beaten, believing the only outcome is death?

Jessica had an explosive temper. And Billy wasn't the type of person to stand down to anyone.

Please be okay, Billy. Please just stay alive.

The front door opened, saving her from further mental torture.

Jason stepped out of the house and plopped next her on the loveseat. "Don't let Mike catch you out here by yourself."

"It's just the front porch. Besides, I have my knife on me." She pointed to the sheath hooked to her belt. "And one right here." She moved her hip from the arm of the chair, revealing the hidden weapon.

"That's my girl." Jason sat back and stared into the forest. "Sami?"

"Yeah?"

"Will you still feel the same way about me if they don't find Jessica in time?"

"You mean if they don't kill her and you turn into a werewolf?"

"Yeah."

She pondered the thought of him as a monstrous beast with the power to rip someone apart with his bare hands. But she couldn't imagine Jason being anyone, or anything, other than his charming, charismatic self. She rested her head on his shoulder.

"Of course, you're one of my best friends," she said.

"Really? I am?"

"Yes, you are." Sami lifted her head and looked at him. His huge grin brought a smile to her face. "What about me? Would you still feel the same way about me if I turned into a werewolf?"

"That's never gonna happen," he said as if he were sure of it.

Her smile faded. "Do you think Billy's okay? Do you think he's a werewolf?"

Jason shook his head. "No way. Billy is cleverly keeping out of any kind of trouble with Jessica."

"Are you sure? I've been worried all morning that he's just gonna spout his mouth off and end up hurt. Or worse." She cringed, not being able to say the word *dead* aloud.

"Billy's smart. He won't do anything stupid. He's doing everything he can right now to get out of this mess. Okay? He's coming home."

She nodded, hoping he was right.

Jason scrunched his forehead. "What's that sound? I think it's a car."

Sami eyed the mouth of their road, seeing and hearing nothing out of the ordinary. "I don't hear anything."

"It's definitely a car, and it's coming this way."

A squad car turned onto their road. As it rolled toward them, Sheriff Briggs's face became visible.

"Oh no! What do we do, Jason?" Sami asked, growing anxious. "What if he hurts us or arrests us?"

"Just keep cool and let me do the talking. We haven't broken any laws, and he's not a werewolf, remember?"

"Okay." She sat back in the chair, hoping he wasn't there to wreak more havoc on their lives.

Sheriff Briggs climbed out of the car and strolled toward them, grinning.

Jason met him at the bottom of the steps. "Sheriff."

"Jason, Sami." His smile faded when he focused on their injuries. "What in the hell happened to the both of you? It looks like you were mugged."

"Oh." Jason glanced at his bandaged arm and back to Sami's bruised face. "We were just in a little car accident."

Sheriff Briggs glanced at Jason's car parked at the dead end, noticing the broken window and the dented trunk. "An accident, huh? I haven't heard of any accidents around here these last couple of days."

"It was in California," Jason said.

"What were you two doing in California?"

"It's personal!" Jason snapped.

The sheriff glared at Jason. When he turned his focus on Sami, his eyes softened. "He didn't hurt you now, did he?"

She narrowed her eyes and pursed her lips, tired of his sick game. "Why do you keep asking that? Jason would *never* hurt me!"

"Just checking." Sheriff Briggs smirked.

Jason glared him. "Why are you here, Sheriff?"

"Just wondering if you two have seen Abby?"

"No, we haven't," Jason said, his voice wary.

The sheriff tipped his hat back put a hand on his hip. "Do you think she's with Mike?"

"No, Mike's here," Jason said.

"Where?"

Jason thought for a moment and shot a quick glance Sami's way, raising one corner of his mouth. "Mike's inside with Billy. We're all just hanging out."

"Billy's *home*?" Sheriff Briggs crinkled his forehead.

Jason squinted at him. "What do you mean *Billy's home*? Where'd you think he was?"

The sheriff shifted his feet and shook his head. "Never mind."

Sami bit her lower lip, trying to contain her excitement. *He knows where Billy is! Do we question him about it? No, Sheriff Briggs is dangerous. We should wait for Rick.*

"If you see Abby, please tell her I'm looking for her." He nodded and tipped the brim of his hat. "I'll be seeing you two around. Stay out of trouble." He settled back into his car and drove away.

Sami jumped up off the chair, the sudden movement sending shooting pains through her ankles. "Ahh!" She cringed and dropped back onto the seat. "Do you think he knows where Billy is?"

Jason grinned. "Sure sounds like it! Or he at least knows where Jessica is." In one long stride, he leapt back onto the porch and helped Sami off the chair and into the house.

Mike was sprawled on the couch, sound asleep.

Jason slapped the top of the recliner. "Sit and prop your ankles up."

Sami did as instructed and pulled back the lever, taking the weight off her aching feet.

"Hey," Jason said, putting a careful hand on Mike's shoulder.

Mike's body jerked, and he pulled a silver knife from under the couch pillow.

Jason jumped back and held his hands up. "Whoa, pal! It's just me."

Mike slumped back and tossed the knife onto the couch next to him. "You scared the shit out of me, Jason! What's the matter?"

"Sheriff Briggs was just here," Jason said.

"What? Why the hell didn't you wake me?" Mike jumped up and looked out the window.

"He already left," Sami said. "But I'm sure he knows where Billy is."

"What'd he say?" Mike asked.

"He wanted to know where Abby was." Jason picked up the knife and plopped down on the couch next to him. "We told him we didn't know."

"Son of a bitch!" Mike shook his head and rubbed his temples. He took the knife from Jason. "What's he trying to do, capture her and kill her this time? What'd he say about Billy?"

"I told him you were inside with Billy, just to see his reaction and to see if he knew anything. He looked confused and said, 'Billy's home?' as if it he thought Billy was somewhere else. As if he *knows* Billy's gone."

"Dammit. I don't think Abby and my dad will be back anytime soon." Mike shoved his knife back into the sheath hooked to his belt and sighed.

"Well, spit it out dammit!" Jason glared at him.

Baffled by Jason's sudden outburst, Sami and Mike glanced at each other and back to Jason.

Jason squished his eyes shut and took a deep breath. When he opened them again, they were green.

"Oh no!" Sami's hand flew to her mouth.

"Holy shit!" Mike belted out.

"What?" Jason grew defensive.

Sami lowered her hand to her chest. "Your eyes are green."

"Very funny, guys!" Jason crossed his arms, taking the time to glare at each of them.

"We're not joking," Mike said.

Jason rubbed his eyes and opened them again. "Are they normal now?"

Sami shook her head.

"Dammit!" Jason hurried down the hall to the bedroom.

Mike jumped up and followed him.

Sami hobbled behind Mike, trying to keep up and wincing with each step.

Jason stood in front of the mirror, rubbing his eyes. "What the hell? Why won't they change back?" His arms fell to his sides. "I'm already turning into an animal!" He flopped back onto the bed and closed his eyes, resting his arm across them.

"Does the light hurt your eyes?" Sami asked.

"It's a little brighter now," he said, pouting like a child.

She pulled the curtain closed, darkening the room. "Are you gonna be okay?"

He moved his arm from his eyes. "I'm just gonna take a nap. Maybe they'll be normal again when I wake up."

"Sorry to break it to you," Mike said, "but they probably won't change back until Jessica's killed or until you gain control of your powers."

"Thanks for that, Mike. I feel so much better now," Jason said with sarcasm.

Sami sat on the bed next to Jason and held his hand. "I'm sorry. It won't be for long. They'll find Jessica. I *know* they will."

"Thanks, Sami, but until the bitch is dead, I'm pretty much screwed! It hasn't even been a whole day, and I already have green eyes, and I'm eating like a pig! Everything's a lot more sensitive too."

"What do you mean *sensitive*?" she asked.

Jason sat up and sighed. "I feel and hear everything ten times more than I used to." He held their interlocked hands up and broke free from her grasp to run his fingers through his hair. "Your hand feels ten times softer than it used to. I could hear Sheriff Briggs coming before he even turned down the road. I can even hear both of your hearts *beating* right now—like a frickin' drum. And I'm *always* starving. I thought I'd have more time before I started feeling different."

"Bummer," Mike said. "We can't fix this until Jessica is dead, but I can go make us some sandwiches." He left the room in a hurry.

Jason fell back and draped an arm over his eyes again.

"I'm sorry, Jason." Sami frowned, feeling helpless. She knew she couldn't better the situation, but she had to try. "Is there anything I can do? Anything you need?" she asked, caressing the back of his hand and trying to soothe his pain.

She gazed at his chest, admiring the way his T-shirt clung to his muscles, defining each one. A sudden desire consumed her and she longed to run her fingertips over each crevice. She slid her hand up his arm, not stopping until she reached his chest, enjoying every bit of his masculinity.

Jason peeked at her from under his arm, his brows furrowed.

"Your eyes, they're different now," she whispered. "They're almost golden. They're beautiful."

Jason sat up, his gaze locked with hers. "You're beautiful," he whispered. His head leaned in until their lips brushed against each other. He paused, mouth hovering over hers, their warm breaths mingling. "Sami," he said under his breath, and pressed his lips to hers, kissing her softly.

She closed her eyes as pleasure consumed her. Kissing Jason was wrong. *Terribly* wrong. But, for some reason, she couldn't push away from him. His kiss deepened, and his tongue slid into her mouth, taking over her senses. She was powerless against his sensual touch, and deep inside, she hungered for more. Giving in, she wrapped her arms around his neck and kissed him harder, pressing her body closer to his.

A low growl radiated deep within Jason's chest, vibrating through her mouth and snapping her back to reality. She tensed and pushed against his shoulders.

He arms tightened around her, and his kiss grew more intense. The more she struggled, the tighter he held her. His lips devoured hers as if he couldn't get enough.

She whimpered and pushed on his chest, trying to break free.

Mike barged into the room, grabbed Jason by the back of his shirt, and ripped him off the bed.

Jason stumbled back and fell to the floor, his eyes a piercing green.

Afraid and ashamed, Sami jumped off the bed and sprinted to the door, covering her swollen lips and trying to hold back tears.

Jason jumped up and a growl tore from his throat.

"Jason!" Mike shouted. "Snap out of it! Calm the hell down!"

He stared at Mike with fury in his eyes. When his gaze shifted to Sami, his eyes softened.

Sami let out a fearful whimper, not knowing what to expect from him next.

Jason pinched the bridge of his nose and shook his head. "I'm so sorry, Sami. I don't know what in the hell's the matter with me." He sat on the edge of the bed, shoulders slumped, and ran a shaky hand through his hair. "I can't stop feeling all these feelings. They're just coming at me all at once."

Mike scratched the back of his head and let out a heavy sigh. "Jason, it's gonna be okay. We'll figure something out."

"No!" Jason jumped up, motioning toward Sami. "Look at her! She's scared to death! I *kissed* her, Mike! My best friend's girlfriend! I kissed her and hurt her, and I couldn't stop! Who knows what would've happened if you hadn't come in here when you did!"

"It's just the overload of testosterone running through you," Mike assured.

"But I can't control it! What if I hurt her again?"

Sami felt awful for Jason. He was just as much a victim as she was. "I'm okay, really."

"No, you're not! You have a bruise on the corner of your mouth!" His emerald eyes glistened with tears, but he didn't let them fall. "I *hurt* you, Sami."

"Jason," she said, taking a step toward him.

"No! You just stay there!" he ordered, and his eyes turned yellow again. "I don't know if I can control myself. You shouldn't be near me."

She couldn't stand to see Jason in so much pain. She had to make him feel better. To soothe and comfort him. "Please don't push me away." She went to him and threw her arms around his neck.

Jason froze, his arms ridged at his sides, before he slowly wrapped them around her waist and hugged her back.

"I think he's right, Sami. You should stay back," Mike warned.

An overwhelming sensation of desire washed over her. She suddenly needed to be closer to him, to mold her body to his, and to kiss him again. Tangling her fingers through the hair on the back of his head, she crushed her lips to his.

"Sami!"

Mike's voice rang through her ears, but she ignored him.

Jason growled and pushed her away, sending her stumbling back.

Mike caught her by the shoulders.

Sami's emotions jumbled together into a confusing mess. Fear, shame, lust—she didn't know what to feel at the moment. One thing she did know was she didn't want to betray Billy. Yet, for some reason, she was powerless to the strong attraction she felt for this golden-eyed man before her.

"I'm so sorry, Jason. I can't control myself either! What's happening to me, Mike?" She spun around to face him

"My guess? Jason is also overloaded with pheromones," Mike said in a flat tone.

"Ugh!" Jason groaned, his face crumpled in disgust. "You mean she's lured to me like Dracula and his wenches?"

"Pretty much," Mike said.

"Billy's gonna be so mad at me." Sami looked up at the ceiling to keep the tears in.

Mike lifted one corner of his mouth. "No, he won't. I know he'll understand."

"But what does this mean?" she asked. "Does it mean I love Jason too?"

"No, it just means Jason is emitting a love potion you can't resist."

Sami glanced at Jason.

He shook his head and backed away, knocking over various items on the nightstand. With his hands in front of him he said, "Don't come any closer! I don't know if I can push you away this time."

Mike grabbed Sami by the shoulders and guided her to the doorway. "Jason, maybe you should stay in here and take that nap like you wanted. Sami and I'll go out in the living room."

"But I'm starving!" Jason grumbled.

"I'll bring you some food. Just chill out in here for a while and watch some TV or something. But don't leave! I don't think anyone else would understand your green eyes…or yellow ones. It seems the pheromone color is more of a golden yellow. Just stay put!" Mike ordered and headed down the hallway.

Sami paused in the doorway and stared at Jason. An intense longing filled her. She wanted to go to him again, but before she could take one step, Mike's hand clasped around her arm and he pulled her out of the room.

"I'll get this door fixed today too," Mike said, irritated.

"No! I'll do it!" Jason said, his tone eager. "It'll give me something to concentrate on. I'll just go get some tools out of the basement." He rushed out the sliding door before Mike had a chance to reply.

Mike didn't let go of Sami's arm. He led her straight to the kitchen table and sat her down in a chair. "You stay put too."

He went to the fridge and gathered everything he needed to make sandwiches.

Sami released a forlorn sigh and rested her head against the wall, staring at the crisscross patterns of her shoe laces.

Buddy pounced at her foot and darted into the living room.

A slight smiled formed, but it disappeared when she thought of Billy and how he would react to her betrayal. But it wasn't important at the moment. All that mattered was Billy's safety.

I wonder if Jessica is treating Billy the same way she treated me, or if—

Mouth agape, she snapped her head up to look at Mike. "Do you think Jessica puts off a love potion too? That maybe Billy can't keep his hands off her either?"

He thought for a moment before he shrugged. "Abby would know."

"When Jessica kidnapped me, that's what she wanted. She wanted my baby. *Billy's* baby. I think that's her plan. To get pregnant with his child."

"Let's just wait until Rick and Abby get back before we jump to any conclusions. Maybe they already found them and they're bringing Billy home as we speak."

Hoping he was right, she nodded and got up to help with lunch.

"I've got it," Mike said. "You sit and rest your ankles."

"They're feeling a little better. I took some ibuprofen a little bit ago. I'll take this to Jason." She reached for his plate, piled high with four sandwiches.

"Oh, no you won't." Mike chuckled under his breath, snatching up the plate. "I'll take it to him. You just sit down and eat before you get sick." After grabbing a cola from the refrigerator, he left the kitchen.

Sami couldn't stand not knowing how Jason was doing. She followed Mike, making cautious movements so he wouldn't hear her.

"Jason?" Mike asked, looking around the bedroom before heading into the backyard.

Sami crept to the glass door and peered outside, just in time to see Mike going down the basement steps. She slipped out the back door, keeping a safe distance behind him.

"Jason?" Mike called out when he reached the basement.

"I'm in here!" Jason shouted.

"What in the hell are you doing?" Mike strutted to the other room.

Sami crept up behind him and stood in the doorway.

Jason was sitting in the cage. His eyes were hazel again.

"Why are you in the cage?" Mike asked.

"Why do you think? I'm rendering myself powerless so I can't hurt Sami anymore. Or you. See—" he looked into the reflective silver bars "—my eyes are normal now." He motioned with his head behind Mike. "I don't even lust after Sami anymore."

Mike turned and glared at her. "I thought I told you to stay put!"

"I was too scared to be alone."

"*You're* too scared to be alone? The same person who runs off into the forest by herself every chance she gets?" With an irritated sigh, he opened the cage door. "Here's your lunch." He slid the plate over to Jason followed by the can of soda.

"Thanks!" Jason grinned. "But I don't think I can eat all that now."

"Then, save some for later," Mike said with a biting tone and closed the door.

Sami went to the cage and grasped the bars, relieved her attraction for Jason had ceased. "I don't want you anymore either." She smiled.

Jason's expression went flat. "Gee, thanks, Sami."

She giggled. "You know what I mean."

He winked and his gaze lowered to her mouth. "I'm sorry I hurt you."

Still ashamed of her actions, she stared at the shimmering red and blue soda can sitting next to Jason's knee. "I know. And I forgive you."

"Are we still friends?" he asked.

"Always."

"So—" Jason picked up a sandwich and chomped on it "—are you guys gonna keep me company? It's a little creepy down here all by myself."

Mike looked at him as if he were crazy. "You're kidding me? You're in the safest possible place you can be right now. Even Sami has more balls than that."

She giggled.

Jason pressed his lips together. "Not funny."

Mike smirked. "I'll go get our sandwiches, Sami.

"Yeah, you do that," Jason said.

Mike pointed to Sami. "Keep Jason safe, but from *outside* the cage."

"Ha frickin' ha, Mike." Jason rolled his eyes and took another huge bite out of his sandwich.

Sami smiled. "Don't be scared, Jason. I've got your back."

Jason shook his head. "Not you, too."

"And you—" Mike pointed to Jason "—stay *in* the cage."

"Trust me, this is the closest thing to normal I've felt all day. I'm not going anywhere."

Mike hesitated in the doorway, eyeing them both, before he finally left them alone.

Spotting a folding chair in the corner, Sami dragged it over to the cage and sat down. Still feeling awkward about their intimacy, she tapped her fingers on her knees, not knowing what to say.

"So."

"So." Jason raised his eyebrows. "Good thing Mike was here, huh?" He smiled uneasily and took a bite of his sandwich.

Sami's cheeks turned hot as she recalled the humiliating moment. "Good thing."

Jason gulped and cleared his throat. "Uh, Sami?"

"Yeah?"

"I know Billy's coming back, but if something should ever wrong—I just want you to know that I'll always be here for you. You know, to take care of you and protect you."

Her heart filled with awe. "I know."

"Good! You both actually listened for once!" Mike's voice broke the awkward moment. He handed a plate to Sami.

"Thanks." She took a bite of her sandwich—just what her grumbling stomach needed. Billy flooded her thoughts again and she wondered if he was eating. She remembered Jessica tossing her a lunch bag of food when she'd been caged up in her basement. But that had only been to keep her strength up for the baby.

Sami stared at her sandwich, with her lips hovering over it, feeling guilty.

"You have to eat," Mike said.

She sighed and took another bite, forcing it down and wondering what was taking Rick and Abby so long.

24

SAMI AND Mike jumped to their feet when Rick and Abby barreled into the basement.

"Why are you guys down here?" Abby asked. Her jaw dropped when she saw Jason sleeping in the cage. "Oh no! That's not good!"

"What? Why?" Mike asked, wide-eyed.

Rick rushed in. "Why is Jason in the cage?"

"He put himself there because he was already changing," Mike said. "His eyes turned green, then yellow. He couldn't control himself. He attacked Sami."

"What do you mean he attacked Sami?" Rick asked.

"He kissed her and couldn't stop himself," Mike said as if it were no big deal. "Sami couldn't keep her hands off him either."

"Uh!" Sami grunted, smacking Mike on the arm. "You didn't have to tell them that part!"

"Don't worry, Sami, its normal," Rick said. "It happens all the time with new werewolves. And human women don't have any control over the overwhelming effects of the pheromones. It's not your fault."

Sami still didn't feel any less guilty, but she nodded anyway.

"But, if he's already changing, you have to get Jason out of that cage now. It's like poison to him. He's not sleeping, he's sick," Rick said.

Mike opened the cage door and grabbed Jason by the ankles. He pulled until Jason's legs were touching the basement floor.

"What's going on?" Jason mumbled and his eyes fluttered open. "I *so* feel like I'm gonna throw up right now. I don't think those sandwiches were good, Mike." His eyes closed again.

"Please don't throw up." Rick gathered Jason into his arms and headed upstairs with everyone following close behind. Once they were in Sami's bedroom, he laid Jason on the bed. "He should feel better in a minute."

Mike's brow creased with worry. "I thought you said silver couldn't hurt him?"

"It shouldn't be able to yet, but when I came in, I could sense it had sickened him. For the next full moon being so far off, Jason's changing at an alarming rate. Usually, this only happens if someone's bitten a few days before the full moon."

"So, what are you saying?" Sami asked. "Do you think Jason's gonna change into a werewolf before the full moon? Before we even get a chance to kill Jessica? Is it gonna be too late to save him?"

"No," Rick said. "We can still save him, and no one has ever morphed for the first time without the full moon. It's just, for some reason, the symptoms he should be getting later have developed sooner."

Sami breathed a sigh of relief and headed over to the bed to check on Jason, but Mike stopped her with a firm grip on her elbow.

"I don't think so." Mike motioned with a nod for Abby to come and take Sami's arm. "You're not getting anywhere near Jason until we can figure something out."

"But I just wanna see how he's doing." She eyed Jason lying on the bed, wishing she could help him somehow.

Abby took Sami by the arm and led her out of the room. "Come on, let's go see if there's some chocolate around anywhere."

"But I'm fine." Sami tried to pull away, but Abby didn't relent. On her way out the door, Sami glanced over her shoulder, trying to get one last glimpse of Jason.

JASON SAT up, startled to see Mike and Rick standing at the foot of the bed, staring at him. "What's going on? Why am I up here again?"

Sami and Abby peeked through the doorway.

"The cage made you sick," Mike said. "Sorry, bud."

"What? That's just great!" Jason grumbled.

"Your eyes are green again, Jason," Sami said.

Jason glanced over at her. She watched him with curiosity in her soft brown eyes. He had a sudden urge to take her into his arms.

"Yeah, this isn't gonna work," Mike said, stepping in front of Jason to block his view.

Abby giggled. "My, what golden eyes you have."

Jason rubbed his eyes. "What, you mean they're yellow again? How in the hell do I control these things?"

"What do you suggest we do now, Dad?" Mike asked.

"I guess we babysit."

Mike pinched the bridge of his nose and sighed. "But how is this gonna work when you two leave to find Jessica? Hey, wait a minute, did you pick up her trail?"

"We went to where Jason and Sami saw her last and found some tracks along a hiking trail in the forest. But we couldn't pick up Jessica's scent, for some reason—only the scents of recent hikers. She didn't even leave any blood behind, so, wherever she went, she was careful. There was some human blood, but thankfully, it wasn't Billy's. We followed the tracks for a short distance, but they backtracked to where they started. She must've gotten away in a car. There were tire marks on the sides of the road all over that area. Did you guys notice a vehicle parked nearby?"

Sami shook her head.

Jason thought for a moment, but couldn't recall seeing any vehicles nearby. "No, but we didn't notice much at the time with a monster chasing us."

"It's not important," Rick said. "Jessica can't be too far. We checked to the west and south but didn't find anything. We're going to rest for a while then head north and east tonight."

"So, what are we gonna do with these two?" Mike asked with a troubled look in his eyes. "Jason's getting stronger by the minute. I don't think I can keep him under control anymore."

Jason glared at Mike. "It's not like I'm gonna hurt you or anything. I'm a protector, right?"

"I don't think you'll physically hurt us, Jason," Mike said. "I meant, how in the hell am I supposed keep you from trying to mate with Sami?"

Jason focused on Sami. Just the sight of her made him horny, let alone her sweet fragrance. He inconspicuously inhaled her scent. *Stop it, dammit! You're acting like a pervert!*

Everyone followed Jason's gaze to Sami, whose cheeks were flushed. She averted her eyes to the floor.

"Wow!" Abby giggled. "He *is* overloaded with pheromones! If I were human, I wouldn't be able to help myself either. I almost can't now."

Mike stared at Abby, then Jason.

Jason raised his hands. "Don't look at me. I'm the victim here, remember?" When he didn't receive a response, he peeled back the bandage on his arm to reveal the bite wounds. "Has everyone forgotten I was bitten trying to save Billy?"

Everyone's eyes widened.

Fear gripped Jason's heart. "Oh shit. Is it infected?" he asked, afraid to look. Cringing, he opened one eye and took a peek. The bite had healed, leaving behind tiny scars decorated with stitches. He took a closer look with both eyes and rubbed a hand over his arm. "What the hell?"

"Wow!" Sami wriggled out of Abby's grasp and moved closer.

Mike grabbed Jason's wrist and flipped his arm over to inspect the other side.

Rick stepped into the huddle. "Huh, you already have healing power. That's amazing!"

Afraid he'd lust for Sami again, Jason avoided eye contact with her but could sense her creeping closer. Distracted by his arm, no one else even noticed. Before he knew it, she was standing right next to him, her presence driving him crazy.

Not being able to stand the sensual torture, Jason wrapped his arms around her waist with lightning speed and whirled her onto the bed, covering her body with his. Everything in the room faded into the background as he gazed into her passion filled eyes.

"Dammit, Jason!" Rick roared and yanked him back.

Jason landed on his feet. Now that he wasn't touching Sami anymore, his lust for her lessened.

Sami sat up and straightened her shirt, looking lost and vulnerable.

"Damn!" Rick's eyes beamed with amusement. "I've never seen anything like it. This is unbelievable. It's *unheard* of."

"This isn't some science experiment, Dad!" Mike retorted. "How in the hell are we gonna keep your future daughter-in-law and your son's best friend *apart*?"

Sami furrowed her brow. "Wait, how'd you know Billy and I are getting married?"

Mike sighed and raised a hand out to his side. "Really? It's pretty obvious."

Sami flashed an uneasy smile and lowered her head.

"Hmm…" Rick rubbed his chin, and his eyes glazed over as if he were on another planet. A few seconds passed before his eyes shot to Jason and he smiled. "Let's see if you're strong yet. Pick me up."

Jason gave him an unsure look, but couldn't resist the temptation of a challenge. He placed a firm grip on each side of Rick's waist and hoisted him over his head with little effort.

"Holy shit!" Jason grinned and lowered Rick back to the ground.

"You are *very* strong," Sami said and reached out to touch Jason's bicep, but Mike slapped her hand away. "Ouch!" She glared at him, rubbing the back of her hand.

"Come on, Jason—" Rick headed for the back door "—let's go outside and try something."

Jason glanced at Sami, fighting the urge to gather her back into his arms.

Abby narrowed her eyes and stepped in front of Sami, blocking his view.

"Get out!" Mike shoved Jason toward the door.

Rick reached his hand in and grabbed Jason by the shirt, yanking him out into the backyard.

"All right! Geez!" Jason snapped, giving up on Sami for the time being.

"Okay, watch carefully." Facing the house, Rick crouched down and leapt straight up, landing on the roof.

"That was awesome!" Jason grinned.

"Holy shit! That *was* awesome!" Mike agreed. He pointed to Sami, who stood in the doorway, and said, "You can watch from right there."

Rick jumped back down and landed next to Jason with a loud thud. "Now, you try."

"Okay, here goes nothing." Jason crouched down just as Rick had done.

"Wait," Mike interjected, "maybe he shouldn't try the roof. What if he can't control his landing and falls through it?"

"Good point," Rick said, eyeing the humongous pine tree in the middle of the yard. "See if you can jump to that branch instead." He pointed to a limb jutting out from the others, with enough clearance above it for Jason to stand.

"Are you crazy?" Jason said. "That's like twenty feet high. What if I fall?"

"I'll catch you," Rick reassured. "Now jump."

Jason took a deep breath and crouched down. Tensing his leg muscles, he sprang from the ground with as much force as he could gather and flew through the air, past the target branch to the one ten feet above it. Needled limbs thwacked him in the mouth, poked his face, and jabbed the back of his neck.

"Ugh!" He sputtered, swatting them away. "Awesome idea, Rick," he said with dull enthusiasm.

"Damn, Jason!" Mike shouted.

"That was unbelievable!" Rick grinned.

"Yeah, really frickin' great! Now, how in the hell am I supposed to get down?" He scratched at the irritation spreading across his neck.

"That's gotta be thirty feet high," Mike said to his dad.

"He probably could've jumped higher if he hadn't been hindered by all the branches above him," Rick said.

"Blah, blah, blah!" Jason snapped. "Either I have fleas, or this shit is poking the hell outta my neck! Now, get me the frick down from here!"

Rick chuckled. "You're going to have to jump down."

"What? I can't *jump* down! I'll break my legs!"

"No, you won't. Just do like I did. Focus on one spot on the ground and jump to it. Pretend you're only jumping four feet down. It makes it easier that way."

"Sure, I'm only jumping four feet instead of almost forty, Rick. Thanks, that really helps," Jason said, oozing with sarcasm. "But I'm not jumping. So, you can just get your furry ass up here and get me down!"

Rick sighed and glanced around, his eyes settling on Sami. He grinned. "You can come out now, Sami."

Abby was reluctant to let her pass, but she stepped aside and motioned Sami forward with a swoop of her hand.

Sami rushed to the base of the tree. "Jason, are you okay?" Her fists rested on her hips and her eyes bore into Rick's. "You have to get him!"

"You're going to have to jump down yourself," Rick said, staring up at him.

"What if he gets killed?" Sami said. "He's not a werewolf yet. Save him!" she demanded.

"I'm not a crazed monster yet, Rick. Not until the full moon. I'll wait until then to jump down if I have to."

"I'll tell you what, if you jump on your own, I'll let you kiss Sami again," Rick said.

"What?" Jason couldn't believe what he'd just heard. Just the thought of kissing her again sparked a sexual desire for her, and Rick's permission just obliterated the last bit of will power left.

Mike looked at his dad as if he were crazy. "What? You can't do that!"

Rick turned to his son. "I'm trying to get him out of the tree."

Ignoring the argument ensuing below him, Jason concentrated on his target—Sami. He let go of the tree and effortlessly leapt to the ground, landing in a crouching position with a loud thud. A twinge of pain shot through his ankles, but he paid no attention to it. He gently cupped Sami's chin and guided her mouth to his. All of a sudden, he jerked back, and Sami stood ten feet away from him with an annoyed Abby at her side. Irritated, he yanked his arm out of Rick's vice-like grip.

Mike jumped in front of Sami and glared at his dad. "What in the hell kind of stupid idea was that?"

Rick sighed. "Damn, I missed seeing him jump."

"Too bad. I'm not doing it again!" Jason said, more frustrated than ever.

Just past Mike's shoulder, Sami's angelic face came into view, but she averted her shame-filled eyes. Abby took Sami by the hand and led her to the back steps.

Jason felt like a complete jackass. "Just frickin' great!" He squished his eyes shut and whirled around to face Rick. "I'm a frickin' animal, Rick! An animal that attacks women!"

Rick shook his head. "You'll learn to control yourself. It's a natural instinct to want to mate with someone you find attractive."

"So, what does all this prove, Dad?" Mike asked, his jaw tense. "That I'm no match for Jason when you and Abby leave tonight? There's *no way* I can keep them apart!"

"You don't have to." Rick flashed a huge grin. "Jason's strong enough to come with us."

Mike stared at his dad with a blank look on his face. Then, he tilted his head back and exhaled as if the weight on his shoulders had been lifted. "You don't know how frickin' relieved I am! I thought for sure Billy was gonna come home and kick my ass." He gave Jason a warning glare. "But he sure as *hell* is gonna kick *yours*!"

Disgusted with himself, Jason grunted. "Yeah, yeah, I hope he does. I deserve it." He glanced at Sami, wishing he could hold her again. A distraction is what he needed, as far from Sami as possible. "Can we go to your house or something, Rick? I can't keep my mind off her when she's this close to me. I feel like the worst friend ever."

"Don't be so hard on yourself." Rick gave Jason a swat on the back. "It's normal. You don't really get control over it until you morph for the first time, but it takes months, sometimes years to gain complete control over your emotions. Lucky for you, you won't get that chance."

Mike harrumphed. "You mean lucky for Billy and Sami."

"I'm going to take Jason up to the clearing to have him practice some more," Rick said.

"Good luck with that," Mike said as if he'd had enough for one day. "I'm gonna stay here and make sure Sami doesn't try to sneak out again. I'm sure she'll try since you're going to the lake." He shot her a knowing glare.

Sami narrowed her eyes at him and stormed into the house.

"Good idea, Son. Abby, you should rest. We have a long night ahead of us. Okay, Jason, see if you can keep up," Rick said.

"Don't you have to morph first?" Jason asked.

"No. I'm not as quick in human form, but I'm still fast. I can outrun most animals."

Jason smirked. Excitement brewed in his chest. This was one lesson he was eager to learn.

Rick grinned and darted into the forest, via the trial.

Jason thrust forward as if he'd been running fast all his life. Instead of following Rick's lead, Jason made his own path straight through the trees. The fresh air rushing against his face was exhilarating, giving him a sense of power and freedom. He sped around trees and leapt effortlessly over bushes, enjoying his newfound ability.

Within a minute, Jason reached the clearing. He jerked to a halt next to one of the boulders overlooking the lake, but the momentum sent him stumbling forward and teetering on the very edge of the meadow. His arms flung up, and he caught his balance and leaned back.

"Whoa that was close." He clutched his chest and sat on one of the boulders.

Rick broke through the tree line.

"It's about time!" Jason shouted, deciding not to admit he'd almost tumbled down the hill. "I was beginning to think you weren't gonna show!"

Rick came to an abrupt stop, his eyes full of amazement. "How in the hell did you do that? No werewolf can run that fast in human form."

Jason's excitement dwindled, and irritation took over. "I guess I'm just special!" he snapped. "And I'm not a werewolf yet! Now, can we get this over with? I wanna get back to Sa—" he almost said her name but quickly corrected himself "—to the house. I'm getting hungry."

Rick gave him a curious stare, focusing on his eyes.

"I respect you, Rick, but if you try to kiss me, I'll hit you!"

Rick chuckled under his breath. "Your eyes, they just switched from yellow to green. Good thing. You were starting to worry me for a minute."

Jason raised one corner of his mouth. "Very funny."

"I know you're having trouble controlling all your emotions, Jason. It'll get easier. But don't worry, we won't be long. I'm getting hungry too."

"Good," Jason said. "So, what do you want me to do?"

"Let's see if you can run fast enough to glide across the water."

He looked down at his running shoes, then the lake. "Seriously? I'm gonna sink."

"You'll do fine."

"Well, I'm not getting my shoes wet." He slipped them off, along with his socks, and rolled his pant legs up to his knees. He took a deep breath, mentally preparing himself for the impossible feat. A bead of sweat trickled down his temple and he wiped it on the shoulder of his T-shirt. The thought of doing a face-plant into the icy water brought a smirk to his lips. "Here goes nothing."

He darted down the hill, ignoring the small rocks digging uncomfortably into his soles, and sped across the top of the water. *Splat, splat, splat.* The sound reminded him of jumping in water puddles as a kid. Each splash faded behind him with every stride forward. Halfway across, his fear of kerplunking straight down dissipated, and before he knew it, he'd successfully glided across the lake and stood on the other side.

He cupped his hands around his mouth and shouted to Rick, "Satisfied?"

"See if you can jump back across!" Rick's voice echoed toward him.

Jason eyed the span of water, about twenty-five yards across, skeptical about a jump that distance. But, after jumping forty feet into a tree and running across the water, anything was possible.

He jumped to the top of the small hill behind him to get a running start. After a deep breath, he sprinted forward to the water's edge and pushed off with one foot. As he sailed over the lake, he spiraled his legs forward, as if he were still running, until the ground on the other side grew near. Right before landfall, he brought both feet together and planted them onto the grassy bank with a jarring thud next to Rick. Jason stumbled forward and fell to his hands and knees. With irritation brewing, he bounced to his feet and spun around to face his hard-core trainer.

Rick closed his gaping mouth and grinned. "Wow! I've never seen anyone in human form be able to run across the top of the water or jump that far."

"What?" Jason barked. "You mean I was a crash test dummy? What if I sank?"

"Well, I know you can swim. We had to test it." He pointed to a cluster of trees. "See how high you can jump. Careful not to land on the very top branches, they might not be strong enough to support your weight."

He eyed Rick suspiciously. "This isn't another test no one else has tried in human form, is it?"

Rick let out a small chuckle. "No. You'll be fine. Now jump."

Ready for testing to be over, Jason stomped up the hill to the boulders. Sitting on the smaller one, he dried his feet with his socks and pulled them back on, followed by his shoes. Hunger pangs rumbled through his stomach, and his irritation grew.

"We're done after this, right, Rick?"

"Yes. Then we'll eat."

Jason tromped through the weeds, to the group of trees Rick had pointed out. He focused on a branch on the largest and sturdiest looking tree in the cluster.

"Okay, here goes nothing." He jutted forward and leapt high into the tree, landing as close to the top as possible. The limb flexed downward, and he scrambled to grasp the one above his head before he plummeted to his death. On his tiptoes, he threw one arm up and clutched the branch. With his heart beating erratically, he let out a sigh of relief.

"Rick is gonna be the death of me," he mumbled under his breath.

"I heard that," Rick shouted. "Good job! Now, jump down!"

Jason eyed the ground and gulped. *Everything down there looks so small. I'm gonna die for sure this time. My legs are gonna jam up into my spine, and I'm gonna die.*

"I don't know, Rick, I'm up higher than I was before. It isn't as easy without Sami standing at the bottom."

"Sami's out of the question this time. Now, jump!"

Ah, screw it! If I can leap seventy-feet across water, I can do this. Right? I mean, Rick wouldn't be having me do this if he thought it would kill me. Would he? He peered down, eyeing Rick's jovial smile—or wicked smile. He couldn't see it clearly from so high up.

Shaking the thought from his head, he inflated his lungs with as much air as he could, slapped a reassuring hand over his racing heart, and stepped off the branch. As the ground neared, the thought of dying sent a fearful twinge through his veins. He held his arms in front of him and planted both feet firmly, hammering them into the hardened dirt at the base of the tree.

Immense jolts of pain shot through his ankles, more so than when he'd jumped down to kiss Sami earlier. "Shit! That one hurt! I'm broken." He cringed and limped away to walk it off. The pain diminished within seconds. "Huh, feels better already." He grinned and jumped up and down to make sure they just hadn't turned numb.

"I can't believe it, Jason! You're just as strong as I am, if not stronger. And you're healing. I heard bone cracking when you landed. Now you're fine. And you haven't even morphed yet. I think you're even stronger than Jessica. Just imagine how powerful you'd be if you did morph."

"Huh uh! I'm not morphing! I'm gonna help you find and kill Jessica before the next full moon, and that's it. I'm tired of all this anger. And all this hunger. And most of all, I'm tired of trying to mate with my best friend's girlfriend!" A ferocious growl rumbled through his chest.

"I don't want you to be a werewolf, Jason. But if you were…" Rick rubbed his chin and a spark flickered in his eyes. "…I believe you'd be the most powerful werewolf ever."

"Sorry, but we won't get the chance to find out," Jason replied. "Can we go now? I'm starving!"

"Race you!" Rick sped off and disappeared into the forest.

Jason grinned and darted after him, gliding with ease over bushes and around trees. Spotting Rick ahead, Jason lunged forward and whizzed past him. Within seconds, he broke through the barrier of trees, darted across Sami's yard, and up the porch steps. He opened the door and it slammed against the wall, bouncing back at him.

Sami screamed and jumped off the couch, clutching her knife. "What the hell, Jason?"

"Sami—" Jason held his hands in front of him "—just don't come any closer, and I think I'll be all right. I feel a little more in control now that I've released some of my frustration."

Mike stood from the recliner and shot him a disapproving glare.

Jason flashed a sheepish grin. "Sorry about the door though." He motioned to it with a thumb over his shoulder. "Guess I still need to work on my strength."

The fear in Sami's eyes dissipated and a smile formed. "Your eyes are normal again."

"Really?" Jason blinked. "Are they still normal?"

Her eyes twinkled. "Yeah. Does that mean you're normal again?"

Rick appeared in the doorway. "You are fast! What happened to your eyes?"

"I don't know. I just came in, and they were normal again." Jason shrugged.

Mike strutted up to Jason and looked him in the eyes. Without warning, he slapped Jason's cheek.

Jason growled, and his eyes turned green. "What the hell was that for?"

"Just checking." Mike grinned. "Your eyes are still green."

"Asshole!" Jason glared at him. "You're lucky I don't hit you back."

Mike smirked. "Guess I am. But you know you deserve it."

"See if you can switch them back to hazel," Rick said.

Intent on payback, Jason closed his eyes and imagined kissing Sami. He opened them again, eager to see Mike's reaction.

Mike's smile turned into an angry pucker. "He didn't say to think about Sami, dumbass!"

Jason let out a devious chuckle before he closed his eyes and tried again. In his thoughts, he sprawled back in the recliner with the remote in one hand and an icy cold beer in the other. His eyes popped open and he looked at everyone. "Well?"

Sami smiled. "It worked! Does that mean we can be in the same room now?"

Rick shrugged. "I guess we'll find out."

"Good." Sami yawned and sat back down on the couch.

"Since you have so much energy now, why don't you help me with dinner?" Mike asked.

"As long as you don't slap me again," Jason grumbled.

Mike chuckled and went into the kitchen.

Jason glanced at Sami, noticing the darkness under her eyes. His chest grew heavy. She suffered from lack of sleep, a broken heart, and now, the burden of betrayal.

"Sami, I'm sorry," he said.

She stared at him with shame in her eyes, but gave way to a smile. "I know. It's okay."

Rick sat in the recliner. "I owe you an apology too, Sami. I shouldn't have used you as a prize for motivating Jason."

Sami's cheeks turned pink and she pressed her lips together. "Apology accepted." She leaned her head back and turned her focus to the TV, obviously wanting the conversation to be over.

Rick's gaze also shifted to the TV.

Stomach rumbling, Jason meandered into the kitchen to help Mike prepare the meal. They chopped potatoes, carrots, and onions, and dumped them around the seasoned pot roast. Jason peered into the living room. Sami and Rick were sound asleep. He nudged Mike with his elbow and raised a finger to his lips.

25

I AM standing on an overgrown path with pine trees towering over me. Dark shadows loom all around this desolate part of the forest, and I am afraid.

"Sami…" Billy's voice echoes all around.

"Billy? Where are you?" I shout, anxious to see him again.

"Sami…I'm here," he calls again.

Following his voice, I glide effortlessly until I reach a mountainous wall of rock—a dead-end.

"Billy! Where are you?" My voice bounces off the rocky wall.

He doesn't answer.

"Billy?" I frantically search along the base of the rocky mountain, but he's nowhere in sight. Desperate to find him, I look up at the trees lining the top of the cliff. One of the pines threatens to fall. Leaning forward, its shadow points to a large hole in the cliff-side.

Sami opened her eyes and sucked in a fearful breath, startled to see Jason, Mike, and Rick standing over her. She sat up and threw a shaky hand over her chest.

"Another nightmare?" Jason asked.

She nodded. "How'd you know?"

"It's a little bit of a heart stopper when you start shouting Billy's name in your sleep," Jason said.

Rick sat beside her on the couch. "Do you get these nightmares often?"

"Sometimes," she answered.

He studied her carefully. "Do they ever come true?"

"Sort of. I guess." She shrugged.

"What were you just dreaming about?" he asked.

"About finding Billy." She ran a hand through her hair to smooth it, trying to preoccupy her mind so she wouldn't cry. Her heart felt heavier and emptier after dreaming about Billy.

"Tell me," Rick urged.

Sami took in a deep breath and exhaled, finally gaining control of her emotions enough to keep the tears in. "He was calling to me. Calling out for help I think." She paused, trying to remember the fuzzy details. "I was in the forest, and I could hear him calling my name, but I couldn't find him."

"Tell me everything you remember," Rick encouraged.

"I was on an overgrown path in an area of the forest I'd never been before. The same one I dreamed about this morning."

"You had the same dream this morning?" Rick asked.

She nodded. "I followed the path, and it led me to a dead-end." Tears threatened again, blurring her vision. She reached for her locket and swirled her finger over the smooth metal.

Rick patted her arm. "It's okay, Sami. I know this is hard for you. Is there anything else you remember?"

She rubbed her forehead, trying to concentrate. "I reached a dead-end at the base of a giant rock wall. Like a mountain or a cliff-side."

"Did you see anything else? Anything out of the ordinary about this cliff?" he asked, his voice growing with anticipation.

"Uhhh." She squished her eyes shut and envisioned the dream. "Oh!" She flung open her eyes again. "There were trees on the cliff, and one was leaning like it was about to fall. Its shadow pointed to a cave."

Rick grinned. "I'll be damned." He shook his head. "It's you."

"What? What'd she do?" Mike asked, his face crinkled with

confusion.

"I know exactly where that cave is," Rick said. "It's to the east of us, deep in the mountains."

They all stared at Rick with dumbfounded looks on their faces.

"You're the one." Rick's eyes danced with amazement. "You're the *seer*."

"The see *what*?" Jason belted out.

"The seer. Seers help protect humans from the dangers of the supernatural, and are naturally drawn to areas of higher paranormal activity. They all possess the ability to see and sense danger, but not always in the same way." He turned to Sami. "It seems, through your dreams, you can see when killer werewolves are a threat to those around you. And, apparently, the dreams don't stop until the endangered person is no longer in danger.

"A lot of side effects come with your powers as your body and mind adapt. The emotional rollercoaster you've been on, and the nausea when you don't eat. You might feel dizzy or faint too."

Sami sat in utter shock, trying to absorb everything Rick had just said. *How can I be a seer? Have powers? I'm even afraid of the dark. He has to be mistaken. I'm not built to handle this kind of responsibility. Am I?*

Mike stared at Sami with a puzzled look on his face. "Are you sure, Dad?"

Rick nodded, his eyes still filled with disbelief. "I'm sure. I should've put two-and-two together and caught onto it earlier. Now, you need to be aware of your symptoms and take necessary precautions. You know, like sitting down if you feel dizzy or faint. It's important to eat when you're hungry too. It'll help you to *see* clearer. You'll also need to consume a few more calories to keep up with your transformation. You'll feel nauseous if you don't. Don't worry, it won't be long before you adapt and feel normal again.

"And, since you're still new, don't be upset if you aren't able to see and help everyone around you right away. It takes time to tune into your power and control it. As you become more skilled, your ability to detect when danger is near will get stronger, like Harry's did."

Sami's breath caught in her throat. "What? My grandpa was a *seer*?

You mean, he knew there were werewolves all this time because he could *see* them?"

Rick patted her on the arm. "Yes, Harry was a seer. That's how he knew about Jessica. He didn't have nightmares like you, but his senses were very astute. He could sense when werewolves where within a ten-mile radius, give or take. If he tuned into them, he could see where they were. He could also feel when danger was near."

Sami frowned as guilt filled her heart. "He warned me in the hospital. He told me and Billy the werewolves were out there and they were gonna get us. But we thought he'd lost his mind. Everyone did." Her shoulders slumped forward. She recalled the last time she'd seen her grandpa, withered and dying in his hospital bed, wishing she had known the truth back then.

"All he needed was someone who believed in him before he passed away. But he had no one. He died alone." Tears brimmed and slipped down Sami's cheeks. "We should've listened to him and helped him somehow. He just died with everyone thinking he was crazy."

Jason placed a gentle hand on her shoulder. "We had no way of knowing then, Sami."

Rick's eyes saddened. "I didn't even know he was in the hospital or of his passing until after the fact. I would've come back sooner if I had."

Mike grabbed a box of tissues from the breakfast bar and held them in front of her.

Sami snatched a tissue and wiped her cheeks dry. "How do you know he was a seer?" she asked and sucked in a ragged breath.

Rick sighed. "Harry. He found me a couple of years back when I was passing through the area, and he tried to encourage me to come home." With guilt in his eyes, he glanced at his son.

Mike furrowed his brow. "You mean Harry knew you were alive?"

Rick nodded. "Only for the last two years. I guess I was finally close enough for him to *see* me."

Sami sat back and crossed her arms, waiting to hear Rick's explanation.

Rick lowered his eyes and let out a heavy sigh. "When Harry found me, I told him about what I'd been through. He told me about him being a seer." His gaze shifted to Mike. "About how you and your brother and sister were doing—" he gulped "—and he told me about your mother. I had no idea what had happened to her until then." He paused and shook his head, as if he were clearing his pain.

"Harry also told me about Jessica being a killer and moving in with her uncle. Harry tried to get me to come home, but I was determined to not drag you all into this life. I made him give me his word he wouldn't say anything to you." Rick shrugged and rested his elbows on his knees, clasping his fingers together.

"I figured if I stayed away it'd be safer for all of you. The sheriff assured me he'd keep Jessica under control. I had no idea Jessica would cause so much trouble. All the killer werewolves I've ever run into have always kept under the radar. They don't want to be discovered."

Mike ran a quick hand across his chin and clenched his jaw. "Why couldn't Harry see you get attacked? Why couldn't he have warned you?"

"Harry didn't have visions of the future. He had a strong sense of werewolves in the vicinity and knew when trouble was near. But he wasn't here at the time of the attack. He was on vacation—too far away to sense anything here.

"Since I was relocated up north right after being bitten, all Harry knew when he came home was that I had been killed by a wolf. When he'd finally found me years later, he'd told me he had a feeling a werewolf had attacked me, and that I might be alive out there somewhere. But, since I was out of range of his seeing ability, there was no way for him to know for sure."

Mike looked at his dad as if he were crazy. "You were *attacked*, Dad. Why did you think *we* were safe here if *you* weren't even safe here? Why didn't you come home?"

Rick stood and looked Mike square in the eyes. "I was a *werewolf*, Son! A *monster*! I had become the very thing you all were afraid of as children. The scary thing that went bump in the night. *I* was suddenly the thing I was supposed to protect you from. To me, there was no coming back." He let out an unsteady breath. "The sheriff gave me his word he would look after all of you and keep you safe. That he would keep killers away from you. He made me believe he had our best interests at heart."

Mike scratched the back of his head and the tension in his eyes softened. "I understand. And, until recently, Sheriff Briggs did watch out for us." He glanced out the window. "We had no idea werewolves were out there until Jessica went off the deep end."

"You have every right to be upset with me, Mike. Not a day goes by that I don't regret my decision. I just hope I can make up for it someday." He turned his attention back to Sami. "And, Sami, we aren't going to let your grandpa's efforts die with him. We're going to finish what he'd set out to do. After we get Billy back and destroy Jessica, we're going to protect Wolf Hill from any more killer werewolves."

A sense of duty replaced Sami's remorse. *Rick's right. Instead of dwelling on Grandpa's suffering, I need to honor his legacy by picking up where he left off. I'm the new generation of seer here, and it's time to embrace my gift.*

Sami took in a deep breath and nodded, feeling more confident than she had in a long time.

"So, you know where Billy is now?" she asked.

"Yes." Rick grinned. He clasped Mike's shoulder. "Son, go wake Abby."

"Hell yeah!" Jason shouted as he punched his fist into his other hand. "Let's go kick some ass!"

Mike sprinted up the stairs, two at a time.

Not able to contain her excitement, Sami jumped up and threw her arms around Jason's neck, giving him a big squeeze.

He chuckled and lifted her off the ground in a tight embrace. "That's right! Billy's coming home."

Sami pulled away and faced him. "Uh oh, your eyes are gold again."

BILLY OPENED his eyes, trying to focus on his blurry surroundings. "Shit!" he mumbled and attempted to sit up, but the movement was cut short by a sharp pain in his side and a rope binding his wrist to a bed post.

"What the hell?" He tried to bend his knees, but his ankles were also tied. His eyes shot to the black satin boxers he wore and the elastic bandage around his ribs.

"Dammit! Where in the fuck are my clothes?" He twisted his wrist and pulled, trying to loosen the rope, but the knot was too tight. "Son of a bitch!" Teeth clenched, he threw his head back against the pillow.

"You like saying that, don't you?" Jessica appeared in the entryway, grinning and wearing a red satin negligee. "Well, you certainly have the bitch part right. How's your face? It looks terrible. I guess I hit you a little too hard." She frowned, and her bottom lip jutted out. "And I'm sorry about your ribs. Or *rib*. I only heard one crack when I kicked you. But it was your fault. You shouldn't have punched me."

"What'd you do with my clothes?" he snapped.

"Oh, come now. Such a lot of hostility for someone's who's completely helpless at the moment, don't you think? Do I hear an apology coming?"

He opened his mouth to tell her off, but instead, inhaled a deep breath to calm the anger. "Sorry."

"That's better."

"Can you untie me now?" he asked in as polite a tone as he could manage. "I'd like to get dressed."

She giggled. "No silly, you wouldn't do things my way, so, now you don't have a choice."

"I will. I'll do things your way," he coaxed.

"Will you wrap your arms around me, make mad passionate love to me, and give me a baby?"

He tensed, realizing what the whole kidnapping was about—the same reason she'd kidnapped Sami—to steal his offspring.

"What's the matter? You're not being shy, are you?"

"No." He gulped, and his gut knotted. "But I can't very well wrap my arms around you if I'm all tied up, can I?"

Her smile fell flat. "Nice try. But I don't need you to wrap your arms around me. All I need from you is your seed."

Shit! This can't be happening! What in the hell am I gonna do?

He yanked at the rope binding his wrist and kicked to loosen the ropes around his ankles, but they didn't budge.

"Maybe you should use your other hand? I didn't tie it up."

He eyed his broken hand, contemplating on whether to use it. "Dammit, Jessica, untie me!"

Her amber eyes brightened and turned to an angry red. "Not until you give me a baby." She sauntered to the bed and laid next to him.

Billy continued his frantic struggle with the ropes, grunting in frustration.

"Stop struggling! You're going to get all sweaty and sticky," she grumbled.

"Then, untie me, and I'll do whatever you want!"

"I don't believe you," she said, running her fingertips across his chest.

"Dammit! Get your mangy paws off me!"

"See, I knew you were lying." She giggled and continued her seductive toying, swirling her fingers over his chest hair.

His mouth crinkled with disgust. "Okay, Jessica. Look, just untie me." He tried to keep the desperation out of his voice, but the closer to her sick ritual they got, the more frustrated he became. "I can't do this tied up! Whatever you want, I'll do it! I'll cooperate!"

"Let's see." She leaned down and pressed her mouth to his.

Billy clenched his eyes shut, resisting the urge to turn his head away. He lay perfectly still, cringing inwardly.

She lifted her head for a moment and kissed him again, lips closed and with more force than the first time.

Billy's stomach flip-flopped. Though he wanted nothing more than to bite Jessica's lips off, he relaxed his tense muscles, letting her have her way.

Jessica's tongue jutted past his lips and into his mouth. Billy flung open his eyes, fighting the urge to gag. It felt as if a slug were crawling in his mouth, slithering around his tongue. The urge to push her away intensified. Instead, he obeyed her unspoken demand, forcing his tongue out to swirl around hers.

She raised her head to look into his eyes.

"Will you untie me now?" he whispered, out of breath, wishing he could spit the residue of her saliva from his mouth.

"Yes." She smiled and untied his ankles first, then his wrist. "I just wanted to see if I could get you to kiss me of your own free will before

I used my magical powers to make you *lust* for me."

He sat up carefully, bearing the pain in his side through clenched teeth. "What do you mean *magical powers*?" It didn't really matter what she meant. He was just stalling for time, trying to figure out a way to get himself out of a hopeless situation.

She eased off the bed and stood at the foot of it. "These magical powers." Her eyes changed from red to pink, almost fluorescent.

He stared at her, waiting for some miraculous phenomenon to occur, but nothing happened. He shrugged his shoulders. "I don't see anything."

"Just be patient. You'll feel it soon." Her lips curled into a seductive smile.

He cocked his jaw to one side, wondering whether to run or make Jessica so mad she'd knock him out again. Either way, he'd probably end up tied to the bed with more broken bones.

A lightheaded tingle clouded Billy's mind, almost as if he'd had a couple of beers. He focused on Jessica's red satin negligee—the way it clung to her curves. Sweeping upward, his eyes met her sultry gaze, which sparked a sudden urge to go to her. To wrap his arms around her delicate frame and pull her against him.

"No!" He shook his head, trying to fight the overwhelming aphrodisiac. "No! I love Sami!"

Jessica pressed her lips into a smug smirk. "No use fighting it. I'm too powerful." With lust in her eyes, she eased onto the foot of the bed, crawled across it on her hands and knees, and perched next to him.

Billy looked away and squeezed his eyes shut, hoping it was just her gaze drawing him to her.

"Look at me." She grabbed his chin and turned his head.

Billy tried to resist, but the euphoria was too strong. He opened his eyes and looked at her.

Jessica released her hold on him and waited.

Not able to contain the mounting desire any longer, Billy wrapped an arm around her waist and crushed his lips to hers.

26

EXCITEMENT BUZZED through Sami as Jason, Rick, and Abby prepared for the rescue mission. The possibility of something going wrong loomed in the back of Sami's mind, but she suppressed the thought. If all went according to plan, Billy would be home by the end of the day.

Mike placed four silver knives and a handgun loaded with silver bullets into a backpack. "Here." He handed it to Jason. "These are for Billy. In case he needs them."

"Right." Jason slid his arms through the straps.

"You guys be safe," Sami said. She gave Rick a quick hug, then Abby. Before she could take one step toward Jason, Mike stepped in front of her, blocking her way.

She crossed her arms and glared at him. "Mike!"

Mike stared at her with an *it's not gonna happen* smirk on his face. He stood his ground, not budging.

Flustered, Sami sighed and plopped back onto the couch.

Jason winked at her. "Don't worry, as soon as I come back human, I'll give you the biggest hug ever. No lips attached."

"Human or not, just come back," she replied, praying they all made it home safely.

"That's the plan." Jason disappeared down the hallway, heading for the back door.

"See you soon. Keep your knives on you and stay safe," Rick said. He gave Mike a swat on the back, winked at Sami, and hurried after Jason.

Mike took Abby into his arms and gave her a passionate kiss. "Stay safe," he whispered.

"I will," she whispered back. She gave him another quick kiss and darted away.

Sami and Mike rushed to the sliding door of the bedroom to watch them leave.

"Let's go already!" Jason said, standing in the middle of the yard with his arms crossed.

"Abby and I have to morph first," Rick reminded him.

Jason sighed and approached the steps, taking a seat on the middle one, while Rick and Abby disappeared into the forest in different directions.

"You bring my brother back safely," Mike said as he nudged Jason in the back with the tip of his boot.

Jason glanced up at him. "It won't happen any other way."

Rick stepped out into the yard, completely werewolf, and motioned for Jason to join them before he sprinted away.

Jason jumped up, his emerald eyes full of excitement. "Finally!" He darted away with lightning speed.

With their departure came an overwhelming silence.

Sami and Mike puttered back to the living room and took their usual seats—Sami on the couch and Mike on the recliner.

"Do you think they'll find Billy?" she asked.

"You're the seer. Do *you* think they'll find him?"

While pondering his question, the last dream she'd had about Billy crossed her mind. "Well, when Billy called out to me in my dream, he sounded desperate to be rescued. But it didn't sound like he was in danger."

"It sounds like they're gonna find him, because you led them right to him. And it also sounds like he's okay. Don't worry, in just a few short hours, Billy's gonna be back in your arms and you're gonna be kissing him instead of Jason." He let out a devious chuckle.

"Ha, ha!" She narrowed her eyes and her face grew hot. "How come Abby doesn't have the love potion effect on you?"

"Unlike Jason, Abby has control over all her powers."

"Good thing Jason's coming back human. I *hope* he comes back human."

Silence settled over the room as their thoughts drifted. Sami recalled Jason's golden-eye power and how she couldn't keep herself off him. Guilt consumed her. "Billy's gonna be so mad at me. What if he doesn't wanna be with me anymore, Mike?"

"Sami, my brother is madly in love with you. You kissing Jason because he had some magical spell over you isn't gonna change that."

"Yeah…I guess you're right," she said, still unsure.

"You wanna watch TV?" he asked.

"Sure, I guess. But no werewolf movies."

He chuckled and reached for the remote on the coffee table. After sprawling back in the recliner, he pointed the remote at the TV.

A banging on the door interrupted his actions.

The remote hit the floor, and Mike jumped to his feet with a silver knife in his grasp. On his way to the door, he raised a finger to his lips, motioning for her to be silent.

Sami nodded and reached under the couch pillow, wrapping her fingers around the handle of the blade.

When Mike opened the door, Sami peered out the window. Sharon stood there with a nervous look on her face, obviously intimidated by Mike's unwavering stare.

"Hi. Is Samantha home?" she asked, her tone timid.

"Who's asking?" He barked.

"Sharon. I-I work at the diner."

Sami went to the door but couldn't see Sharon around Mike's oversized frame.

"If now isn't a good time?" Sharon's voice quivered.

Mike didn't move or make a sound. He just stood there like an angry giant.

"Hi, Sharon," Sami said, standing on tiptoes to see over Mike's shoulder.

"I just wanted to see if you were okay," Sharon said. "You know, after what happened at the diner last week. But I'll come back another time."

Sami grew irritated with Mike's rudeness. "Mike, will you move, please? She's hardly a threat!"

Mike continued to eye Sharon but finally relented and stepped aside.

"Sorry about that," Sami said.

Sharon's jaw dropped open. "Oh, your face!"

Taken off guard by Sharon's reaction, she covered her cheeks with her hands, trying to think of an excuse as to how she acquired the bruises. "Uhhh."

"She was in a car accident," Mike said.

Sharon's brows crinkled together over her sad eyes. "I'm so sorry about that and everything—" she shrugged "—just everything you've had to go through lately."

Sami nodded. "Thank you."

Sharon's gaze fell to Sami's neck. "That's a beautiful locket. Is it silver?"

"Yes! It is!" Mike snapped.

Eyes wide, Sharon took a step back.

"Mike!" Sami smacked him in the arm.

Sharon sighed and turned her focus on Sami. "Anyway, you've had such a rough time lately, I just wanted to let you know, if you ever need a friend…" She shrugged and managed a nervous smile. "Oh, and the job at the diner is still available if you want it. Sheriff Briggs fired the manager."

"Sheriff Briggs owns the diner?" Mike asked.

Sharon shook her head and averted her eyes downward. "No, I mean, Sheriff Briggs got him fired."

Mike's angry glare settled on Sharon's bandaged arm.

Sami chewed on her lip, contemplating on whether to accept the offer. "Well, I do still need a job."

"What happened to your arm?" Mike asked.

"Uh—" Sharon's eyes shifted to the bandage and back to Mike "—

just a cut. I'm clumsy with knives."

"She doesn't want the job. Give it to someone else," Mike said.

"Mike! What are you doing?" Sami didn't understand his hostility toward one of the few people in town who'd actually gone out of their way to be nice to her.

Sharon took another step back. "I'll just come back another time."

"No, wait," Sami pleaded, not wanting her to leave under bad circumstances.

Mike pushed Sami aside, slammed the door shut, and locked the deadbolt.

"What the hell are you doing?" Sami shouted. She rushed to the window, watching as Sharon hopped into her car and shut the door.

"That was completely rude, Mike!"

"She can't be trusted," he said, peering out the window.

"She's only one of two people in this town that's been nice to me so far, and you just scared her off!"

"We're nice to you, Sami," Mike said as he rushed to the kitchen cupboard. He grabbed the pistol he'd hidden on the top shelf and checked to make sure it was loaded.

"What are you doing?"

"She's one of them," he said, tucking the gun into the back of his jeans.

"What? A werewolf? That's ridiculous!"

"No—" he plucked two bottles of water from the fridge and handed them to her "—it's not ridiculous. And keep your voice down." He went to the pantry and grabbed a box of crackers and a can of peanuts. "Grab a bag for this stuff."

Sami retrieved a shopping bag from the hall closet and they dropped the items into the bag.

"Where's your knife?" Mike asked.

Spotting it on the couch, she stomped across the room and snatched it up. "Mike, we can trust Sharon!" She whirled back around to face him, ready to give him a piece of her mind.

He gave her a knowing stare, placed a finger to his lips, and motioned her forward with a wave of his hand.

Realizing something was wrong—something other than Sharon—

Sami tightened her grip on the knife and went to him.

He lowered his lips to her ear. "As soon as were outside, run as fast as you can to the cage and don't look back."

Fear consumed her, sending goose bumps down her arms and legs. She sucked in a shaky breath and nodded.

Mike hurried to the back door in Sami's bedroom and scanned the backyard. When he didn't see anything suspicious, he slid the door open and stepped outside. He adjusted his grip on his knife and pulled the pistol from the back of his jeans. With a nod of the head, he motioned for Sami to follow.

Sami kept a death grip on her knife and stepped outside.

Mike peered down the basement steps, making sure the way was clear. His eyes bore into hers, and he gave her the signal—a jerk of his head in the direction of the basement.

With her heart pounding, Sami ran across the yard and bolted down the steps. The clomping of Mike's boots echoed behind her. She flung open the basement door and sprinted across the room toward the other door. As soon as she reached it, she turned the knob and pushed through it.

A vicious growl erupted through the basement.

Sami turned around. Mike was still at the first door and a large shadow darkened the stairway.

"Mike!" she screamed.

"Go, Sami!" he yelled and slammed the door shut, sliding the steel bar into the latch. "Run!" he ordered as he sprinted toward her.

A metal boom pierced their eardrums as the werewolf plowed through the door.

Sami screamed and rushed into the other room and to the cage. Mike's hands were suddenly on her waist and she flew forward, into the cage.

Mike scrambled in behind her and slammed the door shut with a loud *clang.*

The werewolf appeared before them, its crimson eyes a menacing contrast to its black fur. A vicious growl erupted through its fangs.

Sami screamed and covered her ears to block the horrific roar.

Mike lifted the gun and pulled the trigger, shooting the werewolf square between the eyes.

Sami screamed again, ears ringing and watching in horror as the werewolf stumbled into the other room and crumpled to the ground.

"Shit that was close!" Mike's head slumped forward and his arms relaxed, but he kept the gun pointed at the motionless beast—prepared to shoot again if needed.

Sami sucked in a sob.

Mike raised his head and looked at her. "Are you okay?"

"No!" She cried. "I'm not okay! We almost died!"

"If we hadn't made it to the cage, I still would've shot the fucker between the eyes."

Sami sat in shock, staring at the werewolf and wondering whether or not it was really dead.

The beast's fur began to ripple as if bubbles were forming under its skin.

"Oh no! Is it alive?" she asked.

Mike shook his head. "No. I think it's just changing back."

The beast's snout shrunk as if it had melted into its face, while each limb trembled and quivered. Like magic, patches of skin appeared, spreading through the fur.

Sami covered her eyes, afraid to see who it was. "Who is it? Do we know him? Or her? Is it Sharon?"

Mike didn't utter a word.

"Well?" she asked louder.

"I've never seen him before."

"Is he dead?"

"Yeah, he's dead."

Without looking at the body, she crawled to the other side of the cage and leaned against the bars, her back toward the dead stranger. "I don't wanna see," she said with a shaky voice. She tightened her jaw to keep it from quivering.

Mike sat back, adjacent to her, keeping an eye on the man.

"So, do we have to stay in here until they get back?" Sami wiped her cheeks dry with her shirt, trying to control her trembling hands.

"It would be the smartest thing to do."

"Do you think Sharon had anything to do with it?"

"I don't know. It's hard to tell. She wasn't acting right, and he did show up with her."

"What do you mean *with* her?"

"I saw him hiding in the forest across the street while we were talking to her."

"What? Why didn't you say anything? What if he killed her before he came for us?"

"We couldn't be sure she wasn't with him. I had to protect *you*, Sami," he said, sounding as if he were irritated. "Anyway, I doubt he would've wasted his time on her. He was after you. And I'm sure Jessica was behind it."

"How do you know?"

"Because she knows as long as you're alive, Billy will always love you and only you. You can't trust anyone, Sami. Not anymore." He ran his hands down his face and let out an exhausted sounding sigh.

He was right. Just because Sharon had been nice to her, it didn't mean she should be trusted. Mike had tried to tell her that in the house, but instead of listening to him, she'd wasted valuable time arguing and almost getting them killed.

"I know. I'm sorry I got mad and didn't listen. It was stupid of me."

"Don't worry about it."

She shifted, trying to get comfortable against the cold metal bars. "So, how long do we have to stay in here?"

"Until they get back."

"Great." She crossed her arms and yawned. The horror had depleted all of her energy.

"Are you hungry?"

"No. I'm just tired…and still freaked out," she admitted.

"Come here." Mike scooted into the corner right next to her. "You can lay your head in my lap and rest. I'll keep watch."

"Okay." She repositioned herself and rested her weary head on his thigh. The brown leather on one of his work boots was worn to the steel toe. Something he should replace, but he probably held onto them for the comfort they offered. Something they all needed at the moment to feel a little more safe and secure in this world. Comfort.

"I wonder if they reached the cave yet?" Mike said.

"I hope so. Jessica's crazy and Billy's stubborn. The longer he's with her the more danger he's in." An ache filled Sami's heart again. Her chin began to quiver, and tears burned her eyes.

"It's okay," Mike whispered, patting her hip. "We're safe in here, and there are three werewolves making sure Billy's safe."

Holding onto his encouraging words, Sami closed her eyes and drifted to sleep.

27

RICK MADE a sudden stop along the trail.

"Shit!" Jason cringed, digging his shoes into the dirt to slow down, but it was too late. He plowed into Rick with so much force they smashed into a small tree, sending it crashing to the ground.

A low growl rumbled from Rick's chest.

Jason stood and dusted off his shirt. "Sorry." He chuckled under his breath, a little embarrassed. "I wasn't expecting you to stop so suddenly. Guess I still don't have the whole *brake* thing down quite yet."

Rick growled again. *"Shut up! We don't want her to hear us!"*

He stared at Rick with a dumbfounded look on his face. "Dude, did you just say, 'Shut up. We don't want her to hear us,' through your growl?"

"Good, you can finally hear me. Now, keep your mouth shut from here on out! If she hears us coming, we might not be able to save Billy."

"Wow. This power is totally awesome," he said quietly, beaming.

Rick growled again.

"Okay, okay," Jason whispered. "Geez."

"Now that you can understand us—"

Jason turned his attention to Abby, waiting for her to finish.

"—follow Rick's lead, but not too close. Just get to Billy and get him out of there as fast as you can. We'll take care of Jessica."

"Got it," he whispered and looked at Rick. "But how am I gonna get Billy out of the cave if I turn human again after Jessica's dead? I won't be able to jump down from that high."

"We'll keep her alive long enough for you to get Billy out of there. We're still a few minutes out, but be prepared. It's going to be a bloody battle when we're inside. Don't try to be a hero. Just get Billy out of the cave and a safe distance away."

"Yeah, I got it." Jason grew irritated, feeling like a child. "Let's go."

They all darted toward their destination. Within minutes, they were staring up at the entrance to the cave.

BILLY'S MIND reeled with desire as his mouth devoured Jessica's lips. He couldn't seem to get enough of her. Everything about her drove him crazy, consuming him in a euphoric high. He pulled away to catch his breath.

"Your eyes. They're so beautiful," he whispered huskily, gazing into the liquid pools of pink sapphire.

Jessica smiled with pleasure. "I take it you like what you see?" She climbed off the bed and slipped the thin straps of her negligee from her shoulders. The gown slid down her body to a puddle at her feet.

Billy held his breath, taken away by her naked beauty—every curve, every ounce of sweet, soft flesh. He wanted her, and he wanted her now. He climbed off the bed and pulled her against his chest, kissing her hungrily, while his hand slid down her waist to her supple buttocks.

She pushed away from him, and her eyes turned red. "No!" A deep growl burst from her lungs, and she fell to her knees. Shaking violently, her body jerked this way and that.

Confused and dazed, Billy backed up against the cave wall and watched in shock as Jessica's body twisted and writhed, bulging profusely in various areas until either claws or thick fur pushed through the leathery skin. Within seconds, a killer werewolf towered over him.

Jessica stuck her chest out and roared with fury.

"Get the fuck away from my best friend, you bitch!" Jason boomed from the mouth of the den as another werewolf, with dark fur, pushed past him and leapt through the air.

Jessica spun around, and the werewolf tackled her.

Billy's eyes widened as the beasts barreled straight for him. Firm hands clutched his waist, and after a sudden jerk, he was safely across the room.

"What the hell?"

"You can thank me later!" Jason said.

Billy spun around to face Jason, staring in shock at his vivid green eyes. Before Billy could even think straight, another werewolf pushed past Jason and leapt into the bloody fight.

"Climb on my back!" Jason demanded, keeping an eye on the fierce battle.

"What?" Billy asked in disbelief. "How in the hell are your eyes green?"

"Never mind!" Jason snapped.

Billy was suddenly in Jason's arms, and the stone walls smeared into a dark blur. They jerked to a halt at the mouth of the cave.

The bright daylight bore into Billy's eyes. He squinted and held a hand up to shield the sunshine.

"Hold on tight," Jason warned. "I've never jumped from this high before."

"What the fuck?" Billy peered over the edge. A tingling sensation shot through his palms and the soles of his feet. "No. Wait!"

Jason grinned and leapt off the cliff's edge.

Billy clenched his eyes shut and screamed. A strong jerk and a loud thud jarred his senses. "Are we dead?" he shouted with his eyes squished tight and feeling nauseous.

Jason slid his arm from under Billy's legs, letting his feet flop to the ground. "Not yet."

Billy looked around and straightened as Jason pushed him into an upright position. He exhaled, trying to compose the fear and the sickness. "How in the hell did you do that? Are you a werewolf? Did Jessica bite you that night?"

A vicious roar echoed above them from the cave, followed by a whimper.

"Climb on my back." Jason turned around and squatted.

Billy did as ordered, being careful of his broken hand.

Jason grabbed Billy's arms. "I'm still new at this, so keep your head behind mine in case I run into a tree."

"You better be joking!"

"I'm not."

A sudden rush of wind whooshed through Billy's hair. Blurs of green and brown whizzed by, intensifying the nausea. Tightening his grip, he closed his eyes, praying it would be over soon.

"You okay?" Jason shouted.

Afraid he'd blow chunks any moment, Billy kept his mouth shut and answered by shaking his head back and forth.

Jason slowed down and stopped. "Dude, you can get off my back now."

Billy opened his eyes and breathed a sigh of relief. "Are we still alive?"

"Yes. Now get off my back."

He let go and stood on wobbly legs. The contents of his stomach rose to the back of his throat and out of his mouth into a nearby bush. Pain tore through his side, and he double over, clutching his aching ribs.

Jason grabbed Billy's arm to steady him. "Are you okay?"

"I'm just gonna sit for a minute." He walked over to a fallen log and eased himself down, waiting for the nausea to subside.

Jason sat next to him and gave him a couple of firm pats on the back. "It's so good to see you! I was sure Jessica mated with you, and then ate you. Looks like she popped you pretty good across the face though." He nodded toward the makeshift cast. "Broken?"

"Yeah, broken. I think she cracked a rib too." Guilt took over as Jason words haunted his thoughts. "We almost did, you know, *mate*," he said, disgusted with himself. "I couldn't control myself. It was like

I was under her spell or something."

"You don't have to explain. I had the same effect on Sami. Nice boxers by the way."

Billy furrowed his brow and anger replaced the guilt. "What?"

"No time to explain." Jason stood. "Rick and Abby are coming." He clutched Billy's arm and pulled him to his to his feet.

"What'd you do to Sami? And how in the hell are you a werewolf?"

A strong gust of wind blew Billy's hair back. He shut his eyes to shield them, and when he opened them again, two werewolves stood in front of him—one with rich brown fur and the other a pale sandy color.

"Dad?" Billy asked.

The darker werewolf nodded.

A growl rumbled from the other werewolf's chest.

Billy's eyes widened. "Why is that one pissed at me?"

"It's Abby. She's not mad. She's communicating with me," Jason said. He looked at her and shrugged. "I don't know why they're still green, Abby." He rubbed his eyes and leaned toward her. "Are they normal yet?"

Abby shook her head and growled again.

"Shit!" Jason ran a hand through his hair and started to pace. "Shit! I'm still a werewolf. That means Jessica wasn't the one who bit me." He stopped and looked at Billy. "Who in the hell attacked us then?"

Before Billy could answer, he was in his dad's furry arms, whirring through the forest.

Billy winced, trying to ignore the searing pain in his side. Feeling nauseous again, he turned his focus back to the blur of trees rushing at him, praying they didn't crash into one of them.

SAMI MOANED and opened her eyes, focusing on Mike's boots. She looked past them, to the two blurry figures standing in front of the open cage door.

"Sami!" Billy's voice jarred her from the mental fog.

"Billy?" She sat up, rubbing her eyes. Billy and Jason's smiling faces came into focus. "Am I dreaming?" She rubbed her eyes again.

Mike sat forward. "Good to see you, little brother!" He smiled. "And nice boxers."

Sami glanced down at his satin boxers, then back to his face. *It's him! He's really home!*

Billy climbed into the cage and crawled toward her. "You're not dreaming, Sami. I'm really home."

With tears in her eyes, she giggled and threw her arms around his neck, welcoming his tight embrace. "I can't believe it!" she cried. "I've missed you so much! I was afraid I'd never see you again!"

Billy loosened his grip just enough to look into her eyes. "I love you, Sami." He lowered his lips to hers.

"Why is Jason still a werewolf?"

Mike's gruff voice cut their kiss short. They both turned and looked at Jason.

Abby and Rick emerged through the doorway.

Rick shrugged. "Jessica's dead, so he must've been bitten by someone else. Who in the hell is that?" He pointed to the body lying on the floor and went over to inspect it.

"I don't know." Mike climbed out of the cage and leaned back with his hands on his sides, stretching the stiffness.

Abby threw her arms around him.

"I missed you, too." Mike lifted her off the ground and kissed her.

Billy turned back to Sami, his anguished eyes roaming her bruised face. "I'm glad that bitch is dead. She'll never be able to hurt you again. Come on—" he took her hand in his "—let's get out of this thing."

Jason reached in and helped her out of the cage.

"Thanks, Jason." She smiled, captivated by his golden gaze. Behind her, the shuffling of Billy climbing from the cage faded into the background. All Sami wanted at that moment was to be in Jason's arms again. Her heart fluttered with anticipation and suddenly Jason's supple lips were on hers, engulfing her mind in a sensual fog.

"Oh shit!" Mike's voice bounced through Sami's mental haze.

"Dude, what the fuck are you doing?" Billy's voice boomed, snapping her back to reality.

Sami opened her eyes just in time to see Billy shove Jason against the wall.

A growl erupted through the basement and Jason's green eyes blazed with fury.

Rick leapt between the two angry men. "Cool it, Jason! Control yourself! Just relax and get control."

Billy turned to Sami. "Are you okay?" he asked with a bitter tone.

"Yeah," she said shakily. The euphoria dissipated leaving shame in its place. "I'm so sorry." Her breathing became unsteady, and she started to cry. "I couldn't help it. He has some love power or something he can't control."

Billy's angry eyes softened. "It's okay, Sami. I understand. I'm not mad at you."

"You do? You're not?"

"Yeah, Jessica had the same power." He sighed and averted his guilt-ridden eyes.

Jealousy nipped at Sami's heart and she wiped the tears away with her hands. "She did? Is that why you're only wearing boxers?"

He nodded.

"Well, how did that work out with no one there to stop you?" Sami asked, afraid to hear the answer.

"We got there just in time," Jason said.

"So, you and Jessica didn't…?" She couldn't say the words.

"No, we didn't," Billy said. "But…we almost did."

Sami's gut knotted, and an ache filled her chest. "Did you kiss her?"

Billy nodded, and his eyes filled with moisture. "Sorry," he whispered. "I tried to fight against it."

"Did you touch her? In *places*?" She gulped, fearing his answer.

He shook his head. "I held her and kissed her is all. Maybe my hand touched her butt? It's all kinda foggy. They got there before anything happened. I'm so sorry, Sami."

Sami breathed a sigh of relief. She didn't think it'd hurt so much knowing Billy was intimate with another woman. Especially since she and Jason had kissed, and on more than one occasion. But it did. Instead of dwelling on the hurt, she decided to look at it from a positive aspect—it only hurt so much because they were truly in love and meant to be together. She wrapped her arms around Billy's neck.

"It's all right, Billy. I understand. I'm not mad at you either," she said.

He smiled and his arm tightened around her. "All that matters is we're together again."

"Can I get one of those too?" Jason asked with his arms extended.

"No!" everyone shouted at the same time, glaring at him.

"Geez! I was just kidding." He chuckled under his breath. "You guys are so touchy."

"Hey, your eyes are hazel," Sami said.

"They are?" he rubbed them and blinked.

Sami looked at Rick. "Does that mean he's human again? Maybe it just took time for the whole werewolf thing to fade?"

"I don't know. We'll have to wait until he gets aggravated again before we know for sure," Rick said.

Billy approached Jason and stared into his eyes. Suddenly, he popped Jason in the jaw.

Jason stumbled back, clutching his jaw, his eyes a piercing green. "What the frick? Asshole!"

Billy shrugged. "Guess he's still a werewolf."

Jason gritted his teeth and squished his eyes shut. After a deep breath, he opened them.

"You're eyes are hazel again, Jason," Rick said. "You're gaining better control."

Jason looked at Billy. "Dude, thanks for hitting me. I feel so much better now. I was totally feeling guilty for trying to mate with your girlfriend while you were gone."

"I wish I could've done that to Jessica," Sami said, crossing her arms.

"Don't worry. I did it for you. Twice." Billy gloated.

A smile crept into Sami's cheeks. "You did?"

"Yep. It was worth the broken hand and battered face. Speaking of which—" he inspected her cheeks "—this all happened when we were attacked?"

"Not all of it," Mike said.

Sami cringed, dreading the scolding Billy was about to give her.

"Sami was attacked by a different werewolf at the lake this morning," Jason said. "And if you think her face looks bad, look at these." He lifted her top before she could react, exposing the fingerprint bruises on her sides.

"Holy shit!" Billy glanced at his dad and Mike. "What the hell? How could this have happened with my big brother and two werewolves looking after her?"

"Three," Jason corrected before the others had a chance to answer. He lifted Sami's pant leg to show more of the damage while he explained. "Sami snuck off to the lake, hoping one of Jessica's minions would capture her and take her to you, but another werewolf was there instead.

"Luckily, Rick, Mike, and Abby got there before he raped and killed her. Sucker got his heart ripped out. He would've died anyway though—Sami gutted him with her silver knife right before they got there."

"What?" Billy shouted with a stunned look.

Jason grinned. "I know, right? She's getting better at defending herself." He raised one corner of his mouth, suddenly looking guilty. "Oh, and uh, the bruise on the corner of her mouth—" he chuckled under his breath "—I got a little carried away. But I already apologized to Sami, and I'm sorry again to you. You can hit me again if you want. I totally deserve it." He stepped forward and closed his eyes, waiting for Billy's fist to make contact with his jaw again.

Billy ignored him and looked at Sami, his eyes wide. "My God! Are you okay?" He wrapped his arm around her. "All this time, I thought you were safe, and then I find out you were in more danger than I was." He glared over his shoulder at his dad and brother again.

"I'm okay. And don't be mad at them. It's my fault," Sami admitted with shame. "They thought I was in the shower. I tricked them to get away. Other than that, I was pretty safe. Except for when Mike and I were almost killed by the *other* werewolf, I mean. But Mike took care of that one." She pointed to the dead body.

Billy squeezed her tighter. "I am never gonna leave you again. I promise."

"I'm gonna hold you to that." She snuggled against his chest and smiled, relieved all the pain-staking details were finally divulged.

"Let's go upstairs and talk," Rick suggested.

"What are we gonna do with him?" Mike asked, pointing to the body.

Rick let out a weary sigh. "Same thing as the one from the lake this morning—I'm dumping him at Sheriff Briggs's along with a message on where to find Jessica. This is his mess to clean. Oh, and Billy?"

"Yeah, Dad?"

"You really should get your hand checked out. And your ribs."

"I will in the morning," he assured.

Everyone left Rick in the basement and headed upstairs. Darkness had fallen, ensuring the nightmare of a day was almost over.

Sami helped Billy change into a pair of briefs, sweatpants, and a blue T-shirt.

They both sat on the bed, and Billy put an arm around her. "Thanks for helping me get dressed."

"You're welcome." She ran a gentle finger under his jaw, avoiding the bruises. "We both look like a mess."

"Yeah, but we'll heal with time. And so will our hearts." He leaned down and gave her a long tender kiss.

"Uhhh, sorry to interrupt." Jason stood in the doorway with a sheepish smile on his face. "It was your idea to update you on all the details, bro, and everybody's waiting. So, you guys coming or what?"

Billy groaned and stood, pulling Sami up with him. "I guess, since everyone's waiting on us."

Sami frowned, wishing they could all just talk in the morning. Billy's fingers entwined with hers, and they went into the living room. He didn't even let go of her hand when they sat on the couch next to Rick. He'd missed her as much as she missed him and wasn't afraid to show it.

Mike was sitting in the recliner with Abby perched on the arm of it and snuggled against him. Jason pulled up a bar stool. They all took turns telling Billy about what had happened the night he had been taken and the following morning at the lake, Sami's dreams, her being a seer, and Jason's powers. Then, Mike told everyone about Sharon and the mysterious killer werewolf that had followed.

"Now, back to more important matters," Jason said. "The bitch that bit me last night. It looked just like Jessica. Is it possible it really *was* her, and that it can take a few hours for my powers to go away?"

Rick rubbed his forehead as if he were trying to get rid of a headache. "It should've happened instantly."

"But it looked just like her," Sami said.

"Maybe she has a twin," Jason added with sarcasm.

Everyone turned their attention to Abby.

"She doesn't have a twin, does she?" Jason asked.

Abby flashed a sheepish smile. "Uh, well, it's possible." She stared at the coffee table, away from everyone's accusing glances.

"Please tell me she doesn't have a frickin' twin!" Jason said, his tone bitter.

"Hey, pipe down!" Mike warned.

"It's okay, Mike," Abby said. "Jessica and I were adopted. We are, however, biological half-sisters. Our birth mother had me and put me in an orphanage when I was too young to remember. Then, I was adopted by my foster parents. Years later, she had Jessica and put her in the same orphanage. The administrator there contacted my adoptive parents and told them about Jessica, and they took her in too. It's possible Jessica had a twin that she was separated from before she came into the family."

Rick rubbed his chin. "It's a long shot but a possibility. It's also possible some other werewolf bit you, Jason. We do look an awful lot alike after we morph, especially to someone who isn't used to seeing us that way."

"You mean like getting other people's dogs mixed up?" Jason asked.

"Have a little respect." Mike glared at him.

Abby giggled. "It's okay. He's actually right."

"So," Billy said, "it's not at all possible to get bitten by a werewolf you just so happen to kill before the full moon and still become a werewolf anyway? It's never *ever* happened before?"

Everyone looked at Rick.

"I've never heard of it before. But I know there's a book which contains a lot of facts in it about werewolves, dating back to the last few hundred years. If it has ever happened, there's a good chance it would be in that book. The question is…where is it?"

Billy grinned. "I know where it is."

Rick's face lit up. "Where?"

"At Sheriff Briggs's house," Billy answered. He turned to Sami. "I saw it there when we rescued you that night."

"Great!" Jason said, throwing his hands in the air. "So, we're just supposed to face the *sheriff* uncle of the werewolf we *killed* and ask to borrow his book?"

"Don't worry about him." Abby smiled. "He can't hurt you."

"He *is* the sheriff," Mike reminded her. "He could always arrest us and throw us in jail."

"He won't now that Rick's back," Abby said, her tone confident. "He wants to keep the peace in this town. He doesn't want word to get out about werewolves. All he's ever dreamed of is being a sheriff in a small, quiet town. He didn't expect to run into any werewolves. But now he has, and he knows he has to appease them too."

Sami was confused. "So, we can trust him?"

"Absolutely not!" Abby said. "He'll do anything for the killers as long as they leave him and his small town alone. But I'm sure he'd also do anything for us. Well, for Rick anyway. I don't think I have it in me to persuade him in the way he needs persuading though. You would basically have to threaten him Rick."

Rick nodded. "I'm sure I can handle that."

"So, Dad," Billy asked, "how are we gonna explain to everyone in town why you're not dead?"

"I've given that a lot of thought. We're going to stick to the part of the story that was made up thirteen years ago—I was attacked by wolves. And we can say there was a mix up with charts in the hospital, and they thought I had died, but it was actually someone else. We're also going to say I had amnesia. Then, not remembering my old life, I simply walked away from the hospital and started a new life until recently, when I finally got my memory back."

Mike rose from the recliner and shoved his hands in his pockets. "Could work. Sounds far-fetched, but stranger things have happened. How are we gonna make sure the story sticks?"

"Apparently, Sheriff Briggs has a lot of important connections. That's how he was able to devise the cover up back then. Now, I'm going to make sure he fixes it."

"What about the fake guy in the hospital they mixed you up with?" Jason asked.

"Fake guy would have to remain a John Doe, since he doesn't exist anyway," Rick said.

Billy cleared his throat. "Whose ashes did we bury in the clearing?"

His dad's eyes filled with regret. "Nobody's. They were just ashes from Sheriff Brigg's fireplace. But, for everyone else's sake, it was John Doe. I removed the fake ashes when I came back. The thought of them being buried next to your mother…" He shook his head. "I just couldn't live with it anymore. You know where to put me when my time comes."

Billy let go of Sami's hand and gave his dad a couple of firm pats on the thigh.

Mike pulled a set of keys from his jeans pocket. "Looks like we've covered everything. I'm gonna run to the diner and grab some food to go. Anyone else want anything?"

Everyone raised their hand.

"Okay." Mike chuckled under his breath. "Cheeseburgers and fries sound good?"

"Yes!" Everyone agreed at the same time.

"I'll go with you." Abby hopped up and followed Mike out the door, closing it behind her.

"Oh, and I know you two are anxious for your privacy—" Rick looked at Sami and Billy "—but I think it's best if we all stick together for a couple of days until we know we're all safe."

Billy frowned. "But I thought you said you and Abby can tell when killer werewolves are near? If you're right next door and Abby's just down the street, wouldn't we be safe?"

"Yes, but I don't understand why we didn't sense the other werewolf—the one Mike shot right after we left. You did say Sharon knocked on your door just a couple of minutes after we left, right, Sami?" Rick asked.

"Yes." Sami yawned. Her mind couldn't take much more information. She was exhausted, physically and mentally, and longed for the comfort of her bed.

"Maybe it's possible the werewolf wasn't here yet," Billy suggested.

"You're probably right. But just to be on the safe side, I'd hate for a killer to be faster than me at getting to you two. It won't be long before we can all get back into a normal routine."

"I've heard that one before," Sami said with sarcasm, but followed it with a slight smile.

"Yeah," Jason agreed. "I'm beginning to think this *is* normal for this town."

She yawned again and turned to Billy. "I need to shower and get ready for bed. I'm exhausted. Can you come and get me when dinner gets here?"

"Actually, I need a shower too." Billy stood and helped her off the couch.

"So, where are we all sleeping if we have to stick together?" Jason sounded irritated.

"There are two guest bedrooms upstairs," Sami said. "Plus my old room but there's no bed in there."

"I'll take the couch," Jason said.

"Oh, no you won't, *Romeo*," Rick said. "I'll take the couch. You choose a room upstairs."

Sami's cheeks filled with warmth. Ready to put the humiliating past behind her, she pulled Billy along, not stopping until they reached the bedroom.

28

SAMI AWOKE the next morning afraid the previous night had been a nightmare and Billy wouldn't be there when she rolled over. The steady sound of his breathing reached her ears and she shifted to face him. He'd really been rescued, and they were together again. Smiling, she nestled against him.

"I love you," she whispered. "With all my heart."

"I love you too." He opened his eyes and wrapped his arm around her shoulders, drawing her close. "With all *my* heart. And I really wanna *show* you how much with something else." He rolled on top of her and showered her face with little kisses before he planted one on her mouth.

Sami giggled under his lips.

He pulled away and flopped his head back onto the pillow. "Ugh! We have to get that door fixed today."

Confused, Sami lifted her head and glanced at the doorway. Mike stood there, smirking.

"Sorry. Breakfast is ready." He let out a light chuckle and disappeared down the hallway.

Sami propped herself up on an elbow. "Sorry about the door."

Billy gave her a soft smile. He looked down and noticed the locket she wore. "Jason gave it to you?"

She traced her finger over the smooth heart. "Yeah. He left it on the dresser. I was pretty sad. He thought it might help me feel closer to you."

"I made it, you know."

"I know. It's beautiful, Billy. Thank you." She lifted it from her neck to gaze at it again. "It got me through everything. And it even helped save me from the werewolf at the lake."

"Good. I think I'll make enough silver jewelry to cover your entire body." He grinned.

She giggled. "So, how did you make the locket? I didn't even know you were a jeweler."

"Well, Mike and my dad helped. My dad used to make jewelry. We kept all his old tools and stuff all these years."

"Awe, Billy, I'll never take it off. I love it. I love *you*." She locked her mouth on his, thanking him with her lips.

He held her tighter, intensifying their kiss.

"Oops! Sorry." Jason let out a wary laugh.

"Ugh!" Billy groaned, frustrated.

Sami giggled and rolled off of him.

Mike's laughter made its way from the living room to their bedroom.

"*Mike* just wanted me to tell you—" narrowing his eyes, Jason looked over his shoulder and down the hallway before turning his attention back to them "—after we eat, me, Rick, and Mike are gonna go to Sheriff Briggs's house to get the book. Abby's gonna go with you two to the hospital."

"Oh yeah, I forgot." Billy held up his broken hand, staring at his homemade cast. "Pathetic, huh?"

Sami pursed her lips, trying not to laugh. "A little." She gave him a light peck on the lips.

"Enough already," Jason grumbled.

"Shut up." Billy chuckled, low and devious. "You're just jealous."

Jason turned his head, facing the hallway. "Mike, when are you gonna fix this door?"

"Shut up and eat!" Mike's voice echoed into the bedroom.

"Oooh, it's ready?" Jason grinned, rubbing his hands together and hurried off.

"Come on." Sami climbed out of bed and held her hand out to Billy. "We have to hurry before Jason eats all the food."

"Really?" he asked, taking her hand and scooting off the bed.

"Really!"

They quickly readied for the day and went to the kitchen to join everyone for breakfast. When they were finished, they all parted ways. Sami, Billy, and Abby headed to the hospital to get Billy's hand properly casted and his ribs x-rayed. Mike, Rick, and Jason headed to Sheriff Briggs's house to find the book.

MIKE SPED down the road, dreading having to return to Sheriff Briggs's pig sty of a home.

"It's kind of weird being in a car again," his dad said, staring out the passenger window. "I can't believe Billy kept my Charger all these years. It looks better now than it did when I had it."

"Yeah," Mike said. "I didn't want him to have your motorcycle after all the trips to the emergency room we had to make from him falling off his bicycle."

"I'm sorry I wasn't around to take care of you boys," he said with regret.

"You're here now. That's what matters. And you can have your motorcycle back if you want. I'm gonna get a truck. I need one for all my tools."

"Thanks, Mike. It sure would be nice to be able to get somewhere without having to worry about a change of clothes for once."

"Here we are." Mike pulled up to the house and shut the engine off, hoping the place didn't smell as bad as it had before.

"Looks like a frickin' haunted house." Jason leaned his head forward between the two front headrests.

"Here goes nothing," Mike said.

They all climbed out of the car and clomped up the rickety porch steps.

Rick knocked on the front door.

Soft footsteps approached from inside and the door creaked open. Sharon's eyes widened, and her mouth hung open.

Mike narrowed his eyes. He gave her a quick once-over, noticing the bandage still on her arm. *Wait, Jason cut the werewolf who attacked them in the arm.* He eyed the bandage again, and then raised his gaze to meet hers.

"What are you doing here?" Mike asked.

"Uhhh, just cleaning." She gulped. "The sheriff hired me to clean his house."

"Bummer," Jason said as he peered into the dirty, run-down home. "I hope you brought some gasoline and matches."

"We're here to see Sheriff Briggs. Is he here?" Rick asked.

She shook her head. "Are you a friend of his?"

"A close family friend," Rick said.

"Oh. Hello," Sharon said in a timid tone.

"Nice to meet you, Sharon." Rick smiled. "I left a book here, and I need it back."

"What book? I can get it for you." She lowered her lashes to avoid their stares.

"If you don't mind—" Jason stepped forward "—we'd like to come in and get it ourselves." He grinned and winked, obviously trying to charm her. "We know where it is, and we won't take long. Promise."

She pressed her mouth together to hide her bashful smile and stepped aside. "Okay."

Mike nudged Jason and motioned with his eyes to Sharon's arm.

Jason looked at the bandage and gave a subtle nod.

Mike led the way straight down the hall to a door on the right. He stood in the doorway of the study to eavesdrop on Jason and Sharon's conversation while his dad went into the room to find the book.

"So...*Sharon*, right?" Jason asked.

She nodded and put her head down.

"What happened to your arm?" he asked, his voice overloaded with sympathy.

"Oh, I tripped and fell. I'm clumsy sometimes."

"I'm sorry to hear that," Jason said. "Good thing it wasn't serious."

Mike narrowed his eyes. Sharon had told him that she'd cut herself with a knife. Now, she was telling Jason she'd fallen. He wondered what she was hiding from them. If she were a werewolf, then his father would be able to sense it. He couldn't wait to get out of there to find out if his dad had picked up on anything.

"Got it!" Rick held up the book, grinning.

"Good. Let's get the hell outta here." Mike let him pass and followed him back to the front door.

"Thank you, Sharon." Rick smiled. "We found it."

Sharon eyed the book. "That looks like a very old book. Where'd you get it?"

"Oh, it's been in the family for generations," Rick said.

Mike glanced at her bandage. "Sharon, how'd you say you hurt your arm again?"

"I fell." She averted her gaze and hurried out to the front porch.

The three men followed her outside.

"I'm glad you found your book. I'll be sure and tell the sheriff you stopped by."

Jason grinned and jogged down the steps. "You do that. It was nice talking to you."

"Thanks again," Rick said, following Jason's lead.

As Mike brushed past Sharon, he gave her a warning glare. Without uttering a word, he headed straight for the car. The door slammed shut behind him, followed by the click of the deadbolt. He climbed into the driver's seat with a satisfied smirk, started the car, and sped off down the road.

When they were a safe distance away, Mike said, "She's one of them."

"Sharon?" Jason laughed. "She couldn't hurt a fly. I'm sure her arm injury is just a coincidence."

"She does smell familiar," Rick said. "But that's probably because she lives around here. I didn't sense anything from her."

"I know werewolves can heal instantly from wounds caused by ordinary weapons. And I know they can die from silver weapons if hit in fatal areas of the body like the head or heart. But what happens if they're just *cut* by a silver knife in the arm?" Mike asked.

"They'd be wounded," Rick said.

"How long does it take to heal, though, Dad?"

"It's not instant. It takes some time. At least a few days. It's like poison to us. Our powers help with the healing, but slowly."

Mike glanced at Jason in the rear-view mirror. "When you guys were attacked on your way to Tahoe, where'd you cut the werewolf?"

"In the left arm, to make her let go of Billy," Jason said.

"But, I'd *know* if she was a werewolf," Rick reminded him. "And *Sharon*?" His forehead lined with uncertainty. He stared at the dashboard at nothing in particular, before shaking his head. "She's too submissive. There's no way she's a killer. It can't be her."

Mike pulled over on the side of the road, intent on convincing his dad otherwise. "But didn't you say werewolves all have some sort of unique power? Like, Abby can sense killer werewolves from farther out than you can, and you can track better than anyone."

"What about me? What's my special power?" Jason asked as he stuck his head over the seat.

"You're more irritating than ever," Mike said.

"Whatever." Jason sat back and crossed his arms.

"Anyway," Mike continued, "what if Sharon's special power is that no one can detect she's a werewolf? Is that possible?"

His dad swiped a hand over his mouth as he contemplated the notion. "I've never heard of it before, but it's possible, I guess. It would be one hell of a power to have, to always fly under the radar. That would make her one of the most dangerous werewolves out there."

"You also were saying you didn't understand how you couldn't detect the one I killed last night, especially since he showed up just after you left. Maybe you *were* too far away to sense him, like you said. But what if it was because her power also protects others from being detected while she's around? Or maybe that werewolf also had the same undetectable power?"

Rick let out a long sigh. "Then, that would mean none of us are safe." He turned to face Jason. "Where did Sami stab the werewolf that night?"

"Right here," Jason pointed to his left side.

"Jason, call Abby and warn her. Mike, turn the car around. We're going back."

Mike grinned. "Now we're talkin'!"

"Wait! Just wait a minute," Jason interjected. "What *exactly* are we doing?"

"We're going to see if Sharon's a werewolf," Rick said.

Mike pulled back onto the road, then slammed on the brake, screeching the car to a halt. "We can't just show up there again. She'll know we're on to her. She might run."

"She seemed to be smitten with you, Jason." Rick raised his eyebrows.

"What? What do you want me to do, just go back there and ask her to lift up her shirt?" he asked, looking at Rick as if he were crazy.

"No," Mike said. "Ask her out on a date."

"Hell no!" Jason boomed. "I have preferences you know. I'm not the least bit attracted to her."

"Just close your eyes and pretend she's Sami," Mike taunted.

"Just ask her over for dinner," Rick suggested. "That way Abby and I are close by in case something goes wrong."

"What if my eyes change, then what?" Jason asked.

"They're not changing now. It looks like you're gaining better control," Rick reassured.

"I mean, what if they change to *yellow*?" Jason asked with a disgusted look on his face.

Mike let out a hearty laugh, deeper and louder than usual.

Rick clenched his jaw to keep from chuckling, but it didn't work. He turned his head the other way, hiding his amusement.

"Maybe Sharon would keep you satisfied long enough to keep your paws off Sami until you're normal again," Mike added.

"Whatever!" Jason sighed. "But I'm not going to the door. I'll just call her."

"Fine," Rick said, still chuckling. "Let's get back to the house."

Mike stepped on the gas and sped back to his brother's place. When they arrived, Jason went to the privacy of the upstairs guest bedroom to call Sheriff Briggs's house.

Rick sat in the recliner and began reading through the book.

After calling Abby, Mike plopped on the couch to relax. "Find anything helpful?" he asked his dad.

"Nothing I don't already know," Rick said, his nose still buried in the book. "Wait a minute. Here's something that might tell us Jason's fate. It says here that a woman was attacked by a wolf beast. A few months later, she gave birth to a son that was believed to be the spawn of evil. Let's see.... Oh, here. It says when the child aged he was bitten by another wolf beast and soon the boy's evil powers were unleashed, turning his eyes the color of blood. They tried to kill him, but he seemed to be immortal."

"Does it say anything else about the wolf that bit him? If they killed it or not?" Mike asked.

His father remained silent while he skimmed over the page. "Here, it says they killed the wolf beast who attacked the boy, hoping to free the boy of the evil, but the child remained unchanged. He remained human on the outside, but on the inside, he was evil. He vanished and was never seen again." Rick slammed the book shut and set it on the coffee table.

"Maybe they weren't able to save the boy because they didn't kill the wolf before the full moon," Mike suggested.

"I haven't read anything about the full moon in the book yet. Maybe they didn't realize the full moon and werewolves had a connection back then."

"So, even if Sharon *is* responsible for turning Jason, there's a remote chance that killing her won't bring Jason back."

"You might be right, Mike. There might not be any fixing Jason at all. But in the book, the boy's father was a werewolf, which might be why there was no saving him."

Mike sat forward and clasped his hands together, trying to make sense of it all. "So, you're saying maybe it sealed the boy's fate when he was bitten? There was no saving him since he was born with werewolf blood already running through his veins?"

Rick's eyes filled with dread. "You saw Jason's parents all the time with them living right across the street. Do you think one of them, or both, are werewolves?"

Mike brought his hand to his mouth as he tried to recall any interactions he'd had with Jason's parents over the last thirteen years. "I don't know, Dad. After Jason's dad accidentally shot you out in the forest, then a supposed wolf killed you when he left to get help, Jason's parents pretty much stayed away from us. Me, Billy, Megan…we were pissed at them, and they knew it. But, from what I saw of them from a distance, I never noticed anything out of the ordinary." He shrugged.

"I'm sorry for all of the pain everyone had to go through."

Mike shook his head. "It was a long time ago, Dad. It's done and over with."

His father picked up the book and started flipping through the pages again. "Jason's powers have developed quickly. Too quickly. It's not normal for that to happen. And he's already learning to gain control over some of them. The full moon is still almost a month away. If he was the offspring of a werewolf to begin with, it would all make sense."

"Well, Jason's parents moved to the east coast a few years ago. So, how in the hell are we gonna find out if they're werewolves?" Mike asked.

"Ask him," Rick replied as if it were no big deal, while still browsing through the book.

"Ask who what?" Jason said as he trudged down the stairs.

Though Jason was irritating at times, Mike couldn't bear to traumatize him over something they weren't sure of yet. He jumped to his feet. "Nothing. Abby just said they were on their way back."

"Oh. Did you find anything in the book?" Jason stood behind the recliner, peering over Rick's shoulder.

"Not yet," Mike said with urgency, not giving his dad a chance to answer. "So, how'd it go with Sharon?"

Jason grimaced. "She's coming to my house tonight at seven. Do I really have to go through with this?"

Mike pinched a smirk between his lips. "Don't you wanna know if she attacked you? Don't you want Sami to be safe?"

Jason's eyes turned to angry slits. "Since it was your idea, you can come over and do the cooking. And, when we're finished eating, you can drive your happy ass back over and clean up."

"Sounds fair," Mike agreed.

Jason furrowed his brow. "Really? Why are you being nice all of a sudden?"

"No reason. I just feel bad for your sorry ass is all." He shrugged. "You wanna help me fix the doors?"

"Sure, I guess. It'll get my mind off tonight," Jason said, his tone glum.

"Let's go gather up some tools." Mike slapped Jason on the back and headed out the front door.

29

STANDING ON his front porch, Jason watched Sharon park her car. For the first time on a date, he was a bundle of nerves. *Please don't kill me, please don't kill me....*

As she approached the steps, he put on a fake smile and raised a hand.

"Hello. Don't you look beautiful tonight?"

"Thank you." She blushed, straightening out her white blouse, even though it was tucked in neatly to her red pants. With a quick hand, she felt to ensure her dark curls were still bound in a tight ponytail. She seemed just as nervous.

Jason opened the door and led the way inside.

As she entered, she inhaled deeply and smiled. "Smells good. What is it?"

"What is it?" he repeated, wishing he would've taken the time to see what Mike had prepared before she arrived. "Oh, just a little something I whipped up." He inhaled the hearty aroma. "It does smell good, doesn't it?" Eager to eat, they went right and down the hall, until they reached the dining room.

Jason looked at the table and tensed. It had been romantically set, complete with lit candles and rose petals sprinkled all over.

Dammit, Mike! What the hell?

"Oh, spaghetti. My favorite!" Her eyes twinkled.

Jason pushed his ire aside and pulled Sharon's chair out for her.

"Thank you," she said as she took her seat.

"You're welcome," Jason said, sitting adjacent to her.

He handed her the bowl of spaghetti. "Ladies first."

She smiled and spooned a lump of spaghetti onto her plate before handing the bowl back to him.

Jason eyed her meager helping. *She certainly doesn't eat like a werewolf.* He shoveled more spaghetti onto the serving spoon and held it up. "Are you sure you have enough?"

She lifted her hand. "Thanks. I have plenty."

He shrugged and slopped it onto his plate, along with another heaping spoonful. He eyed the huge bowl of pasta, wishing he could just dig right into it instead. Dinner was going to be harder than he'd thought. Not only did he have to try to figure out a way to see under her shirt, but now, he had to make sure he didn't make a complete pig of himself in front of her.

Eating with as much restraint as possible, he made idle chit chat about her work at the diner, where she was from, and the weather—all the while trying to come up with a scheme to look under her shirt without getting slapped, or worse, eaten.

A spool of spaghetti unraveled from Sharon's fork and slid onto her blouse. "Oh no!" She frowned and un-tucked the shirt to pull the hot food away from her skin. She pinched the blob of noodles between her fingers and tossed them onto her napkin.

Jason smirked. *Thank you, Mike, for making spaghetti!* Before Sharon noticed his amusement, his smile faded. "Oh, no. Here, let me help." He dipped a clean napkin in his water and knelt beside her. With a light touch, he dabbed at the red stain on the lower left side of her blouse.

"Hmmm." He clutched the bottom of her blouse and pulled it up a little, while pretending to work at the stain.

"I'll get it." Sharon snatched the napkin.

He sighed at his failed attempt before an idea popped into his mind. Wearing the slightest of smirks, he stood and pretended to fall forward, bumping into her side.

"Ouch!" She winced and bolted to her feet, holding her waist.

"What's the matter? Did the sauce burn you?" He swiftly lifted her shirt, exposing a white bandage taped to her side. Jason gulped, trying to remain oblivious while suppressing his fear. "Oh, I'm so sorry! What happened?"

Sharon yanked her top from his grip and pulled it back down. "Nothing! It just happened when I fell!" she snapped.

"Sorry," Jason said, trying to sound as genuine as he could. "Must've been one hell of a fall."

"It was, but I don't want to talk about it." She met his gaze with uncertainty and pushed in her chair. I think I just want to go home now."

"I'm sorry. I didn't mean to upset you." He continued his charade with the probable werewolf before him, thankful she didn't appear to want to murder him. Yet, for some reason, deep down he felt bad for his behavior.

"It's okay. Maybe we'll just try this another time?" She took a pen from her purse and jotted her number down on a paper napkin. "Here." As she handed him the napkin her chin started to tremble. "I have to go."

"I'll see you out." He walked her to her car, apologizing to her again before she drove away. When the sound of the engine faded, he darted back to Sami's house.

THE FRONT door banged open.

Sami screamed and jumped up from the couch.

"It's her!" Jason shouted, closing the door behind him.

"Quit doing that!" Sami shouted with her hand clutching her chest.

Billy glared at him. "Can't you be a little calmer?"

"Was her side wounded?" Mike asked, getting up from the recliner.

"Yep! It was all bandaged up. She said it happened when she fell. Then she wanted to leave. Thanks for making spaghetti, by the way."

He grinned.

Mike smirked and sat back down. "It was the least I could do. Didn't wanna make you actually have to kiss the monster that bit you."

"Ew!" Jason cringed at the thought and turned to Rick—who was sitting at the breakfast bar reading the book. "So, now what? We kill her, right? Then I'm all back to normal?"

"It's not so simple, Jason." Rick said. "Her wounds could just be a coincidence. Now, we have to make her mad to see if her eyes turn red."

"Why didn't you tell me that before? I could've done that back at my house."

"We couldn't take the chance of her harming you before we got there," Rick reminded.

Abby descended the stairs. "So, what's next?"

"Let's go piss her off!" Mike jumped up, ready to go.

"Give me a few more minutes." Rick turned another page.

"This is good news, Jason" Billy said. "You're one step closer to being normal again."

Jason dropped next to Sami on the couch. "I hope so."

Billy shot Jason a warning glare and wrapped a protective arm around Sami. "You better keep your eyes their normal color."

"Don't worry, I can control the whole love potion thing now. I think." Jason eyed Billy's cast. "That one's much better. How's the ribs?"

"Not broken," Billy said. "Just bruised."

"That's good. Oh—" Jason gave Mike a dirty look "—the candles and rose petals were a little over the top, don't you think?"

Laughter and snickers filled the room.

"The rose petals were actually my idea." Abby giggled.

Jason scowled at her. "Yeah, well, thanks for that."

Rick sighed and closed the book.

"Are we ready to go rough Sharon up?" Jason asked, his ire suddenly replaced with eagerness.

Rick's expression turned serious. He crossed the room and sat on the coffee table in front of Jason.

Jason's excitement dimmed. "What's going on?"

"I did find something in the book," Rick said. "I found one case like yours—a human bitten by a werewolf. Just like you, he stayed human but had werewolf powers. They killed the werewolf responsible, but it didn't help."

"Are you saying I might be stuck this way? Well, maybe they didn't kill him before the full moon? Or maybe they killed the wrong werewolf? It had to be Sharon who bit me. She was bandaged in the exact same spots we stuck her. If we off her, I *could* turn back to normal."

"Maybe," Rick said, "but there's a possibility killing her won't help you either."

"And why is that?" Jason eyes turned green.

"The boy's mother was human, but his father was a werewolf at the time of conception. The boy was born half-human, half-werewolf. For the first few years of his life, he seemed normal. His powers weren't unleashed until he was bitten by another werewolf, triggering the transformation. His powers developed quickly, within a couple of days, just like yours. And, when they killed the werewolf who had bitten him, the boy didn't change back into a human. Either it was because they failed to kill the werewolf before the full moon, or it was because the boy was never really a human to begin with."

"Well, Rick, sorry to burst your bubble, but I'm pretty sure my dad is *not* a werewolf. And my mom isn't a werewolf either," Jason said, his tone biting. He stood and stormed toward the kitchen and back to the living room with a strained look.

Rick stood to face him. "Are you sure he's your biological father and she's your biological mother?"

With his jaws clenched, Jason let out a deep growl. "Yes, I'm sure! Maybe it didn't work for that kid because they didn't kill the werewolf who bit him before the full moon! Maybe it'll still work for me!"

"Calm the hell down, Jason!" Mike boomed. He sighed and turned to his dad. "So, what do you suggest we do now?"

"Let's start with Sharon. Anyone know where she lives?" Rick looked around at everyone.

"My guess is with the sheriff," Jason said, anger still lining his tone.

"Who's going?" Billy asked.

"Me, Abby, and Jason," Rick said. "The rest of you need to wait for us in the cage."

"What?" Mike jumped to his feet. "We really need to modify that thing and make it bigger. Maybe line the whole damn room with silver instead."

Sami sucked in a quick breath as an idea came to mind. "Wait. I could probably get her to come here. She seemed to really want to be friends. Maybe you all could just hide out in the bedroom until she's in the house. Killers can't sense when other werewolves are near, right? That way she can't run off."

Everyone stared at her with blank looks on their faces, making her feel uncomfortable. "It was just an idea." She shrugged.

Rick finally grinned. "Sami, I think it's the best idea I've heard today. But, if she is a werewolf, we can't utter a sound or make the slightest of movements, or she'll hear us."

"What? No!" Billy said. "It would put Sami in danger."

"No, Son. She would be heavily protected. Three against one, Sharon doesn't stand a chance."

Sami understood Billy's concern for her but was growing tired of being treated like the helpless child. "Billy, we're armed with silver and surrounded by werewolves. We'll be okay." She gave him a reassuring smile.

He sat back again, but from his sour expression, he still didn't like the idea. "Can't she smell everyone?"

Rick nodded. "We'd be in the rooms with the doors shut, which would lessen her chance of smelling us until she's inside. But at that point, we'd have her surrounded."

"Jason, do you have her cell number?" Sami asked, avoiding Billy's gaze. She was going to help whether Billy liked it or not.

"Oh, yeah," Jason said with dull enthusiasm and pulled a folded napkin from his pocket. "Good thing I didn't throw it away yet. And how'd you know she gave me her number?"

"Lucky guess, *Romeo*." She smirked.

Billy's stern look softened, and he let out a slight chuckle. "She must have the *hots* for you."

Jason narrowed his eyes. "Don't even go there. She's the first woman that's repulsed me, aside from Jessica, and I wanna keep it that way." He handed Sami the napkin.

Sami went to the privacy of her bedroom and made the call. Sharon sounded eager to meet but was leery of Mike. Sami assured her that Mike wouldn't be around. With a guilty conscience, she hung up the phone and went back into the living room.

"She's on her way." Sami forced a smile, feeling uneasy about deceiving a possible werewolf.

"Good," Rick said. "Jason, you wait in the downstairs bedroom. Abby, morph and wait at Jason's house. As soon as she's inside, Jason will alert you with a text. Then, get back here as fast as you can to guard the front door. Mike, you wait upstairs with me. Do you have your gun?"

Mike nodded and lifted his pant leg, showing off the gun strapped to his calf.

Billy raised his eyebrows. "Nice."

Mike grinned and nodded. "I know."

"Where's my gun?" Billy asked.

Mike opened the end table drawer next to the recliner and pulled out a pistol. He reached over the coffee table and handed it to Billy.

Billy checked to make sure it was loaded. He stared at his brother with an annoyed look. "You know, it would be nice if you told me where all the guns are stashed."

"Later," Mike said.

"When Sharon gets here invite her in," Rick said. "Make her think everything's safe. Then try to anger her somehow."

Sami suddenly wished she could back out of it. Angering a killer werewolf seemed like a bad idea. "You want me to make her mad?"

"We won't let her lay a hand on you," Rick reassured. "You'll be safe, Sami. I wouldn't let you do this if I thought you'd get hurt."

She nodded, deciding to ignore the knot in her stomach and trust Rick.

"Ready?" Rick asked.

"As I'll ever be," Sami said, her tone unsure.

Billy stood from the couch and tucked the pistol in his waistband. "Don't worry, she'll be surrounded, and nothing will happen to us. Here..." He pulled the locket from under Sami's shirt. "Extra protection."

With a slight smile, Sami took a few seconds to admire the locket, then glanced around the room. Aside from Mike clomping up the stairs, everyone else had disappeared without making a sound. "Hmm, they're already gone?"

"Must be nice to have powers like that," Billy said.

They sat on the barstools and waited. Sami tapped her fingers on the counter, and Billy kept glancing at window. They discussed possible topics of conversation to strike up with Sharon and how to anger her. Within a couple of minutes, headlights illuminated the kitchen window, and the hum of an engine grew near.

"That was fast," Sami whispered, growing anxious.

"It'll be okay," Billy whispered back.

They both stood and faced the door.

Even though she was expecting it, the loud knock rattled Sami's nerves.

Billy rubbed the back of her arm, silently reassuring her. He took a quiet step back and gave her a quick nod.

Sami took in a deep breath and opened the front door.

Sharon stood there, wearing leggings and a blue top.

"Hi, Sharon."

"Hi." Sharon smiled, but her eyes shifted behind Sami toward the kitchen, the stairs, and the living room.

"Sorry about Mike yesterday. He can be a little overprotective sometimes." She stepped aside to let Sharon in.

Sharon entered the house and threw a nonchalant glance over her shoulder, in Billy's direction.

"Hey, Sharon," Billy said in an upbeat manner and shut the door.

"Hello." Sharon gave him a timid smile.

"Uh, you probably already know Billy." Sami motioned toward him.

Not wanting to scare her off, Billy kept a welcoming smile. "How's business at the diner?"

"Um...slow."

Sami tried to think of something to say to absolve the awkwardness, but she couldn't recall one of the ideas she and Billy had just come up with. "Uh, are you thirsty?"

"No, I can't stay. I was just hoping I could talk you about the job at the diner."

"What happened to your arm?" Billy asked casually.

Sharon looked down at her bandage. "I…uh…."

Sami recalled the reason Sharon had given yesterday. "She accidentally cut herself with a knife," Sami said to Billy. She looked back at Sharon. "Right?"

"Right." Sharon smiled. "At work. Someone walked past me holding a knife, and I got a little too close." Pursed lips replaced her smile, and she gave Sami an uneasy look.

"That's strange." Billy narrowed his eyes. "Jason said you fell."

Sharon's eyes widened with fear. "I have to go." She headed for the door.

Billy stepped in front of the door, blocking her escape. "Which is it? Did you accidentally fall, walk by someone with a knife, or were you stabbed?"

Sharon tensed, and her eyes turned green.

Sami screamed, taken off guard by the unexpected change. In a split-second Jason's arms were around hers and Billy's waists and the room spun too fast to see anything clearly. When everything came back into focus, they stood at the end of the hallway in front of the bedroom door.

"What the hell?" Billy asked, stunned.

"Stay put," Jason ordered, his eyes a bright jade.

Sharon opened the front door, but Abby's monstrous frame blocked her escape.

Abby growled, bearing her fangs.

Sharon staggered back before turning and crashing smack-dab into Rick's brick wall of a chest. Eyes wide, she backed up, each step slow and cautious. With nowhere else to run, she simply lowered her head, cowering in shame.

Jason darted into the living room and stopped in front of her.

"Jason?" Sharon asked, her eyes clouded with confusion.

"Surprise!" Jason grinned.

Sharon backed away. "It was Jessica! She made me do it! I didn't want to!"

"Look what you did to me!" An angry growl ripped from Jason's throat. "You turned me into a freak! You hurt my best friends!" He clamped a hand around her throat.

"I didn't mean to bite you! Please!" she begged. "I'll do anything! It won't help to kill me! Please!"

Jason released his hold on her neck. "What do you mean it won't help to kill you?"

"You won't change back to human! I was told that you have to kill your father!" she shouted, her face stricken with fear.

"My father's *not* a werewolf!"

Abby grabbed Sharon's arms, holding her in place.

"Not the father that raised you. Your *real* father!" Sharon cried.

"You're lying!" Jason roared.

"No! I'm not lying!"

"Then, who in the hell is my *real* father, and how in the hell do you know all this?"

"I don't know who our father is! Jessica wouldn't say. All she told me was you won't change back unless he dies."

Jason's mouth hung open. He stared at Sharon's dark curls sprawled about her shoulders, her tan skin, then her hazel eyes. His glared at her suspiciously. "What in the hell do you mean *our* father?"

"I'm your sister," Sharon admitted.

"I don't have a sister!" Jason boomed. "You're just saying that so we don't kill you right now!"

"No! I'm really your sister! We have different mothers but the same father. Please don't hurt me," she cried helplessly. "I didn't mean to bite you! I promise! Jessica just wanted Billy! She said if I didn't do it, she'd kill you!"

"The werewolf who bit me had red eyes!" Jason said.

"They were contacts! They're in my purse!" She motioned with a quick nod to her purse lying next to her feet.

Jason snatched up the bag and emptied it onto the breakfast bar.

"In the white plastic container." She sniveled, sucking in sobs.

He opened the container and sighed. "Shit!" He dumped the red contacts onto the counter.

Rick growled, catching his attention. Since no words were spoken, Sami knew they were communicating telepathically.

Jason turned back to Sharon. "Who bit you?"

"Jessica…almost two weeks ago," Sharon said.

Jason squinted his eyes. "It only took you a week to learn to morph? Is it because of the full moon? Do I have to wait until it's full to morph?"

"I was able to morph a couple of days after I was bitten. So, no, it wasn't because of the full moon. Sheriff Briggs and Jessica think, because both of my parents were werewolves, my powers developed faster than normal. You might be able to change before the full moon, too, since you were born part werewolf."

Jason glanced at Rick and shifted his eyes back to Sharon. "Why can't anyone sense you?"

"When I'm in human form, others can't sense that I'm also a werewolf. That's one of my special powers, I guess. I'm stronger and have more than one power since I was born a werewolf. You probably have more than one power too. Another power is that I don't leave a werewolf scent behind when I'm a werewolf—only a human scent—so it's easier for me to go undetected. But, I also have weaknesses. I can't sense when others are werewolves when they're in human form, and I can't sense when protectors are near—they smell like humans to me. I *can* detect when killer werewolves are nearby, though."

Jason cocked his jaw to the side. "That's why you weren't fazed by Rick when we showed up at the sheriff's house earlier. And you had no clue what you were walking into here tonight, did you?"

Sharon shook her head. "I've heard of Rick, but I didn't know what he looked like. I didn't realize it was him."

The werewolf Mike had shot in the basement crossed Jason's thoughts. "Why can't we sense killer werewolves when you're around? Are you keeping us from sensing them?"

Her eyes filled with uncertainty. "You should be able to. I don't have that power."

Rick darted upstairs so fast all Sami saw was a blur.

"Who was the werewolf hiding in the forest when you came here to talk to Sami yesterday?"

"I don't know. Honest. I didn't even know there was one nearby."

Jason scratched his forehead and sighed. "If our *real* father is a werewolf like you say, is he a killer or a protector?" Jason asked.

"He's a killer." She lowered her head in shame.

"Wait a minute. Was Jessica your sister? *Our* sister?" He asked with a look of horror on his face.

"No. She was just ordered to guide me into being a werewolf after she bit me."

"Oh, thank God!" he breathed a sigh of relief, clutching his chest.

Billy smirked and pressed his lips together to contain his laughter.

Rick darted back downstairs, wearing jeans and a T-shirt, followed by Mike. "It's okay, Abby," Rick said. "You go ahead."

Abby let go of Sharon and disappeared up the stairs.

"Mike...." Sharon backed away from him, bumping into the couch.

"Just hold on, Son." Rick put his hand up, warning Mike to behave. He turned back to Sharon. "That's why you smelled familiar today—you were one of the human scents on the trail in California—it was your blood I smelled. All this time, I thought the human scent on Sami and Jason the night of the attack was from someone they'd come in contact with here, before they left, or from a doctor or nurse at the hospital where Jason had stitches. But it was you." He turned to Jason. "I only smelled Jessica on you guys that night because of the red shirt Sami was wearing."

Jason's eyes widened and he nodded. "It all makes sense."

The men turned back to Sharon.

Sharon shook her head. "I'm so sorry I caused all this trouble. I never wanted to hurt anyone. Jessica said she'd kill Jason and Sami if I didn't do what she wanted. She just wanted Billy for a few days to conceive his baby. She was going to bring him back unharmed and leave everyone alone. I was just trying to save everyone," she said, her tone desperate.

"We call that being a traitor!" Mike snapped. "Why should we trust you now?"

"You have to believe me! You can ask Jessica! She's probably still hiding out in the cave!"

"Jessica's dead!" Jason growled. "We rescued Billy then ripped her evil cold heart out!"

"Sh-she's dead?" Sharon whispered with a shocked look on her face. "Then, it's okay now. We're all safe!" A slight smile formed, and she let out a relieving breath.

Rick narrowed his eyes. "We're not safe! Sami was attacked by two werewolves in one day!"

"I don't know why! Honest, I don't!" Sharon backed farther into the living room.

Sami couldn't see Sharon anymore. She grabbed Billy's hand and went to the entrance of the hallway, against the staircase, to get a better view. Abby darted down the stairs and held a hand up to her and Billy, motioning for them to stay put.

"Please," Sharon pleaded. "You have to believe me."

Jason ran a hand through his hair and exhaled. "I believe you," he said, his voice calm.

"What?" Mike asked incredulously. "She's lying!"

Jason shook his head. "She's not lying. I can feel it."

"How?" Mike asked.

"I don't know. Maybe because she's my sister. Maybe because I have special powers. I just know," Jason said, irritated.

"We're still not safe," Rick said. "We still have daddy dearest to contend with."

"If we find out a way to kill our father before the full moon, whoever he is, will you be normal again too?" Jason asked Sharon.

She shook her head. "No, it's too late for me. My first full moon just passed. I almost told you earlier, at dinner, but I didn't want Jessica to hurt you—" she locked eyes on Sami "—or you. I didn't know she was already dead."

Sami felt awful for Sharon. She wanted to do something to help her—to tell everyone to back off—but they needed answers, and Sharon had them.

"So..." Jason furrowed his brow and stared at Sharon for a moment. "You're all right if I just kill whoever in the hell our real father is? It won't faze you the slightest?"

"I've never really knew him, Jason. Besides, he's a killer, remember? He had me move to this town. He probably had Jessica bite me, for all I know."

"Right." Jason sighed.

Mike took a menacing step toward Sharon. "If Jason's still a werewolf after we kill his father, we're coming after you next."

Sharon gulped. "The sheriff and Jessica said it would work. That I wouldn't have to be killed to change Jason back. But, if for some reason it doesn't…then do what you have to do." She lowered her head.

"Did you know what we were up to earlier today?" Mike asked, his anger more subdued.

Sharon lifted her head. "What do you mean?"

"When I was sweet talking you to get the book at Sheriff Briggs's house," Jason said. "Did you know it wasn't ours?"

"Well, I kind of had a feeling. I have no idea how the book fell into the sheriff's hands, but I know something like that didn't really belong to him. I would've let you have the book, you know. You didn't have to get all cheesy."

Mike and Billy chuckled under their breaths.

Jason glared at them.

"And when you called the sheriff's house and asked me to dinner, I thought it would be the perfect chance to tell you everything. I was trying to work up the nerve as soon as I got to your house, but I was thrown off by the candles and the rose petals. The whole time, I was praying you didn't try to kiss me or something. But then, you started asking about my wound, and I just got scared. I gave you my number to play along. I didn't want to make you feel like I rejected you. You know, lower your confidence or anything." She shrugged.

Mike and Billy chuckled again.

Jason growled at them. "So, Sharon, you can turn me into a werewolf, but you're afraid to damage my ego? That's a new one," he said, his tone dripping with sarcasm.

Still seeing the amusement in it all, Mike and Billy closed their mouths to muffle their snickers, but it didn't work.

"Come on, guys! It isn't funny!" Jason snapped. "I didn't know she was my sister. It's not like I was gonna kiss her or anything. Assholes!"

"Well," Rick said, "if you're Jason's sister, then that means you're on our side now. Where are you staying?"

"In a back room of the diner until I was turned. After that, my father ordered me to stay at the sheriff's house so Jessica could train me."

"How do you know it was really your father who put the order in if you don't even know who he is?" Jason asked. "It could've been Jessica or the sheriff himself."

"I've been talking to him on the phone ever since I was a little girl. Then, when my mom died a few months ago…" Tears glistened her eyes. "He told me to move here. So, I did."

Jason's eyes saddened. He swiped a hand over his mouth. "I'm sorry about your mom. How did it happen if she was a werewolf?"

Sharon lowered her head. "Silver knife to the heart. I don't know who did it."

Sami felt terrible for her. "Sharon, I'm so sorry about your mom." Sami took a step forward, but Mike's sudden ironclad grip on her arm stopped her. "Mike, come on!"

His eyes bore into hers. "You can stand next to Billy or here with me."

Flustered, she yanked her arm from his grasp and went back to Billy side.

Mike turned his cold glare back to Sharon. "So, some guy you don't know claims to be your father and tells you to move here, and you simply do what he tells you to do?"

"I grew up talking to him on the phone. I had somewhat of a relationship with him. My mom just wouldn't let me meet him in person. I think it's because he's a killer. She was trying to protect me from him. Trying to keep him from warping my mind or something. I don't know." She shook her head.

"Did you grow up knowing your parents were werewolves?" Rick asked.

She nodded.

"What?" Jason asked. "Why would you listen to your father and just move here if you knew he was a killer?"

Sharon lowered her gaze. "I had no one after my mom died. He was always nice on the phone. I thought I could come here and meet him and have a real relationship with him. I thought he'd be nice to me since I was his daughter." She lifted her lashes to meet her brother's gaze and tears slipped down her cheeks. "But I haven't even seen him. He's not here, and the sheriff and Jessica wouldn't tell me where he was. They've just been grooming me to be evil like them, ever since I was bitten." She sighed, and a satisfied smirk tugged at the corner of her mouth.

"Boy, were they angry when I turned into a protector instead of a killer like they were hoping." Her smile faded, and pain filled her eyes again. "But they were the closest things to friends or family I've known since my mom died."

"Not anymore," Jason said. He walked right up to Sharon and gave her a huge, whole-hearted hug. "Let's go get your things. I have a big house, and I could use some company."

Sharon wiped the tears away with the back of her hands and lifted her head from Jason's chest to look him in the eyes. "Really? You mean you want me to live with you?" she asked with a confused look on her face.

"Yeah." He grinned. "No sister of mine is gonna live in that rat hole with the likes of Sheriff Briggs."

She smiled, her eyes beaming with excitement. She wrapped her arms around his waist and squeezed. "I'm so sorry I bit you and for everything! I'm gonna make it up to you! You'll see!"

Jason chuckled and squeezed her tighter before letting her go. "Come on, let's go."

"I'm coming with you," Rick said.

"I was hoping you'd say that," Jason said. "The sheriff's house gives me the frickin' creeps."

Mike crossed his arms and grunted under his breath.

Rick glanced at him. "She's one of us, Son."

Mike remained silent, his expression full of skepticism.

As Jason and Sharon went out the front door, Sami smiled. One minute, Sharon was fighting for her life, and the next, she was a part of the family.

"We'll be back in a few minutes," Rick said. "Be on alert. There could be more werewolves around." He paused in the doorway. "It sure is good to have another protector on our side."

"Yeah, well, I'll believe it when I see it," Mike said.

Rick went outside and closed the door.

"So, it looks like we've gained another member of our family." Sami smiled. "See, I knew Sharon was nice."

"You mean before or after she bit Jason, hit you, and kidnapped my brother?" Mike said as he plopped onto the couch.

Sami shot him a disapproving glare. "Yeah, well, everything turned out okay. And she was forced into it, remember?"

"It's a good thing we ran into Sharon," Billy said. "So far, she's our only lead into finding Jason's real father."

Abby sat next to Mike and cuddled against him.

Billy nudged Sami with his elbow and winked, throwing the slightest of nods toward their bedroom.

Knowing exactly what he had in mind, Sami smiled.

"Well, it's been a long day, guys. We're gonna turn in," Billy said.

Abby raised a hand. "Goodnight, you two."

"Night," Mike said, turning his attention back to Abby.

Billy grabbed Sami's hand and led her into the bedroom. "Mike fixed the door," he said as he shut and locked it.

"I see that." She smiled, anticipating their intimacy.

"So, I was saving this for a more normal time…" Billy went to the dresser and opened the top drawer. He pulled out a tiny black box and set it in the palm of his casted hand. "…But I'm afraid this is as normal as it gets." He got down on one knee and opened the box, exposing a beautiful antique-looking, white gold ring. A generous diamond stood in the center, and smaller blue sapphires surrounded it, with a mixture of the two gems adorning each side of the twisted band.

Taken off guard, Sami's eyes filled with tears. She placed a shaky hand over her pounding heart.

"I know I already asked you, but I wanted to do this properly." He inhaled deeply and let out an even, steady breath. "Sami…I love you more than anything in this world, and I want to spend every day showing you just how much you mean to me. I want to spend the rest of my life with you. Will you marry me…?"

Sami's breath caught in her throat, and her heart suddenly filled with more love than she ever thought possible. "Oh, Billy...," she whispered in awe and let out a shaky breath. "Yes! Yes, I'll marry you."

He grinned and removed the ring from the box.

She held her hand out, trying to keep it steady as he slid the ring on her finger. It fit perfectly.

Wearing a proud grin, he stood and encircled his arms around her waist. "I love you, Sami," he whispered.

Elated, she wrapped her arms around his neck and gazed into his eyes. "I love *you*, Billy. And I always will."

He lowered his lips to hers and gave her a long, tender kiss. With each loving mouthful, their passion intensified. As they kissed and caressed, their clothing came off, one item at a time. Standing naked in each other's arms, he eased her onto the bed and covered her body with his.

30

SAMI OPENED her eyes to the sun shining brightly through the sliding glass door. Movement at the edge of the forest caught her attention. A deer lowered its head and nibbled on a wildflower. Seeing a deer in this part of the forest was practically a miracle. She wondered if she should wake Billy to show him.

"Good morning, future Mrs. Billy Holden. Did you sleep well?" he said as he wrapped an arm around her from behind, while nuzzling his chin into the crook of her neck. "Holy shit, is that a deer?"

"Yes. Beautiful, isn't it?" She turned and planted a kiss on his lips.

He grinned. "I love you too."

She giggled and held her hand up. "I love this ring. It's perfect."

"It was my mother's. She got it from her mother. Mike gave it to me when he found out we were getting married. My dad helped me line it with silver. And we made matching white gold and silver bands too."

"It's beautiful." She pulled his head back to hers, eagerly seeking his lips again.

He met her demand, kissing her hungrily. In one swift move he was on top of her, showing her just how much he loved her.

After their morning lovemaking, they readied for the day. Sami chose to wear a white top and a light blue skirt, while Billy slid on a pair of grey shorts and a blue T-shirt.

As she stood from the bed, a strong grumble rippled through her stomach, sending a wave of nausea to the back of her throat. She clamped a hand over her stomach. “I need to eat.”

Billy’s eyes grew wide. “Don’t get sick. Come on. Let’s go see what’s for breakfast. I smell something good.”

She nodded, and they went to the kitchen. Mike and Jason were at the stove, piling pancakes onto their plates. Abby and Sharon were sitting at the table, eating.

A huge grin crossed Abby’s face. “Well, let’s see the ring!”

Sami’s cheeks turned hot. She sat next to Abby at the table and extended her hand.

Sharon sat forward to get a better look.

“It’s beautiful!” Abby said. “Have you set a date yet?”

“No, maybe when things calm down a little around here,” she said, admiring the ring again.

“Hey, Billy,” Mike said. “I have something I wanna show you today if you have some time. It’s in town.”

He shrugged. “Sure. What is it?”

“You’ll see.”

“Can Sami come too?” Billy asked.

“Of course, she can. And Jason.”

“I have to go to work.” Sharon crossed the kitchen and set her dishes in the sink. “Thank you for breakfast. And, Sami, your ring is very beautiful.”

“Thanks, Sharon,” Sami replied.

“You can’t still be working at the diner?” Jason said with a disgusted look on his face. “Sheriff Briggs practically owns the place.”

“Yes, I am,” Sharon said defensively. “I need to make money somehow.”

“I have plenty of money,” Jason said. “You can go to school or something.”

“Sorry to burst your bubble, big brother, but I do need to make a life for myself, you know. I’m a big girl. Plus, I’m a werewolf. I’m sure that wouldn’t go over well in college. It’s best if our kind stays discreet.”

"Yeah, I guess," Jason said.

"Besides, I am the new assistant manager trainee," Sharon said with a smug grin and patted Jason's chest on her way to the door.

"Congratulations!" Sami smiled.

"Yes, congratulations," Abby said.

"Yeah, I was pretty happy myself. And the other waitresses are too. We also have a new manager. He's much nicer than Henry was. And he's younger and hotter."

"Okay, that's enough. I'm trying to eat without getting sick." Jason sat at the table with a mound of food on his plate.

Sharon snickered and nabbed her purse off the counter. "Bye, everyone!" She headed out the front door.

"Bye," they all replied randomly.

"All right, guys," Mike said. "Hurry up and eat. The bus is leaving in fifteen." He looked at Abby. "Are you coming?"

Abby rose and pushed in her chair. "No, I need to go back to the house and make sure everything's in order. Maybe do a quick tidying. I'll meet up with you later." She headed for the door.

Mike followed Abby outside.

Sami and Billy filled their plates and sat at the table.

Heavy footsteps clomped down the stairs, and Rick entered the kitchen.

"So, what are you doing today, Dad?" Billy asked.

"I'm going to scout the area, make sure it's clear." Rick dished himself a plate of food and took a seat.

"So, how long do you think it'll be before we can all get back into a normal routine?" Jason asked Rick. "I really need to sleep in my own bed again."

"Well, with you and Sharon living across the street, me just next door, and Abby just down the road, I think it'll be okay if we all slept in our own beds tonight," he said.

"Good!" Jason said through a mouth full of food.

Excitement brewed in Sami's chest at the thought of her and Billy finally having the house to themselves, but she couldn't shake the fear in her gut. Killer werewolves could be lurking anywhere, and even with silver knives and bullets to protect them, she and Billy were no match against the deadly beasts.

Rick noticed her worried look. "Don't worry, Sami." He winked. "I meant everyone but me. I plan to keep watch at night for a while, just to be sure."

She smiled, relieved, though she felt bad he'd be awake while they slept peacefully.

"That's a good idea," Jason agreed. "I'll switch off with you."

"Thanks, Jason." Rick sounded surprised.

"No problem. I don't sleep much at night anyway. The crickets are annoyingly loud now."

Rick grinned. "You'll get used to your heightened senses."

Sami shot Billy an uneasy stare, knowing every werewolf in the house had heard what they'd been up to last night. His apologetic eyes didn't help to ease the humiliation. She shook her head and took a bite of her pancakes, glad they'd have to the house to themselves from here on out, despite the possibility of killer werewolves nearby.

After breakfast, Sami, Billy, and Jason headed off into town with Mike, anxious to see his surprise.

Mike pulled Billy's car up to an old, run-down building on the outskirts of town, and the rumble of the engine ceased.

They all climbed out of the car and stared at the old auto shop.

Mike looked at his brother. "Well, what do you think?"

"Uhhh, about what?" Billy asked.

"About our new business. If you want it to be."

"Fixing cars?" Billy asked with a confused look.

Mike chuckled under his breath. "No, not fixing cars. It'll be our shop. You know, to store tools and supplies and build shit for houses."

The corners of Billy's mouth curled up and his eyes brightened. "You bought it?"

"I'm about to. I figure if me, you, and Jason pitch in, we can get it fixed up and running in no time."

"Cool!" Jason smiled. "I'm in!"

"Billy?" Mike asked.

"You know I'm in, bro!" Billy said.

"Yeah, I know. You wanna go inside?" Mike looked at everyone.

"Hell yeah!" Jason said.

Mike unlocked the front door, and they followed him inside.

The musty air blasted Sami's nostrils and she cringed. She scanned the dingy room for any signs of decomposing food or dead rodents. "What's that smell?"

Mike pointed to the worn carpet, splattered with stains. "I'm sure it's older than I am."

She nodded, focusing on the dark smudges on the walls, hoping it was just dirt or grease and not blood or feces.

"Don't worry, it's just grease," Mike said, as if he'd read her mind. He lifted his arms and let them fall at his sides. "This will be the office where Sami will be working. If you want to."

Surprised, she giggled under her breath. She'd been so worried about finding a job, she'd actually considered working at the diner, despite many of the local customers still giving her disapproving glares whenever she went in to eat.

"Really? You mean it?" she asked.

Mike nodded, and his lips formed into a smug grin.

"Yes! That'd be great!" She flashed a huge smile.

"Now, we can always keep you safe," Billy said.

Mike led the way through a door on the back wall. It opened up to a large room with a sink and a counter across the left wall, along with an open door leading to a bathroom. "This would make a good break room."

"Yeah," Billy agreed. "There's enough room for a fridge and a couch."

"And a wall mounted big screen," Jason added.

Mike pulled the blinds up along the back wall of the break room, exposing a large window overlooking the warehouse part of the shop. "And this," he said as he opened the door next to the window, "is the shop."

They all followed him in.

Metal cabinets, shelves, and empty peg boards filled the wall space. A couple of flat tires leaned against a wooden work table. Trash and dirty rags were scattered about here and there. The shop expanded around the corner to the right, back toward the front of the building, where two rusted garage doors made up the front wall.

"Wow! This place is huge!" Sami's voice echoed into the rafters.

Jason chuckled. “That’s what she said.”

Billy punched him in the arm.

“Ow, dude!” Jason smirked. “Are you sure you’re not left handed?”

“There’s plenty of room for storage, tools, and work tables,” Mike said with enthusiasm, as if envisioning the finished product.

Billy and Jason wandered off, opening cabinets and messing around with old machinery and tools that had been left behind.

“So, what do you think?” Mike asked.

Billy approached Mike and smacked him in the shoulder. “I’m in, bro!”

Jason held up an old swimsuit model calendar he’d found on a shelf across the room. “As long as we can put Miss July up on the wall, I’m in too.”

Sami leaned against a table and tilted her head back, peering at the industrial lights hanging from the rafters. “Do the lights work?”

“They will soon,” Mike said.

“So, how much will I make?” she asked.

“According to marriage law, what’s Billy’s is yours.” Mike chuckled.

Wearing a loving smirk, Billy crossed the room and wrapped his arms around her waist. “He means, you and I will share my third in the business. *We* will be equal partners. Or, basically, what’s mine is yours.” He gave her a peck on the lips.

“Really?” She wrapped her arms around his neck and giggled. “I’m so glad I don’t have to serve food to any of the mean people in this town.”

“That’s right,” Billy said. “We call the shots here, and our customers better be nice to you—” he leaned his head toward hers, teasing her with the possibility of another kiss “—or they’ll have to find someone else to fix their broken houses.” His lips puckered and smacked against hers.

“Hey!” Jason scolded, pointing a finger at them. “There will be no breaking in tables around here.”

Sami snickered. “So, is Abby gonna be equal partners with you?” she asked Mike.

“Whoa, easy,” Mike said, holding his hands in front of him as if he were trying to stop the thought. “Abby and I are taking things a little slower than you two. Which reminds me, she's drawing up the papers at her house right now. We have to go meet with her."

"All right! Let's go!" Jason grinned, carrying his new calendar.

They left the shop and headed over to Abby's house. After the documents were initialed and signed by all three men, Abby handed a key to each of them.

"Congratulations!" Abby smiled. "You are now co-owners! When do we start the clean-up?"

"I'm sure everyone needs a day off. Tomorrow?" Mike looked around the table at everyone with hopeful eyes.

"Sounds good," Billy said.

Sami nodded.

"You know," Abby said, "if we can get Rick and Sharon to help too, we can probably get the place completely clean and ready for renovation tomorrow. Benefit of having lightning speed powers. Of course, Rick and I aren't as fast in human form as Jason and Sharon, but I'm sure we can keep up."

Jason grinned smugly.

"We should have the place up and running in no time," Mike said.

"We could have a barbecue tonight." Sami suggested. "You know, to celebrate all of the great things happening to everyone."

"Sound like a good idea," Mike agreed.

"I'm in," Jason said.

"I guess Sami and I will go to the store." Billy reached under the table and put his hand on her bare thigh, just below her skirt hem. His eyes widened. With a subtle smirk, he slid his hand up higher.

Sami tensed and grabbed his hand, stopping it mid-way up her thigh.

"You mind if I tag along?" Jason asked. "I'm still not convinced it's safe out there for you two just yet."

"Of course not, Jason," Sami said.

Billy held his hand up. "Keys, bro."

Mike tossed him the keys, and Sami, Billy, and Jason headed outside to the car.

"You can sit in the backseat with me, Sami." Jason smirked.

"Uh!" She smacked him in the arm.

Jason jerked his arm away and winced. "Shit, that hurt! Your ring. Kind of like being shocked, only more intense." He chuckled under his breath.

"Hey, it works." Billy grinned. "Now, I just need to make a silver ring for the other hand."

"I can't wait to be human again," Jason muttered.

They piled into Billy's car and headed to town to shop for the barbecue, ignoring all the curious and disapproving stares they received for their battered faces. Afterward, they stopped at the diner for lunch and to tell Sharon about the celebration.

"Okay, I get off at five," Sharon said as she helped the waitress set their food down on the table. She sat next to Jason, nudging him over with her hips. "Scoot."

"Geez! Pushy!" Jason grumbled, obviously irritated to be disturbed from taking a big bite out of his cheeseburger.

"Congratulations on the new business." Sharon smiled, stealing one of Jason's fries.

Jason growled just loud enough for them to hear.

Sharon smirked.

"Yeah, it's exciting, isn't it?" Sami said. "There's finally gonna be something productive to do in this dull town."

"So, Sharon," Jason said with a mouthful of food, "do we get to eat here for free now?"

She squinted her eyes at him. "No! I thought you *had* money," she reminded.

"I do, but it's always nice to get free stuff." He shrugged.

"Well, I have to get back to work. See you back at the house," she said, stealing another fry from Jason before she slid away.

"I said I'd share my house, not my food!" Jason snapped.

"I'll fight you for it, and I'll win," she teased and sauntered away.

"She probably *would* win." Billy let out a devious chuckle.

"I think I like the old Sharon better!" Jason grumbled.

Sami shook her head. "No, the old Sharon was the sheriff's and Jessica's puppet. I like the *real* Sharon better."

Jason sighed. "I guess you're right."

They continued to eat, and when they finished, they drove back to the house.

Sami and Billy stomped up the steps of the front porch.

Jason stood at the bottom, staring up at them. "I'm just gonna run home and tidy up a bit since a girl is staying in the house now. Apparently, my sister thinks the house needs a good dusting. His face scrunched as if he were repulsed. "Who dusts anyway?" He shrugged. "Oh well. I'll be back later."

"Wait," Sami said. "What if there are werewolves around?"

"There are. Rick's next door." He winked. "Pretty sure he knows we're here."

"I am so jealous of your freakish powers," Billy said.

Jason gave him a pompous grin and darted away.

Billy sighed.

"I happen to be glad you're not a werewolf." Sami smiled. "I like you just the way you are. You are unbelievably handsome..." She caressed his cheek. "And strong..." She ran her fingertips over his chiseled biceps. "And..." She wrapped her arms around his neck, pulling his lips close to hers. "You are the best kisser in the world. Among other things."

Needing no more convincing than that, Billy crushed his lips to hers. After an indulgent kiss, he pulled away and motioned toward the house with a nod. "Let's take this inside."

She giggled and followed him into the house.

"WHAT TIME is it?" Sami asked, climbing out of bed to get dressed.

Billy looked at his watch. "Three-thirty."

"Oh, crap! Come on, we have to hurry," she said, tossing him his clothes. "I hope no one's here yet."

He hesitated and shook his head. "Now that everyone has moved out, they have to knock before barging in. So, I'm sure no one's here yet."

"You're right." She smiled, feeling more at ease in her own home now.

They finished dressing, freshened up, and went to the kitchen to prepare for the barbeque.

Jason barreled through the front door, catching it before it slammed against the wall. “It’s about time you two—”

“Hey!” Billy cut him off and gave him a knowing glare. “Can’t you knock?”

“Oh, right,” he flashed a cheesy grin.

Sami’s face grew hot, but she played along, pretending ignorance to the fact that Jason had been impatiently waiting all afternoon for them to come out of the bedroom.

“Where’s my dad?” Billy asked.

“Down in the basement with Mike and Abby,” Jason said.

“Everyone’s down in the basement?” Sami asked, more humiliated than ever. *Will we ever have any privacy again?*

“What are they doing?” Billy asked.

“Modifying the cage,” Jason said.

Billy smiled. “Cool. Let’s go see.”

“I’ll race you.” Jason smirked.

“Shut up!” Billy snapped.

“Sami, you want a ride?” Jason asked.

“No, I’ll walk. But thanks.”

“Suit yourself.” He shrugged and darted away.

“Show off!” Billy shouted.

When Sami and Billy reached the basement, everyone turned their heads, all eyes on them.

“It’s about time you lovebirds showed up!” Mike said.

Sami’s smile fell flat, and she coward inwardly.

“Wow!” Billy’s eyes twinkled. “The cage looks like a jail cell now. We don’t have to climb up into it anymore. Where’d you get all the silver?”

“From the cage Jessica had Abby in,” Rick said.

“How did you get it over here?” Billy asked.

“My new truck!” Mike grinned.

“You got a new truck, bro? It’s about frickin’ time!”

“Well, it’s not brand new. It’s a work truck,” Mike said.

“Why didn’t you guys tell me? I would’ve helped,” Billy said, sounding disappointed he’d missed out on all the fun.

“Uh, hello. You were busy,” Jason reminded.

Sami averted her gaze to the ground.

"All done!" Rick said as he tightened the last bolt. "I'm going out for some fresh air until I regain my strength." He left the basement, walking at a normal pace.

"I guess Sami and I will start on the food," Billy said.

"I'll go get the barbeque and bring it out front since there's enough seating on your front porch for everyone." Mike headed upstairs.

"I'll help," Jason called out to him and sped off.

"Guess I'll assist you two in the kitchen," Abby said.

Sami led the way to the kitchen, where the three of them marinated steak and chicken, and prepared baked beans, salad, and garlic bread for the feast. When they finished, they went out to the front porch where Mike, Jason, and Rick were tending to the grill. Sharon arrived shortly after.

"Smells good." Sharon sat on one of the porch chairs, next to Abby.

Sami leaned forward from the wicker loveseat, peering around Billy until she had a good view of Sharon. "How was your first day at being assistant manager?"

"A lot better than waiting tables," she replied.

Jason left the grill and grabbed a beer from the ice chest. After pulling the tab and taking a sip, he sat down on the porch steps.

"You're just wasting it," Rick said.

"What? My beer?" He shook his head and took another sip.

Rick smirked. "Your powers have progressed faster than normal. Alcohol doesn't affect werewolves."

"Awww, come on!" Jason belted out as he flung a hand in the air. "You're frickin' kidding me? You mean I can't sit and relax and enjoy a damn beer?"

Billy chuckled. He hopped up from the loveseat and headed straight for the ice chest. After he snatched up a cold beer, he sat down on the step below Jason, leaned his back against the railing, and took a long sip. "Ahhh, so refreshing!" He smirked and proceeded to gulp down his beer, not stopping until it was empty. "Mmmm," he taunted, staring Jason square in the eyes. "I can feel it working already. I'm so relaxed right now."

Mike and Rick chuckled.

"Dumbass!" Jason snapped. He shrugged and drank his beer anyway.

Billy stood and sat next to Sami again.

Sami giggled, and her thoughts drifted to the previous night, when Billy had proposed to her. Turning her focus to her engagement ring, she stared at it dreamily, realizing she had never been this happy in her life. She didn't want to wait to marry him. The sooner the better. She leaned over and pressed her lips against Billy's ear.

"I want to get married as soon as possible," she whispered. "How's next month?"

Wearing a huge grin, he lowered his lips to her ear. "Sounds like a plan."

His gentle finger under her chin guided her mouth to his. For a moment, nothing else existed as they shared their love and celebrated their upcoming union. Reluctantly, they pulled away from each other and turned their attention back to the party, suddenly realizing all eyes were on them.

Sami buried her face in her hands before meeting everyone's gazes again.

"Do you mind telling us what that was all about?" Jason raised his eyebrows.

"Well?" Billy looked at Sami, waiting for her approval.

She nodded.

"We're getting married next month," he announced with a proud grin.

"Oh, that's great!" Abby clasped her hands together, beaming with excitement.

"Cool!" Jason grinned, then his smile fell flat. "But we already knew that because we could hear everything you were whispering." He pointed to his ear and smirked at Billy. "Freakish power, remember?"

"Whatever! I'm gonna have another beer!" Billy taunted.

"Congratulations." Rick winked.

"Yeah, it's about damn time!" Mike raised his beer.

"I wanna get married at the lake while the flowers are still in bloom," Sami said.

"That'll be so beautiful." Sharon smiled, while gazing into the distance, as if she were imagining the wedding.

"You don't have much time to plan," Abby said.

"Well, we just want it to be simple. With all of you, of course. And hopefully my parents. Nothing fancy. The lake is so beautiful, it doesn't need decorations."

"I can marry you if you want," Rick said.

A surprised look crossed Billy's face. "What?"

"A little something I did to try to redeem my humanity." Rick shrugged.

"I never knew that," Billy said. He looked at Mike. "Did you?"

"Yep," Mike gloated.

"It would be perfect if you married us," Sami said, glad Billy had his father here to be a part of his big day and the rest of his life, for-that-matter. She wondered if her parents would make the trip next month, but more so, how they would take the news.

"What's the matter?" Billy asked.

"I still haven't even told my mom and dad we're living together yet, let alone getting married."

"Don't worry." He wrapped his arm around her shoulder. "They'll forgive us once we give them a grandchild."

She giggled and gazed into his eyes. "You think so?"

"Doesn't hurt to try." He winked.

"Ugh!" Jason crumpled his second beer. His eyes turned green. "Do you think a couple of shots of whisky would help, Rick?"

"Nope." Rick shook his head. "Billy, I need something to put all this meat in."

"I'll be back in a minute." Billy went into the house.

"Maybe a nice hot bath would do the trick," Abby suggested to Jason.

"Or maybe you and I could go a few rounds?" Sharon smirked.

"Awww, Jason." Sami got up and sat next to him on the step. "Maybe all you need is a friend." She smiled and nudged his shoulder with hers.

Jason chuckled under his breath. "Actually, feeling human again would be great. I can't wait 'til we find my real father." He sighed and draped an arm across Sami's shoulder, giving her a friendly half-hug.

Suddenly, his eyes turned golden yellow.

THE STORY CONTINUES

WHEN WEREWOLVES FIGHT, DEATH IS INEVITABLE.

After the killer werewolf of her nightmares is destroyed, Sami and Billy are finally able to enjoy their new life together. What they don't realize is a new threat lurks nearby, plotting its revenge. When Billy gets word of the danger, he leaves in search of answers and heads straight into the heart of evil—a decision that leaves Sami to face an unimaginable horror without him and creates an aftermath that will change their lives forever.

THANKS FOR READING!

I hope you enjoyed *Moonlit Shadows Bitten*, book two of the Moonlit Shadows Series. I'd love to hear your feedback. You can leave a review on Amazon.

Thank you!

ABOUT THE AUTHOR

SHAWNA GAUTIER lives in Northern California with her husband, daughter, and two sons. She loves being outdoors, and some of her activities include camping, dirt-bike riding, and going to the beach.

So far, Shawna has written the Moonlit Shadows Series, a four-book YA/adult paranormal fantasy series, and Under the Midnight Stars, an adult contemporary romance.

Please visit Shawna's website to learn more about her books, upcoming new releases, and to sign up for her newsletter:

WWW.SHAWNAGAUTIER.COM

Made in the USA
Monee, IL
25 February 2021